THE
COVER
GIRL

THE
COVER
GIRL

Amy Rossi

/ll MIRA

///MIRA™

ISBN-13: 978-0-7783-6826-7

The Cover Girl

Copyright © 2025 by Amy Rossi

Recycling programs
for this product may
not exist in your area.

All rights reserved. No part of this book may be used or reproduced in any manner whatsoever without written permission.

Without limiting the author's and publisher's exclusive rights, any unauthorized use of this publication to train generative artificial intelligence (AI) technologies is expressly prohibited.

This is a work of fiction. Names, characters, places and incidents are either the product of the author's imagination or are used fictitiously. Any resemblance to actual persons, living or dead, businesses, companies, events or locales is entirely coincidental.

For questions and comments about the quality of this book, please contact us at CustomerService@Harlequin.com.

TM is a trademark of Harlequin Enterprises ULC.

Mira
22 Adelaide St. West, 41st Floor
Toronto, Ontario M5H 4E3, Canada
MIRABooks.com

HarperCollins Publishers
Macken House, 39/40 Mayor Street Upper,
Dublin 1, D01 C9W8, Ireland
www.HarperCollins.com

Printed in U.S.A.

For Jen

2018

I do not receive the sort of mail that comes in thick ivory envelopes. Sometimes junk might mimic the size, the color of personal correspondence, but the envelope is never linen. The cursive address block is always black, always slightly pixelated. If it wasn't for the violet calligraphy looping into a name few people call me anymore, I'd think this delivery was a mistake on the part of the mail carrier.

I ease the envelope flap open with a pearl-handled letter opener. I paid someone to clean out my parents' house after my mother died, and she sent me a box of things she thought I might like to have. Jewelry, mostly, but also some truly ridiculous items like opera glasses, a Christmas card from Pat Nixon, who my mother adored, and this letter opener, which I use in tribute not to my mother but to Barb, who spent forty-six meticulously accounted-for hours sorting through drawers neglected over the rise and decline of several technologies. I imagine how she must have seen me: *This woman who'd rather pay someone to clean up her past seems like the sort who wouldn't want to risk a paper cut opening her mail.*

The letter opener does its job, revealing, of course, an invitation. A startling thing, given that I've cultivated a life that does not require x-ing little cards with my preference for meat or fish. My friend Bobby's wedding three years ago was the first one I'd attended since the '90s, and it will probably be the last.

Fifty years of glamour, the invitation declares. *You are cordially invited to join us as we celebrate Harriet Goldman and the careers she launched.* And a smaller card, separated from the invitation by vellum yet still bound to it with a gold cord: *As one of Harriet's Girls, you will be a special part of this gala event.* And finally, a handwritten note: *Hope to see you there! Therese.*

Therese! My god. How is she still around? Even Debi retired to Prince Edward Island with her wife and is having the time of her life, which she has completely extracted from any tentacle of the industry.

At the time, I admired Debi for this. I still do. Then again, if she were here, she would have warned me.

Pilates stance: heels together, toes apart. The same as first position in ballet, not so different from the Y position one would take at the end of a runway before the turn, or in a photo to angle the hips just so. Nearly every reformer class begins the same way. Lying on the machine, pelvis neutral, heels touching with the balls of the feet on the foot bar, knees as wide as the hips. We'll move into other foot positions, other movements, but it always comes back to Pilates stance. The pose of my life.

Today, though, is jump board class. I hadn't realized the Wednesday afternoon session had switched from the regular sculpt class when I booked, wasn't paying much attention to anything but the gala invitation. "You're going to have so much fun with this," the instructor, Caro, says as she shimmies the board into the end of the reformer.

It's been years since I've taken a jump class; I am fairly certain I will not have fun. All the defined, elegant movement—the return to my body, the escape—that I can retreat into during a

THE COVER GIRL

regular class is off the table with a jump board. There's something unsettling about being on your back and bouncing up and down on a tiny trampoline, two movements that do not go together. It feels like an illusion.

That's a lie.

It feels like a loss of control.

I try to keep my mind on my core, on my pelvic floor, on the flexibility in my ankles as we warm up our bodies and joints for the jumps. I try to enjoy the weightlessness as I spring off the board, try to remind myself I will come back down. Caro walks us through a series with our feet parallel, with our feet in Pilates stance, with one leg raised.

"Now when you push back," she says, "I want you to scissor one ankle over the other three times, starting with the right. I know, it's a lot. You'll have to move fast to fully articulate your foot position at the bottom."

I look up to watch her demonstrate with her arms and I keep my chest raised to ensure my own proper positioning. My legs, long and lifted, toes pointed as one ankle crosses over the other.

Like a good girl. Like a memory.

The feeling crashes over me as quickly as the reformer bed jolts back home. The sound of the machine, the sound of my knees hitting the board. Everyone is looking; everyone is always looking. I am here but not, and still, it is the same silent stares as before.

Caro rushes over to check on me and the equipment, but I'm already on my feet, murmuring a jumble of words that hopefully amount to an apology. It is possible I'm still whispering that I am sorry by the time I am in the car, by the time I am fumbling my key in the door of my home, by the time I am pouring a chilled glass of Sancerre to wash it all away, by the time I am no longer sure what I am apologizing for or to whom.

I take a breath because that's what you're supposed to do in moments like these, take a breath like I am performing Woman

Who Must Recenter Herself After Freaking Out In Public. The role of a lifetime. One breath, then another, and then I take a photo of the invitation and text it to my friend Bernice. Bernice who lives in New York, where it is already 9:00 p.m. Bernice who is so busy that our phone dates require planning and a spot on her calendar so her assistant does not accidentally book over them. Bernice whose name lights up my phone ninety seconds later.

"What are you going to do?" she asks. No time for greetings.

I tell her I don't know. It's in September.

"That's barely enough time to get work done!"

My laugh comes out in a dry bark. But this is why I adore Bernice—she understands where my mind goes first, even if it's not the most flattering place, because her mind has been molded in the same way: around our appearance.

"Well," she says. "You don't have to decide right now."

We both know, though, that the deciding isn't the only problem. It's everything else—the peels and fillers and history and emotions—in between.

Bernice has to go, has to return to dinner. I don't mind; we'll talk more later. What matters in this precise moment is that someone else knows. And I am here, breathing my breaths, feeling the cool tile under my feet, feeling the sweat of the wine bottle against my palm.

I am still here.

But then again, so are all the me's I've been. Those girls and those years have, quite literally, piled up as a stack of portfolios in my living room.

In modeling, a tear sheet is currency. It's exactly what it sounds like, a sheet of paper, torn from a magazine, and also more. It is proof that a model exists. You tear yourself away from the pages you worked so hard to float among so that you may have another page to tear later.

I built myself from my tears. The magazine pages and before

THE COVER GIRL

too, from the beginning. Each tear means something. It has to. For example: birth is a kind of tear, and if that sounds too dramatic, too much like fumbling for a connection between two different things, tell me what to call it, then, when a woman barely has time to feel what's growing inside of her for what it is before the baby girl comes thrashing out. No bond, no hand hovering over fluttery kicks, no dreams of her looking more like Mom or Dad but as long as she's healthy. She is—healthy enough, at least. At first.

Each tear said it louder.

I am here. I exist. Better than before.

Your active portfolio doesn't get longer. Quality over quantity. A solid life philosophy. You rotate pages out, keep them current. The old ones I moved into a different binder. Even though I never open it, I still have it. The proof. And what need do I have to look when I can still see some of those pictures so vividly.

The first shoot, sweet thirteen and never been anything, all big hair and party dress dreams.

The first bathing suit, a year later, no hips, all legs. A pout, nothing yet to put behind it.

Three pictures later, something behind it.

Tanned, hairless thighs. Sunbaked hair removal ad. Later, a commercial.

A fashion show: the wedding dress walk, just a year past old enough to legally wed in the state of California. This bride was crying.

Hint of a smile, face hidden by hair. Truth hidden by face. *You've come a long way, baby.*

Empty years.

Hands smoothing anti-aging cream.

Made into a woman as a girl, then broken into parts once womanhood became too real.

I could say this is the summary of four decades but that would be too simple. *Every picture tells a story* is a cliché until it's not.

1975–1977

Little Miss Dangerous

1

This was the only way I could have been considered in fashion: by accident.

I had no memory of growing. In those final weeks of the school year, when the weather warmed enough for skirts again, I pulled on what had fit fine in the last push of a sticky September. But now, teachers stopped me in the hall and ordered me to press my fingertips to my thighs, reminded me I was breaking the rules.

I spent the summer skulking around shaded rooms or hunched over books, trying to force myself back down to where the normal girls were. I slouched at the dinner table and shuffled the plates to the kitchen, listing to the side like a woman five times my age. Alone in front of the full-length mirror in my bedroom, I confronted the truth: I was a freak. Once, I could stand on the edge of the carpet and see the whole of me. Now in that same spot, I was cut off at the neck. No longer a person. How could I be real without a head or face. This was the first lesson that my body was an uncontrollable thing. It existed apart from me and I watched it with as much wonder and horror as I would a movie.

As our annual trip to New York City for my back-to-school clothes drew closer, I knew I wouldn't be able to hide this development from my mother much longer. I thought about begging her to let me go to Gimbels or Sears by myself, knowing that the answer would be no, knowing that my display of feeling on the subject would be more likely to attract her attention than push it away.

Before I was ever forced to straighten the full length of my legs in front of my mother in the dressing room, though, I was taken to the doctor for my annual physical. The nurse measured me, then the doctor looked at what she wrote down and measured me himself. He said it out loud. "Five feet, ten inches tall. My goodness, that's off the charts for a thirteen-year-old girl."

He told my mother to tell me to stop slouching, while I sat on the examining table, a collection of too-long limbs folded upon themselves. She stared at me for days after, like I'd gone and grown to spite her. No one in *her* family was tall. And then we made it worse by going to New York.

There was a second reason I dreaded the back-to-school shopping trip. My mother had grown up with money, had grown up believing that *the city* was the only place to purchase anything of value. No discount bins, no sales, just rich wools and tweeds, smart suits and hats. Buy quality and have it forever. Make regular excursions so everyone knew you could buy quality and have it forever whenever you wanted. She did this with her own mother as a girl and as an adult and continued with me as a habit.

What I did in this house was watch and listen. My mother was not particularly interested in making room for me in between social events. My father either, but he wasn't the one at home during the day. There was also the fact that my parents never should have been married at all, a drunken truth hurled by my mother at a dinner party I was brought to in Florida when I should have been in school.

I had turned this over and over in my child mind until I

found the proof in a slim leather photo album. My mother had been married before, a nineteen-year-old World War II bride of the kind of society boy she was fated to be paired off with, the kind of society boy who was supposed to do his duty overseas because he was a red-blooded American, dammit, and return home safely to the waiting arms of his wife and the GI bill and a Chevrolet, not get shot down over the Pacific. My father came along after, a safe bet in the fog of grief, flat-footed and turned down for service, handsome and employed, though not from old money. But, from what I pieced together from hissed conversations overheard at holiday gatherings and second-cousin christenings, postwar life brought prosperity and babies to my mother's friends and her dissatisfaction crept in. She pushed my father toward bolder ambitions, a bigger house, a better neighborhood.

They'd long become accustomed to childlessness when I made my surprise entrance, perhaps preferred it, after all. Sometimes I would look through my father's old issues of *Life* and *Newsweek* and consider: they lived through the Great Depression, wars, the Red Scare, radio giving way to television. Sometimes they appeared startled by me, by my wants, by the world I required them to engage with. I was from another time. I should have been born during the baby boom like their friends' children. Perhaps then they would have known what to do.

Or maybe that was the convenient way to explain away the feeling that came every time I heard my mother call me dull. Perhaps if I knew how to be more exciting, there would have been room. It's not that they did anything to me, a fact that cut both ways.

So they thought nothing about sticking me in the middle of an adult dinner party or pulling me out of school for their vacations or arguing at the volume they'd used the whole of their married lives. And it was because of this that I learned that my mother had *what's mine is yours*'ed her inheritance to my father and his every attempt at *for richer* had ended up *for poorer*. It wasn't clear how much money we did or did not have; what mattered was there was far less than she thought there should have been, and somehow less every year. Each trip to New York was weighted with her anger that she should be able to buy me a finer coat or loafers made of softer leather. We did not skip those stores. She made me try on skirts and blouses that she believed it was her right to afford and then she'd sniff at the help and tell them it wasn't quite *our taste*. And then I'd have to do it all again at a place that was within our budget. Or, if she was in a particular mood, she'd take me to the best department stores and shove me into clothing that she would have wanted at my age and then buy her girlhood at me, kneading her bottom lip between her front teeth as she signed the credit slips, gearing up for the fight she would have later, a fight she could always win because it had been her money, even if the credit wasn't in her name. Once I suggested I didn't need all these things. Just once was enough to make clear that these trips were for her, not me.

It was only because of the doctor that my mother started telling me to stand up straight. It was only because she ramrodded her index finger into my spine as we walked into her favorite New York City department store that I was standing up straight at that moment. And it was only because I was standing up straight that day that I was discovered.

I wasn't paying attention. Later, I wished I had been and so I spent a lot of time constructing the scene, trying to see what Harriet Goldman had seen that afternoon. Me, being marched through the door, the pressure of my mother's insistent finger forcing my shoulders back and creating a scowl on my face— a scowl that could be interpreted as a pretty pout, depending on the ambitions or agenda of the beholder. My mother, half a foot shorter, dressed in one of those suits that was supposed to last forever and had, the fabric at least. The style was from another era, a jacket and skirt that would not have been out of place worn by a girl getting discovered at a shop counter in the 1950s. Her blond hair was dyed and set; mine flowed down my back. And leaving from that very same door, a woman I was too irritated to notice but who had been watching me through the window. Sunglasses engulfed her face like two dark moons and she did not wear clothes so much as she allowed the fabric to drape across her thin shoulders. Her dark hair was pulled back in what I would learn to call a chignon. But first, before I could take the time to be intimidated by her, she was just a hand reaching out for my mother's wrist and a deep voice unfurling into a Long Island accent asking, "Darling, does she have representation?"

The way it felt: the three of us melted onto the sidewalk, a flurry of business activity. But that couldn't have been how it really was, not in the city, not with other customers coming in and out and pedestrians with places to be. And she couldn't have signed me that day, of course, not before my mother called the ancient family lawyer and pretended to run it by my father. But even the following night, it was already a blur, like trying to tell a memory from a dream.

The question was about *letting* me model, not whether I wanted to. And what girl wouldn't want to? Maybe a girl who went pink if a teacher called on her, who hid behind her hair at the market. Maybe, but not in this case. I was pleased that I'd been discovered; I separated it entirely from the fact that it meant people would have opinions about me.

Discovered was Harriet Goldman's word. "Look at her," she said to everyone she had me meet in those first few weeks. "I discovered her going into Saks, can you imagine?" *Discovered* was more soothing than exciting. I took it literally. I didn't think about it as validation of my physical appearance, even though I spent more time afterward staring at myself in my bedroom mirror. Someone had seen me. Someone had done the looking and the math and found the result and it was me. Imagine having spent your entire life blending in with the furniture and then to be noticed as decoration.

Discovered was just the beginning. My entire vocabulary changed. Comp cards, go-sees, my book—it became a new language, light on my tongue when I whispered the words to myself at night.

The first time I stood in front of a camera, it wasn't in beautiful clothes or with my hair and makeup done. I was in a tank top and bell-bottom jeans, my hair pulled back from my bare face in a low ponytail. These were the pretest shots. The quiz shots? I thought about making the joke but kept it to myself. Harriet believed I had what it took, but she wanted to see proof before ink was put to paper.

"We just need to see you," the photographer said. "Show me you."

Harriet Goldman sat me in her office the day I signed the contract. My mother settled into the white leather chair next to me. Behind Harriet: the expanse of the city, shrunken by the height of the building and alive under the glass. On her desk: several 8x10 black-and-white photos of me. Harriet delicately ashed her cigarette into a marble ashtray next to the pictures and nodded toward the lobby. My mother didn't move.

"Mrs. Rhodes," Harriet said finally. "She'll come out when we're done."

"I'm her mother."

"Of course you are. I'm the agent. She's the model. We'll see you in a few."

I held my breath, thinking this was it. My mother was going to take back her permission, rip up the paper. But she took a signed document seriously, and so she rose from the chair and left the office, moving as though she were balancing a book on top of her head.

"It's just easier to do this without the mothers," Harriet said once the door was shut. "Sometimes they hear things that aren't there." I nodded. She lit another cigarette and crossed one leg over the other as she slid a hand across those first photos of me. "These are nice." Later I would learn that *nice* could mean *fine* or *good* or *phenomenal*. For now: just nice. She held up a picture so I could see myself—plain but also not. I remembered the Greek myth about the boy who fell into the water staring at his reflection as I leaned forward to get a better look. It wasn't a reflection, though. It was seeing myself for the first time. One eye slightly darker than the other. The chicken pox scar on my cheek masquerading as a dimple. She put it back down before I could fall in.

"So. Birdie. You're very lucky. Know that. Remember it. I get a hundred pictures from girls like you every day, girls who want to be sitting where you're sitting right now." She let that hang like a threat in the air between us. I nodded again. I understood, I thought. "Alright, then. There's a lot of possibility here. You're younger than some editors normally work with, but you're tall enough." She waved off any concern about my youth like it was as inconsequential as a gnat. "We could get you some acting lessons if you think that's something you'll be interested in. And there's the possibility of runway. If you stick with this, you'll go to Paris. Do you have your period yet?" This was spoken in the same matter-of-fact tone she'd used for everything else and it was a moment before I realized what she'd asked. "Oh, darling, there's no use in getting shy now." I told her yes. "Good. Hopefully we're behind the awkward phase, then. That's a mess for everyone."

Harriet stood. She turned toward the enormous window behind her desk. The day was not particularly beautiful, no sun glinting majestically off the Empire State Building, too early for the lights to cast a soft glow to the taxis and sidewalks. It was simply regular. "When you're on a go-see or a shoot, your job is to make them like you. That's how we both get paid. That's how you get more and better work. If you have a problem on a set or if you're not comfortable, you can tell me. Dealing with that is my job. But if a client calls to tell me one of my girls was difficult, it only happens the one time." She was silent for so long that I thought it was my dismissal, and just when it seemed like I must have been failing some sort of test for understanding what she would need from me, she spoke again. "Get your passport if you haven't already. And you're going to need a wardrobe. Basic, quality pieces. Nothing flashy. Show that you know how to wear clothes, they don't wear you. Ask Therese for a list of appropriate designers on your way out."

It wasn't that we couldn't afford such clothes, that it would be a true hardship to purchase them. But if my mother found out there was a cost to modeling, I could see it all slipping through my fingers faster than it had landed in my grasp. I opened my mouth to explain.

Harriet held up a hand. "Expense it to the agency. We'll take it from your earnings." She paused, then her eyes drifted toward the door. My cue to go.

My mother wanted to ask what was said in that office, I could feel it in the purse of her lips, the way she'd glance at me and then look away as we walked back to the car. And I could have told her, but she wouldn't have understood. I had the feeling what Harriet didn't say was just as important, but what that was wasn't clear to me yet.

This was the first time I had something that was mine. I spent too much time around adults to ever feel comfortable around the other kids at school; other than as a target for their teasing remarks about my height, I wasn't of any use to them. I had people to eat next to in the lunchroom, but I wouldn't say I had friends, no one outside of the confines of school hours. Modeling was a decent consolation prize. And my mother wasn't interested in being a stage parent; despite her initial enthusiasm, that would have been too much work. She appreciated Harriet Goldman's eye because it confirmed her long-held belief that she was special, different, even if only through me. A daughter who was a model would probably not get her into the elite circle at the country club that she insisted they belong to, but it was something. And it meant, in her mind, I would be like her.

"I've always been glad you're pretty," my mother said when we were driving back to Connecticut. "It never mattered that you don't have a personality—no one wants that anyway. They want pretty.

"Obviously you'll still want to think about your prospects, and this should help you with poise at your debut in a few years. Perhaps we can do a custom-designed dress—it's never too early to start thinking." She switched lanes sharply. She was a terror on the road, in an absolute boat of a Chrysler: a silk scarf knotted under her chin, sunglasses, lambskin driving gloves. From afar, she might have appeared to be channeling vintage Jackie Kennedy but she most certainly had voted the other way. A well-connected cousin had thrown a fundraiser for Richard Nixon out in the Hamptons during the 1960 election, and for a long time my mother would bring up how Pat Nixon had complimented her hairstyle that night. She only retired that anecdote after Watergate.

"Anyhow," my mother said, "you'll have your own money. That means you don't have to marry for it."

Before I could be sent out for my first job, before I was officially a model, I needed a book. Eventually these pages would be filled with my actual work, but for now, it was important for me to show my potential, not just my bone structure like in those first pictures.

For the test shots, I had my first experience getting styled.

"You don't have to close your eyes," the woman doing my hair told me minutes into her brushing and spraying, but I kept them closed anyway, letting it happen, focusing on the feeling.

It was a tactile world, moving from someone's hands in my hair to hands on my face for makeup and then on my torso to adjust the halter top, to hold up a belt and see if it completed the outfit or not. I didn't mind it, but it made me realize how unaccustomed I was to being touched. I exhaled. I let them mold me. This was what I thought about when I stood in front of the photographer, the one who could build my book and what was next. The first one had said, *Show me you.* This time, I would show all the me's I could be.

It worked. Harriet brought me in to look at the photos, to show me which ones she thought should begin my portfolio. She talked and I tried to listen, but I couldn't stop looking. I handled the pile like it were glass, like touching the paper would crack the vulnerability I had shown. The photographer had caught me laughing, had captured an easiness that I didn't know I possessed. What mystery. What power.

That was the moment I really and truly wanted this.

I booked my first job quickly, an ad for deodorant. It would run in the standard teen magazines, the same ones I had idly paged through when I accompanied my mother to the market. I had to miss school for the shoot, and Harriet wrote me a note to give to my teachers, typed by Therese on thick agency letterhead and bearing the loopy blue *H* and *G* that made up her signature. My teacher had clearly been expecting something from a doctor, and she emitted a small gasp when the text didn't align with the notes she usually received. She looked me up and down as if seeing me for the first time. "Well, then," she said. "Very well."

For the deodorant shoot, they put me in a bright pink dress that firmly failed the fingertip test. I sat in a chair while one

THE COVER GIRL

woman dabbed foundations and powders and mascara onto my face and then in another chair while a different woman rolled my long hair in massive rollers. "She's so quiet," the makeup woman said to the hair woman. "A dream. It's like working on a doll."

I didn't look at myself until I was done and sent to the art director for approval. And for one brief moment, I saw what Harriet Goldman had seen. Not beauty—or not only that, because yes, I did look beautiful and maybe had been all along—but possibility.

The girl in the first photos and the girl in the test shots and the girl in this mirror were not the same. I could carry the weight of transformation, and it didn't matter one bit that I was thirteen years old. With the hair and the makeup and the dress, I had no age unless they gave me one.

The art director approved.

The lights were hotter on this shoot than they had been before. There were more people running around, other girls who were going to be in some of the shots, assistants, music blaring from speakers set up in the corner. There was a set in front of the backdrop, a giant party cake. I wondered if it was real, if the sugary icing would melt under the lights.

"Alright, Birdie, we're going to get started," the photographer said. "Do you have any questions?"

I thought about it. I had many questions and none at all. How did I get here? Was I always headed here? What would happen if I were terrible at this, now that it was for real? How would my face convince girls to buy deodorant?

I looked at him and asked who was singing the song that was playing.

He laughed as though this made me quite clever. "David Bowie."

Someone turned on a fan so that I was bathed in a gentle breeze, so that my hair would achieve a bounce and fullness other girls would want but never find, not unless someone followed them around with large fans too. The making of an un-reachable standard. The photographer took a few test shots. And then it started.

The moment the art director started giving me instruction, I became two people. Or maybe the two people had been there all along and the click of the shutter just freed me. What I was in front of the camera was a body. What freedom in that. He told me to do what came naturally. I leaned over the cake. I blew out candles like I was blowing a bubble with a wad of bubblegum. Someone gave me a wad of bubblegum to blow a bubble with just in case that looked good too. Someone else swapped out the cake with the candles for a fresh cake and when I dipped my finger into the frosting to bring it up to my mouth, the photographer warned me not to taste it because it wasn't real frosting and it would be terrible. He told the other girls to stand behind me and gave me the cake to carry, like I was leading them into some wonderful celebration. They were giggling and laughing behind me; apparently they'd become friends while I was having my picture taken by myself. It didn't bother me. We were having two different experiences today.

And I was the star.

How long could the feeling last? If I'd been alone before I became a model, a new word was needed for after. I was still alone, but full. I did not haunt my house or fade into the hallways. My parents had always treated me like a small adult, and now that I was working, they had even more reason to do so. I had no reason to be unsettled by it. I took the train from Darien to New York by myself for my go-sees and went to my jobs by myself unless someone in charge expressly asked for a parent to be present. Most of the time when that happened, Harriet would send me with a quiet woman named Didi, who had a gray cap of hair and was never seen without a copy of *Cosmopolitan* and the novel *Salem's Lot*.

THE COVER GIRL   29

I didn't book jobs every week, but I didn't need to to feel the gentle expansion of this next self, warming my rib cage and softening the angles of my knees and hips. That was the girl who took over in front of the camera and I wanted to watch her as much as possible. I'd look for her in the mirror. If my body was a screen for others to project onto, what was it that I wanted to project to them? I knew it wasn't okay to want nothing, so I decided nothing *yet* because nothing and everything are closer together than you'd think.

Sometimes I would linger in the city after a go-see or after I dropped off the vouchers that had to be filled out for each job so I could be paid, and I'd duck into stores that were too expensive and what I learned was that if I carried myself like I belonged, I did. No one asked where my mother was or if I was lost. Instead they brought me dresses and skirts and sometimes I charged them back to the agency to be taken out of my pay as Harriet had instructed. I never actually saw a check; the ancient family lawyer made sure it all went directly into a trust that I couldn't touch until my eighteenth birthday.

Eventually word got out around school about this other life of mine, which led to whispers whenever I walked into a room and the occasional direct question that often sounded like some version of *Why you and not me?* When girls were nicer to me than they had been before, I was nice back but also suspicious—if I was only worthy now, how quickly would I become unworthy? Better to save my full self for where it counted.

I was happy. A model is not a doctor, is not a scientist, is not going to solve hunger or deliver world peace, but I was doing something. And this was a world I could understand. There were people to put me in clothes, to roll and brush and spray my hair, paint my face, adjust my hips, tip my chin, tell me how to move, and I didn't realize I'd been waiting for direction until I finally got it. In front of the camera, the rules were clearer than those that governed my home or cliques at school. All I had to do was be a body and listen and the inside Birdie could just float up and watch it happen.

Every time I saw myself in one of those photographs, I stared at the picture too long, a little in love with myself, and mostly stunned that this was what it looked like. This was what it could be.

2

By the time I turned fourteen, I was working often. I wasn't always the star like in that first shoot. Sometimes I posed alongside groups of other girls. Most of the time, it was a catalog shoot or the cover of a sewing pattern. I didn't really care what the job was, not even when I would find the results taped to my locker by classmates—a tampon ad exaggerated with red marker or a catalog photo enhanced with cartoony breasts, maybe a penis scribbled next to my face. How sad for them.

My mother would hand me the envelopes with my bank statements each month, her mouth set in a line, and I kept them all rubber-banded on my dresser as proof of my value. I didn't know if those vouchers I dropped off transformed into a lot of money, and it wasn't even about the money. But one day if all this went away, if my later teen years weren't kind to my appearance or if I just got bored, I'd have a reminder that I had been worth something. That I'd had a dollar amount.

Some girls would be sent right to Paris, right to high fashion, but Harriet said I was still too young. She said with more commercial work, I could build confidence and range before standing in front of the make-or-break Richard Avedons of the world. Even Grace Kelly had started with bug spray commercials, Harriet said. Still, I was turned down for jobs as often as I booked them. The first time Harriet Goldman told me *it was a pass, darling* after a go-see, she called me into the office to do it in person. This was a particular habit of hers. She wanted to see for herself how her girls handled negative feedback. As with all things in this world, there was a right answer that would not reveal itself unless the wrong one was given.

For me, there was no sting. The first job had happened so easily, as if Harriet had willed it. The way her power swirled around her in an almost visible cloud, I could believe that she had. But I was young and fresh to this world and I trusted her more than I had ever trusted anyone. If she believed another opportunity was just around the corner, then I did too. And so when she told me about the pass, I nodded and asked about the next go-see.

I had not yet learned to take a rejection of my appearance as a rejection of myself. I couldn't change how I looked, so there was no sense in being upset if someone else looked more right.

Or: I was used to *no* in all its unspoken forms. The chill of my parents' house. The feeling in my stomach when I saw the children receiving hugs on *The Brady Bunch*. The sensation near jealousy when overhearing girls complaining about their mothers being so nosy in those close quarters where we changed into our gym uniforms. The word *no* was never said but it weighed as heavy as the inherited velvet curtains my mother hung downstairs.

There was relief in finally hearing the word. In experiencing it as more than a feeling.

Each *no* reminded me that this was not to be taken for granted and each *yes* made me a little more powerful. At home, I turned down my mother's meat-and-potatoes-laden cooking, insisting that I had to watch my figure, and she'd halve her own portions, as though it were a competition. Any piece of clothing that I re-

THE COVER GIRL

ceived as a gift, I wore, flaunting skirts and tops that would be out of fashion in months and were still weeks away from being *in*. As long as I was working, I could keep a line between them and me, a line of my own choosing this time.

The first time a photographer told me he needed to come over and adjust my pose, that's what he did. The second and third time too. So the first time a photographer ran his hand up my inner thigh and called it *helping me with my pose*, I believed him.

It was what we called *small things like that*.

If it doesn't seem small, imagine a group of young women standing around a party they are being paid, more or less, to attend. A man walks by, ruddy-nosed, shirt sloppily tucked in. A shadow of his former self. One of the young women laughs humorlessly. Another shudders with her whole body. A couple exchange glances. Finally one places a comment in the center of the table, like a bread basket: *I hear his wife left him.* Silence. And then: *He took me out to dinner a few years ago.* More silence. *Just dinner?* And: *Was it in his hotel room?* And then the details fill in, stories of Quaaludes and promises of stardom. No one cries. Everyone is too relieved that she didn't dream it. Everyone has a story, ranging from mysterious finger-shaped bruises to just a touch, you know, small things like that.

It didn't happen often, anyway, just occasionally enough to seem like part of the job. Why wouldn't someone need to touch you if you were being fitted for a bathing suit? Sometimes you don't know how to move the way they want you to unless they show you how. Most things appear to be normal unless there's something else to compare it to.

My body was a thing that was useful to me and to others in a specific way. They didn't discover us for our minds, our senses of humor.

I had barely been modeling for six months when I was on a shoot with a girl a few years older than me who showed up twenty minutes past our call time, body loose and eyes half-shut. She slid out of poses like unset gelatin, melting into me for support. I tensed my arm, trying to keep her upright with the force of my palm, but whatever she'd taken was stronger than me.

The photographer came out from behind his camera, right up to her face. "Are you on drugs?" he yelled. "Are you on fucking drugs?" Her eyes fluttered shut and her head lolled back and forth, giving her the appearance of a broken doll. He yelled some more but she couldn't muster anything other than a soft whimper, so he reached back and slapped her across the face.

The sound shocked me so deeply that I was the one who screamed. The model blinked three times and unfurled her spine. Wordlessly, hair and makeup appeared on the set, not daring to bring her over to the chair. They combed back loosened wisps and quickly dabbed over the red mark.

We made it through the rest of the shoot, though I knew I wasn't delivering my best work. I was thinking about every movement, the exact opposite of the freedom I normally felt on set. The wet-eyed concentration of the model next to me kept me too close to the ground.

After we were done, I asked her if she was okay. It only seemed right, though I'd never asked a question like that before and my words were halting, like I could sense their inadequacy even as I spoke.

She laughed.

Later, when I was leaving for the day, I passed a half-open office. The model was straddling the photographer's lap, her back to him. Her eyes were closed, his mouth pressed against the same cheek he'd hit.

In our first meeting, Harriet had said if something happened on a job that made me uncomfortable, I could tell her. And that was the name for the feeling blooming inside me: *discomfort*. What right did I have here, though. It wasn't my story.

I turned away.

THE COVER GIRL

★ ★ ★

I didn't make friends with the other models, but I observed them. I listened to the names that floated reverentially from their lips: Beverly Johnson, Lauren Hutton, Margaux Hemingway. These were the women we should aspire to be, the ones who represented a place beyond group shots and catalog work, the ones who became themselves instead of simply modeling it.

Who did I want to be? The woman who held the most mystique for me was not a fellow model, but Harriet. I knew nothing about her, whether or not she was married or had children or what she liked to do outside of work, and not knowing made her seem even more powerful. To me, she represented the *modern woman*, a full rebuttal to the world of cooking and cleaning and homemaking my mother lived in.

This was not something I could say out loud. Very little was. That was the report from every photographer, anyway, every casting director when they conferred with Harriet Goldman over the phone or untouched lunches: *She's so quiet, What a dream to work with, She never says a word, Send her back anytime.*

The other models carried themselves as if they'd been born on a set, as if this was all they'd ever known. It was impossible for that to be true, of course; we were all good at carrying ourselves, even if we didn't feel it. This was the place I should have fit in best: a group of girls plucked from their regular lives because they looked right, girls that made others understand something fundamental about being a girl, a secret shared only with a look, not with words. Still, I was content to sit on the sidelines, unaware that this made me come off as snobbish rather than shy, aloof instead of nervous, cold and not curious.

This was only a problem with the girl models. The boy models were a different story—though it wasn't really fair to call them *boys*, was it, because while we could be put in bikinis and miniskirts and flip our hair just like women at thirteen, there was something *unseemly*, something awkward and gawky about asking a boy that age to do the same. If I was on a shoot with a male model, he was often at least seventeen. And the thing about seventeen-year-old male models is that they heard they were beautiful and special quite often. They didn't receive the same constant reminders that they were replaceable, and they were seldom told *no*.

So I didn't think to say it.

A designer brand, Soleo, was launching a Junior Miss line and Harriet sent several of us to the party to slink by and catch their eye. One of us could be the face of Soleo, or the legs or body. We were to stay overnight in a brownstone with Didi, who would bring us to the party and round us up at a reasonable hour—before all the things happening in corners and bathrooms happened out in the open.

I didn't enjoy parties. The thing about being someone's idea of beautiful was that because people felt comfortable looking at you, they assumed you felt comfortable in the world.

If I'd been in front of the camera in this white ruffled dress, bearing my shoulders, my hair flipped and feathered, lips glossed red, then I would have been okay. I would have known where to stand. But in this dark hotel ballroom, all I could do was linger at the edges of conversations and tell myself this was a job like any other.

It was not the first overly crowded room I had been in, but I grew more and more uncomfortable as the night went on, until my breath was ragged and my heart was racing and I was sure I was going to pass out. I didn't know how to fix it, didn't know if I was dying or having a heart attack. The waiters were not concerned with who was old enough when they passed by with trays of champagne, so I grabbed a glass, hoping it would calm me down. The bubbles made me sneeze and it was sweet and sour at the same time, like something gone bad. I sipped and then gulped until my head was swimming, but my heart was

THE COVER GIRL

still thudding against the walls of my ribs, trying to break free. I was not going to be the face of Soleo Junior Miss. I had to leave.

Didi was nowhere to be found, though my concept of *nowhere* and *found* was limited to what was within stumbling distance. I forced myself through the doors of the ballroom and made it to the elevator bank before sinking against the wall, panting, trying to suck in as much air as possible as the black dots in front of my eyes swam into one.

And then he appeared. *Jasper*, he would remind me later. We had worked together on a catalog shoot a few months earlier. He was tall, golden, a seventeen-year-old everyman who looked like he could win the big game and help you in biology lab and have you home five minutes before curfew. "Are you okay?" he asked. All I could do was vaguely gesture at the noise coming from the ballroom behind us. "Do you want to leave?"

I nodded.

He took me by the elbow into the elevator and didn't let go until we were in the lobby, where he informed the concierge we would need a cab and a glass of water. His voice was firm and friendly, a tone that you couldn't question until it was too late.

Jasper eased me into the cab. I sat in the very corner of the seat, against the door, my hands wrapped around the cup of water. I still felt fuzzy but whether it was the champagne or whatever had overtaken me at the party, I didn't know. Just as I managed to recite the address of the brownstone to the driver, Jasper poked his head in. "I'm going to make sure you get back safely," he said.

He kept a hand on my bare shoulder for the duration of the ride, encouraging me to take sips of water every block. When the cab pulled up to the building, Jasper slipped him a bill or two, no discussion.

Once inside, he gravitated toward the row of liquor lining a gold bar cart that we were supposed to know better than to touch. He poured us each a glass. "This will help," he said.

One drink. Then two. And then I knew why I felt fuzzy and announced I needed to go to bed. Jasper laughed and walked me into the bedroom I was sharing with a girl who was without fear or could hide it better, a girl who still might be the face of Soleo. And then he kissed me.

He had handled me so confidently all night that I had no reason to mistrust him. He knew how to be, how all this worked. I said nothing when he pushed down the top of my dress, nothing when he laid me down on the bed.

And when he left as quickly as he'd come into my night, I didn't say anything then either.

The glass from the hotel sat on the bedside table. I stood up carefully, my head still cottony and aching, and I opened the bedroom window. It was two stories up, but I let the glass fall, tinkling into a burst of nothing on the quiet sidewalk below me.

You know. Small things like that.

3

Then, two years in, the thing we thought I was past happened: an awkward phase.

I had worked consistently, hard even, after the Soleo incident. That was what I thought of it as when I allowed myself to think of it at all: the Soleo incident, the moment where I panicked and lost control, full stop. Perhaps I could have told Harriet, but to do so would have meant crossing the gulf between the story I told myself and the truth. Instead, I worked.

Harriet would read me lists of opportunities for go-sees from her steno pad—the only thing she ever used and so the only thing her assistants used—and her tone of voice was my guide, her words shifting to a nasal register as she curled her lip in disdain for photographers she didn't care for or ads she knew wouldn't show my face. I didn't mind those jobs. Sometimes I preferred them. Then I could truly let go and exist only as a waterfall of hair or pointed toes. It let me move through the regular world mostly unnoticed, like I had a secret. But can anyone name a famous catalog model? Even though the work paid well, no one ever made it without their face as the point of the picture. And that's where Harriet's real percentage lived.

But my face had become a problem. The angles of my hips had softened. I was not well endowed by any stretch, but that wasn't in at the moment and, anyway, what little I had for a chest had filled out. But I stayed too young-looking in the face, too apple-cheeked and innocent, for my body. Youth was prized, but mine was too literal. On one go-see, the photographer declared that I was fifteen "only in the sense that if you averaged what she looks like above the neck and what she looks like below the neck, that might be what you land on," like I wasn't even in the room. All I could do was blink. Better seen than heard. Makeup helped but only somewhat. Harriet would receive notes back saying I was a sweet girl but my look wasn't quite right. Send her again in a year or so.

I wanted to let her know that I was trying, that I would be worth it, but all this went unspoken. Harriet had no patience for people who couldn't fill in their own blanks. She lived between the lines. And I had no experience with any kind of directness. We were made for each other.

My mother saw me leafing through all the catalog shots that weren't right for my book, and she asked where the ads were, the big face shots. I repeated back what I'd been told, that my look wasn't right for those jobs right now.

"You should dress up more when you go on those interviews," she said. "Put on a little rouge. Don't go in there boring them."

I imagined Harriet's reaction to this advice and almost laughed. It was easier to say nothing than to tell her she didn't understand. To keep this world and its rules for myself.

A late winter afternoon in Harriet's office. The sun streaming through that giant window, glowing off her earrings, bouncing from her cigarette holder. Under my coat, I wore a little white outfit, sleeveless, belted at the waist and then flaring out into shorts. I'd thought it was a dress when I tried it on, but I liked

THE COVER GIRL

the way my legs looked, toned and endless, and I could feel spring coming. That was the magic of clothes, I was learning.

"How are you, darling?" Harriet asked. She did this while shuffling through stacks of papers, detached Filofax cards, scribbled *While you were out...* messages, so I assumed she was just being polite and murmured that I was fine. We spent some time going through my book, and then Harriet read me a list of potential jobs that would work with my school schedule.

Most of it was auditions or go-sees I'd gone on before, jobs I was already not getting. When Harriet said the words "album cover," her voice was an eye roll. She didn't bother editorializing. She rattled off a few more: ballet catalog (again), travel agency brochure (could be interesting), cola (not Coke).

I said I looked forward to going out for whatever she sent me on. She appreciated that I did not take the barrage of *noes* personally because I never put my comp card in just one basket. And because I had already given the right answer, I took a chance and asked, my voice unnaturally high, for more information about the album cover.

"You're kidding me." I said nothing. "It's a rock album. Can't read the guy's name. Therese's handwriting is terrible." I knew Harriet had probably written it herself, had stopped trying to fully form letters as her interest waned. "Do you really want to go for that?"

I knew nothing about rock music. I couldn't even conjure up the image of an album cover at that moment. But I knew I should try to be more than a ballet catalog model—Harriet herself wanted me to be more than that—and it sounded different. Interesting, even. A world I had not yet traveled to. I offered her a smile and a half shrug and she shook her head slightly. But she said okay.

The go-see for the album cover was unlike anything I'd gone to see about before. For one, I had no idea what to wear. The latest fashion didn't seem quite right. Neither did the freshly scrubbed, hint-of-mascara and colorless-lip-gloss face I normally presented. It seemed to me that rock music would require something bolder, something louder: black mascara instead of brown, red lip gloss, and my hair flowing long and loose to my elbows.

That was as loud as I could go. I was still one of Harriet's girls, after all.

And then there was the fact that it wasn't a go-see at all. It was much closer to what people referred to as a cattle call, a phrase I hated. This was more for a girl who was hoping to be discovered, not something for a girl with representation.

We were told to stand in line. I stood between a thin redhead who was taller than my own five-ten and had the palest skin I'd ever seen, and a shorter curly-haired girl with the narrow middle and dramatic curves of my mother's favorite vase. I liked to study the other models, not because they were my competition but for the puzzle. You could tell by the way the girls stood what they thought—or had been told—their standout feature was. The redhead's hair, the short girl's breasts. For me, legs, so I had on a pair of white shorts that displayed everything from the two-inch inseam on down.

It was just supposed to be test shots, and they'd bring the photos back to the rock star and he would pick out a few of us he wanted to see, and it would go from there. *We'll take it from there* was something assistants said a lot that day. I would not include this information when I reported back to Harriet. She'd never let me do something like this again.

He wasn't supposed to be there that day. At least no one told us he would be; maybe the people in charge didn't even know. He wasn't there, and then he was. He was taller than us all, even the redhead in front of me, brown hair hanging wild down the back of his mostly unbuttoned shirt, jaw working a piece of gum like it owed him something. He turned, scanning the hallway, then grabbed a man with a clipboard. The men with the clipboards always knew what to do. He pointed and asked my name. The clipboard man looked at me and back to his sheet and told him: *Birdie Rhodes*. It didn't seem to occur to them that we could all hear, and I found myself listening with the other girls, as though they were talking about someone else.

"That's the one," he said.

There were no test shots. He grabbed me out of the line and I had the job, just like that.

The shoot was a week later and like almost every other one I'd done. They blew out my hair, they painted my lips and lined my eyes. They gave me tiny stretchy shorts and a black halter top, two strings sprouting up from the ruched center to tie around my neck. Red high heels topped it all off.

The full treatment, but all I had to be was legs.

I was placed in front of a white backdrop. Feet apart, hands on hips. Right foot forward, left foot back, like ballet. I walked back and forth on an invisible tight rope. I walked like I was born in spiked heels.

All I had to be was legs, and then he showed up. He watched a few poses and listened to the click of the camera, and I looked anywhere else in that room, feeling his eyes on me all the same.

"This is all wrong," he said. "Her legs are supposed to be in the air. That's what I said I wanted."

"Of course," someone responded from a chair near the camera. "We'll flip the photo."

"It won't be the same." He walked across the room, right up to where I was standing. "Birdie," he said. My name coming out of his mouth was a jolt. He looked me right in the eye. "Would you be willing to do it the other way?"

What did it feel like, that first moment, the first time he really saw me?

Like I could see my past, present, and future right there?

Like love at first sight?

Like nothing would ever be the same again?

Like I was looking into the eyes of my soulmate?

No.

Like I was the one with the power.

I nodded slowly. I was a professional. No one would ever tell Harriet I refused to do what I was asked. If he needed me to lie on the floor and point my toes in the air to sell albums, I was being paid to do that very thing.

And then, just as I was about to sit down, he reached out a hand to help ease me to the floor and paused, looking deeply into my eyes. "How old are you?" he asked.

I did not say fifteen. I was possibility, a canvas, not an age. What I said was *old enough*, which is the kind of answer you give when you're learning how the truth tastes when it is bent to meet your needs, how different from a lie it feels in your mouth.

I lay on the floor and pointed my toes to the ceiling, holding different poses: crossed and uncrossed, hinged at the knee, scissored at the ankles, the way nice girls sit in church. I turned to the side and bent my legs slightly, as though kicking off my shoes: a natural act slowed down to the bizarreness of its parts.

All I had to be was legs.

Two days later, my mother handed me the phone and said it was for me. The voice on the other end barely waited for me to finish saying hello before informing me the rock star would like to take me to lunch to thank me for my good work. I was given a time, a hotel restaurant for the next day.

It felt like being underwater, everything blurry and slow as the hours until I would see him drifted by. The regular world but also not.

I stopped at a salon beforehand to have my hair blown out shiny and full right before lunch. I bought a new dress, a black lace shift that barely covered my backside. On my feet: new

THE COVER GIRL

espadrille sandals with thick black ribbons tied at my ankles. I winged out dark eyeliner and dabbed on pale pink lipstick.

The lunch meant nothing.

It could mean everything.

So much fancy food on that restaurant menu, so tempting after days of cucumbers and hard-boiled egg whites to look as slim as possible for the album shoot, and still, I ordered the salad. Even that was impossible to eat in front of him. I tried to ask insightful things about music, but he kept turning the conversation back to me, wanted to know more about what kind of jobs I did and what I liked the most, why I chose modeling.

So I told him that I loved the clothes, that once I'd started putting on different things, I could see the point to all of them—what the right skirt or pants could do.

"You take care with how you dress," he said, looking me over. "You're creating something."

My heart leaped in my chest and I nodded, head bobbing too quickly in my excitement. Yes. Yes. He got it. He was the first person I had met who was not content to just let me listen, and I hoped I sounded smart as I explained to him what it felt like to see those first test shots, to see every photo since as a new reflection—yes, yes, a creation. With the right clothes, I could be anyone.

"So who are you?"

How could I know the answer to this? Is this what my mother meant when she said I had no personality, when she said I was dull? He saw me, though. Saw something. So I asked who he thought I was.

It was an honest question. I wanted him to tell me why we were here, why he cared about anything I was saying. A look I couldn't read passed over his face, and I wondered if I'd said the wrong thing.

But after a moment, he said, "I think you're different."

We talked until the lunch service ended, until the tables were reclothed for dinner, until if he were anyone else, throats would have been cleared to signal we needed to leave.

"Do you have to be anywhere?" he asked. "I'm staying here, and I'd love to get your opinion on this song I'm working on."

Deeper underwater as I followed him to the elevator, up to the top floor into an expansive room overlooking New York. How was I here? Deeper still as he pulled out the guitar and played a few chords. His singing voice was soft in this room, a few lines about a girl he couldn't get out of his head.

"I started working on this right after the shoot," he said. "I think it might be about you."

What happened was my eyes welled up and I didn't know why, so I looked to the side like a picture, like I was told to play bashful. It was too much to receive such attention, like stepping into the Florida sun after a cold Connecticut winter. So when he asked if he could kiss me, I nodded, grateful for a chance to close my eyes for a moment.

He asked how old I was again when we were in his bed, his jeans pushed far enough down his narrow hips for me to see where the trail of hair on his stomach led. He'd slipped my dress over my head and he took in my plain white cotton underpants, my bra with the small pink rosette stitched in the center. I knew how to use makeup and how to dress in women's clothes but failed to account for what a woman might wear under those clothes, that whatever it was wouldn't come from the Young Miss section of a department store. I watched his eyes fall to the little rosette burning through my sternum. And so when he asked how old I was, I told him *almost sixteen*, which weighed as lightly as the almost-truth on my tongue because it was, after all, the age I would turn next. Never mind that I'd just had a birthday.

The times this had happened before felt like an extension of modeling. Take away the camera and what do you have: *Move this way a little, Turn your leg that way, Put your mouth here, just like that, yes.* I could take direction, could adjust myself into any pose necessary, and, just as with the camera, I could turn my head and let my body take over.

I didn't know it could be different until then. He palmed my stomach, as if to press me down to the bed, as if to say: *Stay*. As if I could have done anything else.

Does it matter what happened or not that afternoon?

The truth: he didn't let me touch him. My hands moved without me thinking, and he stopped me every time, folding one over the other in a prayer. It was less than I'd been part of before and also more, because there wasn't a destination he was trying to reach. I could be any girl in the back of a car at the top of a quiet street, just a different kind of captain of a different kind of team.

It felt like hours before he suggested someone might wonder what had kept me so long in the city, and I knew how to take a dismissal. But he pressed a slip of paper into my hand. "Call my driver if you want to come see me tomorrow." Before I could leave, he kissed my cheek and said, "Can this be between us for now? I'd hate for the paparazzi to follow you."

Of course. I couldn't imagine anything worse.

The moment I got home, I found my manicure scissors and sat on my bedroom floor, snipping each thread from the back of my bra until the rosette fell to the floor.

A few days later, Harriet asked me to meet her for lunch, and my first reaction was to wonder what I'd done wrong. She'd never asked me to meet her outside the office before.

We met at the kind of restaurant where people *do lunch*, the kind of place where your people and my people meet for the important business we needed them to discuss with each other. Dim lighting, the low hum of business talk, servers who appear from the shadows to refold your napkin or refill your glass. I wore a

48   Amy Rossi

black dress and a chignon and when I looked at Harriet, I realized what I had done was try to be her mirror. See: I am good.

Once the orders were in—a martini and a steak, rare, *yes that's all, don't insult me with potatoes* for Harriet and another salad for me—she leaned back in her upholstered chair. "How do you feel about runway?"

Runway. She'd mentioned it that first day, but I didn't know much about it, not enough to have feelings.

"It wouldn't pay well starting out," she said. She pulled the silver cocktail pick out of her glass, frowning as she regarded three lewdly stuffed olives. "But you have your whole career in front of you. If you walked for some up-and-coming designers, we could establish very strong relationships. I had a girl end up in *Vogue* because she walked for a designer when he wasn't a big name. I want to start considering you for fashion. You could have the right look. It's a good way to get your name in some different circles if you're open."

Of course I was open, as Harriet must have known I would be.

Once our food arrived, though, her steak naked and seared just to the point of rare, my salad shimmering and ridiculous in its low bowl, Harriet changed the subject. "So. Who is he?"

I shoved a vinegary chunk of lettuce in my mouth, shaking my head slowly.

"Darling." Her tone made it clear she'd detected bullshit. "It's all over you." She cut a precise bite of steak, dragging it through the pool of red. "Does your mother know?"

I shook my head again.

"Of course not." Harriet opened her handbag and slid a card across the table. "Do yourself a favor, darling. Take some time while you're in the city and visit a doctor. No, let me say it clearly so there is no misunderstanding: *get a diaphragm.* Don't look at me like that. It's easier to take care of an *oops* these days, but we don't need to let it get that far. It's so tedious to have to update a girl's measurements. Didi can take you."

There was no point in telling her she was wrong, that I didn't even need a diaphragm, that it was deeper than that. She'd already decided.

Later, I stood in front of the mirror, trying to see what Harriet saw. Was I brighter now that someone else had discovered me?

I saw him every day after that first time. He had a member of his entourage call my house again and ask me to come see him, told me to call the driver when I was ready. He must have known I would never have used the number he'd given me myself, not for lack of desire but because I couldn't imagine someone like him would want someone like me. I needed to be invited.

I was not a girl looking for a secret. It was as simple as this: I went because he asked me to.

And yet. He not only saw me, took in the whole of me, but he wanted to listen to me—he thought I had things to say. In his eyes, I wasn't dull. He saw my shine.

The only other person who ever took an interest in peering below the surface I offered was Harriet Goldman.

I asked him to play a song every time I saw him, and every time, he lit up like I'd plugged him in. I wanted to be where someone wanted me. I wanted to be the girl in his song.

4

I went to the doctor. I got the diaphragm, because Harriet had told me to, even though I didn't need it. Then I needed it. I was booked to walk in a runway show for a wunderkind designer named Azrian de Popa, which gave me an excuse to spend a whole week in the city. I stayed in the agency's brownstone with Didi—who'd upgraded to a copy of *The Shining*—and a few other underage girls of Harriet's on different assignments. Regardless of what our jobs were, we had a nine o'clock curfew each night to ensure we were fresh-faced and rested for our morning call times; he always had me back at the house at eight forty-five.

Runway modeling, as Harriet had said, was an investment in the future. Fashion shows were just that: shows. You wanted to be seen, to show what you could do. Maybe eventually you would become the muse, the body for a Givenchy or the inspiration for an editor like Grace Mirabella.

I spent four days in fittings, half-finished dresses pinned around me on a Monday only to become something completely different by Tuesday. It didn't matter—when I caught glimpses of myself in the mirror, I knew what was being made was art.

It wasn't what you'd find in a store or on a shoot. It was the vision of one person, and I couldn't stop looking.

Azrian's name was uttered constantly, but it wasn't enough to make him appear. He was elsewhere, pondering photographs and sketches, undoing each finishing touch. Pieces of structured suit pants flowed from my waist. One garment appeared to be just a scarf, a silken thing as tall as I was that no one could figure out how to drape properly because it wasn't supposed to be draped at all. *Structure!* was the battle cry. Every hour we spent preparing for the show snapped by in double time; I had no idea how we'd pull it off when everything seemed more like fabric than clothes. This was, I assumed, what it meant to be a wunderkind. This was, to me, magic.

"Look at the way this sits on the hip."

"The torso is too long for that piece."

"This hides the waist. You know how he feels about that."

Always *the*, never *her*. I kept the body parts still as I was measured and remeasured, barely flinching when the assistants missed with the pins.

When I wasn't with Azrian's team, I learned how to walk from a runway coach named Nadine, who had a pixie haircut and a heavy French accent. She was, according to Harriet, the best. Nothing I did pleased her, which only made me want to please her more. But walking was not as simple as one foot forward and then the other, not for a runway. Having to think about it made me as clunky and hesitant as a baby. Nadine showed me grainy footage of the 1973 Versailles show, and I watched, transfixed: the magic of Pat Cleveland, the elegance of Bethann Hardison, the sparkle of Marisa Berenson.

"See how they move? See how they show their personalities?" she barked.

I saw. I walked, inspired by the beauty she'd shown me, and she stopped me after two steps. Personalities, yes, but no smiles.

"Stop it! Stop smiling!"

I hadn't even realized what my mouth was doing.

I molded my lips into the moment before a kiss and Nadine nodded her approval. She handed me five-inch heels and made me walk back and forth: "*Lift* the knee, *lift* the knee."

It became a chant until I developed a kind of prance-like stomp, hips slanting ahead of the ribs, unfurling the whole length of the legs to fully showcase the movement of the clothes, the power of the stitching, the magic of the right angle, the mastery of the fabric.

I practiced my walk without Nadine. I tried it in the clothes being fitted for my body.

And when the rock star asked me to come see him, as the clock ticked closer to my curfew, I did the walk across his room wearing one of his tee shirts knotted at my waist, his music blasting in the background, my hips swaying to the drums. He clapped as if he was delighted, and to me, that was as good as anything that would happen in the hotel bed. I performed bigger and bigger, chasing his reaction. The mirrors offered fragments of leg, a cloud of hair. The mirrors suggested there was confidence in that strut. I kept my eyes on the girl in the glass reflection, but whoever she was inched farther away the closer I got.

Until the final rehearsal, the other models were just bodies in passing, dress forms pinned in possibility. But once we were all in the room together, seamstresses and assistants and Azrian himself, finally, we became a team: the girls.

Azrian was maybe five foot two from the soles of his feet to the crown of his head, but platform boots, a silver-streaked pompadour, and the energy vibrating from his every pore made him tower above the room. There were six of us, our first-walk outfits still basted in some places. Will it be a pocket? One strap or two? Decisions to leave until the final-final moment.

We lined up in order, the first girl disappearing out of our

THE COVER GIRL

sight. Seconds later: a scream. We ran out to the catwalk to find the model splayed across the floor, holding her ankle.

"The shoes!" Azrian wailed. "I knew they would be too slick."

"We'll scuff them," an assistant said, the anxiety still hanging in the air.

Our shoes were all taken away, one at a time, to have the soles scuffed enough to give us traction. Ice appeared for the girl who'd fallen, and she sniffled through the rest of her walk, barefoot.

All this mention of the runway, and there it was in front of me, so much longer and narrower than I had imagined. *Lift* the knee, *lift* the knee; I took each step on the balls of my feet. No use in getting accustomed to feeling the ground under me. It wasn't the same as being in front of a camera, but it was a different kind of freeing, this task of making the clothes come to life, of using my body to show the garment going sheer in unexpected places or the range of possibilities contained within black-and-white fabric. The final walk I took with a hand on my hip, not because it would look good—though I could tell by the release of Azrian's shoulders that it did—but because I had to hold my dress together.

These were the details I kept and cataloged, turning from incident into story so I could report back in the rock star's hotel room that night. So I could watch him watch me tell it.

The rehearsal extended well past my curfew, though, so instead of taking a cab to him, I had to wait for Didi to escort me back to the brownstone. Azrian stood outside alone, staring at the city lights. The day had been tiring for me, certainly, but I couldn't imagine what it was for him—the pressure of this show, the decisions that still needed to be made, the knowledge that other people were waiting on those decisions. He caught me staring and I could see him shift his expression into something somehow both more friendly and more aloof.

"You are one of the girls? Tell me your name again," he said. After I told him, he looked right at me and asked, "What do you think?"

Nobody had asked me that on a job before. My role was, I thought, to say something quick and polite, to take the focus off me and put it back where it belonged. But this show had brought me something new, and maybe he needed to hear that. So I told him the truth: that this week had been incredible. That I had never seen clothes like his before, that it felt like wearing works of art. That he made me think about modeling differently—I could be part of the art. I thanked him for making this happen.

Azrian closed his eyes for a moment, then kissed me on each cheek. "Birdie, my dear, you do understand. I am so glad you have joined us. And I hope after this, our paths will cross again. We have our entire careers ahead of us."

A flash of realization: I could be wanted here too.

I was glowing the entire taxi ride home, barely paying attention to Didi, and it was only a few hours later, just after the sun was up and the nightlife was tucked back into the alleys, that I was back for the blur of the fashion show. There was hair and makeup like on a regular job, yes, though it was friends of Azrian taking care of the six of us. And the drama of it all—a cotton-candy cloud of blond teased out in all directions, eyeliner slashed to my temples. Backstage, a madhouse: models in various stages of dress and undress, the friends following us around with enormous aerosol cans, spritz-spritz-spritzing any head in sight until hair spray hung dense in the air. The girl who had fallen walked carefully, her eyes just to the point of glazed from whatever she'd taken to convince them not to replace her. Azrian ran back and forth across the room, panicking and telling us to be calm, pulling accessories off and putting new ones on only to go back to the original necklace or bracelet, singing, "Where are the shoes, where are the shoes." He lit a cigarette and set it down to fix a problem or create one, then lit another.

THE COVER GIRL

55

I watched this unfold as I stood in my undergarments, waiting for the hem to be finished for my first walk piece.

The assistant in charge of the scuffing rushed in, bleary-eyed. She wordlessly held up three pairs of shoes, no explanation for what happened to the rest.

The room fell silent as we pretended not to look at Azrian. He inhaled so deeply he seemed to grow even taller. Full minutes of silence passed before he said, "Fine. Girls, you will have to share the shoes."

We would share the shoes. It wouldn't matter if someone was a size eight and the only available pair was a seven. This was what we did best.

I stopped for a split second to look at myself. My legs were silhouetted through the fabric of the pants and my white blouse had been molded to my body, one dramatic collar point sweeping out to my shoulder. Nothing I could wear in regular life, but isn't that the magic of fashion? I had never felt more beautiful.

Places.

And then: the lights, the music, the audience, the runway, even longer and narrower than it looked during rehearsal. My first thought: *I can't do this.* There wasn't time for a second one. An assistant shoved shoes onto my feet and the stage manager was shouting, "Go, go, go," in my ear and so I went. Lifting the knee down an invisible tightrope, hips swinging and toes just touching the runway. Turn right, pause for the flashbulbs, turn left, and again. It was over so fast, and then I was backstage again, the pants removed, the shoes whisked away for the next girl, dress held open for me to step into. New earrings, new necklace, hair up and *go, go, go.*

At the end, we all came out together, half of us without shoes, a collection of girls whose individual-*ness* was dwarfed by couture and Breck. It was only here that we could smile, and I did. The girl I walked alongside squeezed my hand and I couldn't help but laugh. What a spectacle it was. What a world that we were needed here.

And then:

Do you see...?

Isn't that...?

That's him! Right there!

The buzz rippled through us girls: A rock star in the front row, watching us. You know the one. He was just on the cover of *Rolling Stone*. Didn't you hear that song all over the radio?

In the post-show throng, when I was still alight from the relentless action of it all, he pressed a bouquet of peonies into my arms. I raised my fingers to his newly bare face, how smooth it looked, but he grabbed my hand and squeezed, returning my arm safely to my side. "You looked amazing out there," he said. "You enjoy all this, okay? Come to the hotel after." He kissed my cheek carefully, our bodies not touching—nothing that would catch the prurient eye of a gossip columnist or paparazzo.

It was enough, though, for Harriet. The moment he was gone, she materialized next to me. "The album cover?"

I nodded. She knew everything anyway, and I didn't want to lie about him anymore, not to Harriet. To lie would be to suggest there was something to hide.

We stood side by side, looking only at Azrian working the room like he hadn't threatened to scrap the whole show or nearly set fire backstage with his unsmoked cigarettes, at the models clinking glasses and laughing with their hair still final-walk big and dresses taking up twice the space of a body. We did not make eye contact as Harriet spoke. "You're fifteen. He's thirty-one."

I hadn't known that, and I was glad we weren't facing each other. If she'd asked, I would have said twenty-five, maybe. But with something so real, did a few years really matter? Harriet, of all people, should understand that some things are beyond age.

"If I were your mother," she continued, "I would go to him and tell him he has no business with you. But I'm not, and if she

THE COVER GIRL

can't see what's right in front of her, I assume she won't hear it either. So I will say this to you, Birdie, as your agent, as someone who is invested in your career. Your focus right now should be yourself. There will be time for all that. Don't do anything that can't be undone."

Since the day I met her, I'd trusted Harriet more than I trusted anyone in the world, even him. I trusted her like she was magic, all-seeing and all-knowing.

I did not trust either of us enough to tell her she didn't understand.

I did not want my focus to be on myself. How lonely that was, and wouldn't I know. There was plenty my mother couldn't see, that was true, but it turned out there were things even Harriet Goldman couldn't see.

At that moment, Azrian arrived in a flurry of champagne and cheek kisses. He pulled me into a cluster of fashion people, people I had to meet. This night was mine.

And then there was the day, three weeks into the affair, when I lied to everyone about where I was and where I needed to be and when, and instead went to the rock star's hotel so that we could have a full night together and wake up in each other's arms. A dinner date. A rooftop bar so he could show me the view of the city and the one he created around us with his presence. A bottle of champagne and a tray of strawberries sent to the room more for the look than for us to consume. He explained his tour would start again soon—he'd been on the road for two years straight, only pausing to finish the album here, and his time with me had made him happier than he'd been in a long while. Silently, I filled in the blank: *this is it*. Of course it was going to have to end sometime. But in the morning, he pressed his face against my back, told me he was in love with me, and asked me to come on tour with him. I laughed because it sounded silly, a wish on a penny or a letter to Santa Claus, and

I said yes because the girl I was in this room always said yes. I said yes because this was too much to be real life.

No one said they loved me in real life. Or that they were in love with me. I couldn't grasp a distinction, having never heard the word. It was safer to believe I had dreamed it in the early morning light, sun lazily pooling through sheer hotel curtains, a what-if sort of hour.

When I went home, I thought about ways we could stay together in the true light of day—he'd have to come back to New York at some point, and maybe Harriet would send me on jobs that required travel. He'd probably send me a plane ticket himself. Maybe it wouldn't have to end, after all.

So it was a surprise to me when he showed up at my house to talk to my parents, a sight so ridiculous it should have been happening to someone else.

What it looked like was this:

The mother and father sat on the brown leather sofa in their special-occasion clothes while the rock star sat across from them, much too tall for the velvet-upholstered chair that used to belong to the grandmother, the rich one, long since dead. He leaned toward the parents earnestly, elbows on knees, in his tight jeans and black shirt—only one-quarter unbuttoned rather than his customary half. He had pulled his hair back and spat out his gum for the occasion. One leg bobbed with energy, and with him in the room, the young model could see how old her parents looked, how creased and tired. She situated herself between the two parties, ankles crossed. Better seen than heard.

They all sat in that living room in Connecticut and the rock star explained to the mother and father his plans for the young model. The traveling part, at least. That, as the face, so to speak, of his album, she'd be an important part of the tour. And it would be good for her career.

The mother and father nodded, their eyes bracketed in bewilderment. They'd heard of the rock star, but they were not

THE COVER GIRL

59

rock and roll people. They were already far out of the target audience and rooted in the decorum of bygone years when Elvis shook his hips on television for the first time, so they had little interest in what had followed over the next twenty-two years, instead preferring crooners and standards. How this man had come to sit in Grandmother Putnam's chair, complimenting the cake as if the mother hadn't bought it at Palmer's Market and asking the father for investment advice, was a puzzle for which they were missing several important pieces.

He told the mother and father how much he cared for their daughter and that he would keep her safe. The young model watched the parents for a reaction, an emotion—how did they feel about this? All they did was nod slowly, like one does at a party when one doesn't understand what one's conversation partner is saying but does not wish to ask questions, lest the conversation continue.

The rock star continued. Traveling with a minor, he explained, could get complicated. Especially with the school year to finish. The model chose not to linger on the word *minor*. No one else did. She was now major. The rock star explained that if the young model wanted, and if the mother and father were willing, the rock star could become her guardian. Oversee her tutoring. Keep her on the right path. He spoke of their daughter so kindly, was so matter of fact in his explanation and so careful not to put the word *legal* before *guardian* that the proposal did, in fact, make sense.

The young model wondered, briefly, if this was too much, too fast. Too big. But all her parents did was bob their heads—*Yes, yes. This sounds right*. Above all, they cared—the mother cared—about how things looked. This looked fine. Special, even.

The mother and father told the rock star that if the young model wished to go on the tour, they would not stand in the way of her career. Though she was not surprised, a part of her had hoped for a fight, something to show they wanted her too.

But because she made her own living and her face and body belonged to magazine pages and album covers, she had already been slipping away bit by bit, and why would the mother and father claim the rest of her? So when they asked if she wanted to go, she said yes. Everyone would get what they wanted.

The ancient family lawyer was called. Papers were signed.

I brought the rock star with me when I went to talk to Harriet, more nervous than I had been when he spoke to my parents. Did we discuss it? Did he ask? Did I ask him? There wasn't a scenario that seemed plausible, and yet there he was. I was too busy rehearsing how to tell her I would be finishing ninth grade on the road and would then be gone for the summer.

The summer. I knew what the papers meant and also I didn't. One season at a time.

I couldn't meet the glossy eyes of the models whose photos lined the hallway. Despite how often I made excuses to come to the city, despite how little authority they had exercised since I became a model, the enormity of leaving my parents was beyond my comprehension. By that, I mean: it was not a thing I thought about. No sooner did it enter my mind than it tumbled into a void. But walking through the halls that day, it felt like the end of something.

He accompanied me, but he stayed in the waiting room, folded into a shiny white chair, knees at east and west while Therese snuck looks from her desk.

I knew Harriet wouldn't like it and expected nothing else beyond that. A small part of me wondered if the fact that she wouldn't like it should tell me something. I trusted her for everything else. She, after all, discovered there was something to me before anyone else cared to look. But surely she didn't discover me to keep me hidden.

When I told her, she didn't nod, didn't adjust her cigarette

THE COVER GIRL

holder, didn't move. "Are you quitting?" she asked. Stone words meeting stone face—this is how you make fire.

I wish I could play a version of this conversation in my head where I sounded sure, strong. A version without childlike fear shimmering out from my corners. I told her I wasn't quitting, not unless she wanted me to, my voice low and quaking.

"Why would I want that? I believe I've made myself clear on that point," she said. "Is this a break, then?"

Not that either. My hands shook as I handed her the mimeographed itinerary, so many stops close to a major airport, see, so maybe there would be fewer go-sees or last-minute bookings, but he was going to fly me to wherever I needed to be. For the summer.

"An itinerary," Harriet said. "How wonderful. I'll pass this along to Therese."

I explained that he was in the lobby if she wanted to talk to him. Maybe we both remembered the first day I'd sat in front of her in that office and she had invited my mother to wait for me outside. "That," she said, "will not be necessary."

The conversation was over, and I had grown quite good at reading when I was supposed to leave. But I couldn't make myself get up. I needed something more from her. A hug? Advice? Mothering? To be told no, I couldn't leave? Nothing I could name and nothing I could ask for, and nothing she could have given. A grasping feeling worked its way from my stomach to my throat to my eyes, and the one thing I knew was I could not let her see me cry. It didn't make sense; this was what I wanted. But maybe that was a childish thought, to expect everything to be simple. I knew better now.

When I finally got up, she asked me to close the door behind me. I was halfway to the lobby when I heard a sound not unlike that of an object being hurled at a wall.

2018

The invitation still sits on the countertop. *Harriet's Girls*. I haven't been called one of those in years.

The legend is this: A young woman answers phones at a famous modeling agency. *The* famous modeling agency. Eventually, she's one of the ones booking jobs and negotiating rates. She sees careers bloom and fall, sees the four seasons of a girl's potential unfold in a week. She sees the distinction between fashion and commercial and what pays what. She sees an assumption that girls will eventually get married and have babies, so who needs longevity, and she sees 1968 on the calendar and knows the times, they are a-changin'.

She sees everything and is invisible to everyone.

She sees a girl leave the agent's office in tears after being told the usual things that boil down to no—too heavy, too plain, too boring, too much in any direction and also not enough—but this one, this one is different. The young woman sees what the agent cannot. She knows about a job. She has earned trust. She has connections.

The girl books the job and then, practically overnight, *Vogue*. She becomes a star. The young woman is fired and lands on her feet at a smaller agency, where the founder is tired of competing with the big famous one and so lets the young woman take the reins. Scouts scout, and agents agent, and bookers book except when the young woman sees true potential and decides a girl is worth taking a more active role for. No need to wait for someone to come to your doorstep when she could be walking down the street. Find them early and build a career. Find them early and help them make some money. Tell the story about Grace Kelly's origins at every chance. Find them early, before the big agency does.

Find them early, and they will always be her girls.

Maybe that last part isn't true.

How much of the rest is?

Does it matter?

I didn't realize we were a thing, that I was a part of such a thing, until months after I started modeling. As in, *Oh, you're one of Harriet's Girls*, said in a way where the capital letters are as pronounced as the words themselves. The implication varied, as it does for women who have never felt the need to shut themselves up or shrink themselves down. But whatever the impressions of Harriet, it could be counted on that we, the Girls, were as quiet and as small as needed. Her voice was enough.

I would walk down the halls of Harriet's office with the photos of the most famous of her girls, the original ones, watching me. And here is how foolish I was: I didn't think of them as my peers. I gave them names like I would have given dolls: Mindy, Rhiannon, Juliet. They weren't so much who I wanted to be as who I imagined watching over me. If I was coming back from a particularly good go-see, it was as if they were signaling their approval in their cocked eyebrows, saucy half smiles. And if it had been a bad shoot, a bad meeting, their expressions would shift into something stern. *Do better, Birdie. We expect more.*

Harriet herself would seldom be so direct. My own mother wouldn't have been able to offer an opinion that held weight

THE COVER GIRL

with me at that time. Perhaps it sounds sad, then, that I leaned on photographs—not even the actual women—for some sort of instruction. Perhaps I should look back and think, of course things unfolded how they did. What other way could they have gone? But even now, years and years later, what I think is: *how resourceful.*

My photo eventually became one lining the hallway. For a couple years I could at least look at myself for some sort of reassurance.

The doctor asks why I am here and I tell her that my previous plastic surgeon died. She blinks at me, keeping her eyes closed just long enough to tell me what she thinks about this as an answer. I see her point but it doesn't make it any less true.

Dr. Rosenthal's funeral was six months ago, tasteful, elegant, the way it is when a death is not foreseen but not unexpected, like a summer thunderstorm. He had just touched up my Botox a few weeks before. At the wake, I stood off to the side, the wide brim of my black hat obscuring my unweeping face. Everyone assumed I was the mistress.

There is a whole scope of human experience out here, yet we can never resist the temptation to distill it down to fucking.

Dr. Rosenthal laid nothing but the most professional hand on me, but I had known him since he rebuilt my nose in the '90s, which made ours one of my longest-standing relationships. Of course the sense of loss is profound; it's why I can no longer visit his practice. My last Botox appointment was too eerie, all these vestiges of him and all these people who thought the length of time I'd been coming meant they knew me. So, a new doctor.

She's not really new, though; her degrees illustrate that she has been practicing for at least a decade, though she is younger than me. This is the world now. They are all younger than me and sometimes that is a punishment and sometimes it is a reward.

"Ms. Rhodes, according to the files sent over from Dr. Rosenthal's office, you went in for a facelift consultation *eight times* over the course of...eleven months?" She shuts the manila folder and stares at me.

I stare back, refusing to be undone by how off-putting it sounds out loud. Why shouldn't making the leap from an injectable to surgery—to cutting open my face—be treated as a serious decision requiring multiple conversations? I do not have to explain myself. The ability to sit in silence is a virtue, and she holds my gaze with admirable steel. When she speaks, it isn't a crack but a doubling down. "Are we doing the facelift?" she asks. "Or do you just want to talk about it? Because if that's the case, I may not be the doctor you need."

And that is how I end up sliding the invitation across her desk.

Dr. Adams picks it up. "So you're preparing for this event?" she asks. I open my mouth, then shut it, and she narrows her eyes. "You haven't made up your mind."

I shake my head.

She glances at the invitation again, then back to me. "Okay, Ms. Rhodes, based on your chart, you're a good candidate for a couple options. You could do a thread lift, which isn't going to last as long, or an upper eyelid lift. You need to decide if that's what you want quickly, so we have time to schedule and give you at least six weeks to heal. You can't rush recovery." Dr. Adams's tone strikes an impeccable balance between kind and firm; she could teach classes.

I tell her I'll decide today. It's too much to choose while sitting there in her office, being watched, knowing I'm already running out of time.

I can't explain why I felt so much comfort going into Dr. Rosenthal's office, beyond the relief of the release of the wrinkles my occasional Botox injection offered. I knew the front office staff thought either I was crazy or we were having an affair, because what I needed was apparently outside their limited imagination. It was a place where it was okay to look older than

THE COVER GIRL

you used to be because he was going to fix it. I liked flipping through his photo books, seeing the examples of what plastic surgery could do. Sometimes I thought about building a whole new face and a whole new life. Sometimes he talked to me about new procedures. I would ask about maintenance: If I had a face-lift now, would I need one every ten years? More frequently? Would what felt like the right thing now become burdensome in the future? I chose not to plumb that one for metaphor.

There is no shortage of things from today's visit to let rattle around my head, and as I drive to my afternoon ad shoot, I am stuck on *I may not be the doctor you need*. What a polite way to say it.

I have tried therapy, more than once. The first one I went to asked, *Do you think you have a before and after?* I didn't answer her because who doesn't have a before and after and also that was the kind of bullshit questioning that made me die a little inside every time someone suggested I talk to a therapist, each one thinking they were the first to say it.

I had avoided that therapist's question. Not because it hurt, because how could it. None of this was real, *I* wasn't real, not in the way other people were. Solid. Corporeal. I was a composite of observations. I didn't need to express how I felt about anything, not then and not even now. Someone was always there to tell me.

But the therapist had pressed further. "Where's the line?" she had asked. "What divides the before and the after?"

I had refused to answer her, but I never forgot the question either. In that way, I suppose, she'd won.

The ad is for a multivitamin. Three postmenopausal women friends, doing postmenopausal women yoga, because they get the nutrients they need to stay premenopausal vibrant from this vitamin.

I know already the yoga will be funny. We are always laughing in these ads, with our fifty-is-the-new-forty humor, unless it's an ad for erectile dysfunction medication. Those might include laughter too, laughter as foreplay, but there's at least a 50 percent chance I'll get to smolder—tastefully, in beige—instead.

If only it were possible to be signed to an exclusive Cialis contract—those kitchens, bathtubs, cars.

But today, it is vitamins. Routine hair, routine makeup, routine expensive yoga clothes and accessories. Routine until I see my postmenopausal women friends. One of them I recognize from auditions. The other I'm certain I've never met until she does a double take. "Oh, my god, Birdie Rhodes! Is that you?"

That name from a stranger's mouth moves through me like the chill of a ghost. I try to correct her: Elizabeth. She doesn't hear me.

"It's me! Sunny! I haven't seen you since New Orleans—that was, what, forty years ago? My god! Remember those days? I had no idea you were still around too."

My first thought is that her *too* is carrying a lot of weight.

My second: that I have two choices. I can let this be uncomfortable for me or I can make it uncomfortable for everyone.

If I focus, if I close my eyes and really think about it, I could probably make myself conjure the job in question. I could make myself remember when.

But I choose not to. It's how I'm still here. Forgetting is not always an accident.

Perhaps I should be more prepared for such things. Perhaps it's only surprising that it hasn't happened sooner. But a career like this is not exactly the standard. There are some women who start famous and stay famous, like Brooke Shields, but there are many more who retire into motherhood or pursue other interests, other careers with more stability and that don't involve the same level of body maintenance and constant rejection. It is a small world, yes, but one we are constantly dropping ourselves off the face of.

THE COVER GIRL

Sunny turns to the other postmenopausal friend, who does not look very post- and could in fact very well pass for peri-. "We did this shoot in New Orleans when we were *teenagers*! That photographer was the *worst*. But those pictures—we had these ridiculous coats. I might be able to find a photo somewhere—you've got to see it. And Birdie completely saved the day, she called her—"

I see I'm going to have to go with uncomfortable for everyone. So I shake my head and interrupt Sunny to say that I'm sorry, but I do not remember.

At first, she laughs. "The fur coats! Gus! Are you serious? You really don't remember this?" When I shake my head again, her expression darkens. "Well," she sniffs. "I guess it *was* forty years ago."

The fitness watch I've been given as a prop flashes with a message: *You're in the cardio zone!* More accurate would be: *Congratulations on your fight-or-flight response! No need to question why.* I fake a few overhead stretches and deep breaths to try to slow my heart.

"Good idea," the other model says. "We should limber up."

Throughout the shoot, I can feel Sunny's glances trying to pin me down, trying to keep me in my head. I close my eyes, let them bounce off. There is no me. There is only a woman who loves yoga and her friends and her vitamins. This is her time.

Later, sitting in traffic, I book the thread lift and the eyelid lift. Why not both? Create a face where the memories should be.

By the time I arrive home, I'm exhausted, and I can hear my landline ringing as I unlock the door. The last thing I want to do is talk to anyone. I know I should become one of those people who only uses their cell phone. There's no reason to pay two bills a month, but I like my old-fashioned avocado-green phone. This old house, built in the 1920s, even came with a little phone nook. What would I put there if not the phone?

But the only people who call me on it are strangers. And

today has included enough of those. So, no, I will not be rushing to answer.

The email pops up on my cell phone ten minutes later. I see the phrases interview request and fifty years of glamour in the subject line. This is what I can look forward to for the next few months. Wonderful.

Dear Ms. Rhodes,

I hope this message finds you well! My name is Michelle Elhert, and I'm a freelance journalist. I've linked to my website below so you can see clips and learn a little bit more about the kind of work I'm doing. I'm working on a piece for a feminist media outlet called *Woolf* about the upcoming celebration of Harriet Goldman and her amazing career. I'd love to speak with you sometime about your experiences modeling, how things have changed over time, and, of course, being one of Harriet's Girls. I've got a couple of the very first models she signed lined up and some of the newest faces too, and it would be terrific to have your voice in the mix. If you're interested, please let me know, or, if you'd prefer, call me at the number below.

Thank you!! Michelle

I have no desire to talk to Michelle Elhert, but I click on the clips she has sent along anyway. She writes for many places, a few I've heard of, about trends on television, the unexpected feminism of a movie that sounded tremendously sexist when I read the review, how the term *beach read* trivializes literature written by and about women and also how we think of our vacations. Her thumbnail photograph is black-and-white. She has wavy hair and thick eyebrows, which are apparently back. One bio mentions she graduated college in 2016. She is young, so

THE COVER GIRL

young, and I imagine it's not terribly lucrative or at least easy to make a career as a freelance writer.

I do not do interviews. There was a time in the late '70s or early '80s when I would answer a few fluffy questions for teen magazines. But I was taught that you don't have to try to control the narrative if you never offer the narrative to begin with, so I have not done an interview since then, not when I was supposedly making a comeback for the first, second, or third time. There have been a few phone calls or emails like this over the years, and I have ignored each one. This is how I have survived, how I have avoided ending up on some sort of internet slideshow or as a talking head—or a subject—in one of those ridiculous *The Outrageous '70s* television documentary things that were so popular as the '90s faded into the 2000s. It was very important we remember what has just happened. Or that we align ourselves with the version of events in the way they are being remembered. Of course I read and watched all those things, the way you watch a horror movie, one eye open, fingers splayed across the face.

There is absolutely no reason for me to do anything other than send this email to the trash and go about my business. Still, it lingers with me into the evening. A narrative is forming, whether I offer it or not. I open her message again, and this time, I see a PS at the bottom:

Sorry if this sounds silly, but I always thought your Swish ad was the most beautiful thing I've ever seen.

It is almost enough to make me crack open that old portfolio.

If you remember a depilatory cream campaign from the '70s or '80s, odds are it was the one with a group of young women kick-lining down a stoop or on the bleachers as they lip-synched a catchy tune that declared Nair a requirement for anyone who dared to wear short shorts like they did. Swish didn't crack the cultural memory. They stopped making Swish more than twenty years ago.

Maybe if I weren't still avoiding my Pilates studio. Maybe if Dr. Rosenthal were still here. Maybe if Sunny hadn't tried to make her memories my own.

Maybe if Harriet hadn't decided what my story would be.

Maybe I would choose differently then.

What I tell myself is that it's the right thing to do. While I'm not an important get for her, I have been modeling for decades. I do, in fact, have perspective on the industry and how it has changed. The way fifteen-year-olds don't walk the runway anymore, at least not as unquestioned as I did. How *Vogue* doesn't book girls under eighteen like they used to. This young woman is trying to make her living, and I am in a position to help.

But also: *come on.* I got my first Botox injection back when it was a whisper among plastic surgeons and dermatologists. There is always a new cream to try, and if they told me rubbing raw meat on my face would eliminate fine lines, I would hold steaks to my forehead.

I don't know how you stick around in this industry as long as I have and not end up at least a little bit vain. And I am. And this writer has done the work to find my name and figure out who I am and how best to contact me.

You also can't be around as long as I have and not be a little grateful when someone knows you as more than a background image in an ad for calcium supplements. When someone thinks you still matter.

Aging is a privilege, and it's also a bitch. And it's further complicated by decades of making a living off the perception that I am pleasing to look at. I don't have the pressure of supermodel fame, but I still know what it's like to have turned heads. To have gotten special treatment. Knowing it was both silly and unfair didn't make me enjoy it any less, nor did it make me any less aware when the attention faded. There were many times

THE COVER GIRL

when I longed for invisibility, but now that it's finally being afforded to me, I realize that what I had wanted was to get to choose when to be seen, and how.

So sometime after midnight, when I finally get into bed, too tired to sleep, I send one word to Michelle Elhert: Okay.

1977–1978

Walk This Way

1

The next part, as it happened, time stilled. The only way to look at it.

The front of the bus declares our first stop is Boston. Both buses—one for us, and one for the equipment and whoever's in charge of the equipment. It isn't a long drive, but that's the purpose of the bus, he explains: it will take you everywhere six, eight, ten hours at a time.

The first time is different and every time after that runs together.

This will apply to everything on this tour.

He told me I'd see the country. He told me the bus was the smartest way to travel, that so many other musicians undertook monster tours only to end up sinking a huge part of their profits into private planes. The planes, he said, were for people who needed the star part more than the rock. He talked about the tour bus as some sort of sacred space.

And then he brings me aboard.

I want to see the magic, but all I see, all I smell is vinyl. The seats are a dull brown, covered in the kind of material no one who has worn shorts or a miniskirt would ever choose—all you have to do is look at it to know exactly how it would feel against your sweaty thighs. I remind myself that this is my new home, at least for now. That in itself is magic enough.

We walk down the center aisle of the bus, and he introduces the band as names and functions. *Eddie. Plays bass.* He says it like that, in two sentences, as though that's all there is to Eddie. Eddie's hair hangs flat down the sides of his face into the collar of his denim shirt. His mustache is thick enough to obscure anything less than a pronounced movement of his mouth—if he is smiling or frowning or sneering at this new addition to the tour bus, I can't tell—and he flicks his eyes up at me and back down again, grunts a sound that could perhaps be construed as a hello. My own greeting comes out whispered and half-formed. That's Eddie.

Beasley. Rhythm guitar. No clarification on whether Beasley is a first name or last. He is, from what I can tell, almost in style, wearing a plain tee shirt tucked into tight jeans, blond hair carefully feathered. It seems like Beasley should have a girl with him too. Maybe eventually. Maybe on the next stop. But just as I'm thinking that perhaps Beasley will be the one to supply me with a girlfriend for the road, someone with whom I can giggle about this bus and sneak off when the men get to be too much, he looks at me and laughs. "You're fucking joking," he says to the rock star, and I don't know what this joke could possibly be, only that I'm the target. We move past Beasley without another word.

Ham. Drums. I repeat the name back, uncertain I've heard correctly; surely he meant Sam. But no. Ham rolls his eyes and leans forward in his seat to shake my hand as he introduces himself as Hamish. The long *a* of his name doesn't really serve as an explanation for why a grown man would want to be called after a lesser lunch meat, but perhaps on a tour bus one doesn't pick these things as much as one is picked by them. Ham unfurls a

THE COVER GIRL

list of questions at me in a heavy Scottish accent, and I do my best to answer—*Connecticut, a model, on a shoot*—but the rock star doesn't let us linger long. There is still one person left to meet.

"And this," he tells me, "is the Doctor."

I hear the capital letter. I hear that this is a man who would not answer to Doc. I am not sure what instruments are left, so I ask what the Doctor does.

"Everything." This answer comes from the Doctor himself.

"If you need anything at all," the rock star says, "just ask the Doctor."

"But let's not need too much." The Doctor laughs, no humor behind the dry *heh, heh, heh*. I cannot fathom needing anything so badly that I would ask this iceberg of a man for it. A weathered cowboy hat obscures his face. He could be the rock star's age or fifty, I can't tell. His voice is harsh gravel, and with his hat pulled down so low, I don't know where he is looking.

The rock star leads me to the back of the bus, where we will have a full view of everyone but be obscured from their view until a bathroom break is needed. He shows me the toilet and I hope I am never desperate enough to need to use it. I don't want to think about peeing with that group of men just outside the flimsy accordion door, let alone anything else.

He takes the inside seat in the second to last row, and I hesitate. There are empty seats on the other side of the aisle, behind and in front of him too. We've been together for the longest stretch of time I have ever spent in the company of a person I'm not related to, and I'm wondering if it's too much, if he'd rather be alone. I wait until he pulls me down beside him, giving me my place.

And then we're off. I'm next to him in that sticky seat, still waiting for something, a signal. He leans back, throws a large hand across my thigh, and is asleep within minutes. The whole bus is quiet, and I wonder if it's because of my presence, if they're holding back on my account or resenting the fact that I'm here at all. If there's conversation, I'm not meant to hear it. It's just the drone of rubber on highway. My eyelids flutter shut.

In some ways, it's more glamorous than I would have thought, but the glamour is always short-lived. The first hotel, for instance—not to be gotten used to, as the bus also means we can drive all night.

It is not our job to deal with the luggage or equipment or wherever the buses need to be parked. It is not our job to check in. We wait while the Doctor talks to the concierge and gets our room keys. He tells everyone what time to be at the arena tomorrow. When we get off the bus, there are screaming fans, all girls, waiting, thrusting their arms and albums at the rock star. I hold my breath as I follow behind, looking down as he waves and says hello.

Because we have barely ventured into the real world together, every time we do, I am reminded he is not a rock star like I am a model. He is not working toward something. He is there. If I looked for him in magazines, I would find him. If I listened for his name in casual conversation on the street, it would come. He is famous.

And he chose me.

We take an elevator to the top floor. This isn't my first hotel room, and it's not even the first fancy one I've visited—after all, I spent plenty of time in his hotel in New York. But he was living out of that room. This one is freshly made up just for him: one bottle of the beer he likes on ice, a can of mixed nuts, three sharpened pencils, two peeled and segmented oranges, a bowl with two steaming washcloths. He takes one and presses it to his face, then sees me watching and passes me the other. I take it and ask why all these things are here.

"Because I asked for it," he tells me. I wonder if this is what the Doctor does.

THE COVER GIRL

"Is there something you'd like in the rooms?" he asks. "I can add it to the list."

I try to think of all the things I like, and my mind goes blank. Surely, there is something I want to have waiting for me in each of these rooms, my new home splintered across states I've only heard about, something that would make me feel at ease and remind me I am where I'm supposed to be. The harder I try to come up with something, the further I fall away from what I know about myself. A new dress? Silly. Chocolate? Bad for the figure. A nail file? Too practical, and is this really what I would want *waiting* for me in hotel rooms across the country? I realize I need to come up with something because if I don't, he might find me as dull as my mother says I am and regret bringing me. Entire minutes seem to have passed before I tell him bubble bath.

"Bubble bath? You got it." He grabs one of the pencils and makes a note on the tiny notepad he keeps in his back pocket. "Any particular scent?"

I can't remember if I've ever had a lavender shampoo or lotion, but it's the first thing that comes to mind. It sounds womanly, sexy.

Within an hour, there's a knock at the door to our room. The rock star disappears for a moment and returns with lavender bubble bath on a silver tray.

I hope I like baths.

The concert isn't until the next day, a luxury that we are only allowed in the breezy beginning of this leg, so that first night in the first hotel we order room service. He gets a steak; unlike Harriet, he wants extra potatoes. There can't be too many potatoes. He wants to swim in potatoes. The steak is a vehicle for the potatoes. I contemplate for a moment getting something different, some kind of extraordinarily French chicken or maybe grilled fish, but I get the salad, with a shrimp cocktail at least to make it a little celebratory. I have a job to do, and when I go back to New York, I will not give anyone the chance to think I look different.

Also, I know I can digest salad. I can't risk what extra butter or a streak of cream sauce would do to my stomach, not here. Not with just a door separating us.

We eat by the window, overlooking the city at sunset: the swirl of roads and cars, the dull green of the baseball stadium, the puff of flowering trees, the slashes of orange sky.

That first night, I am nervous. Him and me and empty hours, not even the hum of the bus or Eddie's snoring. It's a large hotel room and still it's awfully small quarters to share with someone you don't know well, someone like him who takes up space and air at twice the rate of a regular person. It will take time before I can relax into the assumption that we'll go to bed together and go to sleep together and wake up together with rumpled hair and stale breath and smeared mascara, and that that will be okay, that this is a side he wants to see. It will take time before something like washing my face and brushing my teeth before lying down next to him feels normal. It will take time before I stop looking behind me, before I settle into this as my life, rather than something I'm just along for the ride for. That first night, I listen to him breathe beside me for hours before I eventually fall into my own light sleep.

The first concert. He has to leave late in the afternoon for sound check—do I want to come, or do I want someone to bring me later? I don't know what a sound check is, so I pack a bag for my show attire and follow him down to the bus, past a throng of girls.

We duck into the back of the arena, but still there's another cluster of waiting fans shoving albums and posters and body parts at him to autograph. He signs two or three, then grabs my hand. I adjust my sunglasses and keep my face down. The whis-

THE COVER GIRL

pers follow: *Who is that, is that his... I didn't think he was married, I never read anything about a girlfriend.*

The arena is mostly empty during sound check. The Doctor is observing from the wings, and I remember to thank him for the bubble bath. He gives me an odd look; there will be no bonding here. Instead, I pick a seat in the middle of the front section, maybe twenty rows back. The band starts playing—checking—the drums and the guitars, fragments of song but nothing I can put together into one meaningful thing, though I'm not sure I could name that meaningful thing. In truth, the songs he has played for me have all run together. But I'm here now, ready to absorb it. Eventually he emerges, guitar held above his head as he coaxes the strings into the sound he needs. It's so loud it cuts right through me. I move back a section, eventually wandering through upper levels, where he is just a few inches tall and still creating music so powerful I can feel it in my knees.

When it's over, he tells me I can use his dressing room. I change into a satiny cream-colored romper with a pink sash and a cross-front V that peeks open just enough. I mousse my hair and apply what I've heard makeup artists call *a soft look*: pinks and peaches, a sun-kissed glow. Maybe I should buy a magazine on one of these stops so I can figure out what the girlfriend of a rock star is supposed to look like, what kind of clothes will make me fit here, will turn a costume into a uniform. For now, this will have to do.

During the show, I watch from the wings. There will be time enough on this tour for me to find a seat and watch from the same view as everyone else, but this first time I want to see him on my own, as on my own as I can be with a crew rushing back and forth. Someone is on standby when he needs to switch out guitars. Someone else is ready with a towel when he needs to mop himself off. But I pay little attention to all that. I let the music wash over me, into me. I know nothing about rock and roll but I know this is more alive, more electric than what I've heard before, and I am hooked on watching him under the stage lights, the way he commands a microphone and the sound of a crowd singing along.

Beasley and Ham and Eddie are there too, but they could be anybody.

He is another person on stage, screaming to the audience in a throaty pitch I haven't heard before. I'm close enough to see his chest glisten with effort, close enough for it to hurt when I pull off the padded earphones a roadie had slipped onto my head. Close enough to see the women in front bite their lips. To feel his howling vocals shake through my hip bones and the pulse of the drumbeat behind my ears. And to watch him dig into a solo, pull coarse and sweaty sounds from his guitar like his fingers could move through time or fire, watch him lower to the stage floor as if being dragged away by something I can't hear and I will not get him back again. And then he looks up and sees through the song, sees me right on the edge of the audience's sightline, sees me like he doesn't need anything else. Nothing has ever called to me so clearly.

The first time he told me that I should be careful whom I talk to about us, it was only a few days before we left for the tour. He said the guardian label is just a formality, just for travel, and no one else will get it because our world is too different.

"People don't understand what they can't have, Little Bird," he explained.

I thought I understood, but then one night someone asks my name and I start to answer. The rock star reminds me that I don't need to talk to anyone, and I ask what would happen if I mess up.

He takes my face in his hands. "Nothing will happen. But you're newer in your career, and it's better to keep your name out of certain magazines for as long as you can, that's all. Some people will make up lies or try to dig something up about your family, call them for a quote. I just don't want you to have to

THE COVER GIRL

deal with that. If you don't give them a story, you don't have to worry about the story."

The thought of anyone looking into me, figuring out who my parents are and asking them about me, about what they think of me, makes me go cold inside. It's perhaps the worst thing I can imagine and so I vow to never mess up. When anyone wants to know more about me, I let the Doctor step in and tell them they can contact my agent for more information about my rates and how to book me. Money is the best way to end a conversation.

The Doctor really does do everything.

In this little circle, everything seems normal soon enough, even things that shouldn't. Like backstage. After the first few shows, the rock star whisks me back to the hotel or the bus so we can be alone, but in Maryland, we go backstage after, where the same beer he likes, can of mixed nuts, two peeled and segmented oranges, and steaming washcloths await. I take it all in: the haze of smoke, the smell of beer, and so many women, so many girls already cozied up to Eddie, Beasley, and Ham.

The first time I see a girl bend over him—her breasts in his face and her hair flowing down to his lap—and murmur how much she enjoyed the show, I'm sitting right next to him, and I cannot breathe. When he says, "I'm so glad, baby," and thanks her for coming, I think I might throw up. But his hand is on my thigh the whole time, and she soon moves on, and I understand that this too must be part of the show.

It's all about the show. We are a band, an entourage. My backstage pass and big sunglasses make me into a rock and roll princess. I can walk down any hallway in any arena in my short shorts and wedge sandals, and no one asks me a thing. I learn where the most private bathroom in every civic center in the south is located.

The first time Harriet calls me for a job, it's only two weeks later and already I am scared to go without him. I worry I'll fly back to the next city on the tour and be unable to find him.

The first time I leave, I'm reminded that there are people beyond his band, who only look at me when they think I can't see; the roadies, who are an interchangeable bunch with scraggly ponytails forever jamming huge headphones on my ears and muttering about protecting my hearing *goddammit*; and the Doctor.

Outside, people talk. They talk whether I'm there or not, as though I am always only a picture of a person. The makeup woman asks, "Isn't this…?"

"Yeah, that's her," the hair woman says.

"She's only—" Only what? A whisper holds no meaning in a room this size.

"Yeah, well, you know how it is."

"And she's one of Harriet's?"

I can hear the shock, the implication that my new life is incongruous with that of one of Harriet's Girls. Better seen than heard, but my skin burns against the cool foundation she sponges across my cheeks.

I drop off my voucher after the job, an ad for hair lightening spray, another one for the teen magazines. There's a charge in the air, the halls already smell different, even though I've only been away for a couple weeks. I wait in the lobby; Harriet is running behind. It feels as though I am a guest here now rather than a client. There's something lonely in the way Therese feels the need to entertain me with stories of a fashion show gone wrong while Harriet finishes her meeting. I nod along, thinking about when I'll do another show, all the while watching Harriet's closed door. A blonde girl, a teenager not unlike I was, I am, eventually emerges.

"Birdie," Harriet says. I tell Therese it was nice to see her and follow Harriet to her office. I don't wait for her to ask questions. My voice is high and the words tumble out too fast as I tell her about the shoot, how well it went and how they said they'd like to see me again for another campaign, and I debrief her about

THE COVER GIRL

the two go-sees I had while I was in town. She lets me prattle on, regarding me coolly as she replenishes her cigarette holder.

And then she asks how I'm doing. She weighs down those last two syllables with so much emphasis that I choose the most meaningless word I can think of: *fantastic.*

"Well, then. How wonderful." Her tone says something else.

The first time I come back to town, I don't tell my parents. I'll be back again soon enough, I reason, and it seems silly, dramatic even, to visit after such a short time away.

Also, when I called from the road the first time, my mother asked me a series of questions about where I was, what I was eating, what famous people I had met so far. And then, as I was hanging up, she said my name too loudly, almost like a cry. But when I asked what she wanted, all she said was, "There's a good article in *McCall's* this month with tips on how to make conversation. Try to find it. I think it'd help you."

Not the first time I'd been left empty, but the first time I could compare it to feeling full.

That first time I go to sleep in a hotel without the rock star beside me, wrapping his legs around mine, I plan to starfish myself across the entire bed. Instead I wake up curled and cold on the right side, thinking about how he promised me that when I get back, he'll take me to see *Smokey and the Bandit.*

The first time I join back up with the tour, he is waiting for me at the airport gate with a ball cap pulled down low over his face. Just seeing him there makes my heart leap in a way I do not expect. He's here, for me, a pink rose in hand. He picks me up like I am nothing. I wrap my legs around his waist and he holds me like I've been gone for years. I hold on right back.

This is, I decide, what it feels like to be loved. It makes me want to work all the time and also never go to work again.

A few weeks later, I read an article in *Rolling Stone* that describes him as "part of an era bent on redefining rock and roll decadence." That writer must not know he has our itineraries typed up and cross-referenced, drivers holding signs in airports with my name written across them in his handwriting and a tiny heart scribbled in the corner, cheery messages waiting for me when I check into a hotel: *Have fun, You're going to do great, Can't wait to see you in Milwaukee.*

Because his work makes it all possible, I decide it's time to learn more about music. I listen to The Who, Led Zeppelin, The Rolling Stones. When we get to stay in hotels, while he's busy, I call down to the front desk and request that someone please bring me KISS records and also a record player. It's too much to say I like it, but it does feel like knowing him.

I ask him why he isn't in a band like the others, why his is the only name splashed across the album covers. "I write the songs and I play the songs and I sing the songs. I don't need another name," he tells me. "The band is me."

It sounds selfish but when I watch him from my perch in the wings, the way his body contorts to fit the music, the way he'll lean into a gravity-defying backbend because that is what the guitar needs from him in that moment, how his voice leaves nothing behind—the band may as well not even be there. He is all anyone can see.

2

Late at night on the bus, when we're both awake and shouldn't be, I ask him to tell me something. "What should I tell you?" he says. I don't know what I want to know—anything about him, really. I know him now—but what was his life before me? So I ask him to tell me about California.

He smiles. He starts from the very beginning. He was born there, right near the bottom of the state, in San Diego. Whatever The Beach Boys were singing about, he was living it. I want every detail, so I ask what he means.

"You know, 'Surfin' Safari,' all that?" When my face fails to register a hint of recognition, he laughs. "Well, thank god you have me. You have a lot to learn."

I am ready to be taught. He talks about the magic of riding a wave, of surrendering to the power of the ocean. He talks like this is something he loves but doesn't do anymore, and before I can ask him, he tells me about the day he went out, knowing the waves were too big, too dangerous, and he slipped off the board.

"I'm lucky it was only my knee," he says. Blown out ligaments, surgeries. Months of inactivity. "It made me a different person." His voice is soft, almost dark.

The knee injury disqualified him from serving in Vietnam. The knee injury made him pick up a guitar. This is how he says it, one and then the other, as though the instrument was more meaningful than the risk of death in another country, in a war that no one around me could ever define. And maybe for him it was. I hear something bigger: had he stayed home that day, we might not be on this bus tonight. My mind flashes to my mother and her first husband, the picture I found tucked in the back of a photo album, not meant to be seen but not quite hidden. She'd worn a white suit and a fascinator and a smile that didn't exist outside of that photograph. The man next to her looked nervous, though maybe that was the benefit of retrospect. Without that war, my mother would not have had cause to get married again, and the child she should have had would not have been me. And without the surfing accident, maybe he never would have found the guitar or had the drive to get good at it. Maybe he would have died in Vietnam or killed someone and come back haunted by it and everything else, like my father's cousin. One little choice, to go surfing in a storm, set both of our lives in motion.

I consider saying this, some version of this, out loud. But I haven't mentioned my parents since the day we left on tour and I don't want him to think of me as a girl with a mother and father. I just want him to see me now.

He trails off mid-story about his first song. "Are you sure you want to know all this? I'm not boring you?" I shake my head and tell him I want to know it all. He could never bore me. And there it is, that glow, like I've lit him up from within. "You really are different from every other girl I've known," he says.

I lean against his chest as he compares playing his guitar to getting out of the way and letting the wave pull you up and take you where you need to go. It's about understanding where the power is coming from.

THE COVER GIRL

★ ★ ★

June, somewhere in the Midwest, and I have given up trying to keep track of where and when we are. I'm not the one who has to shout *Hello, Cleveland, Cincinnati, Chicago, Des Moines* every night. The sites grow less exciting, and he tells me that the hotel, the landmark, the concert venue isn't as good as it used to be.

It's getting too hot for bubble baths on our hotel stops, which are more infrequent as the cities become farther apart. My luggage has become loaded with partially used bottles of bubble bath and then I started leaving them behind. It turns out it was the hotel staff who procured them, not the Doctor, and I feel bad not making myself take a bath every time since someone else went to the trouble.

We blow a tire one early morning on our way to Nebraska, and we arrive at the hotel hours later than planned. There's a message waiting for me from Harriet: a last-minute go-see for *Cosmopolitan*, tomorrow. Back in New York. I take the details to the rock star. Is this something the Doctor can help me with? I need to leave tonight.

We're still in the lobby, tired from all the sitting and waiting, and I watch as he takes my little scribbled notes to the Doctor, who listens as the rock star speaks into his ear and gives one firm nod. We take the elevator up and I am in the middle of moving clothes from one bag to another when there's a knock at the door. The Doctor fills the frame.

"You shouldn't open the door without checking to see who it is first. You never know who might be trying to get in his room," the Doctor says, and I wonder if he means it to sound as threatening as it does. I think about the fans waiting everywhere we go, and I promise him I'll be more careful next time, trying to use my most earnest face. *Look: I am easy to have around.*

"About New York," he says, eyes slightly narrowed. "The closest airport that serves New York is about three hours away, so six hours round trip on the bus's new tire. A cab would be quite costly, and there's no guarantee we'll be able to find one willing to go that far in time to make the flight. Now, if this is really what you want, we can try to make it happen instead of getting ready for the show. Your choice, just let me know."

I want to choose the go-see, of course I do. It's *Cosmo*. It would be my first editorial go-see. I promised Harriet nothing would change with me on the road, that I could travel easily. Staying here will show her that's not true. But if I go, I will be creating so much work for everyone else and then I'll have to come back to that, the expectation that I will ask for more and more and become a greater and greater burden. And then what.

I probably wouldn't get the job, anyway.

I thank the Doctor for looking into it and tell him I'll be staying.

The rock star must be able to read the disappointment on my face as I turn back to the room. "I'm sorry, baby," he says. "You're so talented, there will be so many other jobs. Why don't you call Helen and then we can take a nap?"

Harriet. I correct him so softly I don't know if he hears me. When I make the call, Therese answers and starts giving me directions and asking for my flight info, and I have to cut her off, explain that I won't be able to make it.

"Oh. *Oh.*" Therese pauses, starts, and stops a sentence about five times. Then, in a soft tone, like we're friends, she says, "How about I just tell Harriet for you?"

This offer makes it clear the right choice on the tour is the wrong choice as a model, and I should be adult enough to have this conversation. I should not be afraid of anything, like the fact that I might cry if I hear the disappointment in Harriet's voice. So many things I should do, and what I choose to do is let someone else handle it for me.

To make it up to me, on our next day off, the rock star asks if I want to learn how to drive. Driving is not something I've ever thought deeply about. I could take the train into the city

THE COVER GIRL 95

and taxis where I needed to go from there. There was no need for a car in that life. But that was before.

He has the Doctor get a sports car for the day, a shiny red Pantera. It's so ridiculous that I laugh when I see it. For a moment, I worry I've hurt his feelings, but he laughs too. I remind him I've never driven before, that we are starting completely from scratch.

He drives us away from the hotel and onto some quiet country road, the kind of place I thought only existed on television: blue-blue sky and cornfields as far as the eye can see. "You ready?" he asks me.

Of course I'm not ready. We switch sides, and I adjust the driver's seat, trying to find some position that feels as natural as sitting on the passenger side. "Alright," he says. "Put the car in neutral. That's this one right here. Okay, good. You always want to start in neutral. Now, put your foot on the brake—no, no, that's the gas, there you go—and turn it on. Okay, now you're going to release the parking brake..."

All these steps and we haven't even started moving. He'd had us on the road in about thirty seconds leaving the hotel, but with me at the wheel it feels like a solid five minutes before the car jerks forward. I ask if it's this much work to get a car going every time.

He laughs. "Only the ones that are worth driving."

There's no one else on the road. He encourages me to pick up speed, and I let it happen. The windows are down and my hair whips around in the wind, in front of my face. He takes it in his hands, holds it in a makeshift ponytail so that I can see the road in front of me. My whole body is thrumming and I don't know if it's the engine or my nerves. This car feels like too much for me to control. How do people do this every day, get in their vehicles and move at forty, fifty, sixty miles an hour without any sort of fear, without it feeling like a roller coaster every time?

"You're doing great," he says. "You've got this. Now you're going to pull off to the side here and stop."

Stopping is more than that. It feels like there are seven steps before I can think about coming to a stop, and when I do, it's too late: we're in the corn. He lets go of my hair as the car jerks to the end of its journey, and I grip the steering wheel with both hands, not daring to look. My first thought is that I am in trouble, but that doesn't seem right, doesn't seem like something he can decide.

"Birdie?" he asks. "Little Bird?" I turn and look. The corners of his mouth are twitching. "You okay, babe?" I nod slowly, watching his mouth. Finally, he gives into the laughter and I'm laughing too. "Okay," he says, pulling me to him. "This is going to take some practice."

We get out of the car to switch sides again, but we both end up in the passenger side. It is a ridiculous thing to attempt, not because it's the middle of the afternoon and anyone could drive by and see us, or not only that, but because the seats were barely made for people of our height sitting still, let alone anything else. And that just makes it funnier. It is more than chemistry this time. More than the physical. He holds my face in his hands and looks at me with sheer delight, like he can't believe his own good luck that I am his.

He told me three weeks after we met that he'd fallen in love with me, and he has not held back from telling me again whenever the moment strikes him: early in the morning before he thinks I'm awake, curling up together on the tour bus, eyes flashing with victory when he leaves the stage. He doesn't need for me to say it back; that is not his motivation. Which is good, because it's not something I can say as easily. The words feel like cotton in my mouth, like there's so much I need to drink before I can get them out. But it's here, in the passenger side of

THE COVER GIRL

this rented sports car that I have no business driving, that this finally feels real. I am in love too.

The first time my picture is in a magazine and I'm not paid for it, Harriet calls.

"Congratulations, darling. You're wanted in Miami."

It seems the editors at *Yes, You!* magazine saw a picture of me in *Circus* and decided mine was the look they needed. We'd been leaving the venue in Indianapolis after the tenth straight sellout in the Midwest, and the press was there. He'd been focused on signing the albums and tee shirts waved at him over the barricade. I'd been aware of the cameras, and behind my big black sunglasses, I could pretend not to be.

Harriet is pleased to send me to Miami, though she is not impressed with the name of the magazine, a new one aimed at young women launching next year. I'm flooded with a strange combination of homesickness and happiness when she announces that *Yes, You!* leaves something to be desired. "My god, it's 1977. We don't need to punctuate our magazine titles."

I call downstairs and ask them to send up a copy of the most recent *Circus*. It arrives faster than should be possible, and there we are, on page eight. My name left out of it, letting me be just a body. *Fans line up for autographs while the model from the cover of* Twice Bitten *does what she does best.*

It is, in fact, what I do best. The picture is spectacular, the kind of shot that comes together when everyone on all sides knows exactly what they are doing, or completely by accident. There are fans behind me, pressed against the barricade. A couple rows deep, someone holds up the album cover that features my legs in the air, toes pointed. And in front, I'm standing in the exact same position as I am on that album, flipped, on solid ground, leaning against the barricade, hips thrust forward. My hair drips down my shoulders; my mouth is fresh lipstick-slick. Anything is a pose if you want it bad enough.

Right after telling me about the job, Harriet said, "This is where we've been wanting to go. This is why we need you to be available." That's the only time she's mentioned the missed job, and every word was pointed—not enough to puncture the occasion, but enough to make sure I know.

This is where we want to go, but it didn't happen because of my usual work or my availability. It isn't the result of my portfolio or a go-see. It isn't even word of mouth from one photographer or editor to another. It's because I am with him. I didn't point this out to Harriet. But alone in that hotel room, while he is at sound check and I am sprawled out on a freshly made king-size bed, I know I am where I'm supposed to be.

Miami will be my first editorial shoot. I will not be selling deodorants or tampons or ballet shoes—or albums. It will be a return to the inspiration I found with Azrian. I will be the girl who illustrates the articles in the magazine. I will be the best spring looks, your getting-ready-for-summer hairstyles, the face alongside a quiz about who your perfect man is. In the late July heat, I will be styled to represent what women will want to look like in the months ahead. It isn't *Vogue*, it isn't *Glamour*, but it is a reminder that it can be one day—the big goal, softly shifting into view.

Miami is a humid blur. The girls on the *Yes, You!* shoot are wild. They want to go out drinking and drugging every night. They shove me into barely-there dresses and drag me into nightclubs like I'm one of them. They hold upturned fingernails to my nose and say, *Just breathe in, silly.*

It's some kind of miracle I have made it this far into my career without being offered pills or powders. A miracle or an innate fear that Harriet would know and she would have strong opinions about it.

THE COVER GIRL

The rock star is not one for drugs, not really. He doesn't mind drinking and will take the occasional puff from a joint, but that's it. It's always our cue to leave the backstage party when everyone starts getting too drunk or too high. He would probably not like it if I told him I tried cocaine in Miami.

But he doesn't have to know.

I breathe in like they say. I expect there to be some kind of smell, but it comes back to me as a taste, acidic and full. The girls clap their hands, laughing at what it's done to my face. "We didn't think you'd actually do it!" It appears to be a victory for them, but they link their arms through mine and pull me onto the dance floor. If I've lost some bet they made, it's worth it.

In the bathroom later, fixing our makeup in the half-lit mirror, one of the girls' reflections catches mine. "Are you the one who's with that musician?" she asks. "Isn't he...*old*?"

I half shrug in a gesture that I mean to mean: *for* you, *maybe*.

"Aren't your parents mad? Mine would never let me date him."

There's an implication there, one that knots my stomach. I tell her I'm different, echoing his words to me as I turn to go.

Sensing she's losing me, her voice drops. "What's the sex like?"

No one has asked me this yet, and I realize I want to talk about it. Not with a stranger, but a stranger is all I have. The only sense of sex I had before modeling was that good girls don't. I was too young to be anything else. And in modeling, it was treated as part of the job, unspoken, just another side of the business. Something I let happen to me rather than participated in.

This isn't that, but the fact is, I wait for the rock star to make any moves. We didn't do it immediately, not all of it, at least—he was the one who wanted to wait. I still leave him in charge because that's what I'm supposed to do—whether that's because he's older than me or because girls aren't supposed to want it, I can't say. Maybe both. But every night when he pulls me to him in bed or on the bus, I take it as proof that I am special. Loved. Wanted.

But she isn't interested in my feelings, just what it is we're doing, and I let her ask questions, but not until she gives me more cocaine. She wants to know how often and if it's different from boys our own age, and I answer in as few words as I can because some things don't feel right to share but also I like the attention, and what does it matter with every third word getting lost under the music or to my high. She nods along like she understands me, like I've completed a transaction. I have successfully performed *girl* in this world: a first.

In the cab on the way back to our hotel, someone shoves a pill between my lips, just as I am starting to feel the comedown creeping in, and in the morning, we make our call times, puffy-faced and hoarse. The hair and makeup staff take one look at us and sigh. Cucumbers and cold rags are procured. Conversations take place over our heads like we're not even there.

"Every time."

"Is it the worst in Miami?"

"I think so. They know New York; they don't get as stupid in New York."

"Any time you put a beach in it, this is what happens."

"They get stupid in Europe."

"Well, I haven't been sent to Europe yet."

"So many boys with accents."

"Oh, god, that's a completely different kind of stupid."

The division of labor allows us to have these conversations in front of each other. They talk about us in front of us; we talk about everything else in front of them. Two of the other models are openly discussing whether the photographer is gay or straight and which one of them should be the one to find out or, hell, should they both approach him?

I just listen—to them, to the hair and makeup people, to the photographer. To the sound of the waves crashing on the

THE COVER GIRL

beach. I let it all unfold around me until it is my turn in front of the camera, and I don't question it when they want pictures of me alone.

When the shoot is over, so is any bonding that occurred in bathrooms. There are no goodbyes. The nights out amounted to just that, and the photos turn out fine.

So fine, in fact, that I am going to be on the cover of the March issue. The news sits on top of me, settling gently but not sinking in.

"Darling," Harriet says over the phone. "When you're back in New York, I'll take you to dinner to celebrate." I can almost hear her smiling.

When I tell the rock star, he announces it to everyone, and as odd as it is seeing Eddie, Ham, and even Beasley clap for me, I don't have it in me to be embarrassed. I just want to watch him be proud of me. We are in a desert state now, and since I've been away for several days, he is like water.

The rock star has the Doctor get a bottle of champagne, and he toasts: *To the most beautiful girl on any coast.*

As we slowly make our way to California, the prospect of that other coast looms heavy. He invited me to come on tour with him. I know—though I spend a lot of time not thinking about it—that he is my *legal guardian*, that the papers signed made us into something, but we never discussed what that means. Is it just for the tour? Is it forever?

Before that's a question that can be answered and long before my face will fill the cover of a magazine, there is a festival. Getting there means hours in the bus, quick stops for shows in between, none of the luxury of getting there the night before and taking in room service and stunning views and decadent baths. We get in and we get out, and he is exhausted. I keep quiet and try to anticipate what he might need: tea, mineral water, extra orders of warm towels. I have never been subject to someone's mood before, not in this way. My mother ran hot and cold, and there was plenty of fighting between her and my father, but their lives and problems existed next to mine, not entwined with.

In this stretch of shows, he worries that the audience isn't responsive enough. He mixes up the name of the city we're in and even though he makes a good joke of it and no one seems to care all that much, he deems the show a failure. Eddie, Ham, and Beasley shrug it off, speaking only to each other. He doesn't hang out backstage with the group, ignores the barely dressed girls trying to eyelash and lip pucker their way in. I follow him through the concrete hallways of the stadium to the un-marked back exit, nearly rolling an ankle in my platform sandals. He doesn't say a word to me in the bus on the way back to the hotel. I sit with my palms pressed together between my knees, legs tucked, trying to take up as little space as possible. It couldn't be my fault; I'm not the travel person. As far as I can tell, it would be up to the Doctor to ensure he was properly briefed on his location. But I feel partially responsible all the same. Maybe a good girlfriend reminds him where he is before every show. Maybe a good girlfriend would make such a comfortable home in a hotel that the blur of the road would never have a chance to set in.

This is the first night we go to sleep right away. In this giant bed, he rests on the outer edge of his side. The hotel air conditioner whirs dutifully and without the weight of him right next to me, I break out in goose bumps. I have no pajamas of real substance. Instead, I wrap myself in one of his heavy black button-down shirts, one that smells like sweat and aftershave. It's warm, but not the kind of comfort I need.

I haven't had time to get lonely on the tour because there is always something new to see or a job to fly out to and the thrill of reuniting in a different place. But tonight, in this hotel room in an unmemorable city, not tired, with his back to me, I am as lonely as I've ever been. It's like something has dislodged inside me, and too many feelings start bubbling up at once.

THE COVER GIRL

I imagine the next day he'll tell me he is done with me, that he is sending me back to Connecticut. There was a test somewhere, one I didn't know I was taking, one I have failed. The tears slide down my cheeks fast and uncontrollable, and I bury my face in the pillow to keep from making any noise. He said he loved me, and I thought that would be stronger. Instead, this is another place I am not wanted.

In the morning, I wake up too hot, my hair stuck to my forehead and his arms heavy around my waist as he pulls me closer. A part of me wants to stay where I am, facing the wall, making clear that his mood, his decision hurt my feelings, but who would I be punishing other than myself? One last time.

After we're done, he tells me he's sorry. This is not what I expected. "Do you ever have a shoot that doesn't go the way you want it to?" I nod. Of course. "And what if you'd tripped that time on the runway?"

I start to roll over. A lecture and a breakup. I will take it, but I don't want to be watched while I do.

He reaches out and tips my chin back toward him. "Little Bird. What I'm saying is we're artists, both of us. And that's what you have that no other woman I've ever known has had. That's what made me fall for you. I couldn't help it. You know what it's like to put yourself out there for a living, how important it is to get it right. You get me." I gasp with relief—it is stronger than that, after all—and wrap my limbs around him as he presses his face to my neck. "I need you to get me."

I stop listening after *I need you.* That is enough.

There's still tension, but it's between him and the band, not us. In the time before we get to the festival, he whispers to me during the day to preserve his voice and sleeps on the bus to save his energy.

The festival. It's all anyone is talking about, but I have no idea what it actually means, how it could be different from a regular concert, other than we have to show up a couple days early and Beasley, Ham, and Eddie don't want to do it. Too long, too many shitty bands ahead of them—what's the point of a prime-time slot when everyone will be passed out by the time they take the stage.

The festival takes place in the middle of nowhere, Nevada, all hot desert and baked earth. When I look out the bus window, it's like we are staying still, the way the landscape doesn't change. There are only a few offerings for gas, so we take whatever stop we can get. There will be no more desperate calls for roadside assistance on the Doctor's watch.

The bus driver, Lenny—who was skipped in the introductions and who I finally had to introduce myself to two weeks into the tour, when I realized we weren't switching drivers in every city and he was just as much a part of this entourage as anyone—climbs aboard after filling up and makes his first announcement since we began the trip: "Cashier just told me Elvis is dead."

Eddie snorts. "Elvis is always dead."

Lenny stares, waiting for more of a reaction, but that is the sentiment of the bus: rumors are rumors. This is a band. What would a gas station clerk know?

When we reach our destination, it is not the lavish, multi-story kind of hotel we've become accustomed to, but a dusty motel. We have crisscrossed the entire country, up and down as we moved westward, and even in the less glamorous cities, there was always one good hotel, always a penthouse. Not here.

There is no lavender bubble bath in the room. For him, one pencil, one orange still ensconced in its peel, one can of peanuts. No washcloths. He rolls his eyes and laughs, showing me the orange, and I realize I've been waiting for an outburst. "If you can't do the rider, you should just not do the rider," he says. "What in the world did they get us into?"

It's late by the time he determines what surfaces are safe to rest our belongings on and we are settled in. We are thinking about dinner, because room service will certainly not be an option here, when there's a knock at the door, one purposeful rap.

The Doctor is outside, and he enters without a word. He turns the knob on the radio and there it is: Elvis Presley is dead at age forty-two.

I could identify an Elvis song if someone played one and I remember seeing pictures of his beautiful wife in magazines, but I know nothing about him, not really. I watch as the rock star sinks onto the edge of the bed, folding his arms across his chest. I know this is big, but my first thought is that the rock star is only eleven years younger than a dead man. "Goddamn," he exhales.

"Goddamn," the Doctor agrees.

Dinner is forgotten. The Doctor fields a flurry of phone calls that continue far into the next day. Our room becomes the meeting place for crucial questions: Does someone from our delegation need to go to the funeral, and what sort of tribute needs to take place? Will it be the opening number or the encore? Which artists in the festival lineup will be invited to participate? The Doctor alternates between negotiations with the festival's promoters and with travel agencies while the band runs down every Elvis song they're comfortable playing. The radio drones softly in the background, live from Graceland. No one seems to know I am in the room, so eventually I sneak out, sure someone else's girlfriend must be here.

I find the women congregated at a wall behind the motel. Some have been crying, most are smoking. They see me coming and slide down to make room, the first time I can recall something like this happening, and I make myself sit down like it's natural. They introduce themselves with the names of those they're accompanying like I must know who they mean: Linda, Gary's wife; Yasmine, been with Peter forever; Holly, engaged to Zeke; Lulu, *shh*, just the road girlfriend. I tell them who I am and who I am with, and after a pause so slight I could have imagined it, they say things like, *How exciting, Is this your first tour?* and *Isn't this fun?*

Yasmine hands me a cigarette. "Welcome to the sisterhood. You're one of us now."

In the end, no one flies to Memphis and the tribute is an opening medley with the three top-billed bands and some members from the lesser-known acts. Few are terribly pleased by this development because it means taking the stage at noon; however, the Doctor refused to cede the spotlight once our group went on as headliners. All the rock star had to do was shrug and say, *He handles the contracts, not me*, and he was excused from any ire that arose, at least directly. Perhaps that was the Doctor's actual job.

The rock star brings me with him in the morning just like any other concert, but when I take my usual place in the wings, it becomes clear that this is not the same, and not just because it's daytime. The stage feels twice the size, and if I angle myself just right, I can see out into the crowd, and it is endless. We have been in arenas and stadiums all summer—finite groups of people, a large bowl of possibility, but with limits. Here, at the festival, it is a crowd as far as I can see, packed in close and moving closer. For a moment, it seems familiar, and it takes a minute before I can place the feeling: the Soleo incident, the buzz, the crush. The after. I find myself drifting out of the wings, toward a wide-open space and away from a memory.

I find Yasmine and the others taking in the opening medley. They are tearful, watching the men they love make the music of the man they must have loved first, and it makes me a little emotional, wondering if I will ever feel this way, maybe about a designer or a photographer. They point out Gary, Peter, Zeke, and Lulu's current boyfriend, who she calls *my guy* and the rest of the women call Phil. I don't have to point out who I am with; they all know. No one makes them wear big uncomfortable headphones, but Holly slips a pair of earplugs into my hand and shows me how to put them in.

After the medley, they decide to search for food. There are hours to kill before the set I want to see, and while I don't want to be a pest, there's also nowhere else to go, and I'm one of them, right? I follow behind, and Yasmine drifts back to my pace, linking her arm through mine.

"How are you doing?" she asks. She looks at me full-on, a gaze like a camera.

I smile faintly. I'm good, aren't I? Overwhelmed by this world, yes, and even more so by what lies ahead and all that I cannot see beyond these final few weeks and where I'll go after that. But I am adored. There's a hand that holds mine.

"I'm not going to ask you how old you are," she says, "so don't worry. Some people have awfully short memories about the girls they were hanging around with themselves. But if it gets to be too much, just know that's okay. I've flown home from the road so many times, and there's no shame in it. This life is not for everyone."

I nod. I don't need to say anything. The number one lesson: keep quiet and make them like you.

3

It is late August by the time we make it to California, a series of concerts that takes us down the state and ends with three shows at the Forum.

Earlier this summer, Led Zeppelin sold out six nights here. The Doctor is furious that our run is shorter, and Eddie isn't having it. "Let him deal with this shit onstage six nights in a row if he wants to so fucking bad," he says.

It is Ham who tells me this is normal, the uptick in bickering, in curse words, after Beasley calls the rock star a shithead for unknown reasons and Eddie announces that everyone on the bus is a shithead. He reminds me how long they'd been on the road before I joined.

"The closer we get to home, the clearer it becomes how long we've been gone. It's safe to get mad now." Ham says this to me quietly as I try to drift to the back of the bus and away from the argument.

The word *home* hangs heavy in the air. There's a part of me that thinks of Connecticut; it has, after all, been my home until now, and there's a part of me that doesn't believe this could be my life beyond the tour. I want to ask what comes next, what it

THE COVER GIRL

will look like. Instead, I continue doing what I am there to do, pose like a pair of legs on an album cover when anyone with a camera asks and act like I am just here on a promotional opportunity.

We stay in a bungalow at the Chateau Marmont during the three shows at the Forum, even though it's not terribly close, and not much farther out than his house in Malibu will be. The rest of the band stays at the Riot House. The Marmont is no fun, they say. No bar, too old-fashioned.

"That's what makes this place great," the rock star tells me. "You get privacy here. The Riot House is all about who's drinking what or shooting what or screwing who. Here, you come and go in quiet. No cameras."

The quiet must be soothing to him after the din of the bus, the roar of the crowd, the fans asking for autographs and more. Everyone here is famous; he is among his kind. I should be happy with this, given how overwhelmed I get in crowds, but there's something about the way he says *no cameras allowed* that makes me itch. Cameras create. There is nothing wrong with cameras. And so I ask him for something for the first time: to go to the Riot House too.

He laughs—a chuckle really, like it's cute that I want to go to the hotel, like the words *Riot House* alone are funny coming out of my mouth.

He relents, though, for the last show of the tour. After telling the crowd how great they are, how he loves every city in America but he has been waiting all summer to come back home to Los Angeles, after a second and third encore, and after we spend enough time backstage for Eddie, Beasley, and Ham to invite the seven or eight girls they want to bring back with them, we take the bus on one last unnecessary drive to the Riot House.

It did not occur to me just how many people would be awaiting our arrival. Cameras and people. The after-party is already in full swing—some bands I recognize from album covers or the festival and women in various stages of dress and undress. One of the girls the band has brought back surveys the scene and realizes her competition is much stiffer than she'd thought, and she turns toward the elevator, gone without a word.

"Birdie!" The last name I'm expecting to hear is my own, but Lulu comes hurtling toward me from nowhere. She's wearing a bathing suit top and short shorts with a silk kimono that flies out behind her. Her platform sandals bring her almost to my height. "I'm so happy to see you! I love your dress!"

I have been waiting all night for someone to acknowledge my outfit. It's a peach Grecian-style minidress, with a narrow V cut nearly to its braided belt, that an aspiring designer sent to Harriet for me. As excited as I am for it, her compliment pales in comparison to her being happy to see me. A sign I belong in this world.

I let Lulu hug me and ask what she's doing here—is her guy around?

"I live here, silly." She dips her head slightly to her right, toward a couple. "And so does his wife. But there'll be a new guy by the end of the night. You want a drink? Some coke?"

The currency of friendship, right, so yes, I absolutely do, but I ask her to give me a moment. Lulu nods like she knows this game. The rock star is surrounded by a throng of people, many of them women, girls, their faces tipped up like flowers to the sun. He pulls me close to him as the girls watch, faces falling, and he lets both hands slide just up under the hem of my dress as he kisses me long and deep. For a moment, I think about abandoning the party. For a moment, I forget everyone and press my hips to his. "Have fun with Lulu," he murmurs. "Just be careful—she's not like you."

I find Lulu in someone's hotel room and she pulls me into the closet, presenting three thick lines on a mirror. She takes one for herself and hands me the dollar bill. I try to remember what the girls in Miami told me as I dip my pinky nail in, up-

THE COVER GIRL

setting her neat work, and bring it to my right nostril. She claps in delight. "Look at you, so delicate. No wonder he loves you."

When we have consumed the contents of the mirror—mostly Lulu, but I dip my nail a few more times—she takes me by the hand and leads me through the suite, as though there aren't people everywhere. My eyes fall on a man and two women somehow all kissing each other at the same time and I quickly look away. "Let me guess," Lulu says when we return to the hallway. "He told you to stay away from me." Not exactly like that, so I shake my head. She laughs. "To be careful, then."

When I take too long to dispute this, she laughs harder. "I know, I know. I'm not wife material and none of them know what to do with me. There are the wives and girlfriends, and there are the groupies, and then there's Lulu."

I point out that no one knows quite what to do with me either, words that surprise me, fueled by cocaine maybe but true all the same, and I feel lighter for having said them. She smiles. She understands. "Look, I wouldn't normally just tell someone this—and I guess normally they'd just assume it—but I'm going to let you know because I don't want you to find out later and get mad. He and I fucked a few years ago, just a couple times. He always gets so itchy when I'm around, like I'm going to suddenly tell him I'm pregnant and it's his."

I consider this as she makes me a drink that is mostly vodka. The thing that hits me first is a deep desire to throw up, but I have a feeling that if I can push past it, I'll get somewhere more interesting. My mind briefly flashes on him and Lulu doing what he and I do, what we'll be doing later, but I shake the image away. No. I can allow him his past, and it's different with me. I know it is. The choice: I can be upset or I can have a friend.

Lulu is watching as I think through it, nodding. "Yes," she says. "There's no need to be jealous. It's a small world here. We all have our place in it. And you—" here she pauses to clink her glass against mine "—you're starting out right on top. You're what I used to want to be. Listen, don't get me wrong. I'll want something steady someday. But right now, this is fine."

What she used to want to be—I honestly can't tell if this a compliment or a neutral statement. I have a feeling Lulu is the kind of girl everything magically orbits around, and I want this to be something more than the bathroom in Miami. We aren't just on a set, we're here, and we're both different. If tomorrow starts a new life in Malibu, I want her in it, so I ask if I can call her sometime.

"Oh, sweetie, sure you can." She leads me through another open hotel room door and picks up the first surface she sees— a paper bag wrapped around a bottle of whiskey. She tears the bag, no concern about who it belongs to or whether or not the bag was necessary, then scrawls her phone number in eyeliner on it. "Here you go. Now, can you do something for me?"

Of course. I want to keep this conversation going.

She glances in a mirror, then sparkles a smile at me. "Perfect. Put me in front of Beasley."

There's no way I keep my face even at this suggestion but if she sees me recoil, she doesn't acknowledge it. Beasley, of all people.

Ham has been pleasant enough. Eddie more or less tolerates me. The Doctor is content to ignore my existence and I do the same. But Beasley—every time I see him is like the first time. *You're fucking joking.* And that's what I feel like around him: a joke. Anything I do in his presence would just prove his point. He looked at me and he saw an end in sight, and I hate it.

But I want a friend.

So I slip my arm through Lulu's and we wind our way around the party until we find him, surrounded by a group of girls. I hesitate.

"Go on," Lulu says in what seems like a whisper but must be a shout. "You're a model, babe. You of all people get to break that up."

THE COVER GIRL

I take a deep breath, wanting to be the beautiful, powerful girl she sees. I shimmy through the group right up to Beasley and singsong his name in a tone I'm not sure I've ever used before, one that throws him so off guard that he forgets to roll his eyes when he sees it's me calling to him. I pull Lulu to my side and announce that I want him to meet my friend. She steps forward, between me and Beasley, and I don't know if I purposefully fade back to let them have their moment or if it just happens, but it doesn't matter. I've done my job.

The party swings on until the sun comes up, and I spend the rest of it by the rock star's side, smiling and not speaking. Turning my head this way and that, delivering *interested, amused, charmed* to his audience. We find a room where we can sleep for a few hours, and when we wake up, for the first time, there is nowhere to go.

It's like any other late morning in any other hotel. There are no phones ringing, though, no knocks from the Doctor. Just the two of us, tangled around each other.

"So," he says, drawing the word out into something else entirely. "Are you ready to go home?"

Am I? I tell him yes, because whatever is next is something I must be ready for.

We are quiet as we gather our things from the Riot House and then from the bungalow, and then as we wait for the car he has called to arrive. We are quiet on the drive, as the city fades away into a less dense version of itself, as buildings give way to the ocean. I look out the window, entranced by how close we seem to be to the edge of the earth.

And then, after a while, we pull into the driveway of one of those large square houses, all windows overlooking the ocean. The driver opens and shuts his door, moves to the back to start unloading luggage. I keep staring at this expanse of a house, waiting to be told for sure what is happening.

He takes my hand in his. "Welcome home," he tells me.

Outside, the huge windows make the house look like glass and inside it is all sharp edges and neutral colors, sleek and modern and like a picture of where someone would live as opposed to the real thing. It is so different from the house I left in Connecticut, with its heavy wallpapers and dark leather furniture and dense burgundy drapes, old family portraits keeping a watchful eye, a house designed to trap everything and let nothing new in. There is no indication this house belongs to him, that he has ever spent more than a few minutes here.

"What do you think?" he asks, and I tell him I love it. It is a house of possibility, a blank slate upon which we can create. It's like a modeling job. I could do a shoot in here, I think. Clean lines matching the surroundings, me as a palette: yellow and orange and teal. The power does not come from what it is but from what it could be. And what it could be includes me. I imagine what my life will look like here: shoots in the mornings, shopping with my new friend Lulu in the afternoons, cozy evenings spent with the rock star watching the waves.

He leads me upstairs, and there is a room for his guitars and a room for business things and rows of bedrooms, but only one of them is ours. In the adjoining bathroom, I shed my clothes and sink into the tub, emptying the contents of one of my endless bottles of lavender bubble bath. But here, it feels like something. Here, it feels like luxury. As I stretch my legs along the full length of the bathtub—my bathtub—I feel like I am truly in this place, rather than just watching myself watch what is around me. A feeling that only comes in front of a camera.

He is waiting for me when I come out. I am not made up; my hair is wet and still shows the lines of my comb. There is no good outfit to do the talking for me. And there is no one else, just us.

I am as nervous as I was the first time in his hotel room in New York. He stands over me, taking me in, and I look away, angle an arm, try to let the light fall across me. He tips my face

THE COVER GIRL

to him. He is my camera, he is what sees me, and so I look back, holding his eyes as long as I can stand it.

For the first few days, it still feels like we are traveling, just taking an extended stay at a place with multiple bathrooms and privacy at last. Our clothes are sent out for cleaning, and there is no food in the house, and if there was, I wouldn't be able to do anything with it and possibly he couldn't either.

But when clothes come back to us, I hang them in the closet together, my dresses and halters and rompers among his jeans and heavy button-downs and weathered tee shirts, and it's something.

Once we're all settled in, I write a letter to my parents to give them my new address, and I call Harriet with that same information, and a phone number too.

"I'll talk to Debi in the LA office. You should go meet her—she'll book you out there." I ask if that means Debi will be my agent now, my voice faltering and small. "No, no," Harriet says, almost gently. "I'll work with Debi, but I'll still be your agent. I'll handle your vouchers, and we'll still talk about big-picture career plans. I want you working, so we need to introduce you to the market there."

I haven't worked in more than a month, and I worry she's angry with me, so I go to meet Debi the next afternoon.

Debi is no Harriet. There is no Long Island accent or cigarette holder or chignon. Her hair is cut into a sensible bob, and she doesn't appear to be wearing any makeup at all. She is not ageless like Harriet, just younger, and she does not call me darling.

Debi gets me a tutor, a real one, and I do lessons instead of going to school, book jobs instead of studying at a library, go to lavish events instead of dances. I ask the rock star if we can do something with Holly, Linda, or Yasmine and whoever their husbands are. He says we will, and I wait, not wanting to ask too often. Lulu and I do go shopping once, in Beverly Hills, but she doesn't seem to share my excitement for the clothes on display, and I can tell she thinks I'm square for not wanting to do key bumps in the dressing room.

For his birthday, we go to a party at the Rainbow. I half wonder if I was supposed to plan it; that seems like something a girlfriend would do, but whatever was arranged went on without me. I wouldn't have picked the Rainbow, anyway. Too expected—even I know that. But we go and I smile prettily at all the other famous men and the women smiling prettily next to them. Lulu's phone rings and rings most of the time when I call, but she's here tonight, hugging me tight and sneaking me into a bathroom stall to do a line.

"I feel like I've been doing shit in this bathroom for half my life." She laughs.

She tells me that she was a *baby groupie*. The term is dubious, two nouns that don't belong together. It conjures nothing.

"You know," she says. "Out here." Like here, here. Sunset.

A few years ago, she explains, there were girls who ruled the Strip—"young, like you," she says—who were wild and beautiful—"models, but I don't think like you," she says—and they could be found on the arms of all the major names in music. At least by night.

"I wasn't one of the important ones," she tells me. "I wasn't in their group."

Maybe I'm adding details to a picture she isn't trying to paint, but I can see Lulu, her halo of copper curls, standing on the edge, wishing she belonged. Maybe we have even more in common than I think.

She tells me that she was on the Strip almost every night as she cuts another line. "Where were my parents, right?" The question had not occurred to me. She doesn't provide any answers either—she goes back to the clubs, the clothes. Everything cooler than it is now. This is one thing I've already learned. Nothing is as good as it used to be. I wonder if we'll all look back to this moment in a few years and think the same thing about now. I

THE COVER GIRL

think of how many times on the tour the rock star would show me something—a restaurant, a hotel, another band—and quickly follow with, "It used to be better." Even the Chateau Marmont. Of course the Riot House. Perhaps the Rainbow too. The thing I know is that I can never truly see what he saw in these places, what they had come to mean to him, because of course they used to be better. If I am disappointed by tonight, for instance, it's only the fault of this thing that has not stood the test of time.

So as we wander back to the party, I let Lulu paint a picture of this exact bar where only the music and the vibe have changed. She would totter along Sunset in unreasonably thick platforms and any array of items that could come together into an outfit—something that hadn't changed, according to the silk pajama shorts, fishnets, and sheer blouse she was wearing, regardless of the memory in her voice. The musicians darkening the corners of the Rainbow or wherever they were that night would notice her. She grabbed their attention.

"And I never left," she says brightly.

I ask what happened to the other girls, the cool ones, and she looks at me like I've missed the point of her story entirely. "Oh." She shrugs. "Some are still around. A couple went to New York." What I hear is that they aren't at the center of the room anymore, their mattering just a moment in time. "Do you know if Beasley is coming tonight?"

I shake my head, and she pouts, so I say I'll ask the rock star. She shoots me a glittering smile. "You're a great friend." The comment buoys me for the rest of the night.

The next day, I buy a cake mix, one that came with its very own packet of frosting and pan and all I have to do is stir. He laughs when I present it to him, one candle lit, something so simple made special because we could have anything.

We eat the cake out of the pan and it tastes good since I haven't had cake in so long. Or maybe it is actually good. When I ask him what he wished for, he says, "For this forever."

★ ★ ★

That fall, *Yes, You!* sends me a little questionnaire to fill out, something they do for all their cover girls. And that's me now, a girl on the cover. The questions are not particularly hard-hitting, but it takes me hours nonetheless.

What is your fashion go-to?

Right away, a question that implies a level of self-knowledge I do not have. A way of thinking I have not adapted to. Not *do you have* but *what is your*. I spend too long thinking about an accessory that I don't leave the house without, a favorite dress or pair of jeans. But my honest go-to, what gets me most excited, is wearing something new—something to be noticed in, clothes to speak for me. This doesn't seem like the right answer, though, and I muddle through my own thoughts for far too long before I realize I can fake it. *No matter what I'm doing, I always make sure I have a good lip gloss*, I write. *Whether I'm on a go-see or going to a party, lip gloss ties the whole outfit together.* Is this true? Does it matter?

What would our readers be surprised to learn about you?

I almost laugh, imagining the answer.

There is nothing your readers could learn about me that I wouldn't also be surprised by.

Oh, did you know I have a boyfriend? He's a rock star. I spent my summer on tour with him and his band. He's older than me. This seems to make some people uncomfortable. Therefore, we could call it surprising. I am answering this little quiz from his—our—Malibu house, which has so many windows they may as well be glass walls. This is better than math class, than drive-in movies, than waiting by the phone for a boy to call, than a curfew that I probably wouldn't have had because my parents would have had to stop and consider me to actually figure out what time is an appropriate time for their teen daughter to come home, and that isn't something I want to even picture them doing because it's like seeing a dog walking on two

THE COVER GIRL

legs. I don't hate them for this. They can't help who they are. This was the best choice for all of us. I nothing them the same way they nothing me and—

This thought presses on something so tender I almost jump. I try to redirect myself, like I can shut my mind up the way I can shut my mouth, like I can't still hear what I was thinking. I start writing furiously anyhow. *I love rock and roll! I love going to rock concerts and listening to loud guitars and screaming fans.* I know what I mean between the lines, and that's the important part.

Who is your favorite designer?

I can name a few holy grail designers off the top of my head— Halston, Vivienne Westwood, Pucci, Missoni. But let's be honest: I am not there yet. And do I know their clothes or just their names? There's only one possible answer for this question. *Azrian de Popa*, I write. That doesn't feel like enough, so I add, *He is an artist. I feel so beautiful in his clothes.*

What makes you—yes, you!—you?

Long blond hair. Long legs. An agreeable nature. Quiet on the set. A broad interpretation of *the set*. What is unsaid.

Or: You took the photographs and picked me for the cover. Could you tell me?

In the cheeriest script I can muster: *The fact that I'm still figuring this out!*

4

We spend Thanksgiving with Ham and his family, a series of relatives and a wife who asks me multiple times if I can eat the food, offers to make a salad if I'd feel more comfortable. "I've never met a model before," she confesses earnestly. "Really met, at least. Had in my house." I assure her it's fine, feeling a small rush of pleasure at the idea that anyone could find having me in their house intimidating. She seems to like me, though—whether that's because of my job or because I offer to stir the gravy in an effort to escape the children some other friends brought along, I can't say. Children, but not small. I hear a reference to junior high school. When we finally sit down to eat, I avoid the eyes of the dark-haired boy and girl only a couple years younger than me. They are the children of someone, here with parents, and a world separates them from me, here with the rock star. He does not hold my hand, but Ham doesn't hold his wife's hand either.

Christmas we spend on our own. He lays a diamond necklace across my throat in the morning. It is both me and not—nothing I have worn and nothing I am but everything I want to be in his eyes.

THE COVER GIRL

My gift is a pair of cuff links. Somehow, even though the magazine had not yet been published, Azrian found out that I had listed him as my favorite designer. The phone rang and when I answered, a soft voice on the other end said, "Please hold for Azrian de Popa."

"Birdie," he said. "I heard about your interview. I am so very touched, my dear."

I told him it was nothing, that he'd done so much for me with the fashion show opportunity and, remembering what he said about our careers lying in front of us, that I hoped we could always work together.

"Of course. We're growing up together, aren't we?"

The thought made me burn happily. See, we were both advanced. Azrian understood me. And then he asked if there was anything he could do for me in thanks for the publicity this would be sending his way, and the thing was, Christmas was coming. The thought of asking to be taken shopping, of trying to figure out what to purchase for this man who could get himself whatever he wanted—or really the thought of what to purchase for a man at all—was beyond me. I'd called Lulu to ask what she thought I should do, but her suggestion was just wrapping myself in a bow. So I told Azrian all I needed was a recommendation for a gift.

He took it a step further. The cuff links arrived soon after, custom designed. I watch now as the rock star opens the box, takes them in.

They are deep purple triangles—scalene, if my tutor would like to know—with sparkling black trim and they could not be less his style, if you would call it a style, if I had tried, but I didn't know what else to do. He smiles, and I can see the furrow of his brow all the same. I try to explain—my *designer friend* made them, they are truly unique, and finally he gets it. "Something I can't find anywhere else," he says. "Like you."

Like me.

Amy Rossi

* * *

It is strange to be the one who travels while he stays still, but Harriet wants me to go out more and more, for editorial jobs, has me booked for Colorado to pose with horses against the mountains and for New Mexico to stand in the desert. I go to New Orleans for a British magazine, and when it's time to get on the plane, I miss him before I even leave the house, but I need Harriet to know that I am still willing to work hard, that I still want this, that nothing has changed.

New Orleans is a place of its own. The soup-thick humidity of Miami with the never-sleep of New York. The party of West Hollywood with the lights of Las Vegas. But all drenched in color and music and the smell of food, and no one performing their daily habits for the sake of attracting the attention of tabloid photographers—they just are.

There's three of us and two rooms. The magazine puts me in a room with a model named Mavis, and they put the other girl, Sunny, in a room by herself. She ends up coming over for the usual: *Don't I know you from this shoot? Were you on that one job? Did you hear about that one girl? I heard something else.* If we were regular girls, we might never say a word to each other. And make no mistake, there will be no exchanging of addresses or phone numbers after this. This is a job friendship and that's it, and the cleanness of it all soothes me. Maybe we'll see each other at a party in six months and wave. But if we are on another job together in two years, the time elapsed will not matter—the relief of a familiar face will make us once again the best of friends.

What designer is your favorite? Don't be alone in a room with that photographer. Someone told me that about this one. Who are you dating? No, really.

"Well, we all know who *she's* dating," Sunny says, gesturing to me.

I'm pretty sure Mavis and I met at a party a year or so ago, but Sunny I am meeting for the first time. It keeps surprising me that

THE COVER GIRL

people know who my boyfriend is without knowing anything else about me. Maybe it would be better to be known for my work instead, but also: he chose me. So I smile softly and shrug, looking at the carpet in what I hope comes across as modesty.

"What's that like?" Mavis asks.

"I think it's weird," Sunny says before I can answer. "Don't you think it's weird? He's dated movie stars, right? And now he's with you? I mean... And your parents are fine with it?"

I can feel my face on fire but I try to keep my tone cool as I tell her that of course they are; they let me go live with him.

Sunny's eyes grow wide. "That's weird!" She turns to Mavis for confirmation, but Mavis just looks at the floor and then at the clock and says we need to get some sleep before our 5:00 a.m. call time.

After Sunny goes back to her room, I want to ask Mavis if she thinks it's weird too, but I don't know that I want the answer. This is why he chose me, I tell myself. I understand that some situations, some people, are special. Maybe Sunny couldn't handle living in his world, couldn't do anything real without her parents, but I'm different.

The shoot starts out normal enough. Hair and makeup and wardrobe. Stockings and dresses to wear under fluffy fur coats, the focal point of today's shoot—girls in luxurious fur along the Mississippi River, strolling through the French Quarter, an homage to the Crazy Horse dancers from the Versailles fashion show, we are told.

The photographer is Gus O'Grady, who I haven't worked with before. Apparently, he's supposed to be an up-and-coming hotshot, and the talk among the other girls is that he has a temper. It doesn't take long for this to prove true.

Nothing we do pleases him. Sunny's eye makeup is too dark; my hair is too big. And Mavis is stupid. Too stupid to take direction, he says. We don't know what to do with this statement—all

we can do is squeeze Mavis's hand and whisper what we think
he is asking for and tell her she looks great.

"Just walk toward me. All I need you to do is walk down the
street. Good fucking god, have you ever walked before?" Mavis's jaw tightens, and he tells her she looks like a man.

"Could you please just show me what I'm not doing?" she asks
after being yelled at for the tenth time that morning.

"You girls get stupider every time," Gus mutters. He points
at me and gestures for me to come toward him. "You. Here."
Like a dog. And I obey. Instead of telling me what to do, he
moves my arms. My legs. No, more open. And then his hand
keeps going.

There's a run in my stockings.

Small things like that.

With all the interruptions, the shoot drags into the afternoon,
one that's unseasonably warm for January, even in Louisiana,
and our too-dark eye makeup is running and too-big hair is
flattening with the humidity. Assistants fan us, blotting beads
of perspiration at our hairlines.

"This is useless," Gus announces. "This shoot is about decadence. Not about sweaty girls. We'll try again tomorrow—nothing under the coats if everything makes them sweat this badly."

Nothing under the coats.

This is what we do: what we are asked. We go back to our
rooms to wash the job off us. We nap. We dress for dinner,
for cocktails, for swaying our hips to big jazz notes. And as we
walk through the French Quarter we spent the early hours in,
this time all lit up and loud and heavy with life, Mavis speaks:
"I didn't sign up for nothing under the coats. I guess I signed
up for him to tell me how bad I am at everything. But not for
being naked under a fur coat."

"They'll let us wear underwear, right?" Sunny asks.

"He said *nothing*."

"They can't really make us, can they?"

THE COVER GIRL

125

"It's not supposed to be nudity, is it? They can't show anything in that kind of magazine. Even if it's British. Right?"

So many theys. Just one us.

"I don't want to do it," Mavis continues. "I don't need a full outfit under my coat, but I want something."

"He's just going to replace you."

"Not if we all refuse."

"They won't just replace us all?"

"You don't think it's worth trying?"

I listen as they agree to try. And then they look at me, waiting for me to join in.

I imagine telling this story to Harriet. *If you have a problem on a set or if you're not comfortable, you can tell me.* But also: *If a client calls to tell me one of my girls was difficult, it only happens the one time.*

I imagine Gus moving my legs again.

"She's not going to join us," Mavis says.

"But she's not even old enough," Sunny says, her voice too loud for a whisper but quiet enough for me to pretend I don't hear. What does she know.

We walk back to the hotel in silence, and as we get ready for bed, in a flash of bravery, I ask Mavis why she said what she said.

She sits at the end of the bed, fingers flying as she braids her hair. "You hear things about the girls you'll be working with on a job sometimes. We heard you weren't friendly. That you act like you're better than everyone since you hang out with rock stars. And that you only care about the photographer and editors, not the other girls."

Oh. Not only do people know things about me now, but they have opinions too.

"I haven't really seen that to be true, if it matters," she adds after we turn out the light. "But I did see what Gus did to you today."

You saw nothing, I don't say. The next morning, we get our hair and makeup done as usual. And then in wardrobe we are each handed a hanger with a coat, a huge strand of pearls, and tiny panties—just a string up the back.

I have modeled in bathing suits, in short shorts and tiny halters. Usually when we're sent on these shoots, though, we know that's what we're doing and can diet beforehand, can do what's required to control how our bodies are perceived uncovered. Can prepare for that feeling. I understand why the others don't want to stand in a vacation destination in coats that do not button or zip with nothing underneath them. I don't want to do it either.

There's a part of me that wonders about what Sunny said, if my age would be a concern, but then I wonder who they'd ask for permission and that thought zaps away as quickly as it came on.

What I do is: I say I need to make a phone call, that it's urgent. Our hotel is right in the Quarter, and I go inside, half done up, and I call New York. It's only seven in the morning there, I don't even know what I can hope for at this hour, yet Harriet answers the line herself.

"Birdie? Is everything alright?"

Is it?

I choose not to tell her about Gus's meanness, the name-calling. I frame it like a question. There has been a change of plans. What would she like me to do?

"How did yesterday go?" she asks. When I tell her I did what I was told to do, she's quiet for a moment, then says, "That's not what I asked. How was he yesterday? Did anything happen?"

My legs, the stockings, the run, his hand. I don't want to make it more than it was, and I don't want her to think I'm calling for no reason. Just one word: yes.

"Don't do anything."

Twenty minutes after I return to set, Gus is removed. The magazine will send a new photographer out first thing. Work will resume in the morning.

THE COVER GIRL

Sunny and Mavis are trying to figure out what happened, and I'm not quick enough to pretend I want to know too. "Did you call Daddy?" Sunny asks.

I understand, by the sarcasm dripping from her voice—and why! I saved the day, didn't I?—that she does not mean my father in Connecticut. The implication makes my stomach turn, but I shove the feeling down.

I don't answer. I force a smile and shrug. They will believe what they want anyhow.

5

The issue of *Yes, You!* with my face on the cover arrives in late February. Outside it should be gray slush and gray clouds and gray moods, not palm trees and sunshine, and that is what awaits me when I fly to New York.

After a go-see, Harriet takes me to dinner to celebrate, just the two of us, and if she's holding New Orleans against me, I can't tell. It's been too long since I've seen her. She looks the exact same but somehow further away, and being in her presence and watching as she effortlessly refuses the first table at which they try to seat us, nothing rude or unkind, just an undeniable refusal, makes me realize how much I have missed her, the concept of her.

Harriet, of course, requests a martini, extra cold, as cold as you can possibly make it. There should be a glass for her in the freezer, Ulrich knows.

Caught up in the moment, I forget the division in my life, the rules of the rock star's world and the rules outside, and I ask for a glass of champagne.

"She's joking," Harriet says, not missing a beat, eyes locked on mine.

THE COVER GIRL

I nod: yes. Just a joke. Just carried away by the excitement of the magazine cover.

My mistake aside, this dinner is a celebration and so she has a regular rare steak and I get *le petit filet* and we split a side of potatoes, the fact that we will barely touch them already understood. That they are there is the important part.

Harriet raises her martini glass. "Cheers, darling. May this be the first of many covers." I raise my glass to that, though I can't picture what it would mean to be that kind of model. "Now, I have an exciting offer for you. Cameo Cosmetics is launching with a fresh face as their Cameo girl. I sent your book, and they want to sign you to an exclusive eighteen-month contract."

A cosmetics contract. I almost drop my fork. The brass ring. I've never heard of this brand, but even so, it has to mean *something*.

"It's a risk," Harriet says before I can get too excited. "The money is good, but remember, *exclusive* means this will be your job. You won't be able to do other campaigns or magazines, and you've just started editorial work. But they would primarily have you working in New York, so you could come back more regularly—that could be a plus while you're in California. There'd be more stability."

I note how she suggests California is something temporary, but I let the *while* slide by. I ask her what she thinks I should do.

Harriet shakes her head. "This has to be your choice, darling. We can keep going on this path and something bigger may come along, or it may not. I certainly won't be mad if you want to keep your options open. Or we can say yes to Cameo and see where that leads. It's a small brand now, but it could be a stepping stone. You'd be the face of something. Exclusive is funny—once someone knows they can't have you, they're willing to do more to get you. You could be fielding offers we can't even dream of when the contract is up."

I sip my water, taking it all in, trying to think of a question to ask that will make the answer clear.

"Again, this is your decision. Some girls work their whole careers hoping for a deal like this and never get it, but that doesn't mean it's right for you, and this has to be right for you," Harriet says.

Because I'm different. This, I tell her, is right for me. When we toast again, I feel as full and warm as if I had the champagne, after all. A contract.

And when I think the night can't get any better, once the plates are cleared away and the ice crusting the glass of her second martini is nearly melted, she asks, "Why bother staying in a hotel while you're here? Why don't you stay with me?"

My first feeling is relief: we have not discussed New Orleans, which I'm glad for, and also she wouldn't ask this if she felt I'd handled it wrong. And then even stronger is pride, pride that I've earned this level of care, of intimacy with Harriet. I have tried to imagine her existing outside the office or richly decorated restaurants, an entire life separate from what goes on in these twelve square blocks, and I have always come up empty. I still don't know if she has a husband or children. There can't be any way, right? Not according to my understanding of husbands and children. But now I can find out. I call the hotel from the restaurant, leaving Harriet's number for the rock star just in case. She will, I'm sure, love that.

Harriet's apartment on the Upper West Side is not unlike my new home—black and white, all the color and its absence, and nothing in between. The walls are peppered with abstract art, also black and white. There are no fashion photographs, none of her girls on display. Not a single face. I want to look in her closet, imagining the same pair of palazzo pants five times, two weeks' worth of drapey black tops. She does not offer me a tour beyond her guest room, though, a small simple bedroom more sterile than my hotel would have been.

She shakes herself another martini while brewing me a cup of unasked for tea. "Will you see your parents while you're back?" Her tone suggests she knows this question is loaded yet she still feels the pull to ask.

It's not that I don't want to see them but also it is exactly that. There's no way to look at them while living the life I have right now. Didn't we agree this was best? But I anticipated the question and to live up to who Harriet thinks I can be, I've planned an actual lunch this time.

"Wonderful," she says. "Perhaps now that you'll be coming back more frequently, you'll be able to have more visits. And please know, I'd be delighted to have you stay with me whenever you're here for your Cameo shoots."

Delighted. The word is almost too much, pressing right on my curiosity. So I ask to be sure—I wouldn't be in anyone's way?

Harriet half smiles. "It would just be my way, darling. And as you can see, no, you would not be."

I find myself oddly pleased by this fact, by this life. I thank Harriet for the offer. No, what I say is that it feels like a dream come true.

"The Cameo contract?"

The heavier meal and cup of mint tea has made me warm and sleepy—almost tipsy in a way that lets words tumble out that would otherwise not. I confess: yes, and also being able to stay with her.

A look I can't read passes across Harriet's face, then softens into nothing. "It's late," she says. "We'll get the Cameo paperwork signed in the morning. Let's get you settled for bed."

It feels silly, to be fussed over, almost *parented*, at this point. I am beyond this.

I am supposed to be beyond this.

Harriet hands me a bath towel and facecloth after she walks me to the guest room. She tells me good-night, then pauses. "Birdie. You're okay after the New Orleans shoot?"

Is it a question or a statement? Is it a choice? Her face is filled with concern, but I don't want to be the cause for concern, not ever and especially not tonight. I want to be the cause for steak dinners and clinking glasses. I tell her I'm fine.

"You did the right thing, calling me," she says. "You can always call me." I nod—I know. Still, she lingers outside the guest room door. "And out there? You're still happy?"

Yes. I am happy still.

I am happy until I arrive at the Four Seasons the next day, ninety minutes before I have to leave for my flight home. Ninety minutes is a reasonable amount of time to go without disappointing each other.

But my mother and father do not enter the restaurant alone. With them is a man I've never seen before, younger than them, perhaps the rock star's age. He wears aviator glasses and carries a yellow legal pad. I stare at him through the stiff-armed hugs until my mother finally introduces him.

"This is Clark Youngs," she says brightly. "He writes for the *Darien Times*. He's going to do a story on you. Now that you're a cover girl."

How dare she.

Before I can say no, we're being seated and orders are being taken. I can't believe she did this, but also, can't I? All it took was a magazine cover for her to look at me, to see I might not be so boring, after all.

"Tell Clark about yourself," my mother says when the drinks are set in front of us. Not *How have you been? What are you in town for? Are you doing well?* Not *We've missed you.* This isn't those words dressed up in a more comfortable outfit. This is *Here is what you are useful for now.* I look at my father, as though he can undo this, as though he hasn't gone along with it up until this point. His mouth twitches and one shoulder shifts up in the ti-

THE COVER GIRL

133

niest shrug. In any other moment, this could be an admission—
you know how she is—to bond over, but not this one.

"You're a model?" Clark prompts me. "For a few years? But
you live in California?"

"For work," my mother interrupts. "Otherwise she'd be at
the Mayflower Debutante Ball!" I cannot imagine anything less
important to Clark or to me.

"How did you get to the West Coast from Darien? Isn't New
York a fashion capital?"

"She was on an album cover too!"

He jots down some notes, and I would give anything to
know what's written on that pad. I live with the rock star, my
parents signed something, all of this happened right out in the
open but I know, *know* that it cannot be a story, that Clark can't
get enough to make it a story. Even if the story is about how
a Darien mother spawned a magazine model, which is really
what she wants.

"But you were discovered in New York?"

"And now she's in a magazine!"

Perhaps she found me dull because she never let me speak.

I consider getting up to call the rock star, to ask what I should
do. But I know what he will say, and anyway, I should be able to
handle this on my own. I need to handle something on my own.
When my mother pauses enough to let me get in a word, that's
all I give Clark—so many single-word answers that he can't hide
his irritation, which I hope is all directed back to my mother.
And then he asks the question: "Which album cover was this?"

There is, I am certain, nothing convincing about the way I
knock over my water glass and squeal with surprise. As we ar-
range linen napkins to sop up the spill, I announce I have a
plane to catch. Clark stares at my mother, who looks at me like
she wants to send me to my room. *Which room, Mother! I don't
have one anymore!*

But, I tell Clark, I'd love to call him and follow up on any questions he might have. If he could just give me a phone number, I'll call when I land, and we can do a real interview.

The business card he gives me is damp from being clamped in my palm by the time I'm back in LA. The longest flight of my life. I know what I have to do. I know I do, in fact, need help. Again.

The driver takes me straight to the Doctor's house. He lets me inside the dark wood-paneled foyer like he's been expecting me.

"What do you need?" he asks. I'm grateful he doesn't bother with pleasantries, that he knows I'd never come see him for anything less than dire. He's the manager. I need him to manage. I hand him the curled-up business card and explain about the lunch, that I need this story to go away.

"And what are you going to do for me?" he asks.

This is possibly the first time he's ever looked me in the eye, and my stomach flips. He runs a hand down my arm, drifting too close to my chest. I feel disgusting and ashamed as I whisper that there's nothing I can do for him. I'm asking him to fix it. Not only for me. For the rock star too.

"You just want me to clean up your messes for free, little girl?"

His voice falls on me, heavy, pressing the air out. I know this feeling, have felt this feeling before. Racing heart, blurred vision, unbreathable air. Not a closing in but a crash, and I am so angry with myself for not having more control. For letting this happen in front of him.

I can't help it—I burst into tears in the foyer, unable to fight the panic roiling inside me, so tired from the travel and so sad about my mother ruining what should have been a lovely trip, and so disgusted by this man suggesting I owe him sex or something like it in exchange for his assistance, and so exhausted by men like him and Gus trying to break me down, trying to take, take, take. He watches me cry huge shuddering sobs, and then he drifts deeper into the house. I can hear the

THE COVER GIRL

135

whir of the rotary dial, the rumble of his voice. I'm still weeping when he returns.

"He killed the story," the Doctor says. I can barely bring myself to thank him. He watches me get the words out with a look of tremendous satisfaction. And I think he gets more pleasure out of seeing me so small than he would from anything else I could have done.

At home, before I can go to bed with the rock star, I take a long bath with a big flute of champagne. I close my eyes, and I imagine the water washing it all away—my mother, Clark, the Doctor, Gus. Sunny. I imagine how it could have gone. How it would have been if I were the only girl on the New Orleans shoot and the photographer was fine. I had a regular lunch with my parents. I have never been alone with the Doctor. The girl in the photo is not always me. Here is how it really went.

And then, finally, I can sink into the relief.

In fact, I am so relieved the story is dead that when March arrives and the rock star asks me what I want for my sixteenth birthday, I can't think of anything. So he takes me to Hawaii, where no one acts like he is any more important than anyone else with money, and we rub each other down with suntan oil and drink out of coconuts and the only time I am not wearing a bathing suit is when we go to dinner. He sings a song about being sixteen, beautiful, and his, strumming a ukulele left in our hotel room, and when we're in bed, we both say it over and over again: *I love you, I love you, I love you.*

When we get back, he takes me to get my driver's license. I pass the written part, and when the instructor asks me to direct her to the car I will be driving for my test, I bring her to his yellow Pantera. He waves from a bench.

"Is that your father?" she asks. I tell her no. I do not offer further explanation.

I have improved since that first lesson in the cornfields, and though I can feel the instructor cutting curious looks at me from the corner of her eye as I follow each of her steps, I concentrate on the road. When we come back, he is sitting on a bench, knees splayed and fingers linked, bobbing his foot up and down. He's nervous for me. I don't get out of the car immediately because I love seeing him like this, a man, not a rock star, human and mine.

Once I am sixteen, he takes me out more. He holds my hand in public, guides me by the small of my back into restaurants. I have learned to angle my face away from cameras when they try to capture us because he suggests that I not give away for free what plenty of others have been willing to pay for.

Then we finally have dinner with Linda from the festival and her husband, Gary, from a band I can never remember the name of, and Lulu and Beasley. I'm still angling for a real position in this sisterhood I was told about, and this seems like perfect progress at last. Time spent with both Linda and Lulu will bring me fully into the group.

No one is quite sure what's happening with Lulu and Beasley on any given day, but they've been attempting something since the night of the tour wrap party. Or Lulu has. It's an on-again, off-again spiral where Beasley shows up at our house late at night, swears he's going to change his phone number, and then three weeks later, they're splashed across a tabloid or seen pressed against a wall at a party, her leg possessively hooked around his waist.

The mood is off as soon as we sit down at Yamashiro. No one else seems excited about the pagoda or the view or the prospect of sushi, and I try to cool my own eagerness while Lulu keeps shooting withering looks at Beasley. As I am trying to think of something mature and insightful to ask Linda, something that will make her think of me as an equal, Gary interrupts to propose a toast to the rock star.

"I think this is the longest I've seen you with one girl," he says, glass in the air. "So, let's drink to your continued happiness."

It isn't lost on me that Gary did not propose a toast to the both of us, but at least I'm included in the continued-happiness part, by virtue of contributing to said happiness. The more important part. Linda raises her drink but doesn't quite lift her gaze to meet ours.

Lulu touches her vodka soda to Gary's glass. "Don't bother drinking to *my* continued happiness, because it doesn't exist with this one."

Beasley clinks his drink to the rest of ours as he nudges Lulu. "That could have been you," he says, nodding to me. "Except he realized you were crazy before you could get your hooks all the way in."

Lulu snorts. "Please. I was already like four years too old."

The table goes silent as Gary realizes he's the only one laughing. "Lulu," Linda murmurs.

Lulu drains her glass and laughs prettily, loose-limbed and pleased by the reaction she's elicited. "What? Weren't we all thinking it?"

Thinking what? Her comment does not absorb; it bounces off me like a returned serve. Like this is tennis and everyone is just batting remarks back and forth. I modeled tennis clothes once. Tennis.

I wait five excruciatingly quiet minutes before it seems like enough time has passed that I can excuse myself without it appearing to be directly related to anything anyone has or has not said. I stand in the ladies' room, hands on either side of the sink, and I stare deep into my reflection, trying to bring myself back, trying to keep those words on the surface, where they can't possibly have any meaning.

It's Linda who comes in after me. She takes a tube of lipstick out of her purse and carefully swipes a nude color across her mouth. Then mascara, though her lashes are already fanned out thick and full. "Are you alright?" she asks when her face is done, is redone.

I tell her I don't know.

"Lulu is Lulu," Linda says. "She isn't trying to say anything about you or him. She's just angry with Beasley and trying to get attention from someone else since he won't give it to her."

Linda steers me back to the table, where Lulu is contrite with a new bigger drink and Beasley's arm is tight around her waist. It would not be there had I not introduced them like she asked, like a good friend. She reaches out to squeeze my hand and I let her, but I don't say anything for the rest of the meal. I let the conversation float above me, smiling and laughing with everyone else without knowing what it is I am smiling and laughing about. Tennis.

When we get home, I finally ask him if it's true.

"Is what true?" he replies.

I want him to know what I'm asking without my saying it. I want him to understand. But he's looking at me, waiting, and I make myself find a paraphrase for Gary's comment about this being the longest he has been with anyone.

We are standing in the kitchen, this huge room we use for nothing except getting ice, and he laughs like what I have said is the silliest and most charming thing. He hugs me so hard my feet come off the ground and he sets me onto the counter, easing his body between my knees. "Little Bird," he says. "You have nothing to worry about. It's true, I guess, but it doesn't matter. When you know, you know. And I knew with you the moment I met you. There's a reason nothing else has worked out until now. We're supposed to be together."

My arms are still looped around his neck as he tells me this, and I pull him down to me, kiss him hard, with my whole self, so I can say all the things I don't have the words for, but that is not how he takes it, and so I let him push my dress up around my thighs and unzip his jeans, because there are plenty of things to say this way too.

THE COVER GIRL

★ ★ ★

We are invited to a movie premiere, my first. Two of his songs were included in the soundtrack. I know there will be cameras, eyes, so I call Harriet to ask what I should do, and what I hoped would happen happens: in return I receive a phone call from Azrian de Popa's personal assistant. *My designer friend.* Azrian has just the thing. Are my measurements the same? He would be so honored if I'd consider it. As if I'd say anything other than yes.

The dress arrives shockingly fast. I unpack it as though it could break, examining seams, touching the fabric. It is filmy black. Diaphanous. I learned that word on a shoot. When I lift the skirt, I am surprised to find a bathing suit–like bottom. A dress with leg holes. And when I step through those holes and pull the top up over me, it's stunning. A head-turner. The bodice structured, black, high-cut neck. A metal cuff choker to hold it together. There is no back. The skirt falls to the floor in two almost-panels, three layers each that ensure it's not totally sheer, just somewhat. The slits up the side, nearly to the hip, let me dramatically display whichever leg I choose. Both legs.

All I have to be is legs.

When I call the assistant, I use the low-toned murmur I have learned to affect for hotel concierges and stewardesses, the overly exquisite restaurant staff member. The voice that says I am accustomed to all this—so grateful, gracious, but not surprised. I tell the assistant that Azrian is a genius. I so appreciate that he thought of me. I look forward to wearing the dress. And, yes, of course my escort will be wearing those cuff links.

The evening of the premiere, I do my own hair and makeup with the products Cameo sent me to wear while I wait to be scheduled for my first shoot. I thought it would be more work, and faster, that I'd get word it was time to stay with Harriet again almost right away, but so far, all I've received is a box of tubes and palettes.

I know what my plan is. A nude lip. The faintest bit of blush.

Dark mascara. Something mod to play with the futuristic dress. I cannot say that I came up with that on my own, but applying descriptions from *Vogue* to my own choice feels clever, like I know what I'm doing. Like I fully belong here.

I pull my hair over my shoulder in a thick heavy braid, like that photo of Twiggy in her pink outfit, so the back of the dress, its lack of, will be on full display. Then I dab some foundation on a sponge, but when I spread it on my face, it's all wrong. The consistency is tacky and the color is too harsh for my skin, and my cheeks start to redden from the effort of trying to blend it in. Maybe it'll look better with powder. I don't have a choice; I'm the Cameo girl now.

The rest of the products are no better. The delicate sweep of blue eyeshadow is lurid, the lip gloss reminds me of something from a child's playset. I look clownish. I cannot attend a movie premiere like this, but I cannot break my contract either.

He calls up that the car will be here in five minutes, and in a panic, I shout down that I'm not ready. It is so unlike me, the me I've always offered him, that he appears in the doorway with alarming speed. He repeats that I have five minutes, and instead of acknowledging the time, I ask him to look at me.

I watch him start to say I look beautiful without looking, but then he catches a glimpse of the sticky mess I've tried to make work. "What is this?" he asks.

I explain to him that it's what I'm contractually obligated to wear. That if anyone asks what makeup I have on, it has to be Cameo.

He bursts out laughing. "No one expects that. Just wear what you normally wear and lie."

I remind him it's a contract.

"It's not that serious, Little Bird," he says. "Three minutes."

His casual dismissal of a signed document is alarming. As is the ease with which he suggests I should—and believes I can—lie.

I don't know whom I'm betraying as I wash and dry my face,

THE COVER GIRL

but that is what it feels like. I signed a paper saying I would follow certain standards, and putting on my usual brand of nude lipstick and false eyelashes is not within those standards. This isn't fudging answers in my *Yes, You!* interview. This is my job, my one job. Harriet told me it was my choice, and this is the choice I made. It can't be the wrong choice. It must just be an off batch of product. It's not that bad. I am not locked into promoting something I don't believe in.

Am I locked into scrubbing my face when he tells me to.

Am I locked into his laughing dismissal of my concern.

Signed papers.

I know he's waiting as I snap the cuff of Azrian's dress around my neck, but still I take a moment for this. For the work of art I have been entrusted with. For a new reflection I have found: a girl who takes a few minutes when she needs to, even when her name is being called.

We're stuck in ridiculous evening traffic—my fault, no one needs to say it—when I remember to ask about the cuff links. "What cuff links?" he asks. One look at my face and he realizes he's said the wrong thing. My voice is a whisper, a jumble of words: *Christmas, designer, the dress, I told you.* I had asked. Why didn't he know what I was talking about? Had he ever intended to wear them at all?

"Relax, Birdie," he says. "Standing next to you, no one will be looking at me, anyway."

As though being told to relax has ever had anything but the opposite effect. Even at the premiere, with the comfortable flash of camera bulbs, this is the tone for the evening. Every few steps, I stop, stick out one leg or both legs, angle a shoulder so my hair and back are on display. I make my eyes say that this is an amazing night. I make my eyes say that this is rare air I get to breathe. I may have failed at giving presents, at getting Azrian's accessories noticed, at being an honest Cameo girl, but I will not fail this dress. In between shots, though, I am wooden.

If he notices, he doesn't say anything. There's no conversation to be made during the movie, the plot of which I can't follow. Instead, I excuse myself to the bathroom, and I stare into the mirror, trying to feel like the person looking back isn't a stranger. I am happy. I am so happy. I repeat it, trying to make myself—no, *remind* myself to—believe it, and it is true I have this dress and this career and this man who does not think about clothes except when I am in them, but this version of the girl in the mirror looks back like she knows something I don't.

2018

A phone call is not enough. Michelle Elhert suggests we meet, since she lives nearby. It becomes lunch. I read other interviews with non-supermodel models to prepare. Surely, we won't tread too deep under the surface; no one knows who I am. To the extent I am compelling at all, I am only compelling as a surface. I consider making notes. I consider what I could be asked.

I consider what will be shown to Harriet now that it's my turn.

Michelle is tiny in person, maybe five-two. She wears a tee shirt tucked into high-waisted pants. Her hair is pulled up into a dark messy bun, and a smattering of freckles dots her nose and cheeks, a garnish doled out by a supple-wristed chef, and her only makeup is a layer of bright pink lipstick. I can picture her applying that lipstick and thinking of it as a power lip, a misconception but a sweet one. Even though I know she must be only twenty-four or twenty-five, she appears even younger than I had imagined. Or maybe that's just what they look like now.

"Okay," she says as soon as we've sent the waiter away with orders for salmon salad and white wine, and *no thank you, sparkling water will not be necessary, still is fine.* "Can I just tell you?"

She opens up her knapsack and pulls out a stack of magazines. I cannot tell if the knapsack is in fashion now or if she doesn't care. I wait for what she wants to just tell me. "My mom kept everything. And I loved looking through her teenage things when I was a kid." She opens to an ad with a blonde girl blowing a perfect pink bubble-gum bubble, holding a birthday cake. "I just loved you. I'm sorry, that probably sounds weird, but I would flip through all the ads looking for you." She splays open another magazine to the Swish ad. "I wasn't kidding when I said how beautiful I thought this was. All the other girls I knew wanted to look like Britney Spears and I was like, no, I want to look like *her!*" She offers a bashful chuckle and I laugh along. It doesn't seem like the right time to share with her that I am deeply invested in the happiness and well-being of Britney Spears. "So we get these press kits about Harriet's Girls, and can you just imagine how much I freaked when I saw you were one of them and I finally got to put a name to a face?" She sips her water, takes a breath. "Sorry, this probably sounds so unprofessional, but I *knew* I *had* to write this story, and you were the only interview I cared about getting. I couldn't find much else out about you, so I guess you don't grant interviews very often, so all this is just to say thank you. Seriously."

I feel like I should be embarrassed for her but instead I find her level of effusiveness impressive. How to live in such a way, how to both apologize for being too much for the world yet remain unshrunk by it. It hasn't become much easier to be a young woman, and for every small way things have lightened, new considerations I've never thought of facing have popped up. I've had the comfort of my own name not surviving because we did not need to know everything then. But I could look Michelle up on the internet and probably find her fourth-grade class picture, her sixteen-year-old self's lovelorn blog, photos from the ill-advised spring break in Cancun. Hers is a world of budget cuts and doing more with less, health insur-

THE COVER GIRL

ance as a luxury. And still, she has kept herself earnest enough to become a fan of something, anything. Maybe I *am* getting older, but I'm touched. I murmur something thankful and deferential, as though this happens all the time.

Her eyes widen as she reaches for another picture in the stack. "Oh, my god, Ms. Rhodes, listen to me, yammering on about looking at your pictures in my mother's magazines. I'm sorry, I hope you don't think... I didn't mean..."

She looks so utterly horrified that all I can do is laugh. She hopes I don't think what? She didn't mean what? I spend a lot of time trying to figure out the best way to keep from looking like a woman in her fifties. Sometimes I wish I wasn't a woman in my fifties and that I had it all to do over again, which doesn't make me special. But I'm also quite aware that I *am* a woman in my fifties, I made it here, and I cannot fathom being offended that both Michelle's mother and I happened to be teenagers in the late '70s and early '80s while Michelle, through no fault of her own, had not yet been born.

I assure her she has not said anything wrong, which clarifies, for me, the balance of power. I start to tell her to call me Elizabeth, not Ms. Rhodes, but I realize that would not be the name she's seen. And then what she said finally registers. Press kits. I was included in the press kit?

"I mean, it was a digital kit, but yeah, they sent some photos." Michelle whips out her tablet and with a few movements, pulls up a black-and-white photograph of me in a dramatically constructed white dress, dark mascara running down my face. I turn back to my glass of water almost immediately; that picture hurts to look at for several reasons. Michelle doesn't notice, keeps scrolling. "And then this one." She pulls up a magazine cover. "That must have been so cool. So yeah, there's your full name at the bottom, and I was just like, *finally*."

The salads and wine arrive, and with the initial awkwardness over, we turn to the task at hand. And it doesn't feel like an interview at all, but a conversation. It is much easier than I thought it would be to talk to Michelle. She is smart and thoughtful and clearly interested in the history of modeling. She asks the basic questions—how long have I been modeling, what job was my favorite—but she also wants to know what it *felt* like. The facts are the facts, but the story is the nerves, the elation, the feeling of power. I have kept all of this so well-preserved that it's eluded my own reach.

It seems like we might get through this without talking about Harriet much at all, but I am careful not to relax into the conversation, mindful of what details I share when Michelle asks about more recent times. I find myself eyeing her stack of magazines, wondering what else her mother collected.

As Michelle asks questions and takes notes, she offers tidbits about herself. I learn that she's been with her boyfriend for six years but it's probably not forever; he doesn't have a lot of ambition, but then again, he might be getting on the right track with an entrepreneur he met, who's trying to disrupt the dog breeding industry. She says this so casually that it takes me a full minute to be disturbed by the air quotes she uses around "disrupt"; already I want to take this girl by the wrist and tell her to walk. Just walk away.

"And is there anything you'd like to say about Harriet, specifically?"

I am so distracted by the concept of dog breeding entrepreneurship that her simple question, one I'd prepared for, catches me off guard. I sip my water to buy time, then smile. What could I say that wasn't better said by her longevity and the careers she launched?

"Sorry to press, but that's the point, isn't it? I can write whatever I want, but it's much better said by you and her other clients."

Though her tone is warm, her gaze is resolute, and I feel caught in my nonanswer. As young as she is, as many apologies as she feels compelled to pepper her conversation with, she is still a professional, and two can play this game. That I have not spoken to Harriet since 1996 is only a story to me, and not the one I'm telling here.

So I take it to the other extreme: I'm not sure I can possibly add anything fresh or new to the Harriet Goldman story, but I am certainly grateful and always will be.

Michelle looks at me for another moment before jotting down a note. "Hm. And are you excited to see her at the gala in September?"

Afraid. Anxious. Resistant. Overwhelmed. I could come up with any number of words that are closer to what I'm feeling than *excited* is, none of which are Michelle's business. The little I shared with Dr. Adams was more than enough. I tell Michelle, with what I hope is a convincing display of earnest dismay, that I'm still not sure I'll be available to attend. Potential conflict. I'll have to see how my schedule shakes out these next couple months. The arrival of the check prevents me from needing to say more. Michelle fumbles for her wallet, but I hold up my hand. I looked up the average per-word rate for an article like the one she's writing. Good god, I could get this one.

"Oh, gosh, are you sure?" As though I would change my mind. "Thank you so much. Let me just look at my notes here— make sure there's nothing we didn't cover if that's okay?" she says. I nod as she scans through an impressive scribble. "Oh! Sorry, I forgot the most obvious thing. How did Harriet discover you?"

Of course. I try to keep my face even as I tell her about walking into Saks on a shopping trip in the city. How everything changed in that moment. How wonderful it has been. Again, I am truly grateful for my career, and for this conversation. I gather my purse, signaling my intention to get up, but Michelle is still scrawling notes.

"And how old were you exactly?"

I tell her I was in my early teens, hoping that is enough.

"That's one of the more controversial elements of Harriet's career, right? How early she'd bring girls into modeling? Can you weigh in on that? Did you experience any harassment or anything like that?"

Two questions at once, posed as if they are linked. Posed as though harassment meant the same thing back then. I tell her no, not anything that stands out. And the fact that I'm still here, still working, shows that Harriet knew what she was doing.

Michelle looks like she wants to say more, but she just makes a note. "What was it like for your family—what did your parents think of your career?"

So much I thought to prepare for, and here we are down a path I didn't anticipate. How foolish of me. Everyone loves context now. Somehow it makes things mean more. I take what should look like a tasteful pause, and I tell her my parents have passed away, and it's still difficult for me to talk about them. Both of these are facts, and if one chooses to adhere to correlation equaling causation, that is not my problem.

Michelle's face collapses into a puddle of sympathy. "Oh, no, I'm so sorry. I totally understand. My mom actually died last year, and I was just like, trying to sound normal when I was talking about her magazines." Her eyes fill as she reaches across the table as if to pat my arm but stops in an awkward fluttering motion. "Thanks so much for sharing with me today."

I resist the urge to shrink in my chair. All this work trying to get an upper hand that doesn't even exist—she's just a grieving girl trying to do a job. I feel so terrible that I end up telling her she can call or text me if she needs anything else, anything at all, for her article. And then I walk away unsettled but also, I think, unscathed.

That evening, I make myself go back to Pilates class. I normally go at least three times a week, and I'm starting to feel the

THE COVER GIRL

effects of skipping, not in my body but in my mind. I pick a different instructor, a different time, make like the jump board incident never happened.

The woman teaching tonight is new to me, which means her language is new too. They all have different ways of saying the same thing, of trying to give a visual to an action that cannot be shown. A strand of pearls, to me, has nothing to do with vertebrae or moving one of them at a time—a thing I am still not sure I've ever really done—but it paints a picture. Years of nonsense instructions from photographers have prepared me for what it means to knit my rib cage, zip my zipper, engage my pelvic floor, but it is not second nature the way performing was—I am a body, but I have to stay in it. The movements are all I can focus on, no room for thinking about anything else. When my mind wanders, so does my posture, so do my knees. This is its own escape.

I make my way through the initial leg exercises, eyes closed so I can feel the movement and be the movement. No need to see it. Eventually, we end up sitting in the short box position, holding on to our magic circles—words that would conjure nothing outside of this space and that bring me something close to delight. We roll down into a C-curve, squeeze the circle five times, and then roll up. Stack your rib cage over your hips.

I have the strength to hold my legs at forty-five as I twist to the back wall and to the front window, but I choose tabletop instead, knees stacked firmly above the hip bones. Nothing to see here.

"Make sure the rotation is coming from your core, not your arms," the instructor murmurs as she walks by. "Mind–body connection."

I can't feel what I'm doing wrong. It feels like my core. But my arms are there too. I want to ask her how I'm supposed to do it, how I'm supposed to know what the right thing feels like. I should know after all this time, though. I should know how to feel it right. For now, I slow the movement down, trying to create resistance in my obliques so I can feel what I'm supposed to.

Late that night, after a dinner of celery smeared with fat-free cream cheese sprinkled with cayenne pepper and thirty-two ounces of water with lemon and ginger, followed by a glass of Picpoul de Pinet, I undress and stand in front of my full-length mirror.

This is not an unusual occasion. I need to know what I look like, as long as I am needed as a smile to sell vitamins or calcium supplements, as slices of hand or cheek to tout the anti-aging prowess of a lotion or cream, as the body in a catalog of clothing for the mature woman. I suppose I'll do it until the go-sees completely dry up, until I am too old even to advertise that getting old does not have to be that bad.

Inventory: the legs are still good. I was an early adopter of the Jane Fonda workout, back when she had her own studio and there was a period where, if you were willing to be there at five in the morning, you could take a class with Jane herself. I only managed it a couple times, but I've adored her ever since. I still do the workout almost daily, in addition to the Pilates classes. I made thousands of dollars off these legs and while no one would pay that much for them now, not even a fraction, they are still toned, defined. Breasts were never my best feature, but their lack of size no longer bothers me. My backside is not as high as it once was, but it isn't a drooping pancake either. In profile, I take in the flatness of my stomach, curving just slightly under the belly button despite all the sets of one hundreds and rare non-wine carbohydrates. Visible arm muscles, triceps fighting a valiant battle against the batwing that eventually comes for us all. The faintest scar on the forearm. The creams and peels and serums and Dr. Rosenthal have kept neck sag at bay. Hair dyed blond, as it has been for years and years after I destroyed it in the '80s, except for that period in the '90s when I just gave up.

And then I stare at my face. What would I think if I saw this face on the street? Would I ascribe an age to it? If I was told fifty-six, would I think *no way* or *yikes?* Did Dr. Adams think either of those things? Can there be a middle ground? Is *yes, fifty-six seems right* so bad?

No. Yes.

I have seen my face reflected back at me in so many pictures through the years that I no longer know what I look like. I can stare at my reflection for full minutes and see it only as a possibility as opposed to fact.

But standing naked in front of this mirror, I cannot hide anymore. And the truth is, my question is not *does this face need a little lift to look good enough?* but *am I willing to show it to Harriet after all these years?*

1978–1981

Stray Cat Blues

1

At the Rainbow, he sat in the back with a dark-haired woman wearing a dress cut to her belly button.

What I had learned was this: if it was anyone else, it was never young and blond. It was always the opposite of me. And there were so many ways for an opposite to oppose.

I stood at the bar in my new Halston halter jumpsuit, sipping a Harvey Wallbanger and watching them. If she were really beautiful, she wouldn't have to wear a dress like that. She was nobody, a hanger-on. I, however, had just launched the Cameo campaign.

I was a face. More than legs now.

The face of what?

His hand moved up her thigh.

I drained my drink and as I turned back toward the bar, I realized that while I watched him, someone watched me. An actor I had seen at several parties, someone on the fringes, bit parts, enough that you turned your head and wondered if he was familiar or if it was the pool he stood next to. The actor took a few steps toward me and told me I looked like Debbie

Harry. It wasn't close to true, but this seemed as good a reason as any to talk to him.

The actor introduced himself as Blaine and after another Wallbanger, I found myself saying it over and over, enjoying the flick of my tongue against the back of my front teeth. Blaine brought his hand to my mouth. Slipped a Quaalude between my lips. His fingers lowered to my arm, my waist. His mouth moved to my neck until I cut through the slow motion to push him away.

Blaine disappeared and I snuck away to the ladies' room to breathe. As I swiped a new coat of non-Cameo lipstick across my mouth, my reflection seemed to move five seconds ahead of the dimensional me, my face and not my face at all. I thought of this Birdie as completely separate. She must have known what she was doing. She must be secure in this world. I wished the Birdie in the mirror could decide things for me.

The rock star was waiting for me when I got back to the bar, the girl with the dress cut down to her belly button nowhere in sight. The clench of his jaw was as still and defined as a painting. I stared, reaching my hand up to touch the jutting muscle, but he grabbed my fingers.

I let him lead me out of the bar and down to the Strip, through the Riot House and up to the room he'd booked as a treat. I had ruined my treat. He jerked me onto the bed but didn't follow. I looked at the pink handprint around my arm and up at him, waiting, breathing tiny breaths. I couldn't tell if he was about to fuck me or yell at me or worse. It was possible he didn't know either.

When he spoke, his voice was a serrated whisper: *Never do that to me again.* I told him I hadn't done anything. He kept repeating it and so did I until finally I pointed out the only reason I'd been talking to the actor was because I saw him with the belly button woman. "It's different," he snapped, and he left me alone in the room.

He was angry. But: he loved me enough to get angry with me.

THE COVER GIRL

I went to the bathroom and stared again at the girl who looked back. The Birdie in the mirror knew it wasn't about Blaine. It was about the awards show two nights ago. He'd been in a mood because they sat us with a heavy metal band from England, and he didn't particularly like British people or heavy metal music. The lead singer was half in the bag and had been looking my way all night, and when the rock star came back from the bathroom, he saw the singer bent down next to my chair. They had to be separated.

What he hadn't known: the lead singer had given me his phone number, pressed it into my palm on a napkin. Even if I wanted to use it, several of the numbers looked like letters. I told him I was spoken for. Just like that—*spoken for*. It seemed an elegant way to put it. That's not what he meant, he'd explained, using half the anticipated number of syllables.

He meant if I needed someone. Some help. If I wanted to leave. I had gotten angry, asked why, and that's when the rock star came back.

I'd just sat with my hands in my lap and let them fight it out, none of us knowing what the fight was really about. I didn't know why I stood out that night. If you looked around the room, any room, I was not the only young one, not by far. I'd seen other girls who couldn't have been much older than me, maybe even younger, dancing in the Whisky, sitting quietly at dinner, laughing loudly at the Rainbow. Our youth made us special; I knew that much from modeling. Who wouldn't want to be around us? We were new. We were lively. We wielded a power no one quite understood. Including that British heavy metal guy—what would I possibly need help with when I had a seat at this table instead of being home doing homework? What could possibly be better than this?

None of this was worth discussing with the rock star, so I poured myself a glass of vodka from the minibar and was asleep, freshly showered and smelling of Love's Baby Soft, by the time he came back. When he reached for me, I kept my body heavy. It seemed like a good time to count my weapons. In the morning, he whispered apologies until I gave in, and when I did, he called what we were doing making love, everything around us soft-focused and gauzy. I was beautiful and special and I never wanted it to end.

This was, by most measures, a standard Saturday night now.

Was it useful to ask how we got here?

Uncertain.

Did I notice the slow climb to this point?

I had seen the flirting backstage when we were on tour. I saw the way women looked at him in restaurants, when he took me shopping at designer boutiques, and I saw the way he didn't avoid looking back. This was part of the job. I flirted too. I turned heads too.

The difference was: he didn't like it when other men looked at me, and what was I going to say when women looked at him? The difference was: attracting attention was a matter of professional course for me and I thought about it in terms of my worth on paper. The difference was: I never did anything about it.

And that could be interpreted however one chose.

Was there a first time it felt like more than him enjoying being a famous man in a hungry world? No, but something shifted after the movie premiere, little ticks pushing us closer and closer to a time I could not make out on a clock I did not want to read.

There was, for instance, the afternoon the previous month at someone's pool in Malibu. I was in a gorgeous white crochet bikini, hair piled on top of my head, and he had been laughing for far too long with some woman wearing even less than I was.

Lulu sat in a chaise longue next to me, balancing a plate of fruit on the considerable table her pregnant belly made. She had, it turned out, already been pregnant during that awful dinner. Beasley resumed a pattern of showing up on the doorstep at all

THE COVER GIRL

hours of the night, alternating between claiming he was trapped and crying over how much he loved their unborn child.

I'd said congratulations and sent a floral arrangement because that seemed like the mature, grown-up thing to do, but deep inside it felt like a betrayal, worse even than her tantrum at Yamashiro. We were supposed to be the ones nobody knew what to do with. We hadn't even gotten started yet!

I was lounging next to Lulu, watching him laugh with this woman who was not me—this woman with a Mia Farrow haircut and most of her backside exposed and a hand running across his arm. He seemed, from here, to like that just fine. And Lulu started laughing next to me.

"You can't possibly be mad about that!" she said. I turned and looked at her, blinking slowly. This girl who had meltdowns for show. Just because she could. "This is just what they do. Come on, Birdie, you know that. He comes home to you. You two are practically married."

Practically, but only he had signed paperwork. Of course I could get mad. Of course I could wonder where it would leave me if he chose someone else. That was a thing Lulu could never grasp.

I had spent so long being seen and not heard. This got me work, made clients ask for me specifically. I did not complain. But around me, there were plenty of loudmouth girls who still worked too. There were the Lulus of the world who demanded attention and got it, no matter what. It seemed unfair that we had to follow two different sets of rules for no other reason than I thought it was what people wanted from me.

On our way home from the pool party, I'd cried. Part of it was real—the loneliness of sitting beside Lulu for hours and knowing too much separated us for us to ever really be friends now, and it had been that way all along. She'd probably just been using me to get to Beasley, but there was no more pretending, and if she pulled me into a closet to do coke with a baby asleep in another room, it would just be sad. And part of it was the vulnerability of knowing everyone saw him cozied up to the woman with the Mia Farrow hair, and everyone knew he had come with me. And part of it was to see what would happen.

He was, of course, beside himself. Taking a handkerchief from his back pocket, pulling me into his lap and smoothing my hair. He hadn't meant to hurt me. Wasn't I used to seeing him talk to women by now? It was just that, talking. Did I really think I had anything to worry about? This big man, so gentle and soothing, damn near clucking and cooing over me made me burn with a pleasure I had not yet experienced.

And so it began.

For a while, we stayed wrapped in a sweet, filmy haze. There was the warmth of the holidays, our cozy Christmas for two, a string of shows I stood in the wings for. But strip it away and focus the lights and there would always be another woman magneting her hip to his, finding some way to be my opposite. And there would always be someone else nearby, someone with pills or powders to speed me up or slow me down, just a little, just enough to let the Birdie in the mirror take over.

When I flew to New York for a Cameo gig, I was docile. The art and marketing people were different from the ones on the first shoot. After hair and makeup feathered my hair and brushed velvety rouge that was not Cameo brand across my cheeks, the art director said, "Too Brooke Shields, change up the look."

"I don't think it's Brooke Shields *enough*," the new marketing person replied. None of this meant anything to me, and I stood there while they argued about how wrong or right I looked for the product I'd been hired to be the face of for a year and a half.

I would not take sides. It was all part of the job, wasn't it? Whatever you ask.

I did one set in a cheerleader sweater and ponytail—the picture of teenage innocence, the art director said, like I knew any-

THE COVER GIRL

thing about that, and then the photographer had me against a different backdrop in jeans and neck-breaking platforms while the art director frowned and the marketing person whispered. I desperately reached for anything to try to get them to see me, what they had in me. If you think it would look better if I run in these shoes, then let me try it. No risk too great. Aren't I doing a good job? Aren't I enough of a Cameo girl?

None of it felt right.

She's so agreeable, the assistants murmured. *So easy to work with*, hair and makeup agreed. *You never give us any trouble*, Debi marveled when she sent me to parties, which was the only other thing I could do with the Cameo contract. *Darling, I'm so glad you're one of my girls*, Harriet said when I stayed at her flat or dropped off my vouchers. So I couldn't tell her how much I missed other jobs, how much I felt like my career was passing me by, how I felt that I had made a mistake in choosing Cameo, that she had made a mistake in trusting me to choose to shill for their sticky makeup by wearing another brand altogether. All I did was pretend now.

So at home, after long nights on the town watching him flirt and touch and whisper to anyone who looked twice at him, anyone who had something other than long blond hair and legs up to there, I cried. I dreamed of marching around in my sheer peach bathrobe and marabou slippers, breaking plates like a woman on a soap opera. I dreamed of finding other ways to capture his attention, of daring to be anything other than manageable. But I still feared he would leave me if I pushed too hard, so all I allowed myself was delicate tears to recreate that moment in the car, the soothing and the apologies. The reassurance. The longer I cried, the more blissful the result. There was jewelry, trips to beaches and islands, places where I could be the star. This must be how Lulu had operated her entire life: with the understanding that it was better to demand attention than to hope it will be given.

But then: a party. Who knows what it was for. Something in a hotel. I went to the bathroom to powder my nose, all senses of the word, and I couldn't find him when I returned. I wandered through groups of people, many whom I recognized with the assurance of being invisible without him. When I found him, I would suggest that it was time for us to go.

What a relief to see him in the coat closet. We had the same idea.

Before I could say anything, though, I saw panic flash in his eyes. And this time it was not just a hand on a waist or foreheads pressed together and giggling, but a woman kneeling in front of him.

A *coat closet*! I could imagine Harriet saying, if I dared tell her such things, disgusted by the outright cliché of it all. I turned to leave, hearing my name, hearing his footsteps. But this, this he couldn't pat and soothe away.

The moment we entered the house, I started screaming. I couldn't help it. I couldn't go down without a fight. Unlike the coat closet woman.

I stood on the furniture, needing to look as big as I felt. The mirror didn't make it. The wall clock either. *Who's lacking personality now, Mother!* He yelled too, and a little voice inside me said to stop, to let him apologize, but that hadn't worked, had it? It was easier to feel the anger than the hurt, so instead I yelled louder, a little in love with my own sound, even if all I was saying was *why* and *how could you*. And when I was done, when I was bored of being angry and wanted instead to be taken care of, when I was ready for a long bath and an icy vodka drink and the suggestion of a Palm Springs getaway, I played the one card I had been saving all this time: I told him I wanted to go home.

I didn't count on him laughing. I didn't count on him telling me this was my home, that my parents could do nothing for me and what was more, they didn't want to, and what did I think those papers they signed meant, after all? He was the one who had to deal with my shit and *you're lucky I'm still here because I didn't sign up for this.*

I couldn't afford to think at that moment, just act.

What it looked like was this: the young model stood on the ottoman. She vibrated with an unnameable feeling, a combination of fear and adrenaline and anger and shock all at once. She had no home if not this one. So she had to have this one. The rock star stood across the room. He looked almost bored. But he was supposed to love her, honor her. Or something. She could no longer pretend to know what he'd signed and why. Why her? A sliver of mirror lay at her feet. She needed him to do something. She needed to feel anything else.

The young model picked up the glass and held it to the roadmap of her wrist. The rock star raised his eyebrows, unmoved. She slashed it across her arm and waited for the blood.

A month, lost. I sat in a room with a view of the ocean and ignored everyone and ate exactly half the food on offer so that I would still have a job to go back to. A job at least, if not my life. The doctors asked me the little questions: *Where are you from? Have you had trouble sleeping? How is your appetite?* They did not ask: *Where is your home? Where will you go after? Would you rather stay sleeping?*

It wasn't that kind of place.

A month lost in a facility for the rich and famous, where you could get the mildest of checking-up-on and the softest robes and proof that someone cared enough to try to do something about you. This place was just for show.

I was always cold and one of the outside doctors suggested it was because I was too thin, and one of the inside doctors explained that they couldn't say that to me because of my job; that wasn't what I was here for. I didn't tell them I was always cold because I wasn't used to sleeping alone.

166   Amy Rossi

I was always cold because I was worried now I would always be alone, *okay*?

He visited every week, between a few concert dates. I had nothing to say. I had done enough already, and I had no words to fix it. I couldn't ask for forgiveness, even though I needed it to go on living as we had been. I couldn't ask him to stop fucking around with other women because I could offer no incentive. I had given him everything I had already. All I could do was wait for the moment he informed me it was over. What had he said about me going against my Cameo contract? *It's not that serious.* How seriously did he take whatever he'd signed for me?

He'd end it. I would have no home. All before I turned seventeen.

When they told me I had a visitor an hour after he'd left, I assumed it was him again, coming back to tell me he wouldn't return the following week. I did not expect to look up and see draped wool crepe and a chignon.

"Darling," she said.

No one told Harriet it was just for show, and for a brief moment, for me, it wasn't. For a brief moment, it was like my mother had come to get me, if I'd had a mother who was interested in doing things like coming to get me. I was walloped by the strength of how hard I loved Harriet and her cool manner, the way she put everything back in control. I could feel the tears surging up hot and fast from my chest, and I wanted so badly to let them go. I wanted to fall into her arms and ask how this had happened to me, ask why my parents had signed away the duty to love me and why he only loved me because he had a document saying he had to. I wanted to ask if she was someone who loved me beyond her percentage, beyond what I could do for her. I wanted to ask what was wrong with me. Was I not wanted? Not by them, not by him, not even by the Cameo people? And I had only a split second to not give in to those feelings, a split second to remember that the thing she complimented me on above all was my compliance. My silence. This wasn't the New Orleans incident. If I spoke now, what was she going to do—whisk me back to New York, move me in, help me start over? An overnight visit for a shoot was one thing, but she had plenty of other girls to worry about. I had slept in her guest room, but I was not her daughter or her sister, I was her client, and it was not her job to love me. It was her job to ensure I could continue making money. And so I kept my voice low and even-toned as I said hello, as I said it was all a misunderstanding and I just needed some rest.

"Darling," she said again, her voice softer, and if I didn't know her better, I would say she sounded near breaking. "It doesn't have to be like this."

What was it supposed to be like, then? I assured her I was fine, and she kept looking at me from behind her giant glasses. I barely met her gaze, staring instead at the spots where her eyeliner had flaked away. It was navy, I realized. Not a neutral. This was what I focused on as her eyes searched for something I hoped I was skilled enough to not deliver.

But the desperation rose again as she stood to leave, the fear that she was going to see me differently now. And I had to keep something for myself. So as carefully as I could, I formed the apology: I was sorry for creating a scene, for worrying her, for causing her any trouble. It was truly just a misunderstanding. It would never happen again; this wasn't who I was and it wasn't who I was going to be.

"Birdie," she interrupted. "I know who you are."

Tell me, I did not say.

When the month ended, he came to get me, and I sat next to him in his ridiculous yellow Pantera, quietly searching for a sign for where he was taking me: a hotel, the airport, Debi's office. He too stayed silent until we pulled into the circular driveway of our—his?—home.

I waited. He cracked first. He said, "Dammit, Birdie." He said, "What was I supposed to do?" He said, "I didn't know if you were really trying to hurt yourself."

I said nothing.

He said, "I'm supposed to look after you." He said, "The label told me I had to do something after you went to the hospital." He said, "They know I'm your…"

I knew what he didn't want to say, so I made him say it.

Legal guardian was a phrase I hated because a legal guardian could set a curfew, make you clean your room, sign your permission slips, commit you to the sanatorium of the stars. A legal guardian had to deal with the shit he didn't sign up for, and I left the facility determined to forget this was his role, because if I could forget that, then it could still be a question of which one of us was in control. But I needed to know that he didn't like it either.

He said all this, and when I finally let myself look at him, his hands were gripping the steering wheel hard enough to make his veins pop, and his eyes were wet. He said, "You scared me." He said, "I love you, Little Bird." He said, "I want you to be mine."

Who else's could I be. I had nothing without him. And look: he cared enough to cry. He cared enough to wonder if I still wanted to be his. He loved me, and papers didn't matter. I was his little bird. I threw my arms around him and pressed my hot face into his neck.

Maybe this was not what a Lulu kind of a girl would have done, but the thing I had come to see, bright and unwavering, was that the difference between a Lulu and a girl like me was I still had something left to lose.

2

The performance with the broken glass wasn't in vain. Things did change. We lay on an island and drank fruity drinks and ate crab cocktail and slept under a canopy. We came back and I turned seventeen and then he did a few concert dates while I did Los Angeles Fashion Week, thank god; something to do since my upcoming Cameo shoot had been canceled, which was also okay because I wasn't ready to see Harriet again, not yet, not with a new coat of failure and bad choices. He and I congratulated each other on jobs well done and ate dinner at exclusive restaurants and bought a waterbed. I called for him when I saw a spider and he killed it. This was how it should be.

But it was always there. The volume was all that had gone down. One night, we were at a party, and I was talking with Yasmine, the one who'd been with Peter from one of the festival bands, who'd welcomed me by saying I was one of them, even though I knew now that was not true. I hadn't passed the test. I was never going to get invited to dinners at Ma Maison, but they'd be nice and pretend when we ran into each other.

And as Yasmine and I were catching up, or at least faking that we cared what the other had been up to and that she hadn't ignored at least three dinner invitations I'd asked the rock star to extend, we both saw Peter slip upstairs with someone who was not her. She heard the hitch of disappointment in my sigh and laughed. She knew, she said. She'd decided it was easier that way, as long as he came home to her. And the way she said it, looking right at me, her head slightly tilted, I knew she meant this was something I needed to learn.

There was more than one way to quantify *easier*.

And so I sought my own easier. Seen and not heard, always watching, taking it in.

We had the waterbed and I had the question of whether or not I wanted to take acting classes while I rode out the rest of the Cameo contract, whether or not I could ever catch up to Brooke Shields, who some days I wanted to be and some days considered my greatest nemesis. The closer I got to eighteen, the more I could feel the power of youthful beauty slipping from my reach. If that sounds like a thing no seventeen-year-old would ever think, bear in mind that one day Brooke Shields was not a name I knew and the next she was everywhere, three years younger than me and more successful by any measure.

The gap between me and the top models, the Janice Dickinsons and Lauren Huttons and Cheryl Tiegses, had always been there and never really felt closeable, not even when my *Yes, You!* cover was added to the wall of faces lining the path to Harriet's office, but maybe I should have been dreaming bigger.

I could think about whether the gap would have closed by now if I'd stayed in New York. If I hadn't chosen the Cameo deal because it had felt like the easiest thing, the one that would keep me closest to the rock star and Harriet. I could think about how I fell into this career without question and if it was something I wanted to continue to do for the rest of my life. I could think about being a model first and a rock star's girlfriend second.

I could think about all that. But no one was paying me to think.

THE COVER GIRL 171

The fact was: Los Angeles was a secondary market. New York was not. But when I went to New York, it was just Cameo, and that was my own fault.

My career was not the only one with growing pains. The days the rock star spent behind closed doors with a guitar grew more frequent. It was time for another album and beyond time for another full-scale tour. There should have been one before now. Other artists put out a record a year, sometimes more, stayed on the road for more extended stretches than even the tour I'd joined two years into its existence. There had been shows, but not enough to count as actually *touring*. There had been a greatest hits repackaging and a live release from the big tour, but those didn't count either, I'd learned from a conversation he'd had with the Doctor, who seemed to believe that since he seldom heard or saw me I did not exist in the home.

Apparently, the rock star had owed his label this record for quite a while. "You'd think I'd have made them enough money over the years to buy myself some time," he'd muttered.

"You did, a year ago. You can either tour or you can record. You haven't been doing either," the Doctor said. "You have to get off your ass."

The idea of him sitting around on his ass was almost funny to me—he was always in motion. I was not sure we'd ever spent a day at this house doing nothing; there was always a dinner out or a party or visitors or work. But the way the Doctor said it, I heard that if I wasn't in the picture, he would have fewer distractions. Fewer responsibilities.

Does it sound paranoid? Consider then: shortly after this conversation, Beasley came over, exhausted by the sound and the reality of a baby that never stopped crying. *But how is Lulu?* no one asked—the rock star, because it probably wouldn't have occurred to him that she could be anything other than happy; and me, because I was being small and mean, both jealous of her settled status and relieved that her life was not mine. I sat in one room reading *Glamour*, and he and Beasley sat in the other, once again assuming that if I was not visible, I must not be able to hear them.

Was I listening?

How could I not?

From what I could gather, he'd shared some songwriting attempts with Beasley. Some words, some chords.

"These are dog shit," Beasley said.

"Oh, come on."

"They're dog shit, and what's worse is you know they're dog shit and you're hoping I'll tell you you're wrong."

A moment of quiet. We all knew it was a moment of desperation for him to show Beasley the songs to begin with—when had he ever needed someone else's opinion?

"The songs just aren't coming."

I held my breath, turning a page without looking at the spread.

"You used to write about what you wanted. Who you wanted. What do you want now?"

If Beasley got an answer, I didn't hear it.

But soon it felt like every day was a workday. I'd leave for a 6:00 a.m. aerobics class and come home to find him gone without a plan to return until after midnight. On other days, he'd be out the door before I had the chance to blink my eyes open.

Did I wonder if all this time was spent at the studio?

Of course, and so I asked if I could come too. I wanted to see him at work, I said. I loved seeing him at work. His creative process. I couldn't even say if these were lies or not, but I was embarrassed by how fawning I sounded all the same. More fan than girlfriend. I kept my eyes big and blinking and my arms looped around his neck, the picture of girlish innocence, and he couldn't say no.

See. I could still undo him.

I spent too long getting ready to go to the studio, finding the minidress from our very first lunch, to surprise him, to spark

THE COVER GIRL

173

a memory, to reignite a spark—whatever it was, I wanted that dress to do something, and I didn't want to think hard about why I wanted it. I was halfway out the door when the phone rang.

"Darling," Harriet said. "I'm afraid I have some bad news. Cameo is shutting down."

I did not hear it as bad news. I heard it as relief.

"Unfortunately, that means they aren't going to pay the last third of your deal."

I still could not touch my trust, still had no idea what the vouchers and bank statements I got actually meant. The lost money would matter for Harriet, but it was not real life to me. I apologized anyway because this whole thing was, after all, my fault. But right next to the guilt over how poorly I'd chosen, going with a company that had launched and folded so quickly, was the excitement to go back to work. After only a few shoots spread out over more than a year, I could be useful again. I could find something outside the mirror, perhaps reflect back a girl I could trust more. Who made better choices.

"Now, I know you've been disappointed in how they used you," Harriet said. I had never said those words, never wanted to implicate myself out loud in my own bad decision, but there was no point in denying the truth. "We anticipated more work than there was, which means compared to girls who have been modeling as long as you, you're behind. Set a meeting with Debi. Call her every morning to confirm your schedule. We must get you back out there."

As I agreed, the real meaning started to sink in. I was free from Cameo, free from the lie, but what was there to tether me to Harriet? Was I still one of her girls?

This was all I could think about as the driver took me to the studio. This was not the mood in which to be around people, or even one person, but I continued on anyway. When I went to enter the studio, I was stopped by a harried-looking older man. "No, no, no," he said. "No little groupie girls here."

I narrowed my eyes, told him I was meeting someone.

"Yeah? Whose kid are you?" he asked.

That stung worse than *little groupie girl*, and I mustered up my most withering glare as I informed him I was no one's kid, I was with the rock star.

"Bullshit."

He might as well have told me to prove it. I invited him to go ask my driver, but instead he shoved open the studio door, calling out for the rock star. "Does this kid belong to you?"

If only it had just been him in there. Or even just the Doctor, who was used to looking past me, even after—no, that was nothing. Back to the present, back to the room full of people, and an audience for which I would have to perform the role of rock star's girlfriend after this humiliation. All I had wanted was him and me and the music, and what I got was a look on the rock star's face somewhere between horror and a question.

It took him too long to say yes, I was with him.

To prove a point to the man holding the door open, I wrapped my arms around the rock star and flicked my tongue past his lips, but he gently pulled away. I did not move. I could not make myself turn around and look at the man who'd insisted I could not belong in this room.

Bearing witness to all of this was Gary from the band that I could never remember, who was adding some additional guitar to the track, and he'd brought Linda with him. Linda was another reminder of where I didn't fit, and all I could think about when I saw Gary was the dinner we'd had with them and Beasley and Lulu and his comment about how he'd never seen the rock star with a girl for as long as he'd been with me. I was used to people talking about me like I wasn't there, and Gary became the place to direct any feelings I might feel about that. When he looked at me, I could only assume he was thinking about all the ones who came before.

Today, I hated Gary.

THE COVER GIRL

175

With producers and other record label people and the Doctor and Gary and Linda pretending they hadn't just seen what they saw, the room already felt too full, like there was barely space for me in it.

And then, since Beasley was recording too, in walked Lulu, cradling the chubby red-haired girl they'd named Pamela. And because this is always the way these things go, I ended up crushed in a corner with the two of them and Linda. Somehow the baby was thrust into my arms and I held her awkwardly, neither of us happy about it. We stared at each other as I listened to Lulu and Linda talk about lunch with Yasmine and Holly, the Palm Springs house they'd all visited sometime not very long ago, a planned shopping excursion, Holly's baby shower.

What would happen if I asked if they remembered Yasmine welcoming me into a *sisterhood* of rock wives and girlfriends, if I reminded them they were having this conversation right in front of me? Or did they, like the men in their lives, only think of me as an image and not a thinking, feeling person? I wondered what I had done to not be invited in.

"Oh, honey," Linda said, looking at me holding Pamela away from my body. "You're going to have to learn how to hold a baby. It'll be your turn before long."

The thought nearly made me flinch. And perhaps it was not the kindest thing, but without breaking eye contact with the staring baby, I shook my head and announced that I had a diaphragm.

They laughed like you do when a child says something unintentionally funny, and I handed Pamela back to Lulu.

"I probably could have used one of those myself." Lulu wandered over to the recording console and pushed the button that would let her be heard on the other side of the glass. "Hey!" she said, holding up the baby. "You ready to have another one?"

Beasley burst out of the booth. "What are you talking about?"

"You knocked me up again." She giggled. It didn't seem all

176 Amy Rossi

that funny to me, but I supposed this was the only reaction to having two literal babies at the same time.

And then Beasley dropped to his knee. "Well, I better make honest women of you both."

Just like fucking that.

And everyone in the tiny room cheered and clapped like this was romantic, like these were people in love, like this was a relationship that was not going to be called off at least three more times before that second baby made its appearance.

Jealousy burned deep inside me, though what it was over I could not name. But I could guess. And it wasn't the baby or the engagement or even the fact that I was not included in the friendship circle of women who lived alongside this music life. No, it landed closer to being both seen and heard, loud and listened to.

Recording was over for the day.

Later that night, as we drove home from celebratory drinks and dinner, I asked the rock star what he thought about Lulu and Beasley.

"Jesus Christ, can you imagine what that's going to be like? Better them than us, right?" he said. "They don't live in the real world."

The real world. A concept so vast, it became much easier to focus on. I asked if he thought we lived there, in the real world.

"Of course," he said. He revved the engine of his tiny sports car, winding us toward Malibu, then gestured at the twinkling lights and flicker of ocean ahead. "What could be more real than this?"

I listened closely to reality. I listened closely to his albums. When I called my parents, they said things like *hello* and *where are you?* and *how's the weather?* but not *how are you?* or *what are you?*

I worked more because I needed to recover from Cameo, because *see, I'm not defined by one bad choice,* because I never tired

THE COVER GIRL 177

of how I could feel so blurry and look so sharp on paper, and a little because *watch out, Brooke Shields.*

And then I landed a job for a bridal magazine—back on the page at last, back in editorial, closer to the next better thing. Harriet and Debi were planning to send me to Paris soon and this would help me make the most of that trip when it happened. I didn't know which pictures had got me the job: the ones of me trying to turn my face away in tabloids, next to him at restaurants and events, or the Cameo ones. But I had a feeling.

It was quickly replaced by another.

I'd wanted to be taken seriously. I'd wanted security. But I hadn't thought about marriage as a real solution rather than a someday thing until Lulu and Beasley's wedding. She walked down the aisle—a dirt path—in white hot pants and a lacy white robe, untied to show off how pregnant she was. Beasley held Pamela as they exchanged their vows on a beach cliff. Lulu looked beautiful and ridiculous, the only way to pull off this sort of thing. How she felt about it all, I didn't know. We barely spoke because what did we have in common now? She was supposed to be wild Lulu, the road girlfriend, the one who pulled me into bathrooms to do a line, like anything we did had to be secret. Who said I was a great friend. Lulu who insisted what I had wasn't what she wanted but decided to get it anyway, had me deliver it to her on a platter. She had leapfrogged right over my life into an air I hadn't yet breathed.

But standing on the bridal magazine set with the top of my hair pulled back with a flower, the ruffle of my baby pink dress fluttering every time I moved, gently placed just to the background of the real star, the bride, it came to me bright and clear: I could get there.

The weeks tumbled on and as we got closer to my eighteenth birthday, I thought about how we'd been living like a married couple since the beginning, and the only thing holding us back was my age. The final barrier in the state of California.

But all that happened when I turned eighteen was he gave me a heavy gold cuff bracelet and also a Ferrari. There was no mention of anything else, and my breath lived shallow in the back of my throat while I waited, wondering. I was dizzy with anxiety, glass-eyed. He thought the flush was new makeup and said I looked beautiful: nerves as cosmetic.

I waited for a day he'd be in the studio, and then I drove the Ferrari to a bookstore to buy a cookbook, moving too slowly for everyone around me, and then to a grocery store for ingredients. I was halfway home before I realized I had no idea if there was cookware in the kitchen, a frying pan to get out of the fire. We'd still only furnished what you could see in that house. Nothing under the surface.

The cookbook came with a letter of encouragement in the front, telling me I was at the forefront of modern cooking for having made this purchase and the recipes that followed were full of touches that would make mealtime a pleasure for my family.

I put one of his records on the turntable and listened to him sing about the woman he wanted and the woman who had broken his heart as I browned the chicken on all sides.

Oh, baby, I want to see what you got. These were the words that had come easily for him.

The book suggested that the browning would be complete after three to four minutes per side, but it took me nearly thirty minutes to achieve a uniform brownness on all surfaces of the chicken. I was not concerned. No need to hurry. I was making mealtime a pleasure.

Honey, you look too good to be true. What he wanted, who he wanted.

I dumped a can of frozen orange juice concentrate on the browned chicken and stuck the pan in the oven. Then I moved on to the rice and the green beans mixed with mandarins.

You're so fine and I'd do anything to make you mine, all mine. Was a rhyme like this so out of reach for his life right now?

THE COVER GIRL

The table he came home to: chicken in orange glop, fast hardening into a shell, surrounded by pineapple that had ceased to be fruit after perhaps the sixth minute of broiling. A mound of slightly charred rice covering the parts that were still hard and grainy. Green beans and mandarin oranges that looked edible enough but were both too sweet and too salty. Me, staring at all of it, lower lip pulled in tight to keep my chin from wobbling. He didn't say anything until after he sat down and tried to cut the chicken. He tapped his knife on the candied orange helmet and looked up at me. I had never seen him like that: a man trying to read a foreign language and desperate for translation. And so I wept in earnest and he asked what all this was about and this time I told him the truth: I wanted to be a good wife.

He lifted me from my chair and carried me upstairs to bed like we were in a black-and-white movie. And I closed my eyes and focused on the rhythm of my body because all that the rhythm of my mind could tap out was *this is not an answer, this is not an answer, this is not an answer.*

3

I called Debi in the morning to confirm my schedule, as was my routine now, but it was Harriet's voice that answered. Had I called New York by mistake, by habit?

"Not at all, darling, I'm in town. I had some business—some meetings, vouchers to handle, that kind of thing. Come on down, and I'll take you to lunch."

There was a time when this was both my wildest dream and also something that would have me convinced the end was here—I was being fired. Neither feeling settled over me now, but there were nerves all the same. I had only seen Harriet a few times, light and in passing, in the year since she'd visited me after the glass incident. This was by my own design. Possibly hers too. I hadn't been to New York recently; instead, I asked Debi's assistant to help me send my vouchers with the office's new fax machine.

As much as I tried to pack it all away, to let it just be the glass incident, I still couldn't unsee the look she'd given me when she told me it didn't have to be like this. I was afraid of seeing it again, of what would be reflected back, of what she had really meant.

THE COVER GIRL

But I couldn't avoid her forever and the lunch invitation was less a question and more a statement, so I agreed to meet at La Scala, arriving almost late, which is to say on time, because I could not decide what to wear, how I wanted to be seen. Would something with crisp lines suggest I was put together, or would something flowy show how easy-breezy I was? Could a purple shirtdress really say *I am wonderful and fine and you do not need to worry about me*? Unlikely, and yet.

We each got the salad, of course we did, *as is* for me and *there is no need to chop it so finely, please, I am perfectly capable of chewing and do not fear texture* for Harriet. For a moment, I forgot that I should not relax into this lunch. For a moment, nothing had changed.

Other times we'd done this, once the food arrived, Harriet would reveal her purpose. This time, however, once the bowls were set down—mine a delicate mince, hers a rough chop—all we did was eat. I tried to come up with something interesting to say, but what? Was I supposed to tell her that I'd found out I was a terrible cook? How is your trip going and also it turns out I cannot even make rice? Could Harriet?

"You're awfully quiet," she said. "Is everything alright with you?"

With the weight of the glass incident newly heavy in her presence, did I want to answer this question? I smiled and told her I was waiting to hear the reason for this visit.

"I didn't realize we needed a reason, darling," Harriet said. "We haven't had this opportunity in a long time, longer than I'd like. You know you don't have to have a reason to come to New York or to call me. You're one of my girls." I nodded. I knew she said that, at least. People said a lot of things. "I know I'm a little late, but I wanted to treat you for your birthday." She reached into her purse and pulled out a tiny box.

The rock star had been the only one to acknowledge it. It didn't even matter to me what was in the box; that she'd remembered was a gift. Of course, what was in the box was exquisite: a small pearl hair comb. Tasteful, elegant—pure Harriet. Perfect for the girl who I wanted her to see me as.

In another world, we'd hug. In another world, I'd apologize for keeping my distance and she'd tell me she understood, that she was giving me space. In this world, though, I tucked the comb in my hair and that was enough.

Debi, after consulting with Harriet before she returned to New York, sent me on a go-see for Swish, a hair removal competitor to Nair and Neet.

All I would have to be was legs.

In my booking spree, I had already been turned down for Nair and their ads featuring four girls, each who fit a type, kick-lining down sets of stairs, mouthing the words to a song about short shorts. I could wear the short shorts and I could do the high kicks and I could even mouth the words in time, but I was too tall to kick alongside other girls.

Even professionally, I did not fit into the group.

But on my own, with the creative team and the photographer, I made myself fit. I watched them flip through my book, take in the album cover, the Cameo ad with the dangerously high platforms—all the things I could do with my body whether it was supposed to be the point or not. I waited until they asked me to walk, and then I did my magic. It was the prance-stomp I'd developed with Nadine before Azrian's show. It was a wrap dress wrapped just so, so that every step brought this group of people closer to understanding what these legs could *do*. It was my moment.

I got the job.

He said he was proud of me, but also: perhaps not. There was no announcement, no champagne. The Cameo months meant that I was, for the most part, at home. Slowly, his schedule had become the one we lived by. And even with the rash of book-

THE COVER GIRL

183

ings Debi got me, most were local. The Swish job upended that by sending me to the Virgin Islands right away.

He came home while I was getting my things together. "What is this?" he asked, gesturing at the array of dresses and slips bobbing on the waterbed. When I told him I had a location shoot, he frowned, a crease I hadn't noticed appearing between his eyebrows. "Isn't this last minute? Shouldn't they have given you more warning? I was expecting you to be here."

The album had been delayed yet again, after the label suggested there wasn't an obvious single. He was in the studio most of the day, trying to pull obvious from nothing, and he was moody when he was home. I tried to stay quiet and out of his way, tried to let him work out his artistic genius without any interruptions, but his conversations with the Doctor and Beasley still rattled around my head.

Maybe I needed to get out. Maybe if he missed me, he could write a good song.

But now, as he seemed to fear the idea of me leaving, I asked if he needed me for anything.

"I always need you, Little Bird," he said.

And even though I should have finished getting ready, I asked him to show me how much in the bed full of clothes because I needed to be needed.

But I needed to be needed in the Virgin Islands too, and oh—it was star treatment. It was not that I hadn't received star treatment before; I was simply never the intended star. I was just included. This was, *Can we help you, Miss Rhodes? Please let us know if this view is not to your liking, Miss Rhodes.* For one full week, this would be my life.

Of course I missed him. But I felt more myself than I had in months, maybe even years. Since before the glass incident. Since before Cameo. The bridal magazine was thrilling but perhaps a fluke. Everything else was regular catalog work or small gigs

184   Amy Rossi

to make up for lost time and remind the world I existed. For this job, I was going to exist so deeply, at the jaw-dropping rate of $125 an hour. I would do whatever they asked, and I would make it look easy.

The Swish representatives were thrilled to see me and happy with their choice in casting. The weather was appropriate—no wearing fur coats in the beating sun or bathing suits in the winter. The only question was the photographer.

His name was Benj Boudreaux. He'd been silent on the go-see. I'd seen him at a party recently, the kind of launch event Debi got me lightly paid to attend, and he'd been described to me by another girl as a bit of a tortured-artist type, silent and unsmiling, always with one model or another on his arm. He was known for moody shadows, the kind of art photography you'd find in *Vogue* or *Vanity Fair*, not in commercial work. My impression at the time had been: perhaps he should have just stuck with Benjamin.

I was prepared for this to be the less easy part. There was a chance that I'd strike my first pose and he'd say I wasn't right for the job. Or he'd have an artistic vision I hadn't done enough editorial work to bring to life. There had to be some catch.

But on the beach, in between the setup and moving to different locations and waiting for a single cloud to pass, what he offered was gentle encouragement: *Beautiful, Birdie,* and *That's perfect, Birdie,* and *Can we see the exact same thing in the red bikini, just like what you did before, that was amazing.*

All I had to be was legs.

For the first time, I was reluctant to let myself go, to just let my body take over, because I was waiting for the other shoe to drop, convinced that the minute I let my guard down the whole thing would fall to pieces. This job could not be that easy. And still, I was there and Benj kept telling me I was doing great. The opposite of how I had always worked. It raised the question: If I could do good work without giving it all over to my body, what else could I be capable of? Would I enjoy other jobs if I couldn't create the separation?

On the third day, Benj decided it was time to play with the light. Let's go into the night. The Swish people agreed—hairless legs are for viewing in the daytime and touching after sundown, are they not?

"If Swish doesn't make you think of legs on sheets..." one of them said.

They put me in a long white wrap dress—not unlike the one from my go-see, except this one touched the floor and shimmered with glamour—and asked me to descend the stairs outside the resort while Benj's assistants tracked me with lights. When I reached the bottom, I let each hand find the railing and leaned back, revealing a full leg. And then I turned, leaned against one side of the handrail while propping a foot up on the other, my hair gathered in my hands as I looked at the camera.

"Stunning," he said. "Absolutely perfect. Can you touch your leg for me now?" Of course I could. "Lovely, now with movement." The kind of direction that made me laugh because really, what did it mean, but okay. Whatever I did wasn't what he had in mind, because he came over to me, camera still in hand. "May I?" I didn't know what I was agreeing to when I nodded, and I was sure he could hear me gasp as he took my hand and demonstrated, trailing my fingertips from my ankle to my knee. "And to the hip, if you could."

He could have used his own hand; the request for permission set off something inside me. I let my fingers glide up and down my leg as instructed, crackling with some kind of energy I could not place.

We then moved to the top of the hotel, to a balcony. I struck any pose I could think of, anything that would show off my legs, and then the Swish people thought of another one.

"Can she sit on the railing?"

I glanced down at the shimmering pool below, the distance,

186 Amy Rossi

and a wave of nausea hit me. *She* did not love the idea of sitting on the thin strip of iron but she would do it anyway. That was who she was.

I gingerly lifted myself onto the railing, and someone asked me to put my leg up too. I could see the picture in my eye as I braced myself against the side with one leg and placed my foot on top with the other. It would be worth it. And then I wobbled. A small scream as I shifted my weight, tipped forward back to stable ground.

"Are you alright?" Benj asked. I nodded, catching my breath. "Do you want to keep going?"

As one of Harriet's Girls, my job was to say yes. Whatever you need. But I flashed back to the *may I* on the stairs and against all my training, I wanted to try something. So I told him no. I did not want to continue in this pose.

"Okay, let's stop here." He turned and, louder for everyone, announced we were done for the evening. "Thanks for all your work today," he said, looking not through but at me.

I don't know what he saw, but it was like something had been unstuck. What it was, I couldn't name. As I walked back to my hotel room, I felt light in a way that was entirely new.

The next morning, though, I woke up wondering who in the world that girl was. I knew better than to say no. That's not what I was being paid for. I was filled with dread during hair and makeup, where they gave me classic Hollywood Marcel waves, where they dusted me bronze while I stood in a tiny strapless nude bikini—not what I would wear, but so the real thing would be clean. "What are we putting her in today?" the stylist asked.

"Let's ask Benj."

I held my breath as he entered the room, steeling myself for the other shoe. It was time.

"Which one do you want her in?" The stylist held up two bikinis, one black and one gold.

Benj turned to me. "Which do you think?"

THE COVER GIRL

A question or a test? I shrugged. Whatever he wanted. I had done enough already.

"No, no. Which would you feel the most powerful in? That's what this shoot is about. Feeling powerful."

I looked at him. He did not look angry, nor did he carry the smug smile of ownership, the one that suggested he wanted to put me in my place. He looked like he wanted to know what I thought, and I surprised myself with how quickly I chose gold. With the fact that I trusted myself to have an answer at all.

"Great. Gold it is," Benj said.

I played around the pool for two hours: sitting at the edge with my legs crossed, floating in an inflatable ring with my legs stuck straight in the air, walking in and out of the water while striking poses that I hoped delivered the power I was supposed to feel.

And then one of the Swish people—an ad executive named Macy, the only other woman on the shoot—came up to me. "Birdie," she said. "We just had an idea. *Don't stop at shorts. Dare to be bare.*"

I nodded, told her that sounded nice. Catchy. I liked the idea of being better, more daring than Nair and its cute little song and cute not-tall girls.

"Are you comfortable with that? What it would require?"

She was so vague it took several seconds of pointed staring for me to realize she was asking if I would get naked.

I had done bathing suits. Underwear in a catalog, no head attached. New Orleans came to mind and as quickly as it did, I pushed it away. That wasn't me. I'd never gotten nude, and my first thought was that I should call the rock star. But it wasn't his body, it was mine. This was about whatever made me feel powerful, right? I glanced at Benj, who was chewing on the end of his thumb. He hesitated for a moment, then walked over.

"I want you to be comfortable," he said. "We can close the set and just have Macy here. But also, you don't have to. Really. We can use what we've got or figure out something with the makeup bikini."

If not the rock star, then I probably should have called Harriet. Instead, I said yes. I wasn't really thinking, I was feeling, and what I was feeling was the power Benj had said was so important. Who knows what would have happened if I'd said no, if it would have been taken as easily as they suggested it would. My no was trusted last night. I believed in my yes.

Benj sent away his assistants, the Swish people, everyone but Macy as promised. The golden hour sunlight glinted off the pool, closed to guests for the shoot. It was far enough from the resort that if anyone could see anything, it was a shape and not me.

"I'm not going to give you direction," he said. "Just do what feels right for you."

I sat on the ground, holding a towel just to my front. I moved so my knees were covering my chest. I laid stomach-down on a towel warmed by the pavement, kicking my feet up toward my head. Benj offered quiet encouragement; Macy was more vocal. "Love it! You're so good!"

It felt fine but not *right*. I thought about the night before—the stairs, my leg up, back arched. And I stood up, keeping the foot closest to the pool flat on the ground while stepping my other leg forward, bent knee, pointed toe. I gathered my hair in my hands, angling my camera-side arm in front of my breasts. The sun hit me as the shutter clicked, and it felt more than right—I felt free. Free from Cameo, free from the pressure to be good and silent, free from myself and all the times I'd decided wrong. I tipped my face to the camera and smiled, then laughed. Yes. Yes. Yes. And for a moment, I understood what *powerful* meant.

4

Almost four years earlier, I'd stood in front of a tour bus not knowing what lay in front of me.

This time, I knew.

This time, Eddie had a girl with him who I knew would be gone by the time we hit Baltimore, and I found myself soothed by the fact that she appeared to have a solid year on me. But I couldn't really know unless I asked, and I was not going to ask.

This time, Ham had been replaced and no one bothered telling me the new guy's name. Ham was happy to record the album but was no longer interested in being on tour for months at a time, and he had made that clear from the moment he hit the studio.

This time, Beasley had also been replaced, but at the last minute.

He'd shown up at our door in the middle of the night, a child on each hip. I stood at the top of the stairs, just out of sight. "She left," he'd said.

I watched as the rock star looked around, like I might conveniently appear from around a corner to take the babies off

Beasley's hands and do my womanly duty while the men discussed the matter.

The truth: a part of me wanted to. A part of me wanted him to see me in this role, one a wife would play; a part of me wanted to hug the children and whisper something soft and soothing.

But the rock star had enough friends with children by then that I'd seen the fading away that signaled the subtle shift from a woman being viewed as sexy to being viewed as a mother, Lulu excepted. Women I used to see on arms at all the parties would be pregnant and then gone. Fully out of sight and out of mind; this world was no longer for them. I wanted to be front and center in my nude print ad, not off to the side being a caretaker. And for all the worry I had for these children, I was also relieved. Lulu never stopped being Lulu, no matter how she tried to tame herself, and there was something soothing in that. While I didn't necessarily agree with her choice, they were Beasley's children too.

So this time, there was no tour for Beasley, because he couldn't find help fast enough and because he didn't want his kids to think he wasn't coming back either. He didn't say it like this, just said he *shouldn't*, but that word carried weight.

This time, the Doctor didn't scare me more than any other man who thrived on making people, and especially girls, fear him. He looked old and a little pathetic. I didn't know why he couldn't just call himself their manager, why he had to make it bigger, but some men are like that, I had realized.

This time, no one worried that I was too young to be there. I had just voted in my first presidential election, after all, and put enough time into it to share the rock star's disappointment when Carter lost.

This time, I had lunch with Harriet before we left, and we didn't talk about the nature of the leaving, the traveling, not at first. We didn't talk about her visit to Los Angeles or her gift, which I'd tucked into my hair and she noted with a small smile.

THE COVER GIRL

Instead, we looked through an issue of *Cosmo* to see the Swish ad in print.

It was the final shot. The one with me looking at the camera, daring to be bare. Daring Jane Customer to join me. The rock star hated it—his exact words were *That's not you*—and I could only assume Harriet would think the same thing, for the same reason, if not the same version of me she wasn't seeing.

"You didn't tell me," she said. An accusation? A question?

I admitted that I was afraid she'd be angry with me.

"Was it your choice?" A nod. "The photographer wasn't inappropriate?" Unsurprisingly, she refused to make her mouth say *Benj*.

I apologized, of course I did. Like I was a child again. I hadn't meant to make any trouble, I explained. It'd felt okay to try it, and so I had.

Harriet waved a hand, still gazing at the ad. "You look radiant," she said, finally looking up at me. "Happy. Happier than I've seen you in a long time."

She left a pause for me to fill in, to elaborate the state of my happiness or lack thereof, but instead I handed her the typed list of where I would be and when.

This time, we agreed Harriet would say I was booked out for several weeks at a time, rather than try to fly to and from the road. The illusion of scarcity.

"You're going to miss opportunities," she said quietly. "This isn't like when you were a girl and we could pick and choose. This industry moves fast. You started young, but the other girls have caught up."

This could be about modeling. This could be about everything. The girls were catching up and my specialness was fading.

"You're just now gaining momentum again."

So much unsaid in that *again*. My specialness had been locked into a contract that failed to live up to expectation, and I was still paying for my mistake. I could tell Harriet thought this was another one.

I wanted to be everywhere at once—on set, on the runway, on the arm of the man I loved. On my first tour, an entire four months had unfurled before me, vast and unknown, scary and exciting. Winter on the bus was completely different, just gray and endless. There was no magic this time, but I couldn't make myself go home because what would happen if I wasn't on tour, if I wasn't there with him? I knew I was making a choice, and I wanted to believe it was the right one for me, for at least a part of me.

I had no newness to rely on anywhere anymore. And while, yes, other women had been a problem, they were just that— women. Younger than him, of course, but older than me, so I still held my power. But this time, I saw his eyes linger on a few girls backstage, and even though I wasn't even nineteen myself, I worried they had something I did not.

The first time we got on that tour bus together, he was at the height of his career. Even when critics didn't fully get what he was doing, they knew he was good at it.

This time, there were negative reviews. The album that had been so hard to write did not coalesce into a sum greater than its parts in the eleventh hour; even I could tell there was something tired about it. The songs were weaker versions of the ones that had come before, rehearsed swagger instead of natural verve. This time, he was out on the road with something to prove.

This time, the rider included the beer he liked, a can of mixed nuts, three sharpened pencils, two peeled and segmented oranges, a bowl with two steaming washcloths, and a chilled bottle of Perrier for me. When he asked what I wanted, if it was lavender bubble bath again, I'd said Perrier with a confidence I didn't know I was capable of. I *knew* I could drink a Perrier in every town in every state in America. I liked Perrier. A simple request, no waste. How I had grown.

THE COVER GIRL

193

We crisscrossed the country, our nights in the bus punctuated by the occasional hotel stay. And for all the ways I could identify how it was different this time, there was another that I could not name.

One of the first things that came to mind thinking about the first tour was noise. The whir of the highway, the squeak of the bus's suspension. The roar of the crowd, the blazing guitar, pounding drums. The Doctor droning on with constant updates, the radio, the stories the rock star would tell me about previous stops and his first shows and about what our life would be like when we got home.

And it wasn't that the noise stopped, but this time the whole thing seemed quieter. There were no stories about other tours or questions about what I liked, what would make me happy. Fewer whispers in the dark. His appetite for me had not changed, but it felt more like checking a task off a list than succumbing to a craving. I worried it was my admission that I wanted to be a wife. I worried he'd realized I was boring. I worried that I needed too much. I worried that he was less attracted to me because I'd posed nude and everyone could see what had once been reserved for him. I worried that, no matter what it was, I was to blame.

There had been a part of me, and not a small one, that hoped he would propose to me on this tour. A perfect circle. This was where we fell in love. This could be where we made it real. And every time we were able to stop for a nice dinner or look out on a hotel balcony, there would be a little catch in my throat, a little flip in my stomach. This was it.

But it was never it.

I hated myself for being desperate. I hated myself for having listened to the women around me talk for four years about how you couldn't tame men like ours, only to think I was somehow different. Like he said I was.

What I mean is: I was not the docile girl who'd gone on the

road four years earlier. I was moody, prone to crying, prone to pressing myself to the edge of the bed so he would have to pull me to him. So he would have to come and get me. And choose me, again and again.

It was a two-day stint at Cobo Arena in Detroit, which meant a hotel suite and stretching my legs outside of that bus. I was reading the latest *Vogue* with Kim Alexis on the cover and drinking my Perrier while the rock star took a shower. When there was a knock at the door, I sighed. He wasn't available and whoever it was would not be interested in talking to me.

The Doctor stood in the doorway. Barely meeting his eye, I gestured at the bathroom and said the rock star would be out soon.

"I'm not here for him. I'm here for you."

I stared at him. There was no good reason for him to need me. There was no good reason, ever, for me to be with him without the rock star.

"I just received a phone call from someone named Harriet." He paused, as though this was not my life but just some drama he was building. "It seems your mother called her trying to get ahold of you."

Every word he uttered was somehow worse than the one before it. I stood cold, waiting for him to continue and unsure if I wanted him to.

"Your father had a heart attack, and your mother wanted you to know." When I asked if my father was still alive, the Doctor said, "She didn't say he wasn't."

He stood in the doorway, and I thought for a moment he wanted to comfort me, but then I realized he was expecting me to thank him. I did, anything to end this, trying to sound more grateful than I felt, before closing the door.

I didn't know what to do. I lay on the bed, staring at the ceiling, waiting to feel something. Was I supposed to be upset about

THE COVER GIRL

the condition of a man I hadn't spoken to in nearly a year? They hadn't even called me on my most recent birthday, or if they had, we weren't home and they gave up quickly. The words coming from the Doctor's mouth were only a reminder of how wrong they sounded—mother, father, *your*. None of them were true, not anymore, even as I still used them. What did it mean that my mother wanted me to know?

The rock star came out of the bathroom, towel wrapped low around his hips, to find me spread out on the bed, staring. "What's happening, baby?"

When I told him, it sounded like I was telling a story about someone else. Even the rock star's reaction looked bigger than my own; as soon as the words *father* and *heart attack* came out of my mouth, he was down on the bed beside me, arms wrapped around me.

I wished I could be sad enough for him to comfort me, to fuss over me and hold me like I might break. But I couldn't muster it even for that. And so I had to tell him the truth: that I didn't feel anything.

"You just found out. It hasn't sunk in. Do you need to go out there?"

The speed at which I said no surprised us both. I did not want to go out there. I did not want to see my father in a hospital bed and my mother fretting by his side, dressed up and hair set because you never know who you might see, even if it was a hospital, even if it was life and death. I did not want to act like a dutiful daughter simply because it was a bad time, when I would not be invited to do so in a good time.

I didn't know how to say all this to the rock star, so to file down my quick refusal, I admitted that I felt bad for not feeling more. They were, after all, my family.

"Oh, Little Bird," he said. "They are, but I'm your family too. We're our own family."

This was, it turned out, what I needed to hear. I curled my

body into his and let him hold me until he had to leave for sound check.

I almost didn't answer the phone when it rang while I was getting ready, though I had no reason to believe my mother would be tenacious enough to figure out how to call me on her own.

"Darling," was the greeting at the other end of the line, and I let myself sink into the relief of Harriet's voice. "Did that man talk to you?"

I told her he did, holding the phone in one hand and brushing on rouge with the other.

"I didn't trust him to give you the message. Is he as unpleasant in person as he sounds?" I laughed. I didn't need to agree out loud. She'd know. "With a bedside manner like that," she continued, "I can only assume his silly nickname is ironic. Did he tell you the heart attack was mild? Your father is expected to recover fully. It's still quite scary, though—are you alright?"

I looked in the mirror, my hair swirling at my shoulders in loose hot-roller curls, pinned back on either side. My tight jeans and the halter top it wasn't warm enough for. I had Harriet and I had the rock star and I had my own little family. Yes. I was okay.

That night, I watched the show from the wings, which I hadn't done in some time. In truth, there were nights where I got bored, where I mouthed the stage banter along with him and rolled my eyes at the cheering fans who didn't question whether he was saying these same things night after night, content to believe they alone inspired him to bigger heights.

But that night, I put in my earplugs and watched him as I had before: like it was the first time. I let myself get lost in the way his fingers moved across the guitar strings, what it made me feel, the way he could bend a single note and create a noise that I felt in the pit of my stomach. He held power in his hands; he made something from nothing. The words, the lyrics, they were just a means to an end, just a part of creation. What it was really about was the sound.

THE COVER GIRL   197

★ ★ ★

This time, the festival was in Florida, but they didn't call it a festival. It was just an all-day concert in as warm a place as we could get this time of year, and we weren't headlining. This time, the death of a music icon wasn't hanging over us, at least not in the same way. The news about John Lennon had been more shocking than even Elvis, and I can't have been the only one wondering if these tours were a curse. But there had been time to grieve.

This time, when I ran into Linda and Yasmine, there was no Holly because she was a mother now, no talk of sisterhood, no taking me aside to teach me the ways of the road. I already knew the ways. There were fake air kisses and *we have to catch up when we're back in LA* and who knows what was going to be said when I turned my back. Instead of Lulu, there was a girl named April who had stepped into the road-girlfriend role, and it wasn't worth asking how she fit in so easily when I was still outside the bubble after all this time.

And this time, when we were leaving the not-festival, the rock star took my hand on the bus and reminded me that this tour wasn't like the last—there was a stint in Europe between the US legs. I had known about Europe, and I had not let myself wonder where I would fit in. I still hadn't been; Harriet refused to send her girls to Milan—too much sex, too much power playing, too much risk—and Paris was up in the air. It felt like it could be a two-birds-one-stone situation, or something else that invoked a little less violence, a little less of my name.

The rock star squeezed my hand in his. "There isn't enough money for anyone but the band to go. I just found out."

I nodded. Of course. The hotels were growing more infrequent and the penthouses were even fewer. The crowds were not as big as they had been the last time.

"Are you angry?" he pressed, threading the other hand through my hair. "You know I wouldn't choose this."

I didn't question whether or not I did know that. Instead, I sunned myself in his attention. I would not be angry. I would be fine. Good, even. Happy. His girl.

5

I spent as much time away from the glass house as possible.

I was a bridesmaid again for the bridal magazine, which seemed a little too much like real life. I was the legs in a pantyhose ad. I was a body in a swimsuit. I was whatever I was booked for, which was a lot after I called Harriet and said I was available again. No, what I said was that I had *decided* it was better for me to stay here instead of going to Europe. I wanted her to applaud my good choices and not read anything into the rock star not taking me.

The house had so many windows, too many windows. It was supposed to be walls that close in. I thought about driving to a hotel just to get some walls, just to get out of the fishbowl. The new spring fashions arrived, and I turned nineteen alone. I had to kill my own bugs. I left the dead ones as a warning to their fellow creatures: this could be your fate.

The record label, it appeared, was a group of useless motherfuckers. I had three different itineraries for the European leg of the tour, and according to the blurry mimeographs, he was in Madrid, Berlin, or Stockholm. No one could tell me, and I didn't speak Swedish or German or Spanish. I spent two days sitting on the floor with the phone and a stack of newspapers, reading my horoscope and trying to figure out international dialing with an old French dictionary in my lap: I am trying to get in touch with someone. *J'essaie de toucher quelqu'un.*

The calendar in my purse listed my jobs, my meetings, my appointments, the little x's marking my period every four weeks, give or take a day or two. With him in Europe, the days were blending together and it wasn't until I wrote down a new go-see that I realized the little x from four days ago had not yet arrived. Only four days, but that had never happened before. I didn't know how worried I should be, and there was no one to call. My mother? Fuck. Debi was good for letting me know I could take an aerobics class taught by Jane Fonda if I was willing to drive to Beverly Hills early in the morning, which of course I was, but I couldn't imagine telling her anything personal. The girlfriends I had were people I worked with sometimes or talked to at parties. Linda or any of the so-called sisterhood? Jesus. And Harriet would listen to what I had to say and immediately tell me what to do about it, would perhaps even fly here and hold my hand while I did it, if I needed her to. But even though it could be undone, it would still disappoint her, and I would have to sit with that: disappointing her once again.

What I needed was to talk to him, to hear something in his voice that said he wanted this.

But he was in Sweden or Germany or Spain, and all I had was a vase wrapped in a black hand towel for practice. I carried the vase everywhere I went: to the bathroom, to bed, to the pool. *This is your baby*, I told myself. *This is your life.*

J'essaie de toucher quelqu'un. J'essaie de toucher quelqu'un. J'essaie de toucher quelqu'un.

I could choose not to tell him, have it taken care of, and be just as he left me when he came back. Or I could have the baby and he would realize that four years was forever and we would sign papers that meant something to us both. Or I could have the baby and end my modeling career and be at home with these window-walls all day, not having the number of where he was and waiting, always waiting.

I could take a test and know for sure. But then I'd know. For sure.

On the third day of trying to reach him, the baby broke. My vase. I dropped my baby.

On the fourth day, Sweden told me the person I wanted *to touch* had checked out two days before and also that my French was terrible.

On the fifth day, the blood appeared and I pressed myself like a bruise but instead of hurt, I just felt relieved. And then I knew.

I spent hours calling the label and Europe until he finally answered. He told me it was four thirty in the morning in Berlin. I listened for the whisper of a woman in the background, convinced I'd hear the rasp of legs against the sheets—*Swish*—if I stayed on the line. When I told him I missed him, he said he missed me too. I asked how much, then hung up the phone.

Enough for him to fly back the next night, but that didn't feel like enough, not anymore. Life was too short to live it like this. While he wiped his eyes and rubbed his forehead, I waited for him to tell me I was wrong. I waited for him to fight for me. I needed him to fight for me, for us.

But there was another show for him to get to, and as I watched him gather his things to leave again, the truth revealed itself at last: there would always be another show, and by that I meant a tour or a woman or a song or something that didn't need anything from him. It was easier to love a concept. And I'd thought I could do it. Be a living photograph. I felt most at home as a concept, but it turned out I didn't want to do this for both work and life.

One had to change.

What it looked like was this:

The model knew she had to leave her glass house. The model

was throwing a stone. She took more Quaaludes than she should have and slept through a go-see for the first time in her life, and when the phone rang, she knew it was New York, not Los Angeles.

A split screen. On the left, a girl—can we still call her a girl now, is she too old?—in bed alone, cheek drool-slicked, hair greasy. On the right, the agent. Round glasses. Cigarette holder. The whole package. A woman who needed an answer.

The model wasn't one to lie, and not to the agent, if for no other reason than the agent had a history of seeing right through it. But she knew on some level that this was what the agent had been waiting for, and what she herself didn't want in this moment was to resent another person she loved. The only other person she loved.

The model apologized. She lied her lie. She said she was sick and had taken something for cramps—always safe to go with cramps, never introduce the question of pregnancy, as close as that question had come. She sat against massive pillows, letting the waterbed gently rock her.

What she needed was a change. She was going to miss that waterbed. Even if it wasn't clear on her face, the missing or the knowledge that the missing was coming, this was the thought that came to her as she crafted the lie the agent did not buy. The model didn't need to see to know the agent was choosing not to press the issue—for now. The agent probably even suspected Quaaludes, though not the reason behind them. The model was meticulous in her timing but she'd grown fond of the blurred edges of pills.

One thing for a party, though. Another when it became a response.

Observe the model hatching her plan. Coming to terms with the fact she needed a plan. She walked through the glass-walled house. She floated on the waterbed again. She would have gathered her things, but she didn't need a lot of them. She wasn't

THE COVER GIRL

going forever. It wasn't the end. It was a pause. She folded a few pieces of clothing. Refolded them. Set them in a suitcase.

She looked like a movie star sitting in the back of a cab on her way to the Riot House, the first place she could think of. Her face half-covered in sunglasses despite the clouds, a smart trench coat despite the temperature. From a distance, she looked like a woman, a girl who knew things. A girl who'd decided.

Or had she just let go?

My stay at the Riot House would, I figured, be temporary. This little break would be temporary. I even left my gifted Ferrari behind—see, this isn't for real, forever. This was the move of an adult woman. No more theatrics with blood and hospitals. Let him live without me and see what it was like. Let him come loping back with a ring and a new beginning.

Living in a hotel made it okay that I knew nothing. How to pay a bill. How to access my own money. I didn't need to. I would be the lady of the glass house soon enough.

One week. Another week. I waited for the hotel mattress to gently rock me to sleep; instead, it held me in stillness. No phone call, no visit, no attempt through the grapevine to contact me. I had left the schedule behind, didn't know when he was supposed to get back from Europe. Maybe he was calling all day, trying to reach me, assuming I was on go-sees and shoots. I tried not to think about the fact he'd know to call Debi if he couldn't reach me. Maybe being in Europe made it harder to call Debi. Maybe he was so lost without me he'd forgotten about Debi and even Harriet. I hoped he was eating. He must be so worried.

Or maybe I'd made a—the word *mistake* was too small for the hole inside me that gaped bigger every day.

I booked jobs and showed up on set. I even filmed another commercial for Swish, and the experience floated right over me. I didn't see anyone outside of work, so even though I could have stepped out into the hallway and waved someone down to provide me with Quaaludes or something slightly better or worse, I showed up bright and unfuzzy. If I wasn't working, I was waiting, and if I wasn't waiting, I was sleeping, phone by my head. No pills needed.

The day there was a knock at the door was the day I was waiting for. I looked in the mirror quickly before answering: clean hair, enough vestiges of work makeup to look put together for something else, not this, not sitting in a room. I softened my face, ready to be the picture of love and reconciliation, and that was the face I ended up making for Harriet. And I didn't want to let her see me cry but it was too late.

"Darling," she said. "Do you want to tell me about it?"

I most certainly did not.

"Alright. Well, then, do you want to go to Paris?"

My first instinct was to say no. He wouldn't be able to find me in Paris. But I had never said no to Harriet before, and if I did, there would be no hiding. I would have to explain this hotel room and the tears and the predicament I had put myself in, and I wanted to avoid that as badly as I wanted to be found.

The answer was to go to Paris, to do the thing that models my age do when they are on the cusp of something more, to take the steps that would make me a name. The answer was to find something to hold on to.

Paris for a girl like me was not the Paris of romantic dreams. It was my life in a different time zone, except instead of living in a hotel room, I was crammed into a flat with seven other models on this high fashion quest, some Harriet's and some from another agency. The rock star had been on tour for weeks before I left, and I was no longer used to being around people. My first couple days in the flat, I felt a little feral, startling around corners, struggling to make conversation with the girl I was rooming with.

The trip began as a chain of go-sees for jobs I didn't book be-

THE COVER GIRL

cause my portfolio was too commercial or because my look was too American or because my face was too sad, but not in a smart enough way. The noes slid off me as quickly as they came in.

After the initial few days of go-sees, my schedule became even more ridiculous. Harriet had sent me and the others here for fashion week, and I was booked for multiple shows a day, for four straight days, mostly for new designers.

The first day of shows exhausted me beyond feeling. I walked for a British designer named Kitty Wyoming, whose clothes were geometric, loud, designed to compete for attention in a week full of shows and names. The show started nearly an hour late, and the narrow catwalk and our angular garments, all pointed shoulders and hips, were a terrible match. When the model walking opposite me refused to twist her torso out of my way, I had to spin to avoid falling off the runway—a move that did not match the clothes and resulted in a rolled ankle. I was late to the next show and completely spent by the third, too overloaded by a language I did not speak and clothes that were a challenge to wear, rather than be worn by, to actually enjoy the buzz of the press and the potential of famous guests.

When the cabdriver brought me back to the flat, he told me my French was bad and, even though he said it nicely, all I could think of was the hotel clerk in Sweden. *J'essaie de toucher quelqu'un.*

My roommate, Bernice, one of the non-Harriet models at the flat, who I'd heard was booked to walk for Oscar de la Renta later in the week, found me weeping on my narrow twin bed—a tiny thing compared to the waterbed or even the one I slept in at the Riot House. Nervously, she offered to take me out for a drink and even though I was so tired from the day, from the time difference, from years of trying so hard to be good, I said yes just to feel something else.

"A man?" she asked over a glass of champagne.

I nodded. That sounded much better than *a breakup*. Because it wasn't that, right? It couldn't be. I apologized for being a bad roommate all week—it had just been hard.

Bernice shrugged a little sadly. "I mean, I'm used to not making friends in these places. It's not my first time being the only Black girl in the house."

I was accustomed to girls ignoring me because they assumed I was stuck-up or because I gave off the air that I was—a different thing entirely from what Bernice was saying. I hadn't considered what my avoidance looked like on her end, sharing a room with a possible mix of jealousy and prejudice. I tried to explain, tripping over my words, and Bernice held up a hand: this was not what she needed. I nodded, and I thanked her for inviting me out.

"Anyway, we should toast this day away," she said. "I had an awful go-see. They didn't even look at my book. They had me walk three steps and then laughed me right out of there. Literally."

This wasn't too far off from my own time in Paris, and I'd heard enough to know it could happen to the best of us, but looking at Bernice, it was still surprising. It wasn't just that she was beautiful, though she was, even plainly styled in a tee shirt tucked into a skirt, her shoulder-length hair clipped back from her face by two barrettes. I could imagine people trying to put her in a box—the next Iman, the next Naomi Sims—for easy translation rather than accuracy. She had perfect sharp cheekbones and wide golden eyes and energy, a smile that felt real and that I could imagine made her pictures sparkle. She had *it*. I'd heard people say that before; such a blank phrase, it sounds stupid until you see it—*it*—yourself. I raised my glass, and our toast was not a standard cheers but a *fuck them*.

We ordered a whole bottle of champagne and when men came up to us, we shook our heads and held up our hands, putting up a wall of ice. For them. For us, the walls came down.

Bernice told me she was eighteen, from Virginia, and had

been modeling for a few months to earn money before she started college at Georgetown, prelaw, in the fall. But then it snowballed, and here she was, excited but nervous about the Oscar de la Renta gig. Bernice, it seemed, was on the Brooke Shields path, the star path, even though she didn't seem quite convinced she should pause college and pursue modeling full-time. Loosened by the champagne, I told her I had a feeling I'd be seeing her again on the cover of a magazine and she just laughed.

Then she asked for the story about the man, and I had to consider what to say. A flash to other conversations, feeling judged, memories shoved deep down. People never understood, and I wanted to be her friend—I couldn't open myself up for misunderstanding. So I gave her the whole story in pieces, designed a story specially for avoiding weird looks and long pauses. A man I loved, who loved me. A house I had to leave because we needed space to get ready for the next step. But: I hadn't heard from him yet.

"How are you paying for that hotel?" she asked. When I said a credit card, she pressed further—the picture of a future lawyer. "Whose credit card?"

It was a card he'd given me, of course.

"You left him and made him pay the bill?" she laughed. "Don't worry, he'll find you."

I wasn't even sure what was funny about it but there was no meanness to her voice, so I laughed too. It was easier than thinking too hard, and anyway, when I laughed, Bernice smiled at me and said, "I've never had this. Hanging out with another model off set. Just being friends. Even our names! Birdie and Bernice. It's like fate."

I loved the idea, fated to a friend, and I wanted to hold on to it as long as possible, but we had call times to make. We started heading back to the flat, then Bernice stopped short. "I'm worried about my walk now, after that go-see. Can I show you?" she asked. "Is that okay?" I nodded, and she walked the length of sidewalk like a runway. She moved well below the waist—*lift the knee, lift the knee*—but the tension she'd released from her lower body was being held in her face and shoulders, all stiffness and grimace that didn't deserve laughter but wouldn't help her on the runway.

I explained what Nadine had told me, about not smiling but showing my personality. That I just picked an expression and studied it in the mirror and practiced until I could hold it like a pose. It was a strange feeling, having knowledge that could be shared with someone else. The realization that I had not just been doing but learning all this time.

We practiced all the way back to the flat, pretending we were the girls in the 1973 show at Versailles—"Those Stephen Burrows dresses!" Bernice shouted, and I agreed—and by the end, she had let go of her concentration and smoothed her expression into a sly *I know something you don't know* smirk, and I had added an extra swivel to my turn. I announced that she was going to steal the show.

"We could be stars," she said, her voice light with champagne and dreams.

It felt a little more possible after that night, until my last show, which was a throwback to my first—Azrian de Popa. He was a late addition and my biggest name at fashion week.

"Look at you, Birdie," he said, rushing by with an armful of white silk. "You're all grown up. You have to wear this one."

His assistant draped it over my head, carefully adjusting the waist. "Perfect. You should keep it. I just made some touches with you in mind."

I didn't realize it was a wedding dress until a fascinator was placed on my head just before the final walk. I could not even celebrate being given this featured role in the show and instead stared at myself until *places*, thinking about how I thought we'd get married, and now that I was finally wearing a wedding dress, bridesmaid no more, it was still just me playing dress-up.

THE COVER GIRL

What if Bernice was right. What if he could find me and was choosing not to.

Later, it would become one of the most famous photos of Azrian's work: the column-like dress with sheer panels from the thigh down, the angular neckline, the tiny fascinator with its wisp of a sheer veil tying it all together, and the model, mascara streaked down her face. They assumed he'd planned it. All you need to pose is to believe in it.

2018

My old friend Bobby is in town, a welcome distraction. It's a different time when I look at him, gratitude and survival. Bobby never knew me with Harriet; there isn't a number of years of glamour that would mean anything to him. He never knew me in a lot of ways—the girl he met was someone else entirely, someone I don't often think about except with regard to the places she brought me. There are ways I never knew him either, the freedom that comes with the removal of context. So much we don't need to know to still truly know.

Like Bernice, Bobby lives on the other side of the country. Unlike Bernice, there are never any plans; it just happens. He'll call me out of the blue, forgetting the time difference, or he'll send a text announcing he's in town to visit his niece who's doing an internship in LA, and here's what we're going to do, so am I ready?

The answer is always yes.

I meet him at the Getty Museum for their exhibit on fashion photography from the past century. Bobby: a consummate itinerary planner. He's outside, standing by the fountain, and though it has been three years since I've seen him, since his wedding, I stop for a moment to take him in—the Roman profile, the close-cropped hair fading from brown to gray, his classic uniform of a short-sleeved button-down shirt tucked into jeans. Just another man enjoying the summer afternoon.

There were times when we thought we'd never get here.

When Bobby hugs me, I breathe in sharply. There's no use in considering when the last time someone wrapped their arms around me might have been, how little touch my life includes outside of someone styling my hair or dabbing makeup onto my face. Back when we first knew each other, Bobby would tease me about how poor of a hugger I was, and I would laugh because it was a ridiculous thing to latch on to and also because I wanted to feel like a regular person and him making fun of me was a reminder I was. But eventually he stopped saying anything, like it occurred to him there might be a reason.

I wonder if he's thinking about that now as I try to force my arms into warm curves instead of cold angles. Perhaps I have improved.

We walk inside as Bobby catches me up about everything—the niece's marketing internship, his husband, married life in general—his slow Southern drawl spilling out like syrup. There's comfort in his lack of hurry, his willingness to let other people go around us.

"Okay, buddy," he says as we enter the exhibit. "Are you ready to be my guide?"

Am I ever. The exhibit had been on my list of things to get around to doing, and to have the opportunity to share it with a friend is more than I'd hoped for. The past hundred years of fashion, all here, everything I'd learned to value. The gorgeous Helmut Newton photographs. Actual Diors. The way a Grace Jones pose takes your breath away. There is such joy in being able to simply appreciate. To see how we moved from Cheryl Tiegs to Kate Moss. To share this part of myself without it being about me at all. To see it all through Bobby's eyes.

THE COVER GIRL

We alternate between appropriate reverence and indulgent gossip—I offer a tidbit about Dianna Vreeland, a story I heard about a party I did not attend—as we make our way through the various exhibits.

And then there are the trading card–style images of Perry Ellis, Way Bandy, Halston, Tina Chow, Rudi Gernreich. Just a few of those taken by AIDS. The feeling swells back and crushes forward, and all I can do is take Bobby's hand. There could be photographs and artfully posed original designs, rooms and rooms full, but the simplicity of this is: we can never know how much was lost, how much genius and creation never came to be.

This is the foundation of my relationship with Bobby. In a better world, we never would have met at all. Together, we hold so many memories of people who are no longer here, and as the years and science move us further from that time, from death sentences and fury and loss, it becomes all the more important that we remember.

There's nothing to say right now, nothing that hasn't already been said, and anyway, this is Bobby's story, my choice but his reality. We stand there until the only natural thing to do is drift away.

I lead us back to the Richard Avedon photos, letting the movement and mood wash over us. It's impossible to look at his work without feeling something, whether that is more of or different from what you're already feeling. The perfect backdrop for the liminal space.

When we return to the brightness of the world outside, I ask Bobby what his plans are for the evening, if we should get dinner somewhere, not ready to say goodbye, and he turns to me, smile bordering on sheepish.

"Well," he says, drawing it out to at least three syllables. "You'll never guess who's playing tonight." He swipes through his phone and presents me with the Whisky a Go Go website: Stinger, playing tonight, to be preceded by a list of opening bands I don't recognize. "Please?" he asks, like he's already certain I'll decline.

I can't help but laugh. It's absurd, the thought of returning to a place I have not been to since 1987. To listen to music that never touched me but worked well enough when I was strung out. To see the fragments of a scene I only skirted.

The other girls? They gave me a nickname, after a particularly rough night.

They called me the Cautionary Tale.

Do I want to go?

I did not envision making my life in California. I purposefully tried to *not* make a life in California. I tried to get out, tried to leave it all, but it never took. What I learned is that New York might be the city that never sleeps and the place that dreams are made of, and when you make it there, you know you can make it anywhere, but there are certain kinds of weird that are best kept in California. This is where I fit in. Which is to say: I don't fit in here, but I don't fit in here best out of anywhere else.

Still, it's one thing to remember where we came from, the binding ties. It is another to trot out the vestiges of our old selves for the purposes of nostalgia-riddled back-in-the-day reminiscing.

"This band is responsible for our entire friendship," he says. "Don't we owe it to them?"

If I decline, what will I do instead? Ponder my impending eye lift? Go to another Pilates class? Look up the cost of a flight to New York for the gala again, compare the dollar amount against the other costs? And I like this version of our story that he has created.

The choice of how to tell it.

It is as profoundly strange to be in the Whisky as I thought it would be. Bobby is talking and I want to listen but I can't help but scan the room for people I used to know, like they all

THE COVER GIRL

still live here too, like they didn't get office jobs and move to Seattle or Denver with their spouses, having children and, oh, god, grandchildren who will never know about all the cocaine and bathroom fucking.

In their heyday, Stinger was a middling group of five musicians. There are still five of them, but now it's two original members, one guitarist from a band they used to play with in the '80s, a drummer from a different band they used to play with in the '80s, and a second guitarist who appears to be in his early thirties. A spinning wheel that allows them to keep living their dreams.

The wheel spins, and one look confirms I have slept with three-fifths of this current iteration of the band. I tell Bobby this, and I am both delighted and chagrined when he identifies which three correctly on the first try.

My connection to the band runs deeper than that, though, depending on how one wishes to quantify depth. I was in the video for their one hit song, your standard scantily clad gyrating girl, the kind of thing second-wave feminists felt undid the cause and third-wave feminists could call empowering. The truth was probably somewhere in between. I was thrilled to see myself all over MTV, not because I thought this was a good direction for my career or because I was particularly well paid for it or because I was invested in the band's success. But the song's staying power made me visible in the music world.

This song, the one everyone is waiting for, is reserved for the end, so there's a lot of other music to get to—a few covers, a few songs from vanity projects, one or two from the bands the newer members used to be in. I watch the crowd as much as I do the stage, wondering what they see. Guys in their fifties trotting out the same half-good songs about sex, drugs, and rock and roll they've been singing for thirty years, hanging on to the same hairstyles, parted carefully to cover bald spots and crow's feet, playing in the same venue that was synonymous with making it back then but now seems to be a place for people who take it far too seriously or whose interest is only ironic.

To me, though, there's something about picking one thing and sticking to it, even if, maybe especially if, there isn't any real demand for it. And so I dance along with Bobby, hamming it up for the video he takes of us for his husband, singing the words I remember and reminding myself I can forget what it felt like back then. The truth is, I fit in better now, in a present where we are all relics.

After everyone has sung through five extra choruses of the last song, the one we all know, Bobby and I make our way to the exit and I feel like I've done something by coming back here. I can touch the past without falling down the hole of it.

So when Bobby wants to stop at the Rainbow for a drink, I decide: Why not?

Everything doesn't have to mean so much.

But as we're standing at the bar, I hear my name.

The old tight, heavy feeling rises from my stomach, winding itself around my chest. Who could know me here? Or: Who could know me here who I would want to see?

Bobby and I both turn around and there, weaving in and out of the crowd, waving a hand, is Michelle Elhert. "Hi!" she says, waving again. "How funny running into you here!"

Is it.

She turns to Bobby, sticking her palm out for a shake. "Hello! I'm Michelle. I just interviewed Birdie for a story I'm working on."

While he introduces himself to her, I can feel his eyes on me. An expression that might mean many things but most likely is intended to convey a question: *We spent all day together, and you chose not to bring this up?* I don't know what to make my face say back. Something like: *Let me not be this person with you?*

"We're here for my boyfriend's friend's birthday," Michelle offers in an unasked-for explanation. I wonder if this is really

THE COVER GIRL

a hip place for a twenty-five-year-old's birthday, but then I remember the boyfriend, the self-proclaimed disruptor of dog breeds, and realize one might need to concede the *hip* point.

Bobby, ever the Southern gentleman, steps in so that my quietness cannot be mistaken for rudeness. Before I can stop him, he's explaining to Michelle about the concert, the music video, pulling up a photo of me artfully arched around a guitar to make it look like that's all I have on—I don't remember what I actually wore and I am certain I did not care—in a listicle declaring "Take It, Shake It" the 79th hottest video of the 1980s.

"How did you not tell me about this?" Michelle says, looking at the photo on Bobby's phone, then back to me. As though it could be a point of pride. As though Harriet considered those kinds of jobs to be a reflection of either of our talents.

I offer a polite shrug, trying to laugh as I turn to grab my drink. And then there it is, visible just out of the corner of my eye. A flash of golden-red curls.

The anxiety I extinguished before roars back, full-on fear now. My heart beats faster, like it did that day on the vitamin shoot. And just like that day, I am not quite certain why my body is rejecting the situation but I can only assume it's for the same reason: I am too close to something that could hurt me. I tell Bobby we have to go.

"Right now?" he asks.

I'm already throwing extra cash on the bar. I scan the room, trying to figure out how close, how far I am.

How safe I am.

Not safe enough.

I don't even know what I'm saying to Michelle, all I can hope for is that it makes sense and the music pumping overhead will cover the rest. I clutch Bobby's hand as we wind our way downstairs and outside and I don't look behind me until we're a full block away.

There is no touching the past. There is only sinking into it.

"Buddy. What was that?" Bobby asks once my pace slows, once he is no longer half running to keep up.

I want to ask if there are things he has put away, parts of his life he decided are better left untouched, and what he does if they come roaring back, but I can hear the gall of me asking him such a question without saying the words aloud. I could have been that to him, a reminder of a time too painful to hold on to, and maybe the only reason I'm not is because he needs someone who can say, *Yes it was real, yes it happened, yes it was awful, yes you remember it right.*

He is still looking at me, waiting. There is only one answer: another life.

He nods. "Sometimes I forget that about you. That you had this whole other thing going on before I ever knew you."

When I say that sometimes I forget too, he laughs, so I do too, and we can both pretend there isn't a truth lurking under that sentence.

In the morning, I meet Bobby for brunch, and the night before never happened. He'll spend the rest of his visit with his niece and then fly back to North Carolina, and it might be years before we see each other again. I hug him first this time, knowing how alien I must look holding out my arms, trying to shape what I am going for.

"Oh, buddy," he says. "We're still hanging on."

Later, I text Michelle an apology for rushing out on her. The words fall heavy and fake from my keypad, forced exclamation points—So fun to run into you last night! Hope the writing is going well!—and glossy veneer. So sorry we had to run off! So sorry you were in the middle of the minefield of my memory!

So sorry that you may have realized I am not a reliable narrator of my own story!

1981–1987

Sick Again

1

When I got back from Paris, Debi set me up with a sensible car and a little flat in West Hollywood, not too far from the Riot House. I couldn't sleep at night, couldn't sleep alone, so I went places I would have never gone to before, listening to music that was nothing like before, no flexing guitar solos and pulsing choruses. Just rage and noise, something to fill the void that stretched wider with each new day.

There was no past and no future, just the moment. There was no pondering going back to Connecticut or even New York because that part of my life was not real. I was not a daughter. And I was, at this exact moment, not a wife-girlfriend-lover-ward either. Most days I felt like I was barely a model, even though I worked often. Just not well.

Catalogs. Brochures. Third-rate ads. A far cry from a magazine cover. A far cry from Swish. My chutes-and-ladders career tumbling almost back to the beginning.

If something big was going to happen, it would have happened after Paris, after the runway photo. It might have been different if I had stayed to capitalize on the buzz after the show. For the first time, everyone wanted to know who that girl was, the one with the mascara tears, but I was already on my way home. Even though I had two go-sees scheduled the next day. Even though I wanted to say goodbye to Azrian and Bernice.

And then I disappeared for days once I was home. Not physically, but I was blank. Nothing showed up on camera. I didn't get jobs and some I'd had but lost. Maybe it was intentional. Maybe if I wasn't good enough for him to try to come back for me and make it work, I wasn't good enough for anything else.

You know. For instance.

I booked a Jean Naté knockoff skin something—did it matter?—where I sat in a tub of fake bubble bath for hours in another version of a tiny flesh-colored bikini. I couldn't let the bubbles remind me of the tour. Instead, I let the bikini remind me of Swish and how I'd liked being away, felt powerful on my own, and then I felt guilty for not appreciating what I'd had, but then again, leaving made me appreciate it, so maybe the same would be true for— And then I turned my brain off.

"What's happening over there? You look like you're about to throw up. Sensual relaxing bath time, remember?" the photographer called.

I apologized. How could I forget? I was Girl in Bath and nothing else mattered. This was the one thing I could count on myself for.

It was better than not working, and better than staying home, and better than going to the mattress store and lying on the waterbeds just to feel something, and that was really all I could say about it. And that was the moment I knew Brooke Shields had won. I was never going to be famous.

Debi got me the apartment on the condition that I stopped pulling stunts like leaving an entire country, and in return, I got a moment of clarity in a fake bathroom.

I was never going to be an It girl, have a doll, a movie, a multicycle ad campaign that made me a household name. It might get bigger than this at times, but not often and not for long.

THE COVER GIRL

Whether it was because I wasn't in the same elite circles as I had been with the rock star or because I just didn't have the same drive to care as much or because I had barely spoken to Harriet since I left Paris, knowing I had yet again disappointed her, I couldn't say. But I guess there was a relief in this too. I didn't have to try so hard.

And when I went to the punk clubs, I didn't have to try at all. No, that's not true. I tried in a different way. I didn't have the right clothes, the right hair, not at first. It took a lot of work to look like I wasn't trying, which I should have been used to. I was nearly six feet tall. Add hair and makeup and I was impossible to ignore in most outfits, let alone the ones I thought were right for going out.

Bad Religion. X. Social Distortion. I thought about the roadies who used to shove headphones over my ears as I let these bands drown out everything. I ended up at my first show after walking around Chinatown one night and hearing the sound from the street. Noise. Noise was what I needed and I found myself drawn inside. Mostly men, mostly young, mostly denim and old tee shirts, some shaved heads and mohawks. It didn't occur to me to feel unsafe, partly because of my height and partly because I had no experience with this brand of danger—before, someone always knew where I was.

I didn't like it yet I couldn't stay away. I chased the music all over town. This was where the outcasts went. This had to be where I belonged.

One night, emboldened by the late hour and the reds I'd got off a model at a silly catalog shoot, I went up to a girl who was also alone at the bar at the Starwood. Technically I was still not of legal drinking age, but no one ever asked; it was like I'd pretended to be an adult long enough that I'd just become one. More likely, in a place like this, no one cared. Rules only existed for certain people, in certain buildings.

I thought I looked like I fit in at last. I'd traded minidresses for jeans that I had to rip with nail scissors and tank tops that did nothing to hide the length of my torso or the narrowness of my waist but at least only cost a few dollars. When the girl ordered herself a vodka soda, I did too, and paid for both drinks.

She stared at me. "What are you doing?" Blonde, a little too well-dressed. A shorter version of me, perhaps, except she knew enough to tease her hair up and slick down the sides to create a kind of mohawk.

When she shouted to be heard above the noise, it sounded normal. As I tried to respond, my own words and volume seemed unhinged. We're both here. Girls. Alone. I wanted to be nice. I tried to keep my face friendly, warm, which was a reasonable thing to do in front of a camera but not in front of another human.

The girl rolled her eyes and walked away. Fine. I would not be deterred.

I wrote down the dates of shows in my little go-see notebook. So very punk. I soon became a fixture, inserting myself into the periphery of the circle in the parking lot for cigarettes before or after shows, desperate for something more than people with whom I was at the same place at the same time. The boys at least paid attention to me. Boys with names like Meat and Drunk Dave.

The blonde girl was there too. I tried to introduce myself again after we'd seen each other a few times but she just looked at me and said, "No."

Any other time in my life, I would have been ashamed enough to evaporate on the spot. I couldn't control where my career was going. I couldn't control when the rock star was going to come get me. I was convinced, though, that I could control how this girl felt about me, that I could control fitting in here.

So this was my double life. I would stay out till two or three in the morning half the week and wake up at five or six on the mornings I had shoots. I iced my face to combat puffiness. I took reds. I revved myself up with coffee and cigarettes. I slept during the day like a vampire. The first time this thought occurred to me, I was delighted. I wasn't sucking blood but I was feeding on something in those dark hours.

I thought I was doing a good job of doing it all. I thought no one was the wiser. I was too thick in it, and by *it* I mean my world, myself, my head, my fears, to see anything else.

Someone on a shoot saw, though, which meant a phone call from Debi. "Do you want to stay in the agency house with all the sixteen- and seventeen-year-olds?" she asked. I didn't think they could actually make me do this—I was nineteen, after all, a woman, an actual adult—and even after all my practice as a good girl, seen and not heard, I told her as much. The words sounded like they were coming from someone else; for a moment, I floated above myself, marveling at the girl below with the nerve to talk back. For a moment, the void that had opened in me in Paris closed. Debi was silent too—for all the problems I might have thrown her way lately, she could at least count on me to be amenable.

"Would you rather have this conversation with Harriet?" she finally asked.

Perhaps the only threat that still held any weight.

I did in fact want to talk to Harriet. But there was a part of me that felt all I had done was waste the faith she had in me, and that was all I could do. How had we gotten here?

How useful would that answer be?

All I knew was that wherever *here* was, I had to get out, had to get back to my old life, my real life, so I imposed my own curfew. I didn't want to leave the parking lot or the music thrashing through me, but I would glance at my watch and disappear into the night, hoping it made me look mysterious rather than square.

The blonde girl caught on, started giving me looks when I left and nods when I arrived. Be less available and become more interesting. The biggest lesson. What a solid foundation. One night I showed up to the club and instead of a punk band, it was something more rock and roll, something I couldn't be around, and I faded into the parking lot. I would catch up with everyone after, pretend I'd been there all along.

But the blonde girl followed me out. We sat on the curb and smoked in silence for a little while before she finally said, "Why do you come here?"

Did I need to know the reason? Why do any of us come here? Why does she come here?

"I asked you first."

Me first. One answer: because I need to. Even though I shouldn't. Maybe that's why I need to. I couldn't tell my words from thoughts. I'm a model. I have to be up early for shoots sometimes, I get scolded for staying out too late, it's the only skill I have so I can't mess it up. She was still looking at me. What did she know? I left school a long time ago. I have a piece of paper, but what is it worth. I had tutors, but I'm not sure what I learned, if it was anything valuable outside of these circles. I read newspapers now because everyone expects me to be a pretty face. I was on the road. Not for my career. Because of him. I was fifteen and now I'm not. He was mine and I was his, and we're just working some things out right now. You know how it is.

I watched her eyebrows raise and her lips twitch around questions she wanted to ask, and I knew I should shut up, that these were my stories and not anyone else's, knew how people reacted to my stories, and finally, I stopped midsentence and told the blonde girl it was her turn.

"Is that you in the hair remover commercial?" she asked instead.

I nodded.

"Gross," she said, like she assumed I'd agree with her. "I come here because it's the furthest thing away from little Mary Grace from Oregon."

I waited for her to say more, but she didn't. One of us had

learned better how to create mystery. But I had opened the door for her, at least. I told her we weren't so different, then.

She looked at me. "We are so, so different. You'll figure it out when your little phase passes."

Two things happened. I woke up one afternoon and needed desperately for something to change, and the only thing I could land on was to dye my hair black, a difference that said it wasn't a phase, and then that night Meat kissed me. I think it was Meat.

I regretted my hair the moment the dye hit it. I knew better than to use an at-home kit, but I also knew better than to walk into a salon and expect them to give me the drastic change I wanted. I did it myself because the void yawned bigger and that's what I could fill it with. What else was I supposed to listen to? I regretted Meat before he even stepped into my space. Did I never have eyebrows to begin with or was it the dye, and was it possible I'd never smelled a twenty-year-old man? I pushed him away, and then I burst into tears because my hair looked terrible. My hair looked terrible because I couldn't stomach the thought of kissing someone else. I shoved him off because Debi was going to be so mad and there was no way she wouldn't tell Harriet.

It was *everything happening at once.*

The other guys didn't take too kindly to me shoving their friend. I ended up on the ground, looking up at the blonde girl and the other boys. One of them felt enough pity to reach out a hand to help me up.

"Don't bother," the girl said. "She's not one of us. She's a model. She's just playing dress-up. She's just a corporate shill."

The hand dropped.

"And by the way, I saw your boyfriend at the Rainbow the other night. With a girl. You two aren't working out shit."

I could have reminded her she didn't belong here either. I could have tried to hurt her right back. But I didn't. I sat on the ground in the parking lot as they walked away from me, wondering how I could have chosen so poorly. Again. I thought I would be okay with the outcasts, but I couldn't even not fit in in the right way.

After I was fired from the job I'd booked, Debi took me to a salon herself. The process of fixing my hair was called stripping. Debi sat there next to me like I was a flight risk. Stripped with an audience; no such thing as too on the nose here.

"It's going to take several appointments," the stylist said. "And it's going to take a long time for it to go back to how it was."

I already knew there was no such thing.

My hair went from black to dark brown to brown. It had to happen in stages; removing color is harder than adding it. I stopped by the office to show Debi the progress.

"Sit down," she said, and I knew good news was not coming my way.

"Harriet and I spoke this morning, and we decided we aren't going to book you for a little while." When I started to protest that I only had two appointments left, she held up a hand. "It's not about your hair color, Birdie. You haven't been the same since Paris. You've been inconsistent, unprofessional, undedicated. I wanted to let you go when you left Paris before you finished your go-sees, but Harriet disagreed. We're in agreement now—you need a break."

I had recently seen an article in *Time* that said Brooke Shields's rate was $10,000 a day.

I started sobbing right in front of Debi. She rolled her eyes and handed me a tissue. She thought it was an act. Who cares about taking a break that much? Not me. No, what hurt was: there was a time, not even that long ago, when this message would have come from Harriet. It *should* have come from Harriet. She said before that she was still my agent; Debi was just my LA booker. For her to not tell me about this, to not give me the *darling* before the bad news, told me more about where I stood than the break itself. I wondered for how long we would do all our communicating through Debi, if I was even still one of her girls.

I went home. I sat with my punishment—the first of my life in fact, only administered when I was at last an adult. I looked in the mirror and watched my hair shift from brown to light brown, its texture growing rougher with each treatment. I drove by the Starwood and saw that it was closed not for the daytime but for good, and I wondered if I had imagined it all. My days were spent coating my head in mayonnaise and olive oil and plastic wrap to put some moisture back in. To be ready. To get things back to how they had been, no matter how long it took.

Then flowers arrived. A knock on the door and a delivery man standing there with an arrangement that could only be described as *avant-garde*—a word I could not define but could identify. Angles and branches and roses, dark colors. The suggestion of a bouquet. If I'd looked closer, I would have known, but what I saw was: flowers. At last. I knew the punk girl was wrong; he wouldn't let me go so easily. That flippy feeling of waiting and waiting for something and finally seeing it happen in front of you, a blend of dream and reality—how could the moment live up to what I'd imagined? My heart fluttered and I was nearly giddy as I took the flowers from the man at the door, thanking him profusely while wondering if my hair would be blond in time for our reunion. I didn't want to be seen like this, different.

I had three outfit options in mind by the time I opened the card.

My dear Birdie,
I called Harriet to see about booking your services, but she said you are under the weather and taking a little break. Please know that I am thinking of you and hope you are feeling better soon.

As ever, Azrian

2

What I did was: I begged.

I called New York. I put on my bravest face and my most model voice, demure and soft and pliable. I put on an outfit that made me feel fashionable and in control, even though I knew she couldn't see it. I tucked the comb she'd given me in my hair. I told her I needed to do Azrian's job. I said that my career had been punctuated by his designs, which sounded right enough, and what I needed was fashion. Creativity. Art. And when Harriet stood firm that I was on a break, I held out the one thing I knew she would not be able to dismiss, a glittering jewel of self-abasement.

So much was different now, I told her. So much had changed and of course I was struggling to keep up, *I had been through a lot*, and I was trying right now, perhaps not very well, but maybe what I needed was to work with someone who knew me, who had seen what I could do and could bring out my best. I needed something to still be the same.

This was as close as I had come to acknowledging to Harriet that the rock star and I were not currently together, and I knew it would count for something in her eyes. And so she said yes.

THE COVER GIRL   233

It occurred to me afterward that this was her plan all along—to make me want it again. She was always a step ahead.

I couldn't even be annoyed that it worked. That she still cared enough to make a plan was enough for me.

Booking my services hardly covered the prominence of the job. Azrian was teaming up with shoe designer Kimmi Colette. KC stilettos were all over red carpets, *Vogue* in every language, and Studio 54. Wherever two or more socialites were gathered, at least one of them would be wearing KCs. It was the magic combination of a price tag just north of accessible and bold shiny colors against heels made from materials like metal, stone, or bone. They weren't terribly attractive and they weren't at all comfortable but they were an *event*. It was fashion as a party, and who didn't want a party?

Compare that with Azrian's clothes—structured, dramatic, asymmetrical, a fondness for going sheer in unexpected ways. The potential excited me in a way I'd forgotten I cared about. And the campaign—billboards for the New York and Los Angeles KC stores. A spread somewhere; possibly the holy grail of *Vogue* itself.

I loved myself for being excited. Look at what I was capable of. Look at what I knew, what I had learned. That moment in the bubble-bath shoot that I thought was an epiphany—I had been wrong. I had been sad. There was still time to make magic, to book a *Vogue* cover, to conquer high fashion. To get a real makeup contract this time. To have Brooke Shields know my name. To get him back.

There was still time.

And—Harriet invited me to stay with her in New York.

It would be my longest trip to the city in some time, and I was newly unsettled by the knowledge I was only a train ride away from my parents in Darien. I had this fear I could end up there by some mechanics beyond my own volition. That my body could buy the ticket for me.

I never called my parents after my father's heart attack. I sent the most generic get-well-soon card I could find, and then I moved out of my house and made myself untraceable except through Harriet. Most of the time I didn't think about it; enough had happened to occupy my mind since then. And what did we owe each other anymore, really? We'd made our choices.

And as I stood in Harriet's apartment, I imagined going back there would feel like a particular version of what this moment felt like: acutely crushed by the passage of time. The first time I had been in her home I was just shy of my sixteenth birthday. I had a magazine cover. A promising makeup contract. The potential of high fashion. A man who loved me. Possibility yet to unfurl itself at my feet.

I could have thought about moving backward, but that would have been the uninteresting choice. Instead, I chose to believe that I had it all to do again.

Harriet was making herself a martini, tea for me, despite the fact I was grown, like she could will me to develop the taste. Harriet herself did not believe in beverages served above forty-five degrees. She shook the drink to the proper chill, arms floating in her draped top. The gray streak that wound its way from her widow's peak to the center of her chignon was more pronounced and that was the only thing that had changed.

That and the gulf between us, as I nursed the hurt over her letting Debi tell me I was on a break.

But I could put that in a box, at least for tonight.

"I'm glad you're here, darling," she said, handing me the warm mug like an offering. Like a new beginning. And I told her I was too.

Did I want us to curl up in the armchairs chosen for style over comfort and make plans for where this job could launch me next? Did I want to discuss another shot at Paris?

Did I want her to say she still believed in me so I wouldn't have to say anything at all?

THE COVER GIRL   235

Instead, she asked, "Have you considered coming back to New York, darling?" and I sat up straighter, almost physically moved farther away. How could she think such a thing? Why would I do such a thing? "It'd be good to have you back in the primary market full-time. And we'd be able to work more closely again."

We looked at each other. I broke the gaze first, too scared of what she might see.

"I just thought—"

I knew what she thought. Me too. Another choice, and the decision was all mine, right? Go with her and decide it was really over with the rock star. Stay in LA and hope that it wasn't. I just wanted to do Azrian's job, not uproot my life more.

Harriet nodded at my silence, then announced she had some work to do. I acted like I was tired from my flight, and we let it lie, content enough to have the other in our line of sight for now.

I knew I was not going to be the only model on the AZ-KC campaign—the new official name of the shoe collaboration, after three scrapped drafts that were perhaps more accurate initial-wise but deemed less fun—but no one had told me who the other girl was going to be. Harriet had just said it was being negotiated, which I understood meant a bigger name than my own. I was fine with that. It was what I needed: elevation.

I didn't expect to know the other model, but when I arrived for the first call, Bernice, my roommate in Paris, was just a few steps ahead of me. We looked at each other and screamed in delight—genuinely, that was the only word that could capture our sound and our joy.

"You look gorgeous!" she said, but no, it was her who was gorgeous. She looked more at ease than she had in Paris, settled into her success, no longer trying to straddle the line between cover girl and college girl. She'd traded her barrettes for the model's chignon, a few curls elegantly escaping.

There could be a world in which I was not happy to see Bernice. One where I remembered who I was when we met, the muck I was still trying to form into a new life. One where, despite my hypothetical calm about working with someone more successful, I let jealousy seep in. And truthfully, part of my happiness was relative to hers. If she'd been indifferent to me or couldn't place me, which happened to all of us, I would have responded in equal measure.

Sometimes, I found myself unable to sleep at night, and in the dark I would think about the ways in which I was alone. The failed friendships—the way Lulu's interest in me flamed out the moment she met Beasley, the wives and girlfriends of musicians who'd treated me like one of them in public but kept their distance. The way the girl at the punk clubs immediately decided I could never fit in. I would consider all the ways in which I was unlikable. Unlovable. And then when it felt too dark, too heavy, I would try to remember the moments I had connected with someone and it had been real, not based on what I could offer at the time. And my mind would go back to Paris and Bernice, to finding something to hold on to when we were both untethered. It was different from the smooth surface of a job friendship. It was just kindness. It was possible.

"I'm nervous," she whispered as we walked to the set. Thank god I wasn't the only one.

We didn't know what to expect. That first fashion show with Azrian, with him making last-minute changes—that was how he worked. Kimmi would be described as whimsical or mercurial, depending on the patience level of the speaker and whether they'd been subject or observer. Combined? Who knew.

This first day, it was hours of jet-black glitter makeup and hair slicked back flat against the tops of our heads and then teased out huge behind us and being styled into various leather outfits, and none of it had anything to do with shoes. We took photos together and separately and we both knew better than to ask about the footwear.

THE COVER GIRL

237

Modeling alongside Bernice felt different than it had with other girls. Maybe it was because I knew her star was rising, but she exuded an energy, one I could respond to: the *it* factor she already had in Paris. She had good questions and bold ideas for posing that inspired me to think bigger. I was so used to letting go and just being a body in front of the camera, but this time, I let myself stay there too. A body and a soul—unguarded, without fear.

We were let go for the day without any mention of shoes and with an invitation to meet Azrian at a place called Paradise Garage at midnight. It wasn't until Bernice and I were having predancing drinks at a restaurant so trendy I hadn't yet heard of it that we could raise the question. And it wasn't so much a question as it was Bernice sipping from her coupe glass and asking nonchalantly, "This is a shoe campaign, right?"

And I laughed. We both laughed, falling over each other and attracting attention because our hair was so big and we were so beautiful, had been designed to be perceived as so beautiful.

It was Paris all over again except without the tears and the heartbreak, just a dull ache below my rib cage that I had learned to live with. Paris with a new ending, my second chance to get it right.

It felt like a sign, then, when we arrived as Azrian's guests—true guests, it was members-only—at Paradise Garage, that to get to the dance floor, we had to walk a runway. Azrian went first with his friends, and Bernice and I walked behind, taking the length of the catwalk like it was the walk of our lives and arriving at a dance floor pulsing with disco, filled with hundreds of people, mostly men, dancing together. It was beauty like I had never seen, the magic of creation, the magic of fashion and makeup and glitter not for a photograph but to craft a person into who they were meant to be, their truest self.

Bernice and I clutched hands as we danced all night with Azrian and his friends. I let myself be filled with the joy of the music, the joy of this space, the joy of being invited in by Azrian. The joy of what was to come.

The next afternoon, when we arrived on set, there was a velvet-covered table and six pairs of shoes. *Shoes.* The word barely began to capture it. They were more artfully posed than perhaps my body ever had been. Bernice and I stood and stared, taking them in. There were hot pink boots with a metal toe and heel, sheer paneling up the side. And then the opposite—another pair of boots that were mesh at the foot and grew more opaque and iridescent as they hit knee-height. Sunset-colored alligator skin pumps with wires coiled at the ankle, formed into a bow. Purple sandals with straps formed from big interlocking circles and springs—springs!—for heels. Silvery boots perched upon quartz stilettos. Lime espadrilles with laces made to look like snakes to be crisscrossed all the way up the calf.

"Wow," Bernice breathed.

I agreed. They were both incredibly ugly and stunningly beautiful. I couldn't imagine anyone who didn't live on a coast wearing any of them, and even then, that someone would have to be used to appearing in the pages of a magazine as gossip or fashion. These shoes weren't designed to convey you from one point to the next but instead to defy what you thought a shoe could do.

Bernice and I looked at each other. This might crash spectacularly but it didn't matter. We would be a part of it.

We were styled the same way as the day before, the hair and the makeup and the leather shorts and leather tank tops and little leather dresses. Bernice was given the springs; I was put into the snaky espadrilles. I touched the laces and inhaled deeply. It was possible these were real snakes, that this was some kind of taxidermy.

This time, I was more than legs. With Bernice and on my own, I was AZ-KC. I was a body and a face, and yes, legs, and also what those legs could do. I channeled myself on the Swish set. I was power and ferocity and I was steady on my feet through sheer force of will. I unleashed the girl I had tried to be at the Starwood. I dug out the concept of punk, as much as I had come to understand it. And I let myself acknowledge the want for this work, for this to work, and I let it pour out of me.

What I'm saying is: I delivered.

It was a long day, but not my longest, and all that was asked of me was to not fall in these shoes that were conceived as art before anything else, so it was not my most difficult day either. But I had never worked harder. And for once it wasn't for Harriet, and it wasn't even for Azrian or Bernice, though I wanted to make all of them proud.

I did this one for me. And not just me, but the me I could be.

I went back to LA, despite Harriet's offer. Her words hurt, and while I knew it was because they held a piece of truth, I wasn't ready to give up. The four years I'd spent with the rock star meant something, had to mean something. I wanted someone to explain it to me, yet I didn't want to talk about it.

While we waited for the AZ-KC campaign to launch, Bernice called to say she'd be coming out to LA for a *Glamour* shoot. It took me a moment to realize why she was telling me—because we were real friends now, we were going to stay friends. I took her to the places I'd been taken, like Yamashiro, and shopping in Beverly Hills, and only part of the time did I imagine him seeing me on the town, happy.

I was even more excited to go back to New York for the AZ-KC launch, to see the results and Bernice. It was, in a word, an *event*. It didn't start with a party but a pre-party. Bernice and I had been given dresses and shoes from Azrian and Kimmi for the occasion—nothing that would spoil the launch. Bernice's dress was white, shaped like an upside-down triangle, pointed at the shoulders, then narrowing just below the hips, flanked by Azrian's signature sheer block panels. Her shoes were silver booties, made from the fur of an animal neither of us could guess. "Muppet, possibly," she whispered.

I was put in a tiny black mesh dress flecked with strategically placed three-dimensional shapes so as to leave something to the imagination. I held my arms just so in order to avoid injuring myself on the point of one of the shapes, a task made more complicated by my shoes, which were basically marble roller skates. There was a brake of sorts at the toe, which reminded me of a tooth. I tested it out in a hotel hallway while Bernice stood on guard to catch me if I rolled too quickly.

It was ridiculous, of course. But there was joy in it too. It was playful and silly and risky and everything I had learned the industry could be at its best. We were conduits of possibility.

We mingled at the pre-party for what felt like hours, champagne in hand. I laughed at terrible jokes, I pointed to my shoes when an unwanted touch seemed in the offing—*it's not me, I'd just roll away from you.* How wonderfully convenient.

And then Kimmi appeared. Dyed hair, thick glasses, dressed like a 1940s pinup girl. Classic to the point of camp. She rapped on her glass three times, then gestured toward the roof, where the true launch would take place.

Because of our footwear, Bernice and I had to take the elevator. Because we were moving slowly, we were beat out by magazine editors and fashion writers and other models and designers and the types whose sole job was to attend these parties. And because we were the last in the room, all eyes were on us when we saw the ads for the first time, blown up on stands across the rooftop bar: my feet and Bernice's face.

A couple photographs focused on both of our legs. And there were some full-length shots of her. I appeared from the thigh down in one. But my face had been cut out of it. All I was, it turned out, was legs.

Kimmi's shoes felt less like fun and more like punishment as I drifted out of the spotlight. I marbled my way across the roof-

THE COVER GIRL

top, feeling Harriet's eye on me and I desperately wanted to go to her, wanted to ask her what now. I should have known. But instead I was the girl who needed too much guidance, reassurance, help. The girl who, when given a choice, always chose wrong. I didn't want to be one of Harriet's Girls out of pity, and if I couldn't earn it—that was a thought I couldn't complete, not tonight. My body sank into the muscle memory. I plastered on a smile and agreed with everything: *Yes, I was in that shot. Yes, such an inventive perspective. Yes, so exciting. Yes, yes, yes.*

Once the initial buzz died down, I sought out Bernice. I had to—both for appearances and because I needed her to know that while I was not happy for me, I was happy for her. Of course I was jealous, how could I not be, but I had been in the shoot right next to her. I knew how talented she was, how hard she worked, and what would holding it against her change? My success was out of my control but our friendship wasn't. I finally caught her eye in a throng of people waiting to talk to her, and her face melted from excitement into concern. I shook my head—none of that. When we broke away, I told her the truth: she looked beautiful in the prints.

"I had no idea it was going to come out that way," she said.

No. She deserved this. She needed to enjoy it. I reached for her hand and whispered that she had something special, something we were all lucky to watch unfold. I meant it.

I slipped one time, when I made eye contact with Kimmi. I knew when she looked back at me with a forced little smile that she had been behind the decision. Someone I could hold it against. I'd had too many drinks by then; not drunk, but less careful than I could be. And I asked her what had happened.

"Nothing happened," she said, her voice tinged with an Eastern European accent. "They are beautiful photographs. You have beautiful legs. But your face, it is not interesting enough for high fashion, as much as Azrian wishes it were. You are very good for the Nair ads, though."

Perhaps with one more glass of champagne, I could have reminded her that she was not from another country, as much as she wished it were true. Everyone knew she was from Iowa. And it wasn't even Nair. We were, in fact, both uninteresting. But I was old enough at that point to have been called ugly and heavy and boring and all the other things that girls like me are told in casting for the simple fact that we had the temerity to believe the person who told us we could make a living off what we looked like. *Uninteresting.* She wasn't telling me anything my own mother hadn't already said.

I smiled thoughtfully and said that I understood, of course. And then I looked her up and down and noted the Chuck Taylors she was wearing with her dress. I complimented the *comfort* in her outfit, letting the word hang for the insult it was. *A smart choice*, I called it. I would not be undone by a woman who didn't even have the fortitude to stand in her own shoes.

I worked the room. I kept it together. I smiled when I noticed Harriet's eyes on me. And then I felt a hand on my wrist as Azrian appeared. "I wanted it to work," he whispered. I shook my head, held up a hand; there was no need to say anything. But he didn't want to leave it. "I was so excited for you to be part of this. You and Bernice are both so wonderful," he continued in that same low tone. "You got me a good deal of early attention, my dear, when you mentioned me in *Yes! You.* I wanted to repay the favor."

His soft words and searching look were going to be what broke me—like he thought there was something for me to forgive of him—and I knew I had to end the conversation before a photo was taken, before a tabloid ran something about a crying and jealous model. Because even though I was not interesting, two women pitted against each other always would be, no matter what the real story was. I did not tell him what I wanted, about my plan for a new beginning, my chance to do it all again. There would be no getting it right this time, not with mod-

THE COVER GIRL

eling. I was not going to be on the cover of *Vogue* or *Glamour* or *Elle* or *Cosmopolitan*. I was going to be legs. It was all I had.

And so, I squeezed Azrian's hand. There could not be any hard feelings, at least not in his direction. It was a business, after all, albeit a painful one. I thanked him for the opportunity. The campaign was bold. It would be successful. Bernice was wonderful. What could anyone say? It was not going to get my face out there, no, but I was still attached to it. They couldn't take that from me.

This is what I told him. This is what I told myself. This was the peace I made as I flew home to my secondary market where I belonged.

3

"One of the top-grossing touring acts of the 1970s is back with a new album that's all '80s—in all the wrong ways. Anyone who's anyone in the LA music scene knows that for every boundary-pushing new act on the Sunset Strip, there's five more bands relying on the style of big hair and cartoony makeup to cover up their complete lack of substance. And perhaps we shouldn't be surprised that the artist responsible for albums with titles like In and Out, Twice Bitten *and* Buckwild *is embracing this new trend, but let's be clear—the style isn't there either. The new album,* Go Down, *is overfilled with the type of songs that could have been jokes in* This Is Spinal Tap. *As the opening track lays out, he's older now but he 'ain't no wiser'—a sentiment that is clear throughout. Listeners will feel wiser for having skipped this one."*

I sipped my Perrier and turned the page.

4

I had my little jobs and my little West Hollywood apartment, and the music got harder to ignore. Every night, the parade of people going in and out of tiny clubs would unleash a blast of un-relenting rock at me, and when it wasn't that, it was screaming, catcalling, partying in the street. I tried earplugs. I tried going to bed earlier. I tried blasting disco records, the only sound that felt right in the face of too much. I thought about moving, but that meant either asking for help from Debi or Harriet or find-ing a place on my own, and I wasn't terribly interested in either option. Here, there was still a chance I'd run into the rock star.

It was also possible I was punishing myself.

Debi had the idea to get me into acting; I'd had the Swish commercials a few years back, after all. She put me in a class, the one she *sent all the girls to*. When I asked if Harriet approved, all she said was *sure*.

I soon learned that everything that made me successful—to whatever degree we assessed—as a model was the opposite of what I should do as an actor. The instructor was a man named Olin who had been in a television Western in the 1960s, one of those things that ran for years and years, and then nothing after that. This one experience informed everything, made him a fount of knowledge, especially about what he called *sense memory*.

It had to do with using real life, real memories, to make the experience deeper than just acting. Something like that, at least; the phrase alone made my mind wander. For me, sense memory was simply two words that didn't go together—where I had memories, there could be no sense.

For Olin, though, it was everything. We would never get anywhere, we would fail at our every desire, if we did not listen to his specific instructions on sense memory.

Perhaps he was the teacher of choice because these warnings were just a version of what we'd heard our entire careers—there are thousands of girls who want to be us, we are replaceable, we must always want it more than anyone else. As though I could possibly forget.

I attended five sessions. I did the unsettling mask work, barely looking at the frozen plaster faces around me. I did the even more unsettling massage train, which required us to sit in a circle and rub each other's shoulders for reasons I could not comprehend—to build trust? To relax? Because he wanted to blend his own touch in? I pretended to remember a time when I was cold, sick, scared, and how it felt, while I was really planning how to describe the class to Bernice.

And then he gave me a monologue from Shakespeare. *Romeo and Juliet*. I may have read it with a tutor years ago, but I hadn't retained it. When the others delivered their monologues, I let the words wash over me while the meaning itself didn't come close to sinking in. When I did mine, I knew I wasn't doing more than reciting lines.

"Stop!" Olin shouted. "Where's the feeling? Where's the emotion?"

I asked if I should start again, knowing it was the wrong question but not sure what the right one was—his response differed every time.

THE COVER GIRL

247

"No, you shouldn't start again! You should *remember*." When I stared at him, my face asking *remember what*, he took a different tactic. "Why are you here?"

Because Debi wanted me to be there. Because I had failed at other things. Because I was in my twenties now—early still, but twenties all the same—and I was very aware that my modeling career had an expiration date and this one might last a little longer. I settled on a neutral summary: to gain experience.

"Okay. Fine. And to this point, you've had experiences, right? A girl like you, you've been in love, right?" I nodded. "And what did it feel like?"

I stiffened, a slight movement that did not escape him. "Oh!" He laughed, turning to the class. "Do you see that? We've hit a nerve. Sense memory! Whatever is giving you that reaction, you must bring it to Juliet. She is in love and afraid. Inhabit her. Make her your own. *Feel it*."

What was I feeling? The memories I tortured myself with every day. The rush of driving into a cornfield with the rock star. The weight of his arm on me at night. The thrill of being chosen, the private view of him performing from the wings of the stage. The way he called me Little Bird. How he always wanted me. How special and beautiful I felt. I delivered the monologue again, and again was stopped halfway through.

"You're still holding back, Birdie. You have to *excavate*." He made a motion with his arms like he was lifting something heavy. "It's just words otherwise. Find your sense memory. What are you drawing from here? What are you afraid of?"

I didn't realize this was an actual question and not part of his show until he repeated it expectantly. I whispered that I didn't know.

"Nothing? You're afraid of nothing? You have all the answers?"

Everything felt closer to the truth. Fine. I told him *failure*.

"That's just a concept. Come on. What are you afraid of?"

I could not respond, and the harder I could not respond, the more he questioned until he was yelling the words at me. "Come on, there's not a right answer. The first thing that comes to mind. *What are you afraid of?*"

I was so broken down from the yelling, from the chipping away at whatever protection remained, that I couldn't stop what he was trying to get me to feel from hitting me. And at last I yelled back. I hadn't yelled in so long that the force of my voice was almost painful. I yelled that I was afraid I'd made a mistake in leaving. Another wrong choice. That I would always regret it. That I'd given up too much for reasons that didn't even feel real anymore. That I was so good at forgetting the things that hurt me, but this I could not forget, and because I didn't want to, I was afraid I would.

It was two people onstage at that moment—the girl screaming her secrets and me, horrified at the loss of control. Horrified by these thoughts that I had known existed but had taken such care to push down as deeply as possible.

Olin lowered his head in a slight bow. "Thank you. Proceed."

I read Juliet's words again. A girl in a love that no one understood. Of course.

My voice cracked as I recited the lines, as I summoned up the courage to keep standing there after laying my soul bare. It was probably not what Shakespeare had been going for but it was at least something. Olin assumed it was acting and applauded me; I let him.

When we paused for a break, I went home, still shaking, trying to pack down the fear that had been unearthed.

And then I called Debi and told her I had gotten what I could out of this class, and she could send me on auditions now. Whatever she had in mind for me wasn't Shakespeare. We both knew I just needed to not be so bad that it would distract anyone from looking at me. And that wouldn't require any further excavation of sense memories.

THE COVER GIRL

★ ★ ★

It worked well enough. I did bit parts on soap operas—a date on *All My Children*, a student nurse on *General Hospital*.

Bernice was on the cover of *Vogue*.

But success did not mean ease. We would go out whenever she was in town and sometimes she'd call me long distance in the middle of the night from New York or Paris because I'd be up. While I knew pressure accompanied accomplishments like hers, I learned that for Bernice there were pressures I couldn't fully understand.

"Did I earn *Vogue*?" she asked over the phone one night, her voice softer and more unsure than I'd heard it before.

I started to tell her not to be silly, but that wasn't what she was asking, what she needed to hear. Instead, I told her that I had known since Paris if she wanted this life, she was going to be a star. Anyone who didn't find her deserving just wanted to make her smaller. And then the real question: What had brought this on?

Bernice explained there were people, even girls she worked with, who felt it was appropriate to say that the only reason she got the cover was because the magazine just wanted to feature a Black model. "Someone said I had less competition, so it was easier for me than it would be for her," she said. "Never mind that I found out she was making twice the hourly rate I was on the same job."

There were also letters threatening to cancel subscriptions, which she hadn't known until a journalist casually and callously tossed off a question about it, like it was something she, Bernice, should have an answer for. And even in the moments she was able to fully celebrate, there was the knowledge that a young girl was going to see her cover like she had seen Beverly Johnson's ten years before—something wonderful, but also a responsibility to live up to.

There was a lot I did not know, but I could tell by the change in her tone that it wasn't insignificant for Bernice to share this with me. And maybe I was glorified scenery at work, but in life I could be a presence on the other end of the phone line.

On my last day at *General Hospital*, one of the doctors asked me if I'd like to go on a date with him, and I laughed, and then I realized he was serious and I had to apologize. What I said was I had not been on a date in a long time.

"That can't be possible," he said. "Look at you." So easy to assume one thing connected to the other.

It was, in fact, possible. I had not been on a date since I left the Malibu house. I had not thought about men other than the rock star in that time, and because I had so deeply not thought about other men in a romantic way, I'd wondered if I wanted to think about women instead, since I knew some girls who did. But no, not that either.

There was nothing wrong with the doctor-actor, whose name was Wesley. He was polite. I wasn't quite sure how old he was— older than me but not by too much. He was handsome in a generic, strong-jawline, chin-dimple, floppy-parted-hair, have-her-home-by-ten kind of way. He kept his hands to himself and looked the other actresses in the eye instead of the chest. He was a helpful scene partner, whispering to me the meaning of certain camera terms or what it meant to cheat my body to the left. I was not sure how long we could sustain a conversation, but I could prepare a few questions should it lag.

I could do worse for a date.

The moment in the acting class had unnerved me, as was Olin's intention. Though no one knew what I was talking about when I screamed what I was afraid of, the fact that I knew what I meant was enough. I wasn't sure I could get over the fear, but what I could do was cover it up.

So I told Wesley yes. I curled my hair and put on a surplice-cut pink dress and flat shimmery pearl sandals, and I let him pick me up at my little apartment and take me to Spago.

And it was fine. I ordered a chopped salad, wondering briefly what Harriet would make of the size of the dice. Wesley got the roasted salmon, and we split a bottle of sauvignon blanc. When he asked me a question, I answered as vaguely as I could—*Connecticut, for a while, since I was a teenager*—while still seeming personable and then deflected it back to him.

The restaurant was still crowded when we left, my hand on the arm he offered. We were just another actor and model taking advantage of our glamorous lives.

And then a few people in front of me shifted to the right and a few others shifted to the left. A literal crowd parting, though it would not have looked as dramatic as that to anyone else.

But seeing the rock star standing at the entrance to the restaurant would not have meant the same thing to anyone else.

Of course he wasn't alone. That wasn't the point.

It had been more than three years. Three years since I'd last seen him, been held by him, heard my name in his voice, and there he stood like nothing at all had changed.

He had the decency to freeze when he saw me, or maybe everything looked frozen because I was. I had been waiting for this moment for so long, and then to have it happen the first time I let myself consider the possibility of letting someone else in.

Perhaps I should have done it sooner.

"Birdie? Are you okay?" Wesley asked when he realized I was no longer keeping pace. "You look like you've seen a ghost."

No, no, the only ghost in this room was the one in the mirror. I turned to Wesley and smiled, clutching closer as I assured him I was fine. I hoped the rock star was looking, could see me happy, assured.

Let him see a life so bright that he ached to feel its warmth shine on him again. Let him remember.

Wesley drove me home, and when he pulled up in front of

my building, he asked to see some of my photos. I knew enough to know that if I said yes to this, it would also be construed as saying yes to more.

And while there was something romantic in saving myself for a reconciliation with the rock star, as a model I also knew that my desirability was linked to others finding me desirable. What had Harriet said about the exclusive contract?

They'll do more to get you once they think they can't have you.

So I watched Wesley flip through my portfolios, marveling at the most basic shots. "You're so young," he kept saying. "How have you done this much?"

I laughed, hoping it sounded tinkly and flirtatious. I told him I wasn't that young, that I'd been working for almost ten years at this point.

"It took me so long to break into this business," he said. "You must be very talented."

It felt too honest to tell him that I felt like I was still breaking into it too, and also unfair, since I had gotten a role on the same show as him with five classes and a gentle audition. So instead I offered him a glass of champagne, the only alcohol I kept on hand and only for when Bernice was in town.

I uncorked the bottle, and it fizzed up over my hand down the front of my dress. I watched Wesley follow the line of foam, not without appreciation.

It was both easier and harder than I thought it would be. I didn't particularly want to have sex with him, but I wanted to want to and I wanted to be wanted. And mostly, I knew I couldn't show myself to the rock star again if I stayed preserved in glass.

Wesley didn't pressure me; he kept asking if it was alright to kiss me, touch me, unzip my dress. This could be happening with someone much worse. But it had also been so long since anyone had tried to learn my body. I wasn't prepared for it to

THE COVER GIRL 253

feel so different with someone else, even after all that time. It was more fumbling than exciting, and every time I thought I knew what to do, it wasn't what he was expecting. And the thing about being professionally attractive was I felt like there was an expectation that I should be amazing at sex, that every part of me should feed the senses in some way. This was a weight I had not felt before.

In the end, he got where he needed to go and I did not but pretended to because I knew there was no way I could give up that particular vulnerability, not now, not yet.

"Is it true you hadn't been on a date in a long time?" Wesley asked when it was over. His tone was teasing, like he thought it was a fib to make myself look shyer or harder to get.

I thought about playing along but instead I told him the truth: three years.

"That's not possible," he said, just like he had when I first told him.

And so I explained that it was. That I had been with someone for a very long time and we'd needed a break, and then the break had extended, and here I was.

"What, were you sixteen when you got with this guy?"

His tone fell somewhere between disbelief and like this was all very funny, look at these young girls and how seriously they take everything, and before I knew it, I let the word *fifteen* fall out of my mouth.

"Ah, young love," he said.

The dismissal in his voice. In that moment, I hated him. I hated the way he was speaking to me, the way he thought he knew my life better than I did, the way he was so comfortable brushing off my experiences into something small and cute and manageable. And so I corrected him—no, not young love. I was younger, sure. But he was probably the same age as Wesley was now. He was, is, quite famous. He was good to me. The words coming so fast, unstoppable, as Wesley sat up and started gathering his clothes.

"Jesus, Birdie. I have a fifteen-year-old niece. No grown man should be sniffing around her. Who let that happen?"

I was closer to this niece's age than his own, and here he was. My words were icy when I reminded him I was not that niece. That I was different. My life had been different.

"No shit," Wesley said.

I thanked him for dinner without leaving my bed, keeping my voice flat. There was a lot he could say about me at the end of this night, but he couldn't tell anyone I was impolite. And then I lay back, and I waited for the person I wanted to hear from to call me, to remind me of what we were and what we had shared and how different it truly was. Beyond what anyone else could understand.

5

It was mind over matter or destroy everything, and I did not believe in the *or*. I woke up in my bed. I woke up alone in hotel rooms. I woke up in other people's beds. I woke up in so many different beds that I stopped counting, and there were plenty of times where I didn't make it to bed at all, where a bar bathroom or someone's pool house or the pool itself worked just fine. I woke up with a urinary tract infection. I woke up next to the British heavy metal singer who'd once thought I needed help. I did a shoot and I could have woken up next to Benj Boudreaux, but it would have been a reminder of a power I no longer held. I woke up a day later and I woke up with a bloody nose and I woke up when science would say I should not have.

I needed my body to belong to something or someone, and it wasn't going to be me.

I saw pictures of him in the tabloids, in and out of the Rainbow and the clubs that lined my neighborhood, and I had to face the music. By that, I mean I had to step outside my apartment and walk the length of the block that separated me and the Sunset Strip and tip my face toward the neon glow and let the actual music hit me. I could not avoid this loud, showy, guitar-heavy rock any longer; it was right there outside my door, and it could bring me closer.

Video killed the radio star. Video revived the not-ever-actually-a-modeling-star.

On a rare call with Harriet—my fault, other music I was avoiding facing—she expressed her displeasure with me taking these music video jobs, rolling around on beds with bands. She wasn't prepared for me to ask what she didn't like about it. What was the worst that could happen? Like it hadn't already.

Video kept me in the almost place, the *haven't I seen you* place, the place where his name was never more than two degrees of separation away from mine. I was the face of a song about love and the body of a song about fucking. When I went out, I looked to the past, looking for him.

I went to shows I wasn't interested in for the sole purpose of being visible. I wondered if I would feel called by the bending wail of a guitar solo, but that had been a different place—big arenas, restricted wings, a concert just for me. Now I went to tiny clubs along with throngs of other girls.

Brooke Shields went to Princeton.

Sometimes I saw the blonde punk girl, the one who thought I didn't belong, who thought we were so different. Her hair hung straight to her waist now, and she was always alone, always holding would-be suitors or friends at arm's length. She saw me too, but she always looked through me. I wondered if this was also a phase. I wondered if it felt as long ago for her as it did for me. Long ago and somehow also yesterday. The only way I ever experienced time in those days, and I didn't think it was just the Quaaludes or the coke.

It was a truly strange scene, all these girls falling over themselves and each other for bands that I would learn did not have record deals, let alone records. Bands who hadn't yet been on tour and instead hopped around the city and maybe the state.

And it wasn't just the blonde punk girl.

One night, I ran into Lulu—*Lulu!*—at the Whisky. My instinct was to pretend I hadn't seen her, but I didn't look away in time. She threw her arms in the air and screamed, like this was some kind of gleeful reunion, and I didn't know what to do with my body as she hugged me, couldn't make my arms do anything more than lift and fall. "Which one is yours?" she asked, nodding her head toward the stage. When I said none of them, she gave me a Cheshire grin. "Me too, but that'll change after tonight."

I didn't ask about Beasley or the children; it was not my world and not my concern if she wanted to be out here tonight. Undeterred by my discomfort over this clashing of old life and new, she continued on, telling me who was a good lay and pointing out the girls she knew by sight, the ones she saw at every show. For every big-haired guitarist, there were at least five girls willing to hold the hair spray, and it seemed to me like a recipe for disaster. It seemed to me going down this road at all would be a recipe for disaster. I didn't even know if she heard me as I said I had to go and faded away. I was a recipe of my own making.

Every day was a fight against the clock, the question of how much longer I could do this before I would be too old. No matter that I still looked young for my age; it didn't change the fact that I was almost twenty-five, and there was too much proof to lie. I didn't make it, Harriet! Maybe it was because I picked Cameo and I picked LA, or maybe it was because I wasn't good enough. It didn't matter. Every door I'd walked through had been the wrong one. I'd missed the boat, but I was going to keep running for it until she told me it was over for good.

The idea of what could be next sat next to me on the couch like a polite dog. I could feed and water it, but it existed fully as its own entity.

I did another day player part on a fledgling soap called *Sunset Nights*, sleepwalking through the whole thing, but apparently I was good enough for Paula, one of the supporting actresses, to ask me to substitute for a class she taught at a hip new acting studio. That or I just happened to be at the right place at the right time, which I'd learned is really how anything happens in this town, even things one has no business doing. What I had was bit parts in soap operas and failed pilots, several commercials where all I had to do was speak a tagline convincingly enough. Who would be silly enough to think I had anything to teach them? Who would possibly pay for that?

"Nineteen-year-old girls from Kansas," said Paula.

It was an unsettling economy.

The class was focused on movement and improvisation. Paula gave me a book, and I memorized some exercises. Walking the class through them felt like the boldest acting performance I'd given to date, but none of them were really concerned about me as long as I offered affirmative feedback, which I did, even for the ones who were truly terrible.

I thought about my own foray into being an acting student, and what I had not needed at the time was being yelled at and prodded into giving something up. What I had needed was anything else. I could be kind for a couple hours. The world would be hard enough on them later.

It was an easy enough night's work and I didn't think about it again until three months later, when Paula called and told me she was going to have a baby, a fact she had managed to conceal for an impressive length of time. The students had liked me. Would I want to cover the next eight weeks?

Want was a strong word but still I said yes—there was something vaguely thrilling about securing work without Debi or Harriet being involved, even if it was work I wasn't qualified for. The entire enterprise was remarkably cynical in a way that I felt oddly comforted by. This was what we were: people who looked right convincing more naive people that they too can one day look right.

THE COVER GIRL

259

For weeks, I entered the studio space in the evenings, runway-walking through rows of girls whose hair colors came from chemicals, who looked to me like coked-up babies, who trusted me for no reason other than I stood at the front of the room, who said they wanted to be me and maybe really did, but not in the way they thought. What I found was that my moving like a model enchanted them, and if I enchanted them enough, it didn't matter that the whole thing was an elaborate performance.

They were, after all, going to have to figure that part out.

I developed a habit—not the drug kind, though also kind of, maybe. But after days of moving in double time, a string of jobs and auditions and go-sees followed by parties or product launches or clubs followed by barhopping, I would crash. It wasn't the cocaine or the pills or the lack of sleep or the barely adequate nutrition. Or it wasn't only that. Mostly, it was the being on, and I would reach a point where I would have to turn myself off. I'd pretend to be too busy for everything, and then I would sit on my tiny balcony with a wineglass filled with Perrier and listen to the world around me and tune everything else out. I didn't even look at *Vogue* or any of the other magazines splashed with girls who had started their careers after me. I just was.

The one thing on this earth that I had claimed for myself was a love of mineral water, and no, I did not wish to do any *excavation work* regarding my attachment to something so minimal, so adjacent to necessity.

One day, as I tipped my little green bottle to refill my glass, it occurred to me that this was the answer. I could call Harriet and ask her to help me land a Perrier spot. Cosmetics and high fashion hadn't worked out, but that didn't mean I couldn't be the face of something. The actual face, not just the legs.

And: Perrier had been my thing on the second tour. It was on the rider. What better way to recapture his attention than to hold a cold bottle on a billboard, in a magazine, on a television. To be as inescapable as the memory.

260   Amy Rossi

I was content to give away as much of myself as people would take. I knew enough from commercial work that a product is never a product—it's a lifestyle, it's a promise, it's the thing that could unlock all your desires. Or it could be the funnel into which you poured your meaning. And I could be a Perrier girl.

Drinking this bottle, I considered myself the picture of health. How charming that my actual vice was water. Everything else was just part of public life, even when I took it to excess.

Then I saw the tabloid.

Of course there were other women. There had been other women while we were together. They were strangers mostly, shadow women who existed on the edges, just present enough to darken the path forward. This wide-eyed, skittery teenage girl in front of the Whisky, hand in hand with the rock star in that tabloid, wasn't any more or less a stranger, but seeing her unleashed a flood inside me. She looked like one of those girls from somewhere else in the silly class I taught—searching, skirting the edge of desperate, hungry for someone to tell her what to do.

In the flood of humiliation and sadness, other feelings popped up, feelings about this teenager occupying what had been my space—was she different too?—and I had to push the thought away like it was something physical. A dresser that had to be moved. One in a list of feelings I could not give in to right now.

Instead, I told myself it was a sign. The photo was taken in front of the Whisky, where I hung out sometimes, an easy walk from my flat. If he was sleeping with girls whose paths crossed with my own, we were closer to running into each other. And perhaps it was even deeper, more intentional—a sign that he had been looking for me, even when settling for lesser versions. What I needed to do was ready myself.

And I was able to hold on to that for a few days. I probably could have made it longer, maybe even made it through, except when I went to a show for a band I wasn't interested in for

THE COVER GIRL

the purposes of being seen and also running into him, instead, I ran into the big-eyed tabloid girl.

I ordered the stupidest drink imaginable. Bright. Sweet to the point of being nearly chewy. Nothing I would ever let cross my lips.

And truly, there was no need for me to throw this drink at the tabloid girl except that seeing her made me feel something I did not want to feel. And I needed to feel something else.

Her response: "What did I do?" Not angry, but honestly asking, assuming I had a good reason. There's the age when you think it's all your fault, and the age when you refuse to believe it is.

I couldn't tell her the answer was both *nothing* and *everything*, and as I turned to walk away, I could hear her trying to explain to an onlooker. "I don't know, I went home with this singer, and it turned out he was engaged. Maybe that's his fiancée?"

Engaged.

Engaged.

Somewhere there was a woman who read gossip rags or didn't, who knew what was involved in yoking her life to a rock star or didn't. Whatever she did or did not know, she was the one who had the right to throw drinks, to scream, to fall.

I caused nothing short of a scene. People encircled me and the girl, itching for a fight, but the humiliation I felt as I sank to the floor was not from my outburst or the stares, but the realization burning through my body like the spark of two twigs catching fire: all this waiting and all this time, it was really over.

He was not going to come back for me.

What I did was: I went home. I went back to my apartment. I did not seek out drugs, booze, a man to fuck it away.

Engaged. I let the word repeat over and over again. I poked at it and let the pain fill me like a toothache. I was not, had not been, would not be enough.

And then I let it grow. Because this was what had been cooking all along, wasn't it?

I wasn't enough for him. I wasn't enough to be a successful model. Whatever I had was an illusion. Something to reel people in and then repel them when they saw me close-up. After all, my closest friend was someone I spoke to a few times a year and saw even less frequently. After all, Harriet. Full sentence. I wasn't who she thought I was, who she wanted me to be, and so she more or less turned me over to Debi, did she not? Like my parents turned me over to him. Could I even blame them at this point?

Fuck.

The last time I let myself acknowledge the truth in all of this was when I had slashed my arm with the glass, and even though what I'd wanted to do back then was make a scene, at this exact moment, I just wanted that version of Birdie to have finished the job. To have avoided this. No downfall, just potential I had never been given the chance to fulfill.

It wasn't like I didn't have sleeping pills.

But I knew myself. I would probably find a way to mess it up, take enough to hurt myself, and then I'd have to live with the consequences. And it wasn't like I had a rock star boyfriend this time to send me to a fancy not-a-hospital to get some rest. Or if I did figure it out, someone would still have to find me. And, oh, my god, what if they didn't? Or, what if they did and they saw the stupid tabloid still lying in my apartment and they put it all together and figured out what I had done and why and then he found out? The thought of dying and him knowing that I still cared enough to be hurt by him after all this time was more humiliating than I could bear, and I was already testing the boundaries of humiliation.

Engaged. To fucking *whom*.

I opened my refrigerator. Three grapefruits. Lettuce, cucumbers. Celery. Hard-boiled egg whites, the temptation of yolks

THE COVER GIRL

already thrown away. Eleven bottles of Perrier. I opened one and tipped it to my mouth, no glass needed. I would never be a Perrier girl, never be able to drink it again, because when I did, I would think about the rider and what his stupid fiancée would want.

Not even water was safe.

I drank faster and the carbonation was a rush and then a burn, the bubbles transforming from a pleasant tingle into something that seared my throat on the way down.

It hurt, so I drank faster.

Here's a fact: not since I became a model and probably before—because just imagine my mother tolerating such a thing—had I burped in any manner other than mouth closed and behind a napkin. But what did it matter anymore?

I burped open-mouthed and loudly and it felt absolutely disgusting, but pleasingly so. That I could even go there. I finished the bottle but it was not enough. There were ten more cold glass reminders sitting there. So I opened a second, forced myself to chug. Forced myself to open up to the pain, because wasn't that what all pleasure would eventually, inevitably become? Might as well skip right to it. The third bottle. Water dribbled down my chin, splashed on the floor, dripped down the front of my dress. I did not care. The fourth. I coughed, I burped, I sputtered. The ends of my hair were wet. It was a miracle, what the body could do, the buildup of pressure and the release of a burp, so tidy, so predictable. Nothing else worked that way. Five. Six. My entire front was soaked now, and I couldn't stop coughing, but also I could not stop. I had a fucking purpose. Seven. I dragged the back of my hand across my mouth like it even mattered and continued on. My stomach felt distended; there couldn't possibly be room for more, but I would find a way. Eight. Three to go and it was a challenge. But when had I ever backed down from a challenge?

I almost laughed out loud at the thought. When had I not!

But not this time.

Nine.

I was dizzy, gulping air in between drinks. I opened the last two together, took one in each fist, and I poured them into my mouth. Some of it went into my nose, more spilled onto my body, the floor. But I had drunk them all.

And then I hiccupped and my stomach turned, and when I vomited eleven bottles of Perrier across the kitchen, it was as cold and fizzy coming up as it had been going down.

6

It had been a long time since I'd picked up the phone to hear a clipped voice tell me to please hold for Azrian de Popa. But I held.

"Birdie," he said. "I need you to come walk for me. In New York."

When was the last time I had walked a runway? A question that did not require an answer; the need to ask it said it all.

What I did now was mostly commercials for pantyhose, razors, shaving cream—not me, just pieces—and bit parts in soaps or made-for-TV movies every now and then. The occasional woman in the back of a fitness home video. Enough to finally make it just a job, to detach from it in the same way I imagined I would if I worked in an office doing whatever women who work in offices do. Enough to make it sound special when I talked to the students in Paula's class, which is still how I thought of it even though she never took it back over after she had her baby and somehow the studio kept giving me a Wednesday night section.

I tried to sound neutral as I reminded Azrian who I was now. It wasn't that I couldn't walk for him, just that I wasn't her anymore. I had let that part of me go.

266   Amy Rossi

There was a lengthy pause on his end. "I think you can make an exception."

Of course I could; for him, there would always be an exception. The fact that he was calling me instead of going through Harriet or Debi meant something. The fact that he was calling at all when our paths had barely crossed since the AZ-KC debacle held meaning too. I asked what the occasion was.

"It's my funeral."

His tone was matter of fact; he did not have to say more. I called a travel agent as soon as we hung up and then I lay back down and waited for the tears to come.

This was what those days were like.

High fashion or commercial, AIDS hit our world hard. Few people called it that, though, called it what it was. You'd hear someone was sick and hear the weight in that word. You'd get your hair or makeup done, get styled, and try not to question if the person doing it looked thinner than he had when you saw him six months ago. And then on the next job you'd hear the news. One loss after another. Joe MacDonald. Way Bandy. Perry Ellis. Chester Weinberg. Models, designers, makeup artists, photographers, hair stylists. And while the names were mostly men, it wasn't all. I read about Gia Carangi in the newspaper, and a few weeks later, Harriet called me, signaling just how serious the matter was. It sounded like she was reading from a hastily prepared script as she explained that this wasn't about the dangers of drug use—we knew all that and they knew we were going to do what we were going to do but also if we were going to do what we were going to do, we must avoid needles at all costs. In a desperate attempt to keep her on the phone, I'd assured her I preferred swallowing and snorting, but the conversation was, of course, much bigger than that.

It was profoundly strange to pack for New York like I would for any job, my suitcase an organized grid of shoes, fashionable dresses, cosmetics, and underthings. I considered calling Harriet to tell her I was coming, like I normally would. I selected an outfit for the return flight, tucked a magazine in my bag like I normally did. Then I started to cry because I wasn't sure anything should ever feel normal again.

I pulled my portfolio off the shelf while I waited for my taxi. My first fashion show, the clothes that had been put together at the last minute. Outtakes from the AZ-KC campaign. The Paris walk in the wedding dress that Azrian had suggested I keep. I wished I had. Or: I wished that it didn't need to matter. I could see a progression in these photos, a rehearsed calm in the early ones giving way to simmering havoc in the Paris pictures. Azrian had been there at every turning point, and I hoped I could give something back to him.

Backstage was a who's who—who was now and who had been and who could have been but never was. It was a reunion of sorts, and emotions hit like a wave—the excitement about seeing someone you hadn't seen in ages would crest forward, only to pull back as we remembered the occasion.

Bernice fell into the *now*; she was on her way to becoming one of the most successful models in the country. Max Factor ads. Spots for GUESS and Ralph Lauren. In negotiations for a major designer perfume, with covers in America and across Europe. She was in such elite air at this show that there was a buffer around her, as much as one could be in a crowded backstage.

I wondered if it would be different for us here, but when we caught eyes across the room, I knew I had been invited in.

"I tried calling you! I wasn't sure you'd be here!" she said, pulling me into a hug. "I'm so glad you are. It wouldn't be right without you."

It had been too long since I'd seen her or talked to her, all my doing. She found the time to call me and I always intended to call back but didn't, inert with the knowledge that I wasn't worthy of her friendship, especially not recently. Like everyone else, she would soon figure out that I was not who she thought I was, that I could not live up to initial impressions, and our friendship would fade. I didn't see the point in delaying that process.

It was easy enough to feel that way when she was traveling, but not while she was hugging me—not the thin-armed air pat that most girls favored, but a real hug with the kind of warmth and meaning I hadn't felt in so long, if ever. I found myself whispering tearful apologies against her shoulder.

"Sh. I know," Bernice said.

I believed her. There wasn't time for more—she had to make a call and I needed to prepare. For the show, for what was next. For all of it.

It was hard not to think of our first show as I found a place to get ready. In fact, I was pretty sure I'd just walked by the girl who had fallen in the slippery shoes. Every girl here was someone Azrian had worked with in the past. The number of models who showed up to walk in this show was evidence that he was cherished by many. For me, our relationship was special not for its depth but for its longevity. The decade I had known him was as long as I had known anyone, other than Harriet. When I saw him, I saw the pompadour and the missing shoes from that first fashion show. He saw the girl who named him her favorite designer in a magazine interview. What we were to each other was the past. How deeply unfair it was that he was not going to get a future.

The clothes were all finished this time, a mix of greatest hits and new creations, like the column dress I had been given, no back, the top constructed in a series of tight silvery black coils that gave way to black hot pants covered by a sheer, narrow slitted skirt. It hadn't occurred to me at the time, because I was still new to the scene, how young Azrian must have been at that first show, barely out of his teens. And he had done all that.

I felt a hand on my wrist as I assumed my position for places.

I had tried to prepare myself for what it might be like to see

THE COVER GIRL

Azrian. He was not the first person with AIDS I had known, but still, it was a jolt to see him so thin and frail. I wrapped my arms around him because there was nothing else I could offer. We were supposed to grow up together. And so I said the only words that seemed appropriate: I thanked him for everything. It wouldn't have been the same without him. My voice caught in my throat before I could finish the sentence.

He raised his hands to my face. "Sweet Birdie." We stood like that for a moment, my own hands over his. And then: "Don't be angry with me for saying this. I know it has not gone as it could have for you. But you would have an easier time if you realized what the worst thing that happened to you really was."

Of course I couldn't be angry at him, not with so much else to be angry about. And I couldn't be angry with him because I had no idea what he meant. There were so many girls, so many years—maybe he'd confused me with someone else.

It didn't matter; I didn't want to let him go. The thought that this could be the last conversation we had brought fresh tears to my eyes, and he held up a hand. "No crying. We already did that photo in Paris. Don't make me look boring."

An assistant walked by and motioned for me to tip my head back as she blotted my eyes. As if he could ever be boring.

After we were properly lined up and before the show began, Azrian stood on a box in the center of the backstage area. "Thank you for being part of this night," he said. "This virus, it is not something I have control of. I cannot control what it does to me, what it has already done to my friends and peers and lovers. I cannot control how or when it will kill me. The only thing I can control right now is how I live. And tonight, my dears, we are going to live fiercely and passionately and ferociously. This is a celebration. I have had my anger and my sadness and my pain. I will have more. But tonight, we celebrate. When you walk down that runway, all I want is for you to walk with joy and pride and life. Whatever that means to you. We are all we have."

This was the only truth.

Proud. Passionate. Ferocious. I stepped onto the runway and into another world. One where we were celebrating Azrian with no *because* other than his brilliance. One where there was no way to do this wrong. I paused to let the slit of the skirt open, to reveal the full length of my leg, one arm up, one down to draw attention to the garment. When I hit the end of the runway, I stopped to shimmy and pulse my hips to the beat of the blasting French punk music. I laughed. And when I turned to walk back, passing the next model, she reached out and we high-fived. Joy. Life. Finding our fire.

The final walk became a dance. The first two girls started it, and the rest of us joined in, clapping our hands above our heads, as we step-step-swiveled down the runway.

And then Azrian came out and the whole place erupted, everyone on their feet, and we hoisted him onto our shoulders because he was already the biggest thing in the room. The ovation lasted for minutes. It could have lasted forever. I looked up at his face, shimmering with both tears and laughter, and I tried to memorize it.

It was the most beautiful thing I had ever seen.

I couldn't sleep when I got back. Usually I found myself on the balcony when I was restless, but that night I found myself in the car.

Lately, I'd started driving out to Malibu. I never had before the rock star's wedding announcement. I thought about my neediness and coldness while I sat there staring at that house on its hill against the cliffs. The new owners had installed curtains so you couldn't see in anymore, though I bet they had nothing to hide. That's how it goes, right? He never hung drapes because we were hiding in plain sight. I parked in a slice of dark and imagined who lived there now. What might they see when they looked into the glass? I wondered whether my ghost lurked behind them when they wiped the fog off the bathroom mirror. They could take out the carpet and replace the countertops, but that didn't change the fact that I'd bled all over that floor. All we did was throw stones in that glass house. What did they do in there now?

By *the new owners*, I mean him and his wife. By *now* I mean forever.

Did it matter who she was? No. A woman, okay? Just a regular-pretty woman who, according to the gossip magazine I'd found the story in, was twenty-eight. It might have been easier if she had been an actress or singer or tennis player. Or maybe it would be harder if she were more successful than me. I felt small and stupid for coming out to the house, but that was better than sad.

I took a handful of sleeping pills when I got home, and when I woke up, I was done. I needed to go anywhere else, do anything else, and that's exactly what I told the girls in my class: fuck all of this, the pretending, the trying to stay relevant, the drugs, the music, the being on someone's arm in a magazine. None of it matters. They applauded when I finished. I wondered how long they stayed there, sitting on the floor, waiting for me to come back, still thinking it was a performance.

Azrian was going to die. He was not alone. We were losing a generation of talent, of vision and verve, yes, but more than that, we were losing *people*. For every Azrian, how many were there who were not famous, who were not given a loving tribute in a terrifying time? He was a brilliant designer but if he weren't, it would still be a tragedy. I thought about the night we spent dancing at Paradise Garage, the runway to the glory of the dance floor, and wondered how many of the people we danced next to were gone too soon. I didn't know what I was going to do, who to even write a check to, but I knew I couldn't stay in this same little apartment and wish for things to be different for myself when there was so much suffering.

It was time for a change. Perhaps it had been for a while now. Perhaps Harriet had been waiting for me to notice since AZ-KC, had given me the pieces so I could put the picture together and see what looked back.

I picked up the phone before I could talk myself out of it. Part of me wanted to be petty and call Debi first, but this was too big for me to be that small. Therese didn't put me right through, though, and I almost hung up five times before I heard Harriet's voice. And then I made myself say the words: I was going to retire.

"Are you sure?"

When I said yes, it was a lie. But it was something. It was movement.

She was quiet for a moment, and for that moment, I was fifteen again, wanting her approval, advice, affection. Did I want her to talk me out of it? I wouldn't have believed her, but also, of course. Did I want her to ask me why? But she already knew, and would I have given her an honest answer if she'd asked? In her silence, I became acutely aware that this could be the last time we spoke. That this could be its own breakup call and all the more devastating. What she said could set the tone for whatever happened next.

But all she did was sigh. "Oh, Birdie. I do hope you'll stay in touch. And you were beautiful at Azrian's show."

I didn't know she'd seen me.

Two weeks later, Azrian was gone. There was a sliver of news in the *Los Angeles Times* arts section. Maybe more in the New York paper. Nothing that could have come close to capturing what he did. Who he was.

A week after that, I left California, left modeling, left waiting for crowds to part so the rock star and I could find each other again. It took six years to say goodbye, and I was the only one who heard it.

In the window seat, the only thing between me and thirty thousand feet of sky was fingerprint-mottled plastic. I could sit back as instructed. I could rip myself open in flight. And as I closed my eyes, it occurred to me: *cloud* and *could* were almost the same word.

2018

Bernice and I have a phone date, one that was already on our calendars before I texted her about the invitation. She gives me an opening to bring up the gala and when I don't, she tells me about the college tours she's taking her daughter, Antoinette, on, as though the child could possibly be old enough for that, and about the terrible game show she had been invited to host.

"I mean, I know they'll make anything into a show now. We've gone far past throwing spaghetti at the wall to see what sticks," she says. "But I did not walk the runway for Oscar de la Renta only to become someone who gets on television and says the words *booty points* and *doody points*." The level of disgust in her voice sends me over the edge and she soon follows. "Okay, okay," she says as we catch our breath. "How are you with everything?"

I know she means Harriet, but I instead tell her about Bobby's visit and the Getty, about the vitamin shoot with Sunny, all the details she had about this job we did in New Orleans and me not remembering a one.

"Were you messing with her?" Bernice asks. "You really had no idea what she was talking about?"

When I tell her I really don't think so, all she does is make a small *hm* sound. "Well, since you're going to make me ask, have you thought more about this Harriet business?" she asks. "I just got my invitation."

Of course she would be invited—even though Bernice wasn't one of Harriet's Girls, she's enough of a star to bless any industry event. I admit I still haven't decided, though if she's going, that maybe changes things. I tell her about the new doctor, the thread lift and the eye lift coming up, booked exactly six weeks out, because there will be an expectation—of what, I can't name, but it's there. I can hear how jumbled my thoughts are, how quickly I'm moving from one subject to another like I am trying to outrun something, because haven't I, all this time—no, no. That thought comes too close to something too deep, too dark, and before Bernice can ask me anything more about the event, I tell her about the email from Michelle and our lunch and running into her with Bobby. I wait for Bernice to laugh at the ridiculousness of it all—an interview, me back at the Rainbow—but all she sounds is confused.

"You talked to her? About Harriet? You went all the way down memory lane?"

I sit up straighter, even though she can't see me. No, not all the way.

Bernice is quiet for a moment. And then she asks: "Who are you doing this for, Birdie?"

So much for avoiding questions.

The thing about Bernice is that we have known each other since I was nineteen and she was eighteen. There is plenty we don't talk about, chunks of our lives that remain untouched by the other. We've gone months without speaking, not out of anger or lack of interest, but because one of us needed to. You don't need to know everything to know someone. That too is a kind of trust. We haven't been through the same things; we just went through them parallel to each other, and we made it to

THE COVER GIRL

this point. And if that does not sound like enough, remember: not everyone did. We never talked about what happened with Harriet, though I have no doubt Bernice knows, that even if she didn't read it, she heard about it. She can see right through me whether or not she can actually see me.

That is not the note I wish to end our call on, so I take a deep breath and ask her if she is going to award me a doody point. The laughter feels good, shorthand for all the years and selves between us.

But before we hang up, Bernice has something more for me. "An investment opportunity. Sort of. An investment of some kind," she says.

She has joined the executive board for J Entertainment, a new booking agency launched by an old friend, one without men's or women's divisions, which will specialize in LGBTQ talent for modeling and related work. "There's going to be an LA office for hosting gigs, spokesperson deals, work like that," she said. "I don't know how involved you'd want to be, but whatever you want to do, let me know. The opportunity's there. It sounded like something you'd want to be a part of."

She's right. I ask her to send me some information when she can.

As we hang up, Bernice tells me to keep her posted about what I decide. "For what it's worth," she says, "I think you should go to the gala. It's time. And you don't have to do it alone." Her voice grows even softer. "I don't want to overstep, but we've been friends long enough for me to say that I don't think your face is where you need to get the work done."

The way she says it makes clear she knows I have been running—have been finding myself chased—since the invitation arrived. The same thing Dr. Adams noticed too. What Bernice is saying is that if I am going to do this, I must consider the whole story of Harriet and me, in its full telling.

Too much? she texts minutes later.

It's okay. A nonanswer. Because yes, it is too much. Because even Bernice does not know the whole weight of it. Because I drew this line. Because I don't know what's on the other side.

Because I don't want to.

I spend the next few days considering the information Bernice sent me about J Entertainment, closing in on my surgery date with my RSVP still sitting on the counter. I don't have the investor funds she has, though I could get involved as a coach or at networking events. I like the idea of doing something hands-on; I used to throw myself into action but in more recent years, I've faded into the edges, giving money and wanting that to be enough. And while it's true that money does solve a lot of problems, it isn't the same as showing up and working to make change.

I did what felt right at the time, but in all of that, I still don't think I ever did anything that honored, in a way that felt true to me, the seismic loss the fashion industry—and so, so many others—endured in the '80s and '90s. All those barriers broken down, all those incredible leaps forward in creativity and representation, only to be ravaged by a virus. Bernice saw it at work. I saw it next to Bobby. If there is somewhere for me in J Entertainment, perhaps it can be a step toward crafting what will finally feel like a proper tribute.

As I'm making notes, I get a text from Michelle, the first since after the Rainbow. She's writing, it's going okay, but she's stuck on terminology, the right words to describe different jobs. Could she call me? A reasonable ask followed by a paragraph-long apology—she knows how lucky she was to get to talk to me to begin with and she doesn't want to be a bother at all, she just feels more comfortable with me than she does with other women she's spoken to but if I want to be done, she understands.

Bernice asked whom I'm doing this for. While I can focus on enjoying the validation that my career has mattered, that I have done anything worth remembering, I know I am looking for Michelle to hold up the reflection I used to seek in my photographs. A reflection that can be shown to Harriet—see, she did turn out okay, right? I know it. What I don't know is whether it will be worth it.

And then I stare at these messages, which are essentially an apology for existing. It's not as though I didn't have my own anxieties at Michelle's age, but I spent so long carrying them in a box—everything was about staying quiet and making people like me. I would never have been in a position to word-vomit all over someone I barely knew. I honestly cannot say which is better, but her message pulls at a sympathy I didn't know I had.

I tell her yes, she can call—I do still have some correcting to do after the Rainbow—and the phone rings a minute later.

"Thank you," she says instead of hello. "I promise I've been looking stuff up, but it would be really helpful to hear it from someone who actually lived it."

With this kind of lead-in, I'm almost nervous; I thought we were talking about words. But a word to me is the difference to Michelle. She is confused about the distinction between fashion and commercial because all the famous fashion models she knows of—Cindy Crawford, Heidi Klum, Tyra Banks—she has seen in commercials. I try to help her wrap her mind around the difference, that it is not literal, necessarily, and more about a conventional beauty versus a unique look, editorial spreads and exclusive contracts versus catalog and ad work. More about luxury and the promise being sold.

"But it is important to models?"

I almost laugh. Some days, it seemed so very. The diplomatic answer: it depends on what you want.

"And could you do both? Would you ever start out commercial and go fashion?"

The fact about Grace Kelly doing bug spray ads is out of my mouth before I have a chance to connect all the dots, where I first heard it and why. I could leave it, but I make myself give Harriet credit. This is part of the story.

Michelle laughs. "Really? No one has told me that one yet!"

I wonder if I remembered it right, then. Or: Did it even happen at all? I start to excuse myself, but Michelle is still talking.

"I'm going to have to find a way to work that quote in. I'm so excited to be working on this, but I'm afraid I'm not going to do it justice. And even though it's about Harriet, it's about everything she put into motion, right? Like every time I think I have my angle, a new one pops up. The more I care about something, the harder it is to write."

This admission hits me like a hammer to a reflex—nothing and a jolt at the same time. I'm glad someone who cares so deeply is writing Harriet's story; I can admit she deserves that. Michelle and I are not entirely dissimilar—impossible careers, wanting to believe in what we do, trying to create something that connects with people in some way. I try to imagine what it would have been like to admit what I was feeling, big and small, when I was her age. When I was any age. Right now. What must it be like to offer your vulnerability and expect someone to hold it with you instead of letting it fall?

And then she asks the big question. "Sorry if this is too much, but I'd love to see the difference between fashion and commercial with someone who knows it. Would you show me your book?"

There's my current portfolio. And there's everything I amassed in the '70s and '80s, the only time I got editorial jobs, got close to real fashion modeling, which is what Michelle wants to see.

I have no interest in looking through it myself.

That's a lie.

I kept these books, and a long time ago I decided it was better never to look because if I did, I'd always want to. And I would live in that place, where possibility and paths still felt available. I know Bernice has framed prints of her best photographs in her

THE COVER GIRL   283

house, but she's had a much more successful career and also has more wall space. The pictures that became her *Vogue* and *Elle* magazine covers should be on display. They're art.

A Virginia Slims ad doesn't have quite the same pull.

I could just let Michelle borrow my book, except, as if it's a passport, I always need to know where it is even though I don't always need it. But can I really sit down and watch her leaf through it and see the pages of my entire life turn so easily? As quickly as it all happened?

But if I attend the gala, would it be any different? Just the live and in-person version.

I could consider this a sort of preparation. If I can make it through this, I can make it through—not everything but perhaps enough.

So I tell Michelle I will meet her at Wally's for a glass of wine. Neutral territory, and if it's awkward or terrible, I can claim a reason to leave.

The occasion calls for an exquisitely preserved Halston shirtdress, bright green silk paired with a wide belt. The armor of a previous life before going into battle with it.

We sit on the patio, enough splash in our surroundings to compete with my book. The photos have aged, even with great care, and I focus on my wine as she flips the pages with a gentle reverence.

"This was your first shoot, right? And what were these ones before this one from?"

I explain to Michelle the concept of test shots, how they helped a photographer gain exposure while also giving me pictures to add to my book.

"Is there one that's your favorite?"

I shake my head. The cover could be it, sure. Or that Swish ad she mentioned when she first reached out, my body golden and toned and powerful. But truthfully, my favorite photo of myself as a model is from my first fashion show—sheer pants, asymmetrical blouse, huge hair. At the end of the runway, I paused and I delivered everything I could. That was a girl who knew things, even just for an evening. Maybe by *things*, I just mean *possibility*. So much still in reach. And so that will be a story just for me.

What I tell Michelle is that my favorite changes all the time. With a career as long as mine, it's best to keep looking forward and let each one become the new favorite. This is, of course, bullshit. And I am sure she knows it's bullshit. But you also don't get to have a career as long as mine—unstoried though it may be—without knowing how to take and deliver bullshit.

She nods and continues turning, picking up a little speed. I catch a flash of legs in the air and she blows past with only a fraction of a pause. No further questions on that one. I will not mind if this exercise has become slightly boring.

Sitting across from Michelle, I can glance at these photographs upside down, from a distance. At this angle, the girl in the pictures is a stranger to me. Everything about her seems like it happened to someone else; there are photos here from shoots I don't even remember. Maybe the one with Sunny. I know I enjoyed myself, at least for the most part. But what I enjoyed was being blank. Being given clothes and a style and a vague set of instructions and becoming anyone else. All I wanted was to give, give, give in front of the camera. I don't know what I kept for myself.

I don't know that this is *not* what I am still doing.

"And we got from here to *America's Next Top Model*," Michelle says, studying a simply styled photo, one with an open-mouthed smile that is pure 1970s. I must make some kind of involuntary face, because she laughs. "I bet that was a weird show to watch as an actual model."

I shake my head. I tell her that isn't it. Or it's only part of it. It was hard to watch because it seemed like a heightened period of punishing young women who had the gall to think they were

THE COVER GIRL   285

pretty enough to make a career of it. It was hard to see the series of humiliations not just on that show but playing out in the news and in pop culture.

Michelle looks at me thoughtfully. "I guess I never really thought of it like that, but it makes sense. Do you think what you went through kind of makes that all stand out more?" I tell her I'm not sure what she means. "The way you were preyed on by that musician. The abuse."

If I can focus on her tone, the carefulness of it, the rehearsal it betrays, I can stay here, but no, it's the words themselves, and they knock the wind from me. I start to tell her she has no idea what she's talking about but I can't even hear my own voice for the blood ringing in my ears. Eventually I settle on a single question: Is this what she was after all along? I don't wait for an answer. I push away from the table, flagging down the server, rushing inside so she can run my card.

Michelle is standing limply at the table when I come back out and I walk by her, out of this conversation, out of this line of questioning. She follows, though, hissing my name to try to avoid a scene, but I don't turn around. She may be younger, but I have a good foot on her, which means she has to break into a run to jump in front of me.

"I didn't lie to you!" she said. "Please, just listen to me. I'm working on a story about Harriet, like I told you. I had no idea about anything. But these pieces kept coming up. And I think I should be writing your story instead."

I tell her she's mistaken, ask where in the world she got the idea there was a story, but I realize the truth as she's saying *the Rainbow.*

And a name I locked away along with so much else.

Lulu.

"She came up to me after you and your friend left and asked if that was Birdie Rhodes I was talking to. She told me she was an old friend and hadn't seen you in years," Michelle says. She tells me how she explained that I was part of a story she was writing and asked Lulu how she knew me. "Then she said you were like this child bride of a rock star?"

Everything is falling apart at once and still, what I think is: *No, never the bride.*

"It sounded weird, but also it made sense—I've gotten the vibe that you're holding something back. It's all right there. I didn't even have to look that hard; all I had to do was put it together. The album cover's in your book. I found his *Behind the Music* where it says he had a relationship with the model on the cover. I read the interview with Harriet. I talked to Therese."

Therese. My god.

"She told me why you and Harriet don't speak anymore. And how Harriet almost fired her for giving him your phone number—Therese said that's how he found you after the album cover. You were fifteen when he took you away from your family. He was in his thirties. That's abuse."

No. I shake my head. I understand that things are perceived a certain way—*are* that way—now, I explain. But this was a completely different time. We had a unique relationship. I was basically an adult. I was different. Where was this even coming from—this girl who ended every sentence like it was a question, who would apologize to a chair if she bumped into it. This wasn't her business. It wasn't anyone's. I was there. I know what happened.

"He hasn't faced any consequences. As far as I can tell, no one has ever asked him a question about it. Don't you think he should be held accountable for what he did to you?"

What exactly was done to me. Why is she convinced something was done to me. I've had enough of her explanations, her 2018 perspective projected onto my 1978 life. I push past her to go to my car, and she doesn't fight me. As I'm stalking away, I hear her shout behind me, "Do you really think you were the only one?"

1987–2000

Look Away

1

You spend half your life under a spotlight, and then it's gone. It was one thing to say the words and get on the plane. It was another thing to live it.

At first, it was a fog. A vacation. I landed in New York, and what I wanted was to go stand in Harriet's apartment, holding a mug of undrunk tea. So many fractures along the way, but as much as I didn't know how to live without modeling, I truly did not know what I was supposed to do without Harriet. *Just keep moving* was the only answer I could come up with. Move so you don't feel.

I stayed in Bernice's apartment for a couple nights while she was in Paris. She'd suggested I join her there. It was tempting, but I wasn't sure I was ready for the mirror she could hold up. Instead, I looked at her walls, lined with beautiful photographs—the AZ-KC ads, artistic black-and-whites, covers. Dresses that swirled like ocean waves. Locations like Madrid, Rome, Tokyo, Milan.

What did I see?

The knowledge that I never once operated on this level, even at my best. The knowledge that I could not be in this city by myself and not be a model.

The gentlest transition possible—money, a place to stay—and it was still difficult.

For a few days, I walked through, around, alongside the crowds of the city. I walked into groups of people chanting with their full voices: *Act up, fight back, fight AIDS.*

I paused. I wasn't loud, but I said the words too, on the fringes of the protest, but doing the one thing I knew how to do: be a body, not as a focal point this time, but in solidarity.

What I did was create a double life. I got it together to move to a small town outside of Boston for no reason other than it was quiet and it wasn't as memory-laden as New York, but it wasn't Connecticut either. I introduced myself to people as Elizabeth. I had an untouched trust and residuals from my little acting jobs. I could afford a break. I could afford to share.

Boston was where I found the right people. Exploring the city, I saw flyers for a walk to raise money for HIV research, organized by the AIDS Action Committee. Yes, I could walk, but I wanted to do more. And now I had somewhere to start.

My first community meeting, I sat in the back. Everyone seemed to know each other, and I wondered how many strangers showed up to these. I still didn't know how to blend in.

Listening to the leaders speak fired me up even more—so much to be done, so many injustices I'd never even thought to think about. I was lingering by the wall after the meeting, trying to plot my next move, when a young man approached me.

"Why are you here?" he asked, not unkindly.

I told him I wanted to do something.

"Then let's do it."

Could it be that simple?

Almost. The young man told me what was needed, told me who to ask how I could help. Soon I was serving meals to people

THE COVER GIRL

living with HIV and AIDS and answering hotline calls about testing. When the other volunteers I worked with mentioned money was needed, I pulled out my checkbook. How much? The first time, they thought I was showing off. And of course— who was this new girl, walking in out of nowhere? Would taking a check be the equivalent of letting a visitor in this space take over? I learned to wait, to do what was being asked in the moment. To earn trust.

I made sure I didn't have the time to miss modeling. I started taking night classes at a community college and briefly considered becoming a nurse, but I didn't want to wait to make a difference. I called Bernice after volunteer shifts. She'd share news about names we'd both come up alongside and also the new ones, the reminders that one can only be on top for so long. She didn't think she was going to do this much longer either, but it's hard to know when to hang it up when you're still getting great jobs, even when the writing is on the wall. Like the letters were there but they hadn't filled in yet. Maybe the law degree she'd planned on was still within reach.

"Or maybe I need to get you to give me an acting lesson," Bernice mused one night on the phone, and we both laughed till we cried, and then I had to catch myself before I started cry-crying because the tears were always right there, just under the surface.

"I know," she said softly when my hiccup threatened to turn into something else. "I was at a show recently, and there were so many women designers, and I thought, oh, this is great! And then it occurred to me *why*. And the mood just completely changed."

Sometimes it felt like Bernice and I had more in common now—the shared language of grief bringing us together in new ways. And, truthfully, neither of us understood our lives. This period gave us a new connection, a tether to who we used to be and a reminder that someone else carried that memory too.

In the back of my mind was what Azrian had told me at the fashion show. I wanted to ask Bernice if he had said anything to her that night too, maybe compare notes, make it make sense. But mostly it was a relief to put that girl away. To be Elizabeth, not Birdie. To act on a moment-to-moment basis.

My role expanded into delivering groceries to people living with AIDS when they couldn't leave their homes, to chauffeuring those who lived too far from a bus or T stop to doctor's appointments, to making hospital visits when family was not going to come. I attended training sessions and studied the handbooks so I could provide quality home care. Sometimes I had an assigned buddy, and sometimes I'd go wherever someone was needed.

Sometimes I'd have a buddy for a year. Sometimes I'd have one for just a few weeks before they died. Once or twice, I knew I would be the last person outside of the medical profession someone saw. I read magazines and books out loud, and I listened to stories about beloved family cats, stories about watching lovers and friends go first and knowing what was coming, stories about seeing a movie for the first time in a theater. Whatever they wanted to tell me. Whatever they wanted to take with them or be carried forward.

With the committee, I found a place where I could contribute, and it was satisfying to help meet a need. But it was also a horrible period, marked with sickness and anger. It was a crash course in all the ways in which a government could fail its people, and it was a tragedy that I was needed at all. There was so much heartbreak, so much loss. A volunteer who'd lived with the virus for years would suddenly fall sick and never recover. Or a young man would join for reasons like I did, just to be helpful, and then find himself testing positive, a life trajectory dramatically changed at nineteen, twenty, twenty-one.

It was after a particularly hard week that I became friendly

THE COVER GIRL

with a fellow volunteer named Bobby when he walked up to me and said in his deep Southern drawl, "I know who you are."

I hadn't realized I was waiting to be found out until he said it. Found out for what, I couldn't tell you. I sat, frozen, and waited to hear what kind of fraud he'd figured me to be.

"You're the girl from the Stinger video! The 'Take It, Shake It' girl!" he announced in an exaggerated whisper. When I nodded in confirmation, he threw back his head and laughed. "I fuckin' loved that song. What made you end up here?"

There was a time when I would have tried to vague my way out of it, but I decided to tell him the truth: I just needed to do something.

He accepted that as a full answer. Over the months that followed, I learned he'd moved to the area for love, for his partner who'd died three years ago, in '89, and as he himself tried to grapple with what it meant that he would likely eventually get sick, he'd thought about going back home to North Carolina. But he wasn't sure there was a place there for him anymore.

"I mean, Momma and Daddy knew I lived up here with Michael. They sent us both Christmas presents. My sister's kids called us Uncle Bobby and Uncle Michael. But we never talked about it. We can't *not* talk about it now. And I don't want to know, you know?"

I understood the not wanting to know, though it wasn't my job to offer advice. It was my job to do the tasks Bobby gave me, like stuffing the letters we were writing to state officials about the importance of providing resources for unhoused people living with AIDS, and to listen while he talked it out. I wanted to believe the parents who sent presents and the sister whose children didn't question having two uncles would welcome him back and take care of him when needed. But I'd already heard a lot of stories about accepting families and friends who suddenly changed their tune when their loved one revealed their HIV-positive status. I already knew that the family who gave birth to you and raised you as a child was not always the family a person deserved in their corner.

"What are you doing tomorrow night?" Bobby never stayed on one subject too long, a habit I'd grown used to. "I got an extra ticket to a concert. You want to go?"

I knew who it was going to be before I asked. I'd seen the billboard. But maybe, I hoped, I had gotten the dates mixed up.

Of course he said the rock star's name, but he said it like he was embarrassed. "I know, I know. All that guy sings about is chasing pussy and chasing it some more." How *something* to hear him described by someone else, in such plain words. What a thing to feel and not name. "That's all I listened to when I was a teenager in the '70s. Michael too. Isn't it wild?"

It would have been very easy to tell Bobby no, that this music was not for me. Or that I wasn't a concert kind of girl. There must be another person he could go with. But he'd become my friend, and he'd asked.

And I was curious about what the years had done. What marriage and divorce and remarriage had done, because I still read celebrity gossip. I still enjoyed a little indulgence.

So I went with Bobby to the Boston Garden. The show hadn't changed much in fifteen years. I could have mouthed along with a full two-thirds of the banter. Shockingly, jokes about Gerald Ford's ineptitude had been swapped out for jokes about Bill Clinton. I wondered when that changed, wondered when the girls who had clung to his every note in the front row had been replaced with grown women.

I surprised Bobby by singing along to the songs I knew. We danced and laughed and for a moment it felt like the two halves of my life could fit, maybe not together but next to each other.

And then there was the banter I couldn't mouth along to. "This next song is real special," the rock star announced. "I wrote it for my baby girl, who's due any day now. She's not

THE COVER GIRL 295

even born yet, but I don't think anyone has ever shaken my world like she has."

In a flash, I was back in the glass house. Coming from dinner late at night, talking about how glad we were that we were not Lulu and Beasley. No babies here. Fucking on the countertop because we could. The broken vase.

I sank in my seat, somewhere between throwing up and passing out and angry at myself for falling so easily back into that life.

The joy and freedom I'd felt didn't return, though I tried to fake it. And when Bobby asked if I was okay when we walked back to the T, I wanted to try out the truth. The factual truth at least, because who knows what the meaning of it all was. But I remembered the last time I'd tried this, with that actor Wesley, and I didn't want to have to explain it away, shrink my life down into something careful. Bobby probably wouldn't ask that of me, but it was easier not to risk it. To not be understood at all rather than misunderstood. What I settled on: I had been on the cover of one of the rock star's albums when I was a teenager.

His eyebrows only raised slightly, as if he knew there was more. All he said was, "Yeah, that makes sense."

I wondered in what way.

A month later, I hugged Bobby goodbye in front of Logan Airport. He had finally made the phone call. He was going to live with his sister. He was going to be Uncle Bobby full-time. I didn't know what had changed for him; it wasn't my business. It felt like all we did at that time was say goodbye, but this one was his choice. There was power in that.

"Stay weird, buddy," Bobby said. "It's going to be alright."

If he could believe it, I could too.

2

The phone call came directly to me this time. No news relayed through another party. No buffer to bump my feelings against. I hadn't heard her voice in years but I knew that rehearsed Rose Kennedy–meets–Katharine Hepburn tone immediately.

"Birdie. Your father has died. I thought you would want to know."

Imagine giving birth to a child and raising that child, for at least a period of time, only to make that phone call and deliver that news in such a way.

Believe me, it would have been worse if she'd made a big emotional production of it, if she'd called me crying and expected me to fall apart at the news too. So in that sense, I couldn't blame her. There were a few other senses, though, where blame felt comfortable.

The politest thing was to thank her for telling me. I hastily added that I was sorry to hear.

"Do you plan to attend the funeral?"

She was really going to make me say no to her out loud, so of course I said I would. I wrote down the information, all the while feeling not grief for the man, for what might have been, but anger.

The day of the funeral, I twisted my hair into a chignon and put on a simple black boatneck dress, one that showed off my daily dedication to Jane Fonda's workout—which I now did on the VCR like a regular person—but was also appropriate for the occasion. You can take the girl away from Harriet but you can't take the Harriet out of the girl.

Let's not act like this was an easy day, though. Like I wasn't shaking the entire drive, the knowledge that I was going to see my mother after all this time, that I was going to have to at least gesture toward something like being a daughter. Would it be unforgivable to sneak in at the back and leave just as quietly? Would it be worse if I was there and she didn't recognize me?

I chose the second to last row in the church. I could see my mother at the front, her hair still set like it was 1956. The thought of her going to the salon to get her funeral hair done saddened me more deeply than the reason I was there.

Because, truthfully, it was hard to get sad. He'd lived for a long time. I assumed he had died with loved ones. I'd seen too much, was aware there was so much more that I had not seen, to find much tragedy in a man dying in his late seventies.

I watched the church fill with people I did not recognize, who did not recognize me. This completely different life my father had, separate from my own. Did they know he had a daughter? Did he tell them what she did, used to do, where she went? Did they wonder why he never had answers to questions about her, or did he just make them up?

Eventually, I stopped looking around and instead focused straight ahead, lest I accidentally attract unwanted attention. And that was what I was doing when I felt the presence of someone settling in next to me.

"Darling."

It was only then I realized my mother would have called the agency to get my phone number.

"I hoped you'd be here," Harriet said, looking straight ahead. "And I thought you might appreciate a familiar face. I can leave if you would like."

I shook my head. I didn't know what this meant, only that I didn't deserve such kindness after everything. She held out her hand and as the reverend shuffled up to the pulpit, I took it.

He talked about God and death and eternal life. I half listened. A man a bit older than me went to the front to deliver the eulogy. He called my father Uncle Peter.

Harriet gave my hand a final squeeze before slipping out as the service ended. She could not follow me to the gravesite because of her schedule and also because there was a boundary between the world in which she knew me and the one my mother had been a part of. And I belonged to neither right now, just floating.

I stood away from the rest of the family, the people I guessed were family, not listening to whatever was being said over the casket. What I was trying to do was recall one memory where my father said something to me instead of silently bending to my mother's will. What did women remember about their fathers?

The first thing that came to mind was learning to drive.

Is that your father? the driving instructor had asked.

Being walked down the aisle?

Well. That boat came in the form of paperwork.

I thought harder. Christmas? What was that shaped like before? My birthday? Blank days, greeting-card images, nothing real.

Florida. Winter in West Palm Beach. The Coolidges were having their annual February party. My mother wanted to go. She could use the family condo. They should consider buying one while they were down there. My father did not want to pull me out of school. My mother said it was the second grade, what did it really matter? She's pretty. She'll be fine.

I remembered following behind them into the party. Itchy

lace collar on a dress I did not care for. Tights that were already sliding down. There was food, music, lots of drinks, and no other children anywhere. My mother disappeared into the crowd with her friends, and my father found me a place to sit and set me up with several tiny pastries. I listened to the sound of the party around me, a brassy ringing laugh that my mother never laughed at home. And then I must have fallen asleep because the next thing that happened was my father lifting me up and settling me against his shoulder. "This is ridiculous," he had said. "You should be in bed."

It was possible I would have liked to know him. It was possible I could have done more.

I still hadn't exchanged a word, a glance, a touch, with my mother since arriving, and I wondered for how much longer this could be avoided. One final hurdle. The reception at that cold brick house.

My chest tightened as I turned onto Edgerton Street. I hadn't been here since 1977, seventeen years earlier. More than half my life. I had been at least three different people since then.

Truthfully? I sat in the car for a long time. At least a dozen mourners had come and gone before I could make myself cross the threshold. There was nothing to be undone by going in. But maybe the man who'd wanted me to sleep in a bed at a reasonable hour deserved me trying.

I shouldn't have expected anything less than a house untouched by time and yet it still knocked the breath from me. Those same terrible burgundy velvet curtains hanging in the front room and I knew—*knew*—that somewhere in a closet was a canister vacuum with a long hose connected to it. My mother vacuumed those curtains. Or maybe she paid someone to do it. The point was: that vacuum. Those curtains. That tiny view of the world.

While I didn't know anyone here, what I did know was that this was a reception for WASPs, so there would be plenty to drink. I poured myself a double vodka and slipped down the hallway. Up the stairs. The door to the room that had been mine was closed.

Lace bedspread. Lace shams. Lace curtains. A little girl's room, preserved in time. I sat on the bed, the mattress creaking under me. I sipped my vodka, and that was where my mother found me as the late-afternoon sun cut shadows across the room.

"Thank you for coming," she said stiffly.

I nodded. We looked at each other, not hiding that we were trying to find the secrets of these elapsed years in the other's face. Of course she looked older but then again, she'd always seemed old to me. I must have looked like a completely different person.

The silence became too much to bear, so I said I was sorry for her loss.

It was not the kind of thing a daughter says to a mother, and by the way her mouth twisted, I knew she knew it too.

Fine. I had done enough today, hadn't I? I told her I thought I should leave.

"Already? Birdie, you're here for the first time in I don't know how long, and you already want to run away again?"

The *again* seared through me white-hot. There was no *again*. I asked what she could possibly mean.

"You left us, and you never looked back." Like she had been waiting to say it.

There's a view from which a person could have watched and listened to this conversation and felt so sorry for this older woman with her heavy dated clothes in this heavy dated house, voice cracking as she summoned the courage to say those words to her daughter, who factually had left home at age fifteen and factually had scheduled a few lunches in the city at first and then let it all fade away. That view was not mine.

I didn't look back, but she didn't want to see me.

I reminded her that she was the one who'd made that decision. I wouldn't have left if I hadn't been told to go.

THE COVER GIRL

"We thought it was what you wanted. You had your career. This life we didn't understand."

My career. Like I put on blouses and went to an office building.

"Birdie, what do you want me to say? This famous man came to our home. He wanted good things for you. We wanted good things for you."

Is that why she constantly told me how dull, how lacking in personality I was?

"Maybe I wanted you to do more than I did. And didn't you?" she asked.

All that was left in my cup was melted ice, but I swirled it in my hand as I stared at her again, still standing in the doorway as I remained perched on that uncomfortable bed. Like everything else in this house, appearance was what mattered, not functionality. I asked if she knew he had been my boyfriend. That it was about us, not my career.

I watched her decide what to tell me. I watched her think about that day in the drawing room—of course she called it a drawing room—him sitting in her grandmother's chair holding a slice of grocery store cake on her grandmother's china. What wonderful cake. Him barely even looking my way. Her barely even looking my way. My father the far point on the triangle of adults, looking back and forth, telling the rock star that it was a bear market right now. Diversify your investment portfolio. The rock star repeating this phrase like it was genuinely unique advice and not something read in a magazine. The rock star saying that he cared for me. Something about education, tutors. Album cover. He cared for me. I'd watched her think about those words. What other interest could this man have in her daughter?

"I didn't want to know," she said finally, and this was the most honest thing my mother had ever said to me. And then because it was the truth, she immediately began walking it back. "He had the money to take care of you. And you were always so busy. You were part of this completely other world. We didn't make a habit of standing in your way. We asked if you wanted to go and you said you did. I didn't think you meant forever."

What in the world, then, had she thought it meant? I knew why I had been confused about where I'd go after that first summer, but she was the one who'd signed the papers.

"We thought it was for the summer! We didn't know what we were signing!"

What it looked like was this: there was no dramatic swell of music, no drink falling to the floor. No slow zoom on the former model as the words sank in. She sat, still and cold, as the mother shared what she remembered, as everything around her crumbled, as much as it might look the same.

The mother explained that the rock star came back over with a document. The former model tried to remember if she knew that. It had already been drawn up by his team—they went to Yale Law by the way. All the parents needed to do was review and sign, and he would handle the rest. No need for them to worry about anything. Afterward, a man called and asked if they had any questions. The man was so sorry he had missed meeting them, but he was in charge of the entire tour and would personally see to it that the girl was safe and taken care of every step of the way. They had nothing to worry about. This was also news to the former model but of course that man would have been involved. He'd suggested the father consult his own lawyer if he wished, not knowing this would need to go through the mother. And when the mother signed anything, she always went to her family lawyer, so that's what she did. She said she wanted to give the young model permission to travel the country for the summer. The family lawyer didn't question how strange this sounded, said everything looked fine, and both parents signed.

Months later, after the tour was over and the young model was living in a glass house in Malibu and had not come home, the family lawyer, well into his nineties, was deemed unfit to prac-

THE COVER GIRL

tice due to cognitive decline. And when his grandson looked at files for the lawyer's recent clients, he knew enough of the family involved to know Virginia Putnam Rhodes could not have possibly meant to give custody of her teenage daughter to some rock singer, but that's what she and her husband had agreed to.

Surely, the grandson must have offered to undo it. Surely, that piece of paper had no real legal merit at that point.

"It would have been so messy."

Unbelievable that there were words remaining that could shock me back into the room.

So she told the grandson that I was a model and things worked a little differently for me.

So she chose to avoid admitting her own mistake because people may have found out and gossiped.

So even as she sought out the newspaper to give legitimacy to what had been done, she didn't care enough to seek the truth.

So even if it had not been her choice to begin with, it became her choice.

So because she had felt the need to use the phrase *family lawyer* in front of the rock star's Yale graduates and because she did not feel the need to read what she was signing since her mother and father and aunts and uncles had all trusted this man and surely he must know better, I had left.

So it wasn't that she didn't want me, it was just that she wanted other things more.

What useful information.

I stood up. Any stiffness in my body from sitting down for so long went unregistered. I picked up my clutch and let my glass tip over on the bedspread, the melted ice creating a darker shade of white. And then I walked past my mother down the hallway, down the stairs, past the terrible but dustless burgundy drapes and out of the house, and if there had been any question about whether or not I would return when I left in 1977, there absolutely was not this time.

3

I did not go back. And when the grandson of the ancient family lawyer called a year and a half later to tell me that my mother had passed away, I felt nothing.

That's not true.

I felt nothing, and I felt terrible for feeling nothing, but not terrible enough to actually feel something.

I didn't attend the funeral because there was nobody to disappoint. Because it was symbolic at this point, right? Because I was officially untethered now.

She left me the house, which felt like a fuck-you more than anything. As if I would ever sort through half a century of things she kept because of who they'd belonged to before. I contemplated selling it as is, but I realized an estate sale could be better. I had an accountant for the first time in my life. He told me how much money I could give away while continuing to live within my means, and the house and its contents were going to change that budget significantly.

I could say with 100 percent certainty that my mother had voted for Ronald Reagan in both elections, and there was no better way to honor her neat Reagan life than to sell it off and give the proceeds to AIDS organizations.

I assumed money donated from a place of spite still did good.

I hired a woman named Barb to pack up the house—to dispose of trash, to organize anything of value for the estate sale, and to put anything that looked like it needed to be dealt with aside for me. We only spoke, never met, and I could hear how prepared she was to comfort the grieving. I lied and told her the house belonged to a great-aunt I never knew, that I was the only known living relative.

"Are you sure there's nothing you want?" Barb asked.

I asked her to send me the drapes from the drawing room. I did not call it a drawing room. She could send anything else later, but I needed that box as soon as possible.

It arrived as a rectangle of banged-up cardboard on my steps, heavier than it should have been. Heavy with the weight of expectation and memory and years.

My plan had been to douse the drapes in gasoline and light them on fire, but when I opened the box, the smell of the house hit me. A smell I would never smell again, didn't want to smell again—the age of the house and the motor of the canister vacuum and lemon cleaning products and Yardley April Violets perfume and the hundreds of other small scents melding together into what I had called home. I closed the cardboard back up. There could be relief in giving in to the pettiness. I was entirely convinced that burning these curtains would set something free inside me. But I lived in a small house on a small street, and really, where had I thought I was going to do this?

In the end, I tipped it all into a dumpster, and that had to be enough.

Barb sent me her invoice and a box of items she thought I might want to have. I put them in the back of a closet and paid her double. It would have been worth double even that and then double again to avoid going back.

I wondered if the papers were in there, the ones my mother had signed, convincing herself—on the surface or truthfully—that they meant one thing when they meant another. I was curious and also deeply unprepared to face the typewritten evidence of myself as a transaction. Maybe one day I would have the courage to look. Maybe one day, when I could say for certain what I would do after.

Debi's voice was one I didn't expect to hear coming through my answering machine on a Sunday morning, yet there she was, too early her time. I could hear the hour in her voice as I played the message again. "You aren't going to like it," she said. "I think she was hoping for more context—she didn't want to hurt you. But I wanted to warn you."

The *Times* had arrived heavy and Sunday-thick, and the last thing I expected to see on the cover of the Arts & Leisure section was a photograph of Harriet. "Good as Gold." The story of Harriet. Perhaps if I hadn't retired, she would have warned me herself.

Perhaps if I hadn't retired, a lot of things.

...Ms. Goldman's long storied career is not without controversy. For her first two decades in the business, she had a habit of scouting and signing models barely in their teens, believing talent was talent and it should be developed immediately. There was a time when Harriet's Girls were the youngest on a go-see.

When asked if there was anything she would have done differently, Ms. Goldman does not answer right away. She lights another cigarette in her signature cigarette holder. "About seven years ago, I was talking to a client of mine, a young girl who seemed to have...lost interest."

I could hear her voice, the ellipsis.

"And that happens, of course. What seems glamorous at fifteen and sixteen can be a lot of work at seventeen and eighteen when your friends are at dances and malls, eating pizza and dating boys. So I was digging, trying to figure out if she was over modeling or what and finally

THE COVER GIRL

she said, 'It's not worth it.' And it turns out there had been an incident with a photographer. I asked why she hadn't said anything. I always told my girls that I would deal with any problems they faced on set. And she said, 'Yes but you said my job was to make him like me.'"

Ms. Goldman looks away. She appears to still be shaken by the conversation. "I almost quit the business then and there. My god. I thought I had set my girls up for success by telling them they could bring me any problem, but it was all drowned by the other things I'd said. It was my fault. It was a tremendous reckoning."

The conversation stuck with Ms. Goldman. She wondered what else the teenagers and young women entrusted to her business savvy had not told her, what else she could have done. And she thought back to another regret.

"There was a model who I still wish I'd handled differently. I pushed her too fast when she was too young."

Had she? Hadn't it been what I wanted?

"… I looked for ways to keep her close. I even ended up coaxing her into a cosmetics contract that I knew wasn't a good move—the company was too new, the product was subpar. But they were only shooting in New York, so I could at least keep an eye on her."

The contract didn't work out, and Ms. Goldman says she did what she could for the former client, but as the years passed, the damage had been done. She declines to give further detail. "I wonder what would have happened if I'd waited. What a waste of potential."

I didn't need to read more. None of it had meant anything.

What I did was: I threw up, and then I gathered myself. I drove straight to the agency. This was not any way I would have wanted Harriet to see me. My hair was a nothing shade of blond. Though I was still exercising every day and watching my diet, I was softer than I wanted to be. At this moment, it didn't matter.

I walked directly to Harriet's office. Therese couldn't stop me. I barged right in and told her she had no idea what she was talking about and I did not appreciate the details of my life being put on display. And to have to hear about it from Debi! And perhaps my potential would have been fulfilled if I hadn't spent my prime locked into a contract she knew was bad.

"Darling," Harriet said. "You have every right to be angry with me." She got up from her desk and, in a stunning move, for the first time in the twenty years we had known each other, she laid her hands on my shoulders. There was something so whole, so needed, about the weight of her hands on me that I almost broke right open. "I let him—"

No. I remembered why I was there and what she believed about me and my waste. I shrugged myself out of her grip and walked out.

My time in Massachusetts showed me what else I could be in this world, and that I could be more than one thing at the same time. Leaving wasn't easy because of the likelihood that I would not see any of my fellow volunteers again for a number of reasons, but with the new antiretroviral drugs, the tide was finally, hopefully, starting to turn. I got addresses. I knew I'd still send money. They knew me enough to believe me. They knew me enough to give me names in my new-old neighborhood, to tell their friends to look me up. That I'd help.

Bernice had told me about a tiny bungalow on Cynthia Street in West Hollywood, not far from where I used to live. She knew the real-estate agent. One bedroom, one bathroom. A small contained house for a small contained life. The accountant told me I could do it. That it would be smart to do it, in fact.

So yes. I was going back to California. Because it turned out I belonged there, and I was not going to belong as well anywhere else, no matter what community I found myself in.

I was going back to California because although I was good at more than just one thing now, I had unfinished business as a model, even though I'd been old at twenty-five and was now ancient in my thirties. I was in my thirties, and I did not need

THE COVER GIRL

to reveal more about that number. Once you used it in the plural, everyone knew what it meant. The gaps could be filled in.

I didn't know who would sign me, but I had a good portfolio. I had a good comp card. I had a reputation of silent professionalism and acquiescence. There were advantages to the secondary market, were there not? It was time to leverage them.

The fact was, I bought the house sight unseen. I trusted Bernice, so I trusted her friend. And when I walked in, I started to cry.

One of the important things about what I'd built in Massachusetts was that it didn't involve me at all. I had spent so long thinking about my relationship with the rock star, about my career, about what hadn't shaken out the way I wanted; focusing on others, recalibrating to a real crisis, had shifted my worldview, who I was and wanted to be. And I'd learned to trust strangers.

But I had been careful not to do anything that required trusting myself. Too much had happened.

The house, though. It was right. I had chosen correctly. I had done the right thing.

For the first time in my life, I was home.

4

Of *course* Brooke Shields got her own sitcom. Of course.

5

Debi, shockingly, took me back on.

It was going to be Spiegel catalogs and a lot of beigey wide legs, but it was a paycheck for both of us. I could be of more use to the cause when I was working, and that was where I found my purpose. I had tried to remove the pressure before, to treat it like a job, but now that I'd aged out, I could actually do it. There were no more tiny hopes lurking in the background. I was truly relieving myself from the burden of making it, of covers, of the high fashion leap, and putting myself in Debi's capable hands.

I hadn't been fair to her in my first go-round. She was different. She didn't have the mystique, the gravitas that I had associated with her job. I'd treated her how I imagined I would have treated a stepparent—you're not my real mom, you can't tell me what to do. But it turned out she was both direct and empathetic, with a shrewd approach to the business.

Or maybe we had all just grown up.

Debi had started her own small agency, one that focused more on her talent for building hybrid careers—modeling, television hosting, acting. And while one could say she signed me because she was still building her client base, she told me she believed in the second and third act. Lauren Hutton made comebacks chic. Why not me?

We signed a contract. Everything had changed, but also nothing had changed. I'd call to get bookings. There would be vouchers. And before I left, I asked who to drop them off with.

"Anyone here can handle them," Debi said. She peered up at me over her glasses, still typing away on her orange iMac. When I didn't react, she spelled it out.

"That's always been the case. She just wanted to keep you close."

Bernice got married in the Blue Ridge Mountains of Virginia. After years of being photographed on the arms of Oscar winners, Grammy nominees, 40-under-40s, she met a high school English teacher on an incognito run to Duane Reade. His name was Marcus, he made her happy, and he would have wanted to make her happy whether she was a model or not. He was taking two weeks off to go to St. Barts and then returning to the classroom to start a new unit on *All the King's Men*. To hear him tell it, the honeymoon was purposefully scheduled so his substitute would have to teach *A Separate Peace* in his stead—he shared that fact with anyone who asked about their honeymoon and giggled every time with the joy of a man who believed he'd pulled a fast one. I didn't know the book, but I found myself laughing along with him, found myself meeting Bernice's eyes and nodding through unexpected tears: yes, this is so right.

I had my nose done for the wedding, just a light adjustment after having my perforated septum repaired. I hadn't even realized the hole had emerged until a young stylist on a catalog shoot fitted me into a sensible bra, the kind no one would want to see waiting under the clothes of a potential sexual partner, and told me she could hear the whistling sound of my breathing and I needed to go to an ENT.

"You did coke?" she asked.

THE COVER GIRL 313

Who didn't? Which sounded like the setup for an anemic standup comedy bit where the answer was the '90s.

She shook her head. "I honestly don't understand how any of you have noses anymore. I hear that whistle once a week."

The ENT referred me to a Dr. Rosenthal, who made sure I still had the nose of a model, a nose that could convince you support and sensibility were more important than sex appeal when it came to choosing a bra. I made a passing comment about my forehead in my post-op visit and he said he could give me something off-label—not surgery, but an injectable.

Bernice booped me on the nose with a wink when I arrived in Virginia. Noticeable, but only if you knew.

Long after the wedding, I kept looking at myself in the mirror, in a way I had not since I first started modeling and discovered the power of my appearance. The changes had been so subtle over time. Now I was drunk on the rewind button.

And it was a good time for that button, for Debi's second and third acts. Bell-bottoms were back. Sitcoms were set in the '70s. The cable channels that used to run the music videos I'd starred in were now running constant retrospectives on those videos, on the era, on anything from the previous two decades they could fill an hour with.

I found this packaging and commercializing of nostalgia at best strange and at worst willfully ignorant. The '80s weren't even ten years in the rearview mirror. Was it really time to revisit? Where was the presence of those who didn't make it out of the decade? Veronica Webb just became the first Black model with an exclusive contract for a major cosmetics brand—in 1992. For instance. How wistful were we supposed to get?

As with everything, it was easier to wax nostalgic about it if you weren't there.

For Bernice, it was an opportunity to take control of her career, her location, and the narrative. As she contemplated getting pregnant, she calmed her travel and reinvented herself as a television personality, hosting fashion retrospectives and counting down the best one-hit wonders of the day—"Here's number 79, 'Take It, Shake It,' one of my personal favorites because the video vixen? That's my friend, the gorgeous Miss Rhodes!"—while also reminding her audience that all her credentials and the trails she herself had blazed with Max Factor and by raising her voice for pay equity and her AIDS philanthropy and scholarships were not as rooted in the past as they might want to believe.

Some similar, less high-profile auditions for retrospectives came my way. "I think we'd rather look forward, right?" Debi asked the afternoon I came in to review my updated portfolio.

And how.

I was gathering my things to leave, half turned toward the door when she said quietly, "There's going to be a *Behind the Music*." It felt like slow motion as I turned back toward her. She looked at me above her glasses. "I thought you should know."

I nodded. Right. Yes. I should know.

"I had planned to communicate to our staff that you would not be available if they reached out. Is that your preference?"

Was it? I tried to picture myself against one of those unflattering backdrops, being asked questions about my life. A chyron identifying me as what? A person who existed.

My voice was a whisper when I said it was my preference. But also I wanted to know if it happened. So I had the option to change my mind.

I split my time modeling sensible swimsuits with flattering, flattening tummy panels—yes, *tummy*, this was what the copy said, like anyone looking for *tummy control* wasn't also a grown adult who would use any other word in conversation—and watching cable news about the impeachment trial and waiting for my phone to ring. Waiting was different from wanting. Wanting was different from hoping. Hoping could cover a lot of things.

THE COVER GIRL

I *hoped* to be a class act. I *wanted* something shaped like an upper hand. I had done enough *waiting*.

It was Debi's suggestion that I talk to someone. There was a time when this would have been enough to ensure I never stepped foot in the office of a therapist, but look at how far I had come.

Look at how far I had come and still not outrun the feeling, not really.

My nose looked great. My forehead looked great. Maybe a therapist could help my insides match my outsides. It was worth a shot.

The therapist's name was Julie. I had modeled the exact outfit she was wearing in an Eileen Fisher catalog, and she was, in fact, the exact woman they were trying to appeal to. Smooth-skinned but gray-haired, chunky rings. She could be forty. She could be sixty. It was anyone's guess.

The first thing I said to her was not a complete sentence but a proclamation: *Irish linen blouse.*

Julie's face suggested she'd expected fertile ground. Joke was on her.

Irish linen blouse. From Eileen Fisher.

"Oh, yes," Julie said mildly.

I explained about the catalog but it was clear this was not the bonding moment I had thought it might be.

"What does that feel like?" she asked. "You wear these clothes, you're tasked with selling these clothes. And then you see someone in that outfit. What's that like? Have you accomplished a goal?"

This was testing my newfound respect for Debi. I explained that I was not connected to my jobs like that anymore, and I watched her eyes as she prepared to jump on my final word.

"Was there a time you were?"

I supposed this was safe enough territory. I tried to explain the difference in feelings to her. How when I started, they saw me as a look that could be used to sell something in a magazine and how the goal was becoming the art those ad pages buy. Working toward the goal felt like one thing. Dancing around the goal felt like that thing, only more. Irish linen blouse felt like nothing.

"When you started," Julie repeated. "And when was that?"

Had I ever really been thirteen?

"Isn't that rather young for the industry?"

It was as if I'd been training my entire professional career for this moment. Every comparison I'd clocked. Every milestone I'd watched unfold. It was all so I could correct this therapist and tell her that actually, Brooke Shields appeared on the cover of *Vogue* at age fourteen.

There was child modeling and there was modeling-modeling and we had both existed in the in-between. Kate Moss had been a teenager too. It wasn't quite as common anymore, but it was a different time then.

"Well, I think there are plenty of people who thought Brooke Shields was being exploited too," Julie said. The *too* hit like a jolt, a signal that this could go wrong, and I turned to the window. Julie waited a moment and continued. "So you felt connected to your work when you were a girl, and you've since lost that connection. Is there a before and after for you, Elizabeth?" She watched me roll my eyes. "What bothers you about this question?"

I turned it back to her. I was not special—doesn't everyone have a before and after?

"I suppose you can look at it that way. But if we do, it would be unique to every person's life circumstances, and we're talking about yours. What's the dividing line for you? Where does before end and after begin?"

The question sent my heart racing. Give me a thousand needles to the face. Give me the swelling and bruising before the healing. Anything but this.

THE COVER GIRL

"Let's go back to the beginning. What brought you here?" Julie asked.

I told Julie my agent thought it might be helpful.

"How did that make you feel?"

Like I should listen to her, obviously. As airily and as casually as possible, I shared that I was nervous about being approached for a television special about my ex-boyfriend.

Julie made the fertile ground face again. I wondered if she was that obvious about it with everyone, or if all those years in front of the camera had made me particularly skilled at reading when I had landed on the desired result. "What makes you nervous?"

I let the question sit. And it sat so heavily that I couldn't breathe. Couldn't think.

Sense memory.

I picked up my purse, explained that this had been a mistake, and thanked her for her time.

At home, the television glowed with more news to watch, more discussions of anything related to the impeachment. As I waited to hear from Debi, I spent my time reading, learning about Monica, who I thought of by first name, like a friend. Wanting to know as much about her as possible. What would happen to her with the trial over? I approached it the way I imagined people watched horror movies. It made me sick to my stomach to see the way late-night hosts, comedians, talking heads chewed her up and spit her out as though she was not real. A concept. An avatar for everything they didn't like about women, about girls. As if by making a choice, she had vacated herself of feelings, of humanity.

And then moving from that to MTV, where teen girls lip-synched in music videos dressed in pigtails and short skirts and knotted tops that displayed acres of tanned skin and toned stomachs—no tummies here—to be alternately fawned over and chided for being too sexy. As though these girls were responsible

318   Amy Rossi

for styling themselves. No, I wasn't the one with the song, but I knew what it was to be in a video. It made me uncomfortable in a way I couldn't quite name, a bruise Julie would have delighted in pressing on. Instead, I focused on being glad that while I was expected to be thin, no one had ever expected me to have abs.

All through this, Debi continued to only call for the expected reasons. And in the end, months later, I saw it in *TV Guide*. I asked Bernice if she would watch it with me. I could hear her trying to not ask a hundred questions as she said of course she would.

You could count the number of times I had spoken to Bernice about my relationship with the rock star on one hand, and that hand would include the night we met in Paris. And still, she knew more than most. And it wasn't that I didn't trust her—it was me I didn't trust. I had given up on figuring out how to explain it in a way that people understood.

My phone rang two minutes before the program started, and Bernice and I sat on our couches, three thousand miles apart. For the most part, we didn't speak for the next hour, but I knew she was there.

She heard my gasp the first time his face filled the screen. I knew how old I was, what I looked like, and still it was a shock to see his graying hair and crow's feet. And then there was the Doctor, who they identified as Norman Clay. Beasley. Eddie. Ham.

Lulu.

She heard me barely breathe the word *no* when Lulu appeared, her red-gold hair still curly and wild, her makeup still impeccable. Lulu Dawn. Friend. Her laugh as big and attention-demanding as ever.

"I showed up on the Sunset Strip, this naive teenager just wanting to live and breathe the rock and roll world. He was the first real friend I made on the scene. And, yes, we were more than that." She paused to laugh, to deliver a girlish grin. *"But if you were a pretty young*

THE COVER GIRL

thing in his path, of course you were more than that. That's what it was then. Just a completely different time."

"What a piece of work," Bernice muttered.

And then what they did was blur through those four years, only showing the album and *after which, he began a relationship with the model on the cover.* They did not use my name or mention my age. They did not mention what kind of relationship we had, who he really was: the one whom my tutor called when I started blowing off my math assignments, the one who took me to get a wisdom tooth removed, the one who could admit me to the hospital and take me out again. The one who taught me how to drive.

All I had to be was legs.

And then they skipped ahead to the wives, an interchangeable trio with shiny-shiny hair and shiny-shiny voices, and to present-day clips of the current iteration of family lining up for portraits, him running around in a yard with the little blonde girl he had talked about that night at the concert with Bobby and also two more, all the children sharing the same *K* first initial while the current shiny-shiny wife looked on, rubbing her hand over the growing fourth and probably thinking of her own *K* name. In keeping me out of it, I wondered if he thought he had given me something. And after Bernice whispered that she was there if I needed anything later and hung up, crying was not the noise I made as I remembered him waiting for me to come back in that ridiculous yellow Pantera, waiting to see if I'd passed or failed my test to get a license, and I wondered how there was so much I had forgotten, yet all this still burned brightly in mind, and even though I was not fifteen or sixteen or nineteen anymore, I feared in a way I would never not be, with half of what-if always lingering.

2018

By the time I get home from meeting Michelle, my pulse has slowed and I can inhale without breaking my breath into ragged pieces, but it's still just static in my mind.

One thing at a time, but where to even begin?

I don't know what I do need, but what I don't is to be alone with my thoughts. I call Bernice, and she answers on the second ring. I tell her I have a strange question—does she remember Azrian's final fashion show? Did she remember him telling her anything?

"Remember? I damn near stitched it on a pillow," Bernice says. "He told me, 'Bernice, you are going places, but when someone tells you the struggle is worth it, you have to start asking if they're part of the struggle or if they're making it worth it.' It floored me. So many people wanted me to do more for less because they thought I should be grateful for getting as far as I had, and I started saying no a lot more after that. What made you think about it?"

I explain that he'd said something to me too, something I'd never been able to quite make sense of. And when she asks what it was, I repeat the words that have been rattling in my head for thirty years: he knew things had not worked out the way I wanted, but it would be a lot easier if I realized what the worst thing that happened to me was.

"Oh," Bernice says after a minute of silence. "Are we finally doing this?" She gives me a chance to say something and when I don't, she sighs.

"You don't talk to a single person you knew when you were with him. You've cut them all out. The models you were friendly with. The other day with that Sunny woman—I know we've all done a lot of jobs, but how many did you do in New Orleans? Why do you think you didn't remember her? And don't you even say you kept talking to Debi, because if she hadn't retired, I guarantee you would have found a reason to stop speaking to her too. Like you did with Harriet. That article wasn't great— yes, I read it, I know what you've been holding on to—but at some point in the last twenty years, did you even consider what she was trying to say?"

This doesn't quite seem fair, but now that the door has been opened Bernice is going to push on through. "You never talk about it. Why is that? I didn't even know how bad it was until you asked me to watch that show about him with you. I knew you were young, sure. But I did the math, and, Birdie, honey, you were a child. Younger than Antoinette. And then you went around for years acting like leaving him was the worst thing you could have done when it's probably the only kind thing you've ever done for yourself."

I keep my voice even as I thank Bernice for her honesty. My hands are shaking as I hang up the phone.

In the corner of my living room is the tall seldom-touched shelf my portfolios rest on. I pull down the whole stack of books, nearly knocking over the entire thing. I don't want the one I showed Michelle, with the highest profile pictures. These other books, the ones that hold everything else, are my proof that I wasn't so young. The experience wasn't for everyone, yes, but

THE COVER GIRL   325

neither was modeling. And things had changed. A girl couldn't
have the kind of career I did at my age anymore. There are different rules now, different rules for different times. I flip through
the pages like they could burn me until I find a photo of myself in a bubble bath. See, that was a young woman, not a girl.
And then I see the label: 1981. Okay. Fine. The Swish ad? No,
1980. But it can't have been that different.

The answer wasn't going to be here.

I had a photo album tucked underneath my portfolios. I have
kept this one unopened even longer than my books; I have to
brush off the dust before I turn the cover. I know there's a photo
in here that will prove what I know to be true, prove my own
memories, no matter what the Michelles of the world think.

I find what I'm looking for creased and tucked behind another picture—a photo torn from *Circus* magazine. He's signing autographs, and I am in this frame somewhere. If this is the
one I remember. There was a photo from that magazine that I
looked so good in, all legs and attitude, not unlike the little girl
in the background of this one.

The words sit there in my mind for what feels like full minutes
before I make myself look, before I make myself confirm what it
is I already know, what I have spent so long trying not to know.

The girl in this photo is a child. I am the girl in this photo.

I saw this person and I thought: *Little girl*.

What it looks like is this: the aging model—

No.

Not this time.

I try to catch my breath, try to stay here. I have to stay here.

It's an underwater feeling as I paw through the album, pull
out something only a desperate person would have saved, an
image from a tabloid. The rock star and a girl I threw a drink
on in a club one night and the caption.

Hope this one's legal.

It was not that different of a time.

It's right there in the picture.

Lulu said it at dinner once—she was already too old when she met him. I had to force myself to focus on other parts of that conversation, to seek something else to be hurt by, because the truth was too big for me.

The family lawyer's grandson knew. Even Bernice has known all these years.

Everyone, everyone knew. Everyone but me.

I lie on the floor, somewhere between throwing up and hyperventilating. And when I close my eyes, I am fifteen on a tour bus.

The bus is dark. After months of miles and room service and waking up hours away from where we went to sleep, all the highway signs look familiar. My head is on his shoulder, both of us nodding off. The bus stops, and while we wait to see if it's for the night or for another reason, I ask where we are. He thinks Arizona. And soon, he tells me, we'll be in Malibu. We'll be home. I'll be able to listen to the ocean.

The highway light washes through the window and catches us looking, the kind of searching you only let yourself do in the dark. He takes my face in his hands and asks if I know what drew him to me that day in the line. I do know: my legs. He shakes his head. Not at all. He tells me I didn't even look real to him that first time he saw me, the face of a girl on the body of a woman. Like a dream, he tells me. Like something he would always have to come back to. "You look like a song I don't even know how to write," he says. I think: *He saw me.* I think: *I can be that girl.*

I open my eyes.

Yes, I had wanted to believe I was the only one. An exception.

I was. But only for so long. I was always going to be chasing an idea he had of me, a still and unchanging one: me at fifteen. That was what he wanted.

Even he knew.

THE COVER GIRL 327

★ ★ ★

I don't talk to anyone for days. Bernice texts several times, and I respond with as few words as possible. I'm not sure anything I say makes sense. Why would it. Nothing else does. My life was a lie. Things I thought I forgot come rushing back at random times of the day, and I don't know what is true or not. I'm getting plastic surgery for an event that I have not responded to, an event whose meaning I cannot even begin to parse anymore.

The day before my surgery, the office calls because I forgot to sign something. Of course I did. And standing at the desk, with the receptionist watching and Dr. Adams looking over a chart, I freeze.

I do not think plastic surgery is wrong. I've watched enough young people die to know that aging is better than the alternative, but I've also seen my face in print enough to know what it should look like and to want it to stay that way. And I know I am going to need an extra layer of confidence beyond what good styling can do to be able to do whatever comes next.

But when Dr. Adams asks if something is wrong, what falls from my mouth is an announcement: that I don't want the surgery. And I am so surprised to hear these words in my voice that she asks if I'm sure. And I realize yes, I am, because what I need is to finally see myself for who I am. I need to present the face that went through it all.

Then I do the thing I have been on the verge of for several days: I cry. Deep wracking sobs for the girl I was, the girl I refused to see all these years, the girl I am not sure I even know.

Dr. Adams says nothing, just guides me into her office until I calm down, and when I start to apologize, she waves her hand. "My rule for crying in public is you just don't want to do it where the people there haven't seen it before. David's Bridal? Okay, you've probably never set foot in one, but still. Cry away. The airport? Sure. Here? You are absolutely not the first."

328 Amy Rossi

She tells me I can schedule a Botox appointment at the front. And when she slides me a card for a therapist, I take it.

Back home, I find myself in front of my laptop, searching for Harriet's old interview in the *Times*. Still online, no paywall. 1996. A profile where she was asked about the new supermodels, her career, her regrets. I take a deep breath.

"There was a model who I still wish I'd handled differently. I pushed her too fast when she was too young, and she ended up in a relationship with a much older man. She moved in with him eventually, and it was terrifying to me. I tried to book her on location shoots to get her away from him. I looked for ways to keep her close to me. I even ended up coaxing her into a cosmetics contract that I knew wasn't a good move—the company was too new, the product was subpar. But they were only shooting in New York, so I could at least keep an eye on her."

It has not gotten any easier to read, but this time I find myself settling on the part about Cameo for a different reason. I had been so angry when I found out she'd known it wasn't going to be a good deal, that she'd let me waste my time—my prime—on it anyway. But now I see: that was Harriet's living too, her reputation.

All this time I'd thought it was me, that I was the result of my own poor decisions. But all that time, so much was happening that was beyond what I understood.

And I could be mad now, mad at how little control I'd had, but—how worried Harriet must have been, how much she must have wanted to help me for her to take that risk. How she had gambled to keep me close. How she searched for reasons to stay connected.

How long I spent pushing her away for it.

What a waste of potential. Those lines had hurt me so deeply that I hadn't bothered to read the ones that followed: *I feel responsible. She was like a daughter to me.*

The memory of bursting into her office flashes in front of

me, just another thing begging to be held up to the light after years of being tucked away, and what she said before I left. That I had every right to be angry with her.

"But please be angry for more than that," she'd said. "I let him take you. I should have protected you from him, and I didn't. It will forever be my regret. And when you're ready, we can talk about it."

I had been unwilling to hear what she was saying then. I have not seen or spoken to Harriet since.

It's time.

Time holds no meaning in the days and weeks that follow. One hour, then another, until they stack together and fall apart and I am in New York taking the giant sapphire cocktail ring Bernice hands me. "I think that ties it together."

My hands shake as I slip the ring on. Yesterday I was in California and this morning I woke up in Bernice's guest room.

I had planned to stay in a hotel, had told Bernice that when she first invited me to stay with her and her family. But one of the things I've begun to question is how I hold even the people I care most about at arm's length. There is a long, long way to go, but here I am. Drinking coffee with Bernice and Marcus in the morning. Waving along with her when he and their daughter, Antoinette, leave for school. And when she said, "See you later, Aunt Birdie," like she was six and not sixteen, I let myself feel it: what I am to Bernice. What she is to me.

It has been the shortest and longest few weeks of my life, and now we stand back and look at me in Bernice's full-length mirror. Impeccable makeup. A half updo that would make Brigitte Bardot proud, held by an antique pearl comb. A shimmering black one-shouldered dress that hugs my body down to the floor. And a statement ring to tie it all together.

If only it were as easy as letting the ring do the statement-making.

"Are you sure you don't want me to come early?" Bernice asks.

I thank her, shaking my head. Of course I want her to come with me. But I need to do this part alone.

Though she still has to finish getting ready herself, she pours us each a glass of champagne and hands me one. "To good friends. And to next steps. And to the Azrian de Popa Award."

We had finalized the paperwork earlier in the day. While it was not going to be formally part of J Entertainment, the company would administer the award—an annual cash prize to support rising LGBTQ designers in advancing their careers. I wanted as few strings as possible; the designers could use the money to go to school if they chose or they could start building a collection. And J models would be ready to show off their creations when the time came.

We lost a generation. What I wanted was to help the next one find their way.

What I wanted was to make sure Azrian's name was not forgotten.

I clink my glass to Bernice's as we toast to each other and to our friend. And then for the first time in all the years we've known each other, I look Bernice in the eye and tell her that I love her. I am grateful for her. It is better with her.

"No crying," she says. "We spent too long on that face." I laugh, but we are both sniffling as she pulls me into a hug. "You know I love you too," she says. "And I'm proud of you. And Marcus and I will meet you there."

My phone buzzes: the car is here. It's time.

I look out the window as the city blurs by. I text Bobby: I'm on my way to the gala. He texts back: Good luck, buddy!!!!!! We arrive at the hotel so quickly, too quickly.

Inside, the gala is the calm before the crush. I am given a name tag with a purple ribbon to indicate my status as one of Harriet's Girls—as though we would ever sully our outfits with

THE COVER GIRL 331

name tags—then I'm directed to a green room, one where the other girls and Therese are waiting.

Therese. Though she's gone gray now, I still see the effervescent front desk presence. Recognition washes over her face, a roller coaster I can't quite read, but then she stands and gathers me into a hug. "I saw your name on the RSVP list, but I still wasn't sure you were going to come. It's so good to see you," she whispers, her voice thick with emotion I'm not prepared for. "This will be such a lovely surprise for Harriet."

I tell her it is nice to see her too, then politely, I hope politely, extract myself from her arms. The panic hits, a bottoming-out like the ground could drop from under me at any moment. I push my way out, follow the signs for the ladies' room and tuck myself into an opulent stall. The floor-to-ceiling door, solid wood, is what I need right now. A barrier between me and everything that comes next.

I spent so much time wondering if I was ready to see Harriet that I didn't even get to the question of whether she would be happy to see me. This could be a terrible mistake. Too many years, too many things unsaid, too much to undo. Perhaps it is too late for us.

I pull out my phone to text Bernice, to ask her to come meet me. But then I thumb my way back to the email I received a few hours ago:

Dear Birdie,

Thank you so much for your sweet message. I know we spoke briefly after Wally's but honestly I wasn't sure I'd ever hear from you again. (And I would have understood!) It means so much to me that you read and enjoyed the piece about Harriet—and that it felt honest and true.

And, most importantly, YES. I would be so honored to write your story when you're ready. Whether that's in five months or five years, I'll be here.

I hope you enjoy the gala tonight. And, sorry to be blunt, but I also hope you know that you're not only beautiful—you're brave as all hell.

Love, Michelle

I'm not that brave. But I've come this far.

The little girl walking into Saks came this far.

At ten minutes after eight, we're brought into the event space, all tasteful gold and minimalist decor, and arranged in a receiving line. I can hardly listen as the retired CEO of a rival agency begins the welcoming address, telling us all about Harriet Goldman, things I knew and experienced and let myself forget. How young she was when she started. The trails she blazed as she rebuilt an agency from the ground up. How hard she fought to be taken seriously.

How hard she fought for her girls.

"Ladies and gentlemen," the speaker says. "Please join me in welcoming Harriet Goldman."

The room is a thunder of applause, everyone on their feet, and then Harriet emerges. Her evening gown is tastefully draped, her gray hair styled in its signature chignon. She looks smaller, but her presence still could knock us all down. I watch her make her way down the line, my chest pounding as she grows closer.

And then she's here, right in front of me. I take her hands in mine, and the years fall away. "Oh, Birdie," she says, her eyes filling with tears. "It's you."

"Yes," I say. "It's me."

★ ★ ★ ★ ★

ACKNOWLEDGMENTS

Gratitude does not begin to cover what I feel for my agent, Penelope Burns. Thank you for believing in me and my writing and for never giving up. I'm so glad we made it to the other side together—I couldn't have done it without you. Many thanks to Deborah Schneider, Cathy Gleason, and Abby Knudsen at Gelfman Schneider, and Brian Lipson at IPG, as well.

I am overwhelmed with appreciation for my editor, Leah Mol. Your thoughtfulness and vision have made this book shine. Thank you for seeing me and Birdie and for taking such good care of both of us. Thank you, too, to the entire MIRA/HTP/HarperCollins teams who helped bring this book to life, including art director Tara Scarcello, copy editor Dana Francoeur, typesetter Amanda Roberts, proofreader Susan Dyrkton, and the marketing, sales, and publicity teams, especially Pamela Osti and Laura Gianino.

My research included the following books and films: *Model: The Ugly Business of Beautiful Women* by Michael Gross; *There Was a Little Girl: The Real Story of My Mother and Me* by Brooke Shields; *What You Want Is in the Limo: On the Road with Led Zeppelin, Alice Cooper, and the Who in 1977, the Year the Sixties Died and the Modern Rock Star Was Born* by Michael Walker; *The Face That Changed It All* by Beverly Johnson; *No Filter: The Good, the Bad, and the Beautiful* by Paulina Porizkova; *About Face: The Supermodels, Then and Now* (2012); *United in Anger: A History of ACT UP* (2012); *Versailles '73: American Runway Revolution* (2012); and *Look Away* (2021).

This book began as a short story while I was in the LSU MFA program. Thank you to my professors and classmates for your thoughtful discussion.

Thank you to Moriel Rothman-Zecher, whose generous feedback and keen eye gave me the push I needed, and to the Ice Queens: Kimberly Morton, Anika Gzifa, and Rachel Sanderford. Your insights are invaluable, as is the space we created.

Thank you to Erin Fitzgerald, who helped me see what this book could be at Barrelhouse Writers Camp. Many early pages were written on a hammock at camp—thank you to Dave Housley, Becky Barnard, Chris Gonzalez, and the whole crew.

Balancing a book and an office job is much easier when you have a Wolfpack behind you. Thank you to Amy Feriozzi, Lisa Hall, Emma Ross, and the DCS, Ucomm, and TIDE teams.

For reading early pages, inspiration, and support, thank you to Katie M. Flynn, Kaitlyn Andrews-Rice, Becky Robison, Marianne Chan, Clancy McGilligan, and Maureen Langloss.

Jake Zucker, thank you for helping me tinker with sentences and for always being there.

Meghan Phillips, there is a reason long-distance friendship became a thread in this book. You made finishing that first draft possible. I am so lucky to know you.

Stef Rowley, I cannot thank you enough for your guidance and steadfast belief in me.

Edan Lepucki, Amy Kiger-Williams, and group two of the Fuck You, Write Your Pages contingent: thank you for helping me get to the finish line.

Thank you to the friends who have been on this ride with

me: Alyson Ritter, Ariel Lewis, Kathryn Steed, Leland Sage, Dan Hellebuyck, Corey Milbert, Michelle Witt, Susan Carr, Katie Oldaker, Samara Pearlstein, XRC, Brittany M., Dana Dubis, Jessie Blekfeld-Sztraky, and Erin Zanders.

A lot of pets, only a few mine, rolled around on the printed pages of this manuscript to provide expert canine and feline editorial support: Kitty, Baby C, Cain, Koji, Fancy, Sadie, Waylon, and Kodiak.

The Perrier scene and also more than twenty years of good things in my life would not exist without Christopher Coletta. Anyone can have a best friend, but I have a mist, and a Laura too.

My uncle Bobby gave me so much, and this is but a trib to his memory.

To anyone who sees themselves in Birdie's story, thank y for sharing these pages with me.

Lastly, to my family: you mean everything.

Rocky, thank you for building a life with me and for t my partner in the truest sense.

Patrick, thank you for late-night texts and numbers-guy ques- tions. A little brother like you makes the middle the best place to be. Alexis, thank you for all the support and hype.

Jen, sisters means not writing it out. Matthew, thank you for accepting this package deal.

Mom, thank you for printing countless manuscripts, writing encouraging sticky notes, giving me a soft place to land, and always believing in me.

And finally: Dad, we did it. Thank you for everything you taught me along the way. I would give anything to share this with you. I love you, I miss you, and I hope I've made you proud.